Romance readers around the world were sad to note the passing of **Betty Neels** in June 2001. Her career spanned thirty years, and she continued to write into her ninetieth year. To her millions of fans, Betty epitomized the romance writer, and yet she began writing almost by accident. She had retired from nursing, but her inquiring mind still sought stimulation. Her new career was born when she heard a lady in her local library bemoaning the lack of good romance novels. Betty's first book, *Sister Peters in Amsterdam*, was published in 1969, and she eventually completed 134 books. Her novels offer a reassuring warmth that was very much a part of her own personality. She was a wonderful writer, and she is greatly missed. Her spirit and genuine talent live on in all her stories.

BETTY NEELS

Caroline's Waterloo
& Fate is Remarkable

H HARLEQUIN® SPECIAL RELEASE

ISBN-13: 978-1-335-04514-0

Caroline's Waterloo & Fate is Remarkable

Copyright © 2019 by Harlequin Books S.A.

The publisher acknowledges the copyright holder
of the individual works as follows:

Caroline's Waterloo
Copyright © 1980 by Betty Neels

Fate is Remarkable
Copyright © 1971 by Betty Neels

Recycling programs
for this product may
not exist in your area.

Printed in U.S.A.

TM www.Harlequin.com

CONTENTS

CAROLINE'S WATERLOO

Chapter 1

The narrow brick road wound itself along narrow canals, through wide stretches of water meadows and small clumps of trees and, here and there, a larger copse. Standing well away from the road there were big farmhouses, each backed by a great barn, their mellow red brick glistening in the last rays of the October sun. Save for the cows, already in their winter coats, and one or two great horses, there was little to be seen and the only other movement was made by the four girls cycling briskly along the road. They had come quite a distance that day and now they were flagging a little; the camping equipment each carried made it heavy going, and besides, they had lost their way.

It had been easy enough leaving Alkmaar that morning, going over the Afsluitdijk and into Friesland, pedalling cheerfully towards the camping ground they had decided upon, but now, with no village in sight and the dusk beginning to creep over the wide Friesian sky, they were getting uneasy.

Presently they came to a halt, to look at the map and wonder where they had gone wrong. 'This doesn't go anywhere,' grumbled the obvious leader, a tall, very pretty girl. 'What shall we do? Go back—and that's miles—or press on?'

They all peered at the map again, one fair head, two dark ones and an unspectacular mouse-brown. The owner of the mouse-brown hair spoke:

'Well, the road must go somewhere, they wouldn't have built it just for fun, and we've been on it now for quite a while—I daresay we're nearer the end than the beginning.' She had a pretty voice, soft and slightly hesitant, perhaps as compensation for her very ordinary face.

Her three companions peered at the map again. 'You're right, Caro—let's go on before it's quite dark.' The speaker, one of the dark-haired girls, glanced around her at the empty landscape. 'It's lonely, isn't it? I mean, after all the towns and villages we've been through just lately.'

'Friesland and Groningen are sparsely populated,' said Caro, 'they're mostly agricultural.'

The three of them gave her a tolerant look. Caro was small and quiet and unassuming, but she was a fount of information about a great many things, because she read a lot, they imagined with a trace of pity; unlike the other nurses at Oliver's, she was seldom invited to go out by any of the young doctors and she lived alone in a small bedsitter in a horrid shabby little street convenient to the hospital. She had any number of friends, because she could be relied upon to change off-duty at a moment's notice, lend anything needed without fuss, and fill in last-minute gaps. As she was doing now; the nurse who should have been in her place had developed an appendix and because four was a much better number with which to go camping and biking, she had been roped in at the last minute. She hadn't particularly wanted to go; she had planned to spend her two weeks' holiday redecorating her room and visiting art galleries. She knew almost nothing about art, but she had discovered long ago that art galleries were restful and pleasant and there were always other people strolling around for company, even though no one ever spoke to her. Not that she minded being alone; she had grown up in a lonely way. An orphan from childhood, the aunt she had lived with had married while Caro was still at school and her new uncle had never taken to her; indeed, over the years, he had let it be known that she must find a home for herself; her aunt's was too small to house all three of them. If she had been pretty he might have thought differently, and if she had tried to conciliate him he might have had second thoughts. As it was, Caroline hadn't seen her aunt for two years or more.

'Well, let's get on,' suggested Stacey. She tossed her blonde hair back over her shoulders and got on to her bike once more, followed by Clare and Miriam with Caro bringing up the rear.

The sun seemed to set very rapidly and once it had disappeared behind them, the sky darkened even more rapidly. But the road appeared to run ahead of them, clearly to be seen until it disappeared into a large clump of trees on the horizon. There were distant lights from the farmhouse now, a long way off, but they dispelled the loneliness so that they all became cheerful again, calling to and fro to each other, discussing what they would eat for their supper and whose turn it was to cook. They reached the trees a few minutes later, and Stacey, still in front, called out excitedly: 'I say, look there, on the left—those lights—there must be a house!' She braked to take a better look and Clare and Miriam, who hadn't braked fast enough, went into her, joined seconds later by Caro, quite unable to stop herself in time. She ploughed into the struggling heap in front of her, felt a sharp pain in her leg and then nothing more, because she had hit her head on an old-fashioned milestone beside the cycle path.

She came to with a simply shocking headache, a strange feeling that she was in a nightmare, and the pain in her leg rather worse. What was more, she was being carried, very awkwardly too, with someone supporting her legs and her head cradled against what felt like an alpaca jacket—but men didn't wear alpaca jackets any more. She tried to say so, but the words didn't come out right and she was further mystified by a man's cockney voice close to her ear, warning someone to go easy. She wanted to say, 'My leg hurts,' but talking had become difficult and when she made her eyes open, she could see nothing much; a small strip of sky between tall trees and somewhere ahead lights shining. She gave up and passed out again, unaware that the awkward little party had reached the house, that Stacey, obedient to the cockney voice, had opened the door and held it wide while the others carried her inside. She was unaware too of the size and magnificence of the hall or of its many doors, one of which was flung open with some force by a large man with a sheaf of papers in his hand and a scowl on his handsome features. But she was brought back to consciousness by his commanding voice, demanding harshly why he was forced to suffer such a commotion in his own house.

It seemed to Caro that someone should speak up and explain, but her head was still in a muddle although she knew what she wanted to say; it was just a question of getting the words out. She embarked on an explanation, only to be abruptly halted by the harsh voice, very close to her now. 'This girl's concussed and that leg needs attention. Noakes, carry her into the surgery.' She heard his sigh. 'I suppose I must attend to it.'

Just for a moment her addled brain cleared. She said quite clearly: 'You have no need to be quite so unfeeling. Give me a needle and thread and I'll do it myself.'

She heard his crack of laughter before she went back into limbo again.

She drifted in and out of sleep several times during the night and each time she opened her eyes it was to see, rather hazily, someone sitting by her bed. He took no notice of her at all, but wrote and read and wrote again, and something about his austere look convinced her that it was the owner of the voice who had declared that she was concussed.

'I'm not concussed,' she said aloud, and was surprised that her voice sounded so wobbly.

He had got to his feet without answering her, given her a drink and said in a voice which wasn't going to take no for an answer: 'Go to sleep.'

It seemed a good idea; she closed her eyes.

The next time she woke, although the room was dim she knew that it was day, for the reading lamp by the chair was out. The man had gone and Stacey sat there, reading a book.

'Hullo,' said Caro in a much stronger voice; her head

still ached and so did her leg, but she had stopped feeling dreamlike.

Stacey got up and came over to the bed. 'Caro, do you feel better? You gave us all a fright, I can tell you!'

Caro looked carefully round the room, trying not to move her head because of the pain. It was a splendid apartment, its walls hung with pale silk, its rosewood furniture shining with age and polishing. The bed she was in had a draped canopy and a silken bedspread, its beauty rather marred by the cradle beneath it, guarding her injured leg.

'What happened' she asked. 'There was a very cross man, wasn't there?'

Stacey giggled. 'Oh, ducky, you should have heard yourself! It's an enormous house and he's so good-looking you blink...'

Caroline closed her eyes. 'What happened?'

'We all fell over, and you cut your leg open on Clare's pedal—it whizzed round and gashed it badly, and you fell on to one of those milestones and knocked yourself out.'

'Are you all right? You and Clare and Miriam?'

'Absolutely, hardly a scratch between us—only you, Caro—we're ever so sorry.' She patted Caro's arm. 'I've got to tell Professor Thoe van Erckelens you're awake.'

Caro still had her eyes shut. 'What an extraordinary name...'

Her hand was picked up and her pulse taken and she opened her eyes. Stacey had gone, the man—presumably the Professor—was there, towering over her.

He grunted to himself and then asked: 'What is your name, young lady?'

'Caroline Tripp.' She watched his stern mouth twitch at the corners; possibly her name sounded as strange to him as his did to her. 'I feel better, thank you.' She added, 'It was kind of you to sit with me last night.'

He had produced an ophthalmoscope from somewhere and was fitting it together. 'I am a doctor, Miss Tripp—a doctor's duty is to his patient.'

Unanswerable, especially with her head in such a muddled state. He examined her eyes with care and silently and then spoke to someone she couldn't see. 'I should like to examine the leg, please.'

It was Stacey who turned back the coverlet and removed the cradle before unwinding the bandage which covered Caro's leg from knee to ankle.

'Did you stitch it?' asked Caro, craning her neck to see.

A firm hand restrained her. 'You would be foolish to move your head too much,' she was told. 'Yes, I have cleaned and stitched the wound in your leg. It is a deep, jagged cut and you will have to rest it for some days.'

'Oh, I can't do that,' said Caro, still not quite in control of her woolly wits, 'I'm on duty in four days' time.'

'An impossibility—you will remain here until I consider you fit to return.'

'There must be a hospital...' Her head was beginning to throb.

'As a nurse you should be aware of the importance of resting both your brain and your leg. Kindly don't argue.'

She was feeling very peculiar again, rather as though she were lying in a mist, listening to people's voices but quite unable to focus them with her tired eyes. 'You can't possibly be married,' she mumbled, 'and you sound as though you hate me—you must be a mi—mi...'

'Misogynist.'

She had her eyes shut again so that she wouldn't cry.

He was being very gentle, but her leg hurt dreadfully; she was going to tell him so, but she dropped off again.

Next time she woke up it was Clare by the bed and she grinned weakly and said: 'I feel better.'

'Good. Would you like a cup of tea?—it's real strong tea, like we make at Oliver's.'

It tasted lovely; drinking it, Caroline began to feel that everything was normal again. 'There's some very thin bread and butter,' suggested Clare. Caro devoured that too; she had barely swallowed the last morsel before she was asleep again.

It was late afternoon when she woke again. The lamp was already lighted and the Professor was sitting beside it, writing. 'Don't you have any patients?' asked Caroline.

He glanced up from his writing. 'Yes. Would you like a drink?'

She had seen the tray with a glass and jug on it, on the table by her bed. 'Yes, please—I can help myself; I'm feeling fine.'

He took no notice at all but got up, put an arm behind her shoulders, lifted her very gently and held the glass for her. When she had finished he laid her down again and said: 'You may have your friends in for ten minutes,' and stalked quietly out of the room.

They crept in very silently and stood in a row at the foot of the bed, looking at her. 'You're better,' said Miriam, 'the Professor says so.' And then: 'We're going back tomorrow morning.'

Caro tried to sit up and was instantly thrust gently back on to her pillow. 'You can't—you can't leave me here! He doesn't like me—why can't I go to hospital if I've got to stay? How are you going?'

'Noakes—that's the sort of butler who was at the gate

when we fell over—he's to drive us to the Hoek. The bikes are to be sent back later.'

'He's quite nice,' said Clare, 'the Professor, I mean—he's a bit terse but he's been a perfect host. I don't think he likes us much but then of course, he's quite old, quite forty, I should think; he's always reading or writing and he's away a lot—Noakes says he's a very important man in his profession.' She giggled, 'You can hardly hear that he's Dutch, his English is so good, and isn't it funny that Noakes comes from Paddington? But he's been here for years and years—he's married to the cook. There's a housekeeper too, very tall and looks severe but she's not.'

'And three maids besides a gardener,' chimed in Miriam. 'He must be awfully rich.'

'You'll be OK,' Stacey assured her, 'you'll be back in no time. Do you want us to do anything for you?'

Caro's head was aching again. 'Would you ask Mrs Hodge to go on feeding Waterloo until I get back? There's some money in my purse—will you take some so that she can get his food?'

'OK—we'll go round to your place and make sure he's all right. Do you have to pay Mrs Hodge any rent?'

'No, I pay in advance each month. Is there enough money for me to get back by boat?'

Stacey counted. 'Yes—it's only a single fare and I expect Noakes will take you to the boat.' She came a bit nearer. 'Well, 'bye for now, Caro. We hate leaving you, but there's nothing we can do about it.'

Caro managed a smile. 'I'll be fine—I'll let you know when I'm coming.'

They all shook hands with her rather solemnly. 'We're going quite early and the Professor said we weren't to disturb you in the morning.'

Caroline lay quietly after they had gone, too tired to feel much. Indeed, when the Professor came in later and gave her a sedative she made no demur but drank it down meekly and closed her eyes at once. It must have been quite strong because she was asleep at once, although he stayed for some time, sitting in his chair watching her, for once neither reading nor writing.

She didn't wake until quite late in the morning, to find Noakes' wife—Marta—standing by the bed with a small tray. There was tea again and paper-thin bread and butter and scrambled egg which she fed Caro just as though she were a baby. She spoke a little English too, and Caro made out that her friends had gone.

When Marta had gone away, she lay and thought about it; she felt much more clear-headed now, almost herself, but not quite, otherwise she would never have conceived the idea of getting up, getting dressed, and leaving the house. She couldn't stay where she wasn't welcome—it was like her uncle all over again. Perhaps, she thought miserably, there was something about her that made her unacceptable as a guest. She was on the plain side, that she already knew, and perhaps because of that she was self-effacing and inclined to be shy. She had quickly learned not to draw attention to herself, but on the other hand she had plenty of spirit and a natural friendliness which had made her a great number of friends. But the Professor, she felt, was not one of their number.

The more she thought of her scheme, the more she liked it; the fact that she had a considerable fever made it seem both feasible and sensible, although it was neither. She began, very cautiously, to sit up. Her head ached worse than ever, but she ignored that and concentrated on moving her injured leg. It hurt a good deal more than she had expected, but she persevered until she was sitting untidily on the edge of the bed, her sound foot on the ground, its stricken fellow on its edge. It had hurt before; now, when she started to dangle it over the side of the bed, the pain brought great waves of nausea sweeping over her.

'Oh, God!' said Caro despairingly, and meant it.

'Perhaps I will do?' The Professor had come softly into the room, taking great strides to reach her.

'I'm going to be sick,' moaned Caro, and was, making a mess of his beautifully polished shoes. If she hadn't felt so ill she would have died of shame, as it was she burst into tears, sobbing and sniffing and gulping.

The Professor said nothing at all but picked her up and laid her back in bed again, pulling the covers over her and arranging the cradle just so over her injured leg before getting a sponge and towel from the adjoining bathroom and wiping her face for her. She looked at him round the sponge and mumbled: 'Your shoes—your lovely shoes, I'm so s-sorry.' She gave a great gulp. 'I should have gone with the others.'

'Why were you getting out of bed?' He didn't sound angry, only interested.

'Well, I thought I could manage to dress and I've enough money, I think—I was going back to England.'

He went to the fireplace opposite the bed and pressed the brass wall bell beside it. When Noakes answered it he requested a clean pair of shoes and a tray of tea for two and waited patiently until these had been brought and Noakes, accompanied by a maid, had swiftly cleared up the mess. Only then did he say: 'And now suppose we have a little talk over our tea?'

He pulled a chair nearer the bed, handed her a cup of

tea and poured one for himself. 'Let us understand each other, young lady.'

Caroline studied him over the rim of her cup. He talked like a professor, but he didn't look like one; he was enormous and she had always thought of professors as small bent gentlemen with bald heads and untidy moustaches, but Professor Thoe van Erckelens had plenty of hair, light brown, going grey, and cut short, and he had no need to hide his good looks behind a moustache. Caro thought wistfully that he was exactly the kind of man every girl hoped to meet one day and marry; which was a pity, because he obviously wasn't the marrying kind…

'If I might have your full attention?' enquired the Professor. 'You are sufficiently recovered to listen to me?'

Her head and her leg ached, but they were bearable. She nodded.

'If you could reconcile yourself to remaining here for another ten days, perhaps a fortnight, Miss Tripp? I can assure you that you are in no fit condition to do much at the moment. I shall remove the stitches from your leg in another four days and you may then walk a little with a stick, as from tomorrow, and provided your headache is lessening, you may sit up for a period of time. Feel free to ask for anything you want, my home is at your disposal. There is a library from which Noakes will fetch a selection of books, although I advise you not to read for a few days yet, and there is no reason why you should not sit in the garden, well wrapped up. You will drink no alcohol, nor will you smoke, and kindly refrain from watching television for a further day or so; it will merely aggravate your headache. I must ask you to excuse me from keeping you company at any time—I am a busy man and I have my work and my own interests. I shall

of course treat you as I would any other patient of mine
and when I consider you fit to travel, I will see that you
get back safely to your home.'

Caro had listened to this precise speech with astonishment; she hadn't met anyone who talked like that before—it was like reading the instructions on the front
of a medicine bottle. She loved the bit about no drinking or smoking; she did neither, but she wondered if she
looked the kind of girl who did. But one thing was very
clear. The Professor was offering her hospitality but she
was to keep out of his way; he didn't want his ordered
life disrupted—which was amusing really; now if it had
been Clare or Stacey or Miriam, all pretty girls who had
never lacked for men friends, that would have been a different matter, but Caroline's own appearance was hardly
likely to cause even the smallest ripple on the calm surface of his life.

'I'll do exactly as you say,' she told him, 'and I'll keep
out of your way—you won't know I'm here. And thank
you for being so kind.' She added: 'I'm truly sorry about
me being sick and your shoes…'

He stood up. 'Sickness is to be expected in cases of
concussion,' he told her. 'I am surprised that you, a nurse,
should not have thought of that. We must make allow-
ances for your cerebral condition.'

She looked at him helplessly. Underneath all that pedantic talk there was a quite ordinary man; for some
reason, the professor was concealing him. After he had
gone she lay back on her pillows, suddenly sleepy, but
before she closed her eyes she decided that she would
discover what had happened to make him like that. She
must make friends with Noakes…

She made splendid progress. The Professor dressed

her leg the next morning and when Marta had draped her in a dressing gown several sizes too large for her, he returned to lift her into a chair by the open window, for the weather was glorious and the view from it delightful. The gardens and the house were large and full of autumn colours, and just to lie back with Marta tucking a rug over her and settling her elevenses beside her was bliss. She had been careful to say very little to the Professor while he attended to her leg; he had made one or two routine remarks about the weather and how she felt and she had answered him with polite brevity, but now he had gone and despite his silence, she felt lonely. She sipped the warm milk Marta had left for her and looked at the view. The road was just visible beyond the grounds and part of the drive which led to it from the house; presently she heard a car leaving the house and caught a glimpse of it as it flashed down the drive: an Aston Martin—a Lagonda. The Professor must have a friend who liked fast driving. Caro thought that it might be rather fun to know someone who drove an Aston Martin, and even more fun to actually ride in one.

She was to achieve both of these ambitions. The Professor came as usual the following morning after breakfast to dress her leg, but instead of going away immediately as he usually did he spoke to Juffrouw Kropp who had accompanied him and then addressed himself to Caro.

'I am taking you to the hospital in Leeuwarden this morning. You are to have your head X-rayed. I am certain that no harm has come from your concussion, but I wish my opinion to be confirmed.'

Caro eyed him from the vast folds of her dressing gown. 'Like this?' she asked.

He raised thick arched brows. 'Why not? Juffrouw Kropp will assist you.' He had gone before she could answer him.

Juffrouw Kropp's severe face broke into a smile as the door closed. She fetched brush and comb and make-up and produced a length of ribbon from a pocket. She brushed Caro's hair despite her protests, plaited it carefully and fastened it with the ribbon, fetched a hand mirror and held it while Caro did things to her face, then fastened the dressing gown and tied it securely round Caro's small waist. Like a well-schooled actor, the Professor knocked on the door, just as though he had been given his cue, plucked Caro from the bed and carried her downstairs where Noakes stood, holding the front door wide. The Professor marched through with a muttered word and Noakes slid round him to open the door of the Aston Martin, and with no discomfort at all Caro found herself reclining on the back seat with Noakes covering her with a light rug and the Professor, to her astonishment, getting behind the wheel.

'This is your car?' she asked, too surprised to be polite.

He turned his head and gave her an unfriendly look. 'Is there any reason why it shouldn't be?' he wanted to know, coldly.

She said kindly: 'You don't need to get annoyed. It's only that you don't look the kind of man to drive a fast car.' She added vaguely: 'A professor...'

'And no longer young,' he snapped. 'I have no interest in your opinions, Miss Tripp. May I suggest that you close your eyes and compose yourself—the journey will take fifteen minutes.'

Caroline did as she was bid, reflecting that until that

very moment she hadn't realised what compelling eyes he had; slate blue and very bright. When she judged it safe, she opened her eyes again; she wasn't going to miss a second of the ride; it would be something to tell her friends when she got back. She couldn't see much of the road because the Professor took up so much of the front seat, but the telegraph poles were going past at a terrific rate; he drove fast all right and very well, and he didn't slow at all until she saw buildings on either side of them and presently he was turning off the road and stopping smoothly.

He got out without speaking and a moment later the door was opened and she was lifted out and set in a wheelchair while the Professor spoke to a youngish man in a white coat. He turned on his heel without even glancing at her and walked away, into the hospital, leaving her with the man in the white coat and a porter.

How rude he is, thought Caro, and then: poor man, he must be very unhappy.

She was wheeled briskly down a number of corridors to the X-ray department. It was a modern hospital and she admired it as they went, and after a minute or so, when the white-coated man spoke rather diffidently to her in English, showered him with a host of questions. He hadn't answered half of them by the time they reached their destination and she interrupted him to ask: 'Who are you?'

He apologised. 'I'm sorry, I have not introduced myself. Jan van Spaark—I am attached to Professor Thoe van Erckelens' team. I am to look after you while you are here.'

'A doctor?'

He nodded. 'Yes, I think you would call me a medical registrar in your country.'

The X-ray only took a short while, and in no time at all she was being wheeled back to the entrance hall, but here, to her surprise, her new friend wished her goodbye and handed her over to a nurse, who offered a hand, saying: 'Mies Hoeversma—that is my name.'

Caro shook it. 'Caroline Tripp. What happens next?'

'You are to have coffee because Professor Thoe van Erckelens is not quite ready to leave.'

She was wheeled to a small room, rather gloomy and austerely furnished used, Mies told her, as a meeting place for visiting doctors, but the coffee was hot and delicious and Mies, although her English was sketchy, was a nice girl. Caro, who had been lonely even though she hadn't admitted it to herself, enjoyed herself. She could have spent the morning there, listening to Mies describing life in a Dutch hospital and giving her a lighthearted account of her own life in London, but the door opened, just as they had gone off into whoops of mirth over something or other, and the porter reappeared, spoke to Mies and wheeled Caro rapidly away, giving her barely a moment in which to say goodbye.

'Why the hurry?' asked Caro, hurriedly shaking hands again.

'The Professor—he must not be kept waiting.' Mies was quite serious; evidently he had the same effect on the hospital staff as he had on his staff at home. Instant, quiet obedience—and yet they liked him...

Caroline puzzled over that as she was whisked carefully to the car, to be lifted in by the Professor before he got behind the wheel and drove away. Jan van Spaark had been there, with two other younger men and a Sister, the Professor had lifted his hand in grave salute as he drove away.

He seemed intent on getting home as quickly as possible, driving very fast again, and it was a few minutes before Caroline ventured in a small polite voice: 'Was it all right—my head?'

'There is no injury to the skull,' she was assured with detached politeness. 'Tomorrow I shall remove the stitches from your leg and you may walk for brief periods—with a stick, of course. You will rest each afternoon and read for no more than an hour each day.'

'Very well, Professor, I'll do as you say.' She sounded so meek that he glanced at her through his driving mirror. When she smiled at him he looked away at once.

He carried her back to her room when they reached the house and set her down in the chair made ready for her by the window. 'After lunch I will carry you downstairs to one of the sitting rooms. Are you lonely?'

His question took her by surprise. She had her mouth open to say yes and remembered just in time that he wanted none of her company.

'Not in the least, thank you,' she told him. 'I live alone in London, you know—I have a flat, close to Oliver's.'

He nodded, wished her goodbye and went away—she heard the car roar away minutes later. Not a very successful morning, she considered, although he had wanted to know if she were lonely. And she had told a fib—not only was she lonely, but the flat she had mentioned so casually was in reality a bedsitter, a poky first floor room in a dingy street... She was reminded forcibly of it now and of dear old Waterloo, stoically waiting for her to come back. She longed for the sight of his round whiskered face and the comfort of his plump furry body curled on her knee. 'I'm a real old maid,' she said out loud, and then called,

'Come in,' in a bright, cheerful voice because there was someone at the door.

It was Noakes with more coffee. 'And the Professor says if yer've got an 'eadache, miss, yer ter take one of them pills in the red box.'

'I haven't got a headache, thank you, Noakes, not so's you'd notice. Has the Professor gone again?'

'Yes, miss—Groningen this time. In great demand, 'e is.'

'Yes. It's quiet here, isn't it? Doesn't he ever have guests or family?' Noakes hesitated and she said at once: 'I'm sorry, I had no right to ask you questions about the Professor. I wasn't being nosey, though.'

'I know that, miss, and I ain't one ter gossip, 'specially about the Professor—'e's a good man, make no mistake, but 'e ain't a 'appy one, neither.' Caro poured a cup of coffee and waited. 'It used ter be an 'ouse full when I first come 'ere. Eighteen years ago, it were—come over on 'oliday, I did, and took a fancy ter living 'ere after I met Marta. She was already working 'ere, kitchenmaid then, that was when the Professor's ma and pa were alive. Died in a car accident, they did, and he ups and marries a couple of years after that. Gay times they were, when the young Baroness was 'ere…'

'Baroness?'

Noakes scratched his head. 'Well, miss, the Professor's a baron as well as a professor, if yer take my meaning.'

'How long ago did he marry, Noakes?' Caroline was so afraid that he would stop telling her the rest, and she did want to know.

'It was in 1966, miss, two years after his folk died. Pretty lady she was, too, very gay, 'ated 'im being a doctor, always working, she used ter say, and when 'e was 'ome, looking after the estate. She liked a gay life, I can tell you! She left 'im, miss, two years after they were married—ran away with some man or other and they both got killed in a plane crash a few months later.'

Caro had let her coffee get cold. So that was why the Professor shunned her company—he must have loved his wife very dearly. She said quietly: 'Thank you for telling me, Noakes. I'm glad he's got you and Mrs Noakes and Juffrouw Kropp to look after him.'

'That we do, miss. Shall I warm up that coffee? It must be cold.'

'It's lovely, thank you. I think I'll have a nap before lunch.'

But she didn't go to sleep, she didn't even doze. She sat thinking of the Professor; he had asked her if she were lonely, but it was he who was the truly lonely one.

Chapter 2

The professor took the stitches out of Caro's leg the next morning and his manner towards her was such as to discourage her from showing any of the sympathy she felt for him. He had wished her a chilly good morning, assured her that she would feel no pain, and proceeded about his business without more ado. Then he had stood back and surveyed the limb, pronounced it healing nicely, applied a pad and bandage and suggested that she might like to go downstairs.

'Well, yes, I should, very much,' said Caro, and smiled at him, to receive an icy stare in return which sent the colour to her cheeks. But she wasn't easily put off. 'May I wear my clothes?' she asked him. 'This dressing gown's borrowed from someone and I expect they'd like it back. Besides, I'm sick of it.'

His eyebrows rose. 'It was lent in kindness,' he pointed out.

She stammered a little. 'I didn't mean that—you must think I'm ungrateful, but I'm not—what I meant was it's a bit big for me and I'd like…'

He had turned away. 'You have no need to explain yourself, Miss Tripp. I advise you not to do too much today. The wound on your leg was deep and is not yet soundly healed.' He had left her, feeling that she had made a mess of things again. And she had no sympathy for him at all, she assured herself; let him moulder into middle age with his books and his papers and his lectures!

With Marta's help she dressed in a sweater and pleated skirt and was just wondering if she was to walk downstairs on her own when Noakes arrived. He held a stout stick in one hand and offered her his arm.

'The Professor says you're to go very slowly and lean on me,' he advised her, 'and take the stairs one at a time.' He smiled at her. 'Like an old lady,' he added.

It took quite a time, but she didn't mind because it gave her time to look around her as they passed from one stair to the next. The hall was even bigger than she had remembered and the room into which she was led quite took her breath away. It was lofty and square and furnished with large comfortable chairs and sofas, its walls lined with cabinets displaying silver and china and in between these, portraits in heavy frames. There was a fire in the enormous hearth and a chair drawn up to it with a small table beside it upon which was a pile of magazines and newspapers.

'The Professor told me ter get something for yer to

read, miss,' said Noakes, 'and I done me best. After lunch, if yer feels like it, I'll show yer the library.'

'Oh, Noakes, you're all so kind, and I've given you all such a lot of extra work.'

He looked astonished. 'Lor' luv yer, miss—we enjoy 'aving yer—it's quiet, like yer said.'

'Yes. Noakes, I've heard a dog barking...'

'That'll be Rex, miss. 'E's a quiet beast mostly, but 'e barks when the Professor comes in. Marta's got a little cat too.'

'Oh, has she? So have I—his name's Waterloo, and my landlady's looking after him while I'm away. It'll be nice to see him again.'

'Yes, miss. Juffrouw Kropp'll bring coffee for you.'

It was indeed quiet, sitting there by herself. Caroline leafed through the newspapers and tried to get interested in the news and then turned to the magazines. It was almost lunchtime when she heard the Professor's voice in the hall and she sat up, put a hand to her hair and then put on a cheerful face, just as though she were having the time of her life. But he didn't come into the room. She heard his voice receding and a door shutting and presently Juffrouw Kropp brought in her lunch tray, set it on the table beside her and smilingly went away again. Caro had almost finished the delicious little meal when she heard the Professor's voice again, speaking to Noakes as he crossed the hall and left the house.

She was taken to the library by a careful Noakes after lunch and settled into a chair by one of the circular tables in that vast apartment, but no sooner had he gone than she picked up her stick, eased herself out of her chair and began a tour of the bookshelves which lined the entire room. The books were in several languages and most of them learned ones, but there were a number of novels in English and a great many medical books in that language. But she rejected them all for a Dutch-English dictionary; it had occurred to her that since she was to spend several more days as the Professor's guest, she might employ her time in learning a word or two of his language. She was deep in this task, muttering away to herself when Noakes brought a tea tray, arranged it by her, and asked her if she was quite comfortable.

'Yes, Noakes, thank you—I'm teaching myself some Dutch words. But I don't think I'm pronouncing them properly.'

'I daresay not, miss. Tell yer what, when Juffrouw Kropp comes later, get 'er ter 'elp yer. She's a dab hand at it. Nasty awkward language it is—took me years ter learn.'

'But you always speak English with the Professor?'

'That's right, miss—comes as easy to 'im as his own language!'

Caroline ate her tea, feeling much happier now that she had something to do, and when Juffrouw Kropp came to light the lamps presently, she asked that lady to sit down for a minute and help her.

Caro had made a list of words, and now she tried them out on the housekeeper, mispronouncing them dreadfully, and then, because she was really interested, correcting them under her companion's guidance. It whiled away the early evening until the housekeeper had to go, leaving her with the assurance that Noakes would be along presently to help her back to her room.

But it wasn't Noakes who came in, it was the Professor, walking so quietly that she didn't look up from her work, only said: 'Noakes, Juffrouw Kropp has been such a help, only there's a word here and I can't remember...'

She looked round and stopped, because the Professor was standing quite close by, looking at her. She answered his quiet good evening cheerfully and added: 'So sorry, I expected Noakes, he's coming to help me up to my room. I'd have gone sooner if I'd known you were home.'

She fished the stick up from the floor beside her and stood up, gathering the dictionary and her pen and paper into an awkward bundle under one arm, only to have them removed immediately by the Professor.

He said stiffly: 'Will you dine with me this evening? Since you are already downstairs...'

Caroline was so surprised that she didn't answer at once, and when she did her soft voice was so hesitant that it sounded like a stammer.

'Thank you for asking me, but I won't, thank you.' She put out a hand for the dictionary and he transferred it to the other hand, out of her reach.

'Why not?' He looked annoyed and his voice was cold.

'You don't really want me,' she said frankly. 'You said that I wasn't to—to interfere with your life in any way and I said I wouldn't.' She added kindly: 'I'm very happy, thank you, I've never been so spoiled in all my life.' She held out her hand; this time he gave her the dictionary.

'Just as you wish,' he said with a politeness she found more daunting than coldness. He took the stick from her, then took her arm and helped her out of the room and across the hall. At the bottom of the staircase he picked her up and carried her to the wide gallery above and across it to her room. At the door, he set her down and opened it for her. His 'Goodnight, Miss Tripp' was quite without expression. Caroline had no way of knowing if he was relieved that she had refused his invitation or if he was angry about it. She gave him a quiet goodnight and went through the door, to undress slowly and get ready for bed; she would have a bath and have her supper in her dressing gown by the fire.

Marta came presently to help her into the bath, turn down the bed and fuss nicely round the room, and after her came one of the maids with her supper; soup and a cheese souffle with a salad on the side and a Bavarian creme to follow. Caroline didn't think the Professor would be eating that, nor would he be drinking the home-made lemonade she was offered.

The house was very quiet when she woke the next morning and when Marta brought her her breakfast tray, she told her that Noakes had gone with the Professor to the airfield just south of the city and would bring the car back later.

'Has the Professor gone away?' asked Caroline, feeling unaccountably upset.

'To England and then to Paris—he has, how do you say? the lecture.'

'How long for?' asked Caro.

Marta shrugged her shoulders. 'I do not know—five, six days, perhaps longer.'

Which meant that when he came home again she would go almost at once—perhaps he wanted that. She ate her breakfast listlessly and then got herself up and dressed. Her leg was better, it hardly ached at all and neither did her head. She trundled downstairs slowly and went into the library again where she spent a busy morning conning more Dutch words. There didn't seem much point in it, but it was something to do.

After lunch she went into the garden. It was a chilly

day with the first bite of autumn in the air and Juffrouw Kropp had fastened her into a thick woollen cape which dropped around her ankles and felt rather heavy. But she was glad of it presently when she had walked a little way through the formal gardens at the side of the house and found a seat under an arch of beech. It afforded a good view of her surroundings and she looked slowly around her. The gardens stretched away on either side of her and she supposed the meadows beyond belonged to the house too, for there was a high hedge beyond them. The house stood, of red brick, mellowed with age, its many windows gleaming in the thin sunshine; it was large with an important entrance at the top of a double flight of steps, but it was very pleasant too. She could imagine it echoing to the shouts of small children and in the winter evenings its windows would glow with light and guests would stream in to spend the evening…not, of course, in reality, she thought sadly; the Professor had turned himself into a kind of hermit, excluding everyone and everything from his life except work and books. 'I must try and make him smile,' she said out loud, and fell to wondering how she might do that.

It was the following morning, while she was talking to Noakes as he arranged the coffee tray beside her in the library, that they fell to discussing Christmas.

'Doesn't the Professor have family or friends to stay?' asked Caro.

'No, miss. Leastways, 'e 'olds an evening party—very grand affair it is too—but 'e ain't got no family, not in this country. Very quiet time it is.'

'No carols?'

Noakes shook his head. 'More's the pity—I like a nice carol, meself.'

Caro poured out her coffee. 'Noakes, why shouldn't you have them this year? There are—how many? six of you altogether, aren't there? Couldn't you teach everyone the words? I mean, they don't have to know what they mean—aren't there any Dutch carols?'

'Plenty, miss, only it ain't easy with no one ter play the piano. We'd sound a bit silly like.'

'I can play. Noakes, would it be a nice idea to learn one or two carols and sing them for the Professor at Christmas—I mean, take him by surprise?'

Noakes looked dubious. Caroline put her cup down. 'Look, Noakes, everyone loves Christmas—if you could just take him by surprise, it might make it seem more fun. Then perhaps he'd have friends to stay—or something.'

It suddenly seemed very important to her that the Professor should enjoy his Christmas, and Noakes, looking at her earnest face, found himself agreeing. 'We could 'ave a bash, miss. There's a piano in the drawing room and there's one in the servants' sitting-room.'

'Would you mind if I played it? I wouldn't want to intrude…'

'Lor' luv yer, miss, we'd be honoured.'

She went with him later that day, through the baize door at the back of the hall, down a flagstoned passage and through another door into a vast kitchen, lined with old-fashioned dressers and deep cupboards. Marta was at the kitchen table and Juffrouw Kropp was sitting in a chair by the Aga, and they looked up and smiled as she went in. Noakes guided her to a door at the end and opened it on to a very comfortably furnished room with a large table at one end, easy chairs, a TV in a corner and a piano against one wall. There was a stove halfway along the further wall and warm curtains at the windows. The

Professor certainly saw to it that those who worked for
him were comfortable. Caroline went over to the piano
and opened it, sat down and began to play. She was by
no means an accomplished pianist, but she played with
feeling and real pleasure. She forgot Noakes for the moment, tinkling her way through a medley of Schubert,
Mozart and Brahms until she was startled to hear him
clapping and turned to see them all standing by the door
watching her.

'Cor, yer play a treat, miss,' said Noakes. 'I suppose
yer don't 'appen to know *Annie Get Yer Gun?*'

She knew some of it; before she had got to the end
they were clapping their hands in time to the music and
Noakes was singing. When she came to a stop finally, he
said: 'Never mind the carols, miss, if yer'd just play now
and then—something we could all sing?'

He sounded wistful, and looking round at their faces
she saw how eager they were to go on with the impromptu
singsong. 'Of course I'll play,' she said at once. 'You can
tell me what you want and I'll do my best.' She smiled
round at them all; Noakes and Marta and Juffrouw
Kropp, the three young maids and someone she hadn't
seen before, a quite old man—the gardener, she supposed.
'Shall I play something else?' she asked.

She sat there for an hour and when she went she had
promised that she would go back the following evening.
And on the way upstairs she asked Noakes if she might
look at the piano in the drawing-room.

She stood in the doorway, staring around her. The
piano occupied a low platform built under the window
at one end, it was a grand and she longed to play upon
it; she longed to explore the room too, its panelled walls
hung with portraits, its windows draped with heavy bro-

cade curtains. The hearth had a vast hood above it with
what she supposed was a coat of arms carved upon it. All
very grand, but it would be like trespassing to go into the
room without the Professor inviting her to do so, and she
didn't think he would be likely to do that. She thanked
a rather mystified Noakes and went on up to her room.

Lying in bed later, she thought how nice it would be to
explore the house. She had had glimpses of it, but there
were any number of closed doors she could never hope
to have opened for her. Still, she reminded herself bracingly, she was being given the opportunity of staying in
a lovely old house and being waited on hand and foot.
Much later she heard Noakes locking up and Rex barking. She hadn't met him yet; Noakes had told her that he
was to be kept out of her way until she was quite secure
on her feet. 'Mild as milk,' he had said, 'but a bit on the
big side.' Caroline had forgotten to ask what kind of dog
he was. Tomorrow she would contrive to meet him; her
leg was rapidly improving, indeed it hardly hurt at all,
only when she was tired.

Her thoughts wandered on the verge of sleep. Would
the Professor expect to be reimbursed for his trouble and
his professional services, she wondered, and if so how
would one set about it? Perhaps the hospital would settle with him if and when he sent a bill. He wouldn't be
bothered to do that himself, she decided hazily; she had
seen a serious middle-aged woman only that morning as
she crossed the hall on her way to the library and Noakes
had told her that it was the secretary, Mevrouw Slikker,
who came daily to attend to the Professor's correspondence. Undoubtedly she would be businesslike about it.
Caro nodded her sleepy head at this satisfactory solution
and went to sleep.

She walked a little further the next day, following the paths around the gardens and sitting down now and again to admire her surroundings. She wondered if the Professor ever had the time to admire his own grounds and thought probably not, he was certainly never long enough in his own house to enjoy its comforts and magnificence. She wandered round to the back of the house and found a pleasing group of old buildings grouped round a courtyard, barns and stables and a garage and a shed which smelled deliciously of apples and corn. It was coming out of this interesting place that she came face to face with an Old English sheepdog. He stood almost to her waist and peered at her with a heavily eyebrowed whiskered face. 'Rex!' she cried. 'Oh, aren't you a darling!' She extended a closed fist and he sniffed at it and then put an enormous paw on each of her shoulders and reared up to peer down at her. He must have liked what he saw, for he licked her face gently, got down on to his four feet again and offered a head for scratching. They finished their walk together and wandered in through a little side door to find Noakes looking anxious.

'There you are, miss—I 'opes yer 'aven't been too far.' His elderly eyes fell upon Rex. ''E didn't frighten yer? 'E's always in the kitchen with Marta in the mornings. I'll take 'im back...'

'Oh, Noakes, please could he stay with me? He's company and ever so gentle. Is he allowed in the house?'

'Lor' yes, miss. Follows the Professor round like a shadow, 'e does. Well, I don't see no 'arm.' He beamed at her. 'There's a nice lunch for yer in the library and Juffrouw Kropp says if yer wants 'er this afternoon she's at yer disposal.'

So the day passed pleasantly enough, and the following two days were just as pleasant. Caro did a little more each day now; the Professor would be back in two days' time, Noakes had told her, and she had to be ready to leave then. She had no intention of trespassing on his kindness for an hour longer than she needed to. Of course she would have to get tickets for the journey home, but that shouldn't take long, and Noakes would help her and perhaps the Professor would allow him to drive her to the station in Leeuwarden; she had already discovered that the train went all the way to the Hoek—all she would need to do was to get from it to the boat. She had mentioned it carefully to Noakes when he had been clearing away her supper dishes, but he had shaken his head and said dubiously that it would be better to consult the Professor. "'E may not want yer to go straight away, miss,' he suggested.

'Well, I should think he would,' she told him matter-of-factly, 'for I'm quite well now and after all, he didn't invite me as a guest. He's been more than kind to let me get well here and I mustn't stay longer than absolutely necessary.'

Noakes had shaken his head and muttered to himself and then begged her to go down to the sitting-room and play for them all again—something she had done with great pleasure, for it passed the evenings very nicely. When she was on her own she found that she had an increasing tendency to think about the Professor—a pointless pastime, she told herself, and went on doing it nonetheless.

It rained the next day, so that she spent a great deal of it in the library, with Rex beside her, poring over her dictionary. She was making progress, or so she thought, with an ever-lengthening list of words which she tried out on members of the staff. All rather a waste of time, she knew that, but it passed the days and in some obscure way made the Professor a little less of a stranger. She went earlier than usual to play the piano that day, perhaps because the afternoon was unnaturally dark and perhaps because she was lonely despite Rex's company. And Noakes and his staff seemed pleased to see her, requesting this, that and the other tune, beating time and tra-la-ing away to each other. Presently, with everyone satisfied, Caroline began to play to please herself; half forgotten melodies she had enjoyed before her aunt had married again and then on to Sibelius and Grieg, not noticing how quiet everyone had become; she was halfway through a wistful little French tune when she stopped and turned round. 'Sorry, I got carried away,' she began, and saw the Professor standing in the doorway, his hands in his pockets, leaning against the door frame.

He didn't smile, indeed, he was looking coldly furious, although his icily polite: 'Pray don't stop on my account, Miss Tripp,' was uttered in a quiet voice.

Caroline stood up rather too hard on the bad leg so that she winced. 'You're angry,' she said quickly, 'and I'm sorry—I have no right to be here, but you're not to blame Noakes or anyone else—I invited myself.'

She wanted to say a great deal more, but the look of annoyance on his face stopped her. She wished everyone goodnight in her newly acquired Dutch and went past him through the door and along the passage. He caught up with her quite easily before she could reach the staircase, and she sighed soundlessly. He was going to lecture her and she might as well have it now as later; perhaps she might even get him to see that no harm had been done, indeed he might even be glad that his staff had enjoyed a pleasant hour.

She turned to face him. 'It's a pity you frown so,' she said kindly.

He looked down his splendid nose at her. 'I have very good reason to frown, Miss Tripp, and well you know it. I return home unexpectedly and what do I find? My butler, my housekeeper, my cook, the maidservants and the gardener being entertained by you in the servants' sitting-room. Probably if I had come home even earlier I should have found you all playing gin rummy in the cellars.'

She made haste to reassure him. 'Not gin rummy—it was canasta, and we played round the kitchen table—just for half an hour,' she added helpfully. 'You see, I'm learning Dutch.'

His fine mouth curved into a sneer. 'Indeed? I cannot think why.'

Caroline said in her quiet hesitant voice: 'Well, it's something to do, you know. I'm quite well, you see.'

His voice was silky and his voice cold. 'Miss Tripp, you have disrupted my household—when one considers that I have done my best to help you and I find your behaviour intolerable.'

She stared back at him, her lip caught between her teeth, because it was beginning to tremble. After a long moment she said: 'I'm sorry, Professor.'

He turned on his heel. 'I'm glad to hear it—I hope you will mend your ways.'

He went into his study without another word and she went to her room, where she sat on her bed to review the situation. The Professor was going out to dinner that evening, she had heard Noakes say so—to one of his grand friends, she supposed, where the girls knew better than to play the piano in the servants' room and said things to make him smile instead of frown. Oh well...she got up and went across to the tallboy where her few possessions were housed and laid them on the bed, fetched her duffle bag from the cupboard and began to pack. She did it neatly and unhurriedly. There was plenty of time; she would eat her supper alone presently, as she always did, and when everyone had gone to the kitchen for their own meal, she would slip away. She would have to leave a letter. She frowned a long while over its composition, but at length it was done, neatly written and sealed into an envelope. She would have to leave it somewhere where Noakes wouldn't find it at once. The Professor's study would be the best place, he always went straight there when he came home, shutting himself away in his own learned lonely world—for he was lonely, Caroline was sure of that.

She finished her packing and went down to her supper which this evening had been set in the dining room, a richly sombre place. She felt quite lost sitting at the great oval table surrounded by all the massive furniture, but she made a good meal, partly to please Noakes and partly because she wasn't sure when she would have the next one. And Noakes was uneasy, although the Professor, he assured her, hadn't been in the least angry—indeed, he had hardly mentioned the matter. Noakes hoped—they all hoped—that tomorrow she would play for them again, but first he would ascertain if the Professor objected to her visiting the servants' sitting-room.

Caroline made some cheerful reply, finished her meal, mentioned that she would go to bed early and went upstairs. When she crept down half an hour later there was no sound. Everyone was in the kitchens by now and she wouldn't be missed, probably not until the morning, or at least until the Professor came home, and that would be late. She had put on her anorak, counted her money carefully and carried her bag downstairs before going to the study and putting the letter on the Professor's desk. She paused in the doorway for a last look; his desk was an orderly clutter of papers and books and his chair was pushed to one side as though he had got up in a hurry. She sighed deeply, closed the door gently, picked up the duffle bag and went to the door. Her leg was aching a little and she had bandaged it firmly because as far as she knew she would have to walk quite a distance before she could get a bus—the nearest village wasn't too far away, she had found that out from Juffrouw Kropp. If there wasn't a bus she would have to thumb a lift.

She put out a reluctant hand and opened the door. It was heavy, but it swung back on well-oiled hinges, revealing the Professor, key in hand, about to open it from outside. Caro, taken completely by surprise, stood with her mouth open, gaping at him. He, on the other hand, evinced no surprise, nor did he speak, merely took her duffle bag from her, put a large hand on her chest and pushed her very gently back into the house, and then just as gently shut the door behind him. Only then did he ask: 'And where were you going, Caroline?'

'Home—well, the hospital, actually.' He had never called her Caroline before—no one called her that, but it sounded rather nice.

'Why?' He stood blocking her path, the duffle bag on the floor beside him.

It seemed silly to have to explain something to him which he already knew all about. 'I've upset your household. I can quite see that I've been a perfect nuisance to you. I'm very grateful for all you've done for me—and your kindness—but I'm quite able to go back now and... Well, thank you again.'

His harsh laugh made her jump. Quite forgetting to be meek, she said severely: 'And there's no need to laugh when someone thanks you!'

'It strikes me as ironic that you should express gratitude for something you haven't had. I cannot remember being kind to you—I merely did what any other person would have done in similar circumstances, and with the minimum of trouble to myself. If I had been a poor man with a wife and children to care for and had offered you help and shelter at the cost of my and their comfort, that would have been quite a different kettle of fish. As it is, I must confess that I have frequently forgotten that you were in the house.'

Caro didn't speak. A kind of despair had rendered her dumb; her head was full of a mixed bag of thoughts, most of them miserable.

He put out a hand and touched her cheek awkwardly. 'Have you been lonely?'

Living in a bedsitter had taught her not to be lonely. She shook her head, still feeling the touch of his finger.

'And you will be glad to get back—to your flat and your friends. I doubt if you will be allowed to work for a little while.'

She had found her voice at last. It came out in a defiant mutter: 'I shall be awfully glad to get back.'

The gentleness had gone out of his voice; it sounded cold and distant again, just as though he didn't care what she did. 'Yes—I see. But be good enough to wait until the morning. I will arrange a passage for you on the night ferry tomorrow and Noakes shall drive you to the Hoek and see you on board.'

Caroline said stiffly: 'Thank you.'

'You have sufficient money?'

She nodded dumbly.

'Then go to bed.' His eye had caught her bandaged leg. 'Your leg is worse?'

'No. I—I put a crepe bandage on it because I thought I might have to walk for a bit.'

He stared at her without expression, then: 'Come to the study and I will take a look and if necessary rebandage it.'

He prodded and poked with gentle fingers, dressed it lightly and said: 'That should see you safely to Oliver's— get it looked at as soon as you can. It will do better without a dressing.' He held the study door open and offered a hand. 'Goodbye, Caroline.'

His hand was cool and firm and she didn't want to let it go.

'Goodbye, Professor. I shall always be grateful to you—and I'm sorry that I—I disturbed your peace and quiet.'

Just for a moment she thought he was going to say something, but he didn't.

Chapter 3

Caro arrived back at Meadow Road during the morning and the moment she opened the door of number twenty-six, Mrs Hodge bounced out of her basement flat, avid for a good gossip.

'Your friends came,' she said without preamble, 'said you had a bad cut leg and concussion; nasty thing concussion; you could 'ave died.' She eyed Caro's leg with relish and then looked disappointed, and Caro said almost apologetically:

'I don't need a bandage any more. Thank you for looking after Waterloo, Mrs Hodge.'

'No trouble.' Mrs Hodge, a woman who throve on other people's troubles, felt her sympathy had been wasted. 'Your rent's due on Monday.'

Caro edged past her with the duffle bag. 'Yes, I know,

Mrs Hodge. I'll just see to Waterloo and unpack and then go back to the hospital and see when I'm to go back.'

She went up the stairs and unlocked the door at the back of the landing. Not one of Mrs Hodge's best rooms, but it was quieter because it overlooked back yards and there was a tiny balcony which was nice for Waterloo.

He came to meet her now and she picked him up and laid him on her shoulder while he purred in her ear, delighted to have her back. Caroline sat down on the divan which did duty as a bed at night and looked around her.

The room was small and rather dark and seemed even more so after the Professor's spacious home; she had done the best she could with pretty curtains and cushions and a patchwork cover for the divan, but nothing could quite disguise the cheap furniture or the sink in one corner with the tiny gas cooker beside it. Caro, not given to being sorry for herself, felt a lump in her throat; it was all such a cruel contrast... She missed them all, the Professor, even though he didn't like her, Noakes and Marta, Juffrouw Kropp... She had been utterly spoilt, waited on hand and foot, and she, who had never been spoilt, had loved it. Right up until the moment she had gone on board, too, with Noakes seeing to her bag and getting her magazines to read and having a word with someone or other so that she had a super cabin to herself and a delicious meal before she had gone to bed. She had tried to pay him, but he had said very firmly that the Professor would deal with that later. Caroline had hoped that although he had said goodbye to her, she would have seen the Professor again before she left, but he had left the house after breakfast and wasn't back when she went away, with the entire staff gathered at the door to see her off.

She roused herself, gave Waterloo a saucer of milk and put on the kettle; a cup of tea would cheer her up and when she had drunk it she would unpack, dust and tidy her room and go round to Oliver's, and on the way back she would buy a few flowers to brighten up the place.

In the office at Oliver's, standing in front of Miss Veron's desk, she was astonished to hear from that lady that the Professor had written a letter about her, suggesting in the politest manner possible that she should have a few days' sick leave before she resumed work on the wards.

'A good idea, Staff Nurse,' said Miss Veron kindly. 'I expect you would like to go home or visit friends—suppose you report for duty in five days' time? You'll go back to Women's Surgical, of course. I'm sure Sister will be glad to see you.'

Caro thanked her and walked slowly back through the busy streets to Meadow Road, stopping on the way to do some shopping and indulge in the extravagance of a bunch of flowers. She would have been glad to have gone straight back to work, for she had no family and although she had a number of friends, to invite herself to go and stay with them was something she had never even dreamed of. So she spent the next four days giving her room an extra clean, reading the books she fetched from the library and talking to Waterloo. She hadn't let anyone at the hospital know that she was back; they would have been round like a flash with offers to go to the cinema, invitations to go out to a meal—morning coffee. But most of them had boyfriends or family and she shrank from being pitied; only a few of her closest friends knew that she had no family and that she hated to talk about it. Actually she need not have worried about being pitied, for she turned a bright face to the world; those who didn't know her well considered her a self-sufficient girl bent on a career, and her close friends took care never to mention it.

She went back on duty on the fifth morning, but she didn't see her friends until the coffee break when they all met in the canteen. The precious fifteen minutes was spent in answering questions; Clare, Stacey and Miriam were all there, wanting to know how she had got on, whether her leg was quite better, whether she had enjoyed herself, whether the Professor had entertained her...

'Well, not to say entertain,' observed Caro. 'He was very kind to me and saw to my leg and took me to be X-rayed at the hospital in Leeuwarden. I—I kept out of his way as much as I could—I mean, he is an important man, Noakes says, and had very little leisure.'

'I could go for him,' said Stacey. 'A bit old, perhaps, but very elegant and a man of the world, if you know what I mean, if only he'd come out from his books and lectures. He must have been crossed in love!'

Caro didn't say anything. She wasn't going to tell them about his wife; it was all a long time ago and besides, it had been a confidence on Noakes' part. She shuddered, imagining the Professor's cold rage if he ever discovered that she knew about his past unhappiness, and Miriam, noticing it, asked: 'What's worrying you, Caro? Is the ward busy?'

Caro was glad to change the subject and talked about something which lasted them until it was time to return to their wards.

Women's Surgical was busy all right; what with Sir Eustace Jenkins' round, a twice-weekly event which was stage-managed as carefully as any royal procession; yesterday's operations cases still attached to drips and tubes

and underwater pumps and needing constant care and attention, and over and above these, the normal ward routine of dressings and escorting to X-Ray, Physiotherapy
and the usual thundering round looking for notes and
Path. Lab. forms which somehow always got mislaid on
round days. Caro, hovering at Sister's elbow, ready to
interpret that lady's raised eyebrow, shake of the head,
or lifted finger and smooth her path to the best of her
ability, was quite glad when it was dinner time. She left
Sister to serve the puddings and went down to the first
meal, queuing for her portion of steamed cod, mashed
potato, and butter beans, and devouring it with the rest
of her friends at speed so that there would be time to go
over to the home and make a pot of tea.

She had more tea presently in Sister's office, having
been bidden there to be told that Sister would be going on
holiday in a week's time and Caro would be taking over
the ward. 'Just for two weeks,' Sister Pringle smiled a little. 'Good practice for you, Caro—you're in the running
for my job. I'm leaving to get married in a few months'
time and they're keen to get someone who's likely to stay
for a few years. After all, I've been here for eight years—
they wanted me to stay on, but I've had enough of being
a career girl. I'll make way for you.'

Caro, not sure if this was a compliment or an admis-
sion that she was unlikely to get married, thanked her
superior nicely and hoped that she would be adequate
while left in charge.

'Well, I can't see why not—Sir Eustace likes you and
you have a nice way with the student nurses. There are
some heavy cases coming in, though, and it'll be take-
in week…'

Caro bowed her head obediently over the notes Sister had before her. She wouldn't mind being busy, if she kept her thoughts occupied sufficiently she didn't have time to think about the Professor—a bad habit she had got into, and one which she must conquer even if only for her own peace of mind.

But she continued to think about him a great deal, picturing him alone in that great house, leading a hermit's life. It was a pity, she told Waterloo that evening as she cooked their supper, that he couldn't find some beautiful girl, exactly suited to him, and fall in love with her and get married. No sooner had she thought that than she left the sausages in the pan to fry themselves to a crisp because following hard on its heels was the second thought—that there was nothing in the world she would like more than to be that girl. Only she wasn't beautiful and she certainly wasn't suited to him; she had annoyed him excessively and he must have been delighted to see the back of her.

She sat down on the divan with Waterloo tucked under one arm. On the other hand, if she were given the chance, she would make him happy because that, she knew all at once, was what she wanted to do more than anything else in the world. She gave a watery chuckle. A more ill-suited pair than herself and the Professor would be hard to find, and why, oh, why had she fallen in love with him? Why couldn't it have been someone she might have stood a faint chance of attracting; someone insignificant and uninteresting and used to living on not much money, just sufficiently ambitious to wish to buy his own semi-detached in a suburb and keep his job, recognising in her a kindred spirit.

Only she wasn't a kindred spirit. She hated her narrow life, she wanted to be free; she wasn't sure what she wanted to do, but certainly it wasn't to be tied to a man who didn't look higher than a safe job.

She went on sitting there, oblivious of the sausages and Waterloo's voice reminding her about his supper, lost in a happy daydream where she was beautiful, well dressed and the apple of the Professor's eye. A changed Professor, of course, enjoying the pleasure of life as well as his work, discussing his day with her, planning it so that he could see as much of her as possible—wanting to be with her every minute of his leisure. She would play to him on that beautiful piano in his grand draw-ing-room, in a pink organza dress, and when he came into his house each evening she would meet him in the hall with their beautiful children around her. It was all absurd and impossible and very real in her mind's eye: if it hadn't been for the smell of burning sausages it might have gone on for hours. As it was, she came back to real-ity, removed the charred bits from the pan, opened a can of beans, fed Waterloo and made tea before going round to the local library to change her books. She came back with Fodor's Guide to the Netherlands and then spent the evening reading about Friesland, with the Professor's handsome severe features superimposed on every page.

Sister departed a week later, thankfully handing over the ward keys to Caroline with the heartfelt wish that she would be able to manage. 'Not that you're not capable,' said Sister, 'but it's take-in tomorrow.' She added hap-pily: 'We shall be on Majorca—and in swimsuits—can you imagine it? In November, too.'

But there was no time to be envious of Sister Prin-gle. Take-in weeks were always busy, and this particular one was worse than usual. Several young women were admitted with black eyes, broken noses, cracked bones and severe contusions after taking part in a demonstration march about something or other and falling foul of a rival faction on the way. These had been followed by two victims of a gas explosion in one of the small terraced houses close to the hospital, and no sooner were they settled in their beds than an old lady who had fallen over in the street and cut her head was admitted for observation. Caro found her hands full and they remained like that for most of the week. She sighed with relief when she went off duty on the seventh day. After midnight they would have comparative peace on the ward; she would catch up with the paperwork, see to the off-duty and have time to chat to each of the patients as she took round the post—and the nurses should be able to catch up on their off-duty. She rose from her bed at the beginning of the second week of Sister's absence in the pleasant expectation of an uneventful week.

And so it was for the first few hours. The nurses, happy in the knowledge that there would be no urgent call to ready a bed for yet another emergency, began on the morning's routine with a good will and Caro, having fulfilled her ambition to have a nice long chat with each patient in turn, organised the day's tasks, made a sortie to the X-ray department with the firm determination to discover the whereabouts of a number of missing films, and answered the telephone at least a dozen times, before she settled herself in the office to puzzle out the off-duty for the following two weeks. She was halfway through this tedious task when there was a knock on the door and before she could say anything, it was opened and Professor Thoe van Erckelens stalked in.

Caroline didn't speak, she was too surprised—and besides, after the first second or two, her heart raced so violently that she had no breath. She just sat where she was and stared at him with huge hazel eyes.

'Ha,' observed the Professor, 'you are surprised to see me.'

He looked ill-tempered, tired too. It was an awful waste of one's life to love a man who didn't care a row of pins for one. She took a steadying breath and said in her quiet voice: 'Yes, Professor, I am. I expect you have a consultation here? Shall I...?'

He came right into the office and shut the door. 'No, I came to see you.'

She opened her eyes and her mouth too. 'Whatever for?' She went on earnestly: 'I can't really spare the time unless you wanted to see a patient—there's Mrs Possett's dressing and two patients to go for X-ray.'

He dismissed Mrs Possett with a wave of his hand. 'What I have to say will take five minutes—less.'

Caroline folded her small, nicely cared for hands in her lap and gave him her full attention. He didn't move from the door. 'Will you marry me, Caroline?'

She stayed very still. After a moment she asked: 'Me? Is this a joke or something, Professor?'

'No, and if you will be good enough to give me your full attention and not interrupt I will explain.'

She glanced around her just to make sure that she wasn't dreaming. The office was much as usual, its desk an orderly muddle of forms and charts and papers, chilly, foggy air coming in through the open window, the radiator as usual gurgling gently into tepid warmth. The only difference was the Professor, taking up most of the available space and apparently suffering from a brainstorm. She said in a tranquil voice which quite masked her bewilderment: 'I'm listening,' and made herself look at him. She was rewarded by a forbidding stare.

'I'm forty,' he told her almost angrily. 'I have been married before—thirteen years ago, to be precise. My wife left me for another man within two years of our marriage and she—both of them—were killed in an accident a year later. I have had no wish to marry again.' He shrugged huge shoulders, 'Why should I? I have my work, enough money, a well run home and there are always girls—pretty girls if I should wish for female company.'

He paused to study her and she flinched because no doubt he was comparing her homely face with the young ladies in question. 'However, after you had left my house I missed you—my household miss you. They have worn gloomy faces ever since you left—quite ridiculous, of course—even Rex and the cats...' He paused again, searching her quiet face as though he were trying to discover what there was about her that could disrupt his organised life. Presently he went on. 'You are an extraordinary girl,' he declared irritably, 'you have no looks, no witty conversation, quite deplorable clothes—and yet I find that I am able to talk to you—indeed, I find myself wishing to discuss the various happenings of my day with you. I am not in love with you and I have no wish to be; I need a calm quiet companion, someone sensible who isn't for ever wanting to be taken out to dinner or the theatre, nor demand to know where I am going each time I leave the house. I need... I need...'

'A sheet anchor,' supplied Caro in a sensible voice. 'No demands, no curiosity, just a—someone to talk to when you feel inclined.'

He looked surprised. 'You understand then; I have no

need to explain myself further. And above all, no romantic nonsense!' He gave her a bleak look which wrung her soft heart. 'You will have a pleasant life; the servants are already devoted to you and you will have my friends and sufficient money. And in return I ask for companionship when I need it, someone to sit at my table and play hostess to my guests and run my home as I like it. Well?'

Caro studied his face. He meant every preposterous word of it and he expected her to say yes then and there. I must change him just a little, she thought lovingly, he must be got out of his lonely arrogant world and learn to enjoy himself again—he must have been happy once. Aloud she said in a tranquil voice: 'I must have time to think about it.'

'Time? Why should you need time? You have no family.' He looked deliberately round the little room. 'And nothing but a hard-working future.'

Here was another one who took it for granted that no one wanted to marry her. 'You make it sound like a bribe,' she told him.

His mouth was a straight bad-tempered line. 'Nothing of the sort. I have offered you marriage. I hope that I am not such a hypocrite that I pretend affection for you— liking, yes; you annoy me excessively at times and yet I must admit that I like you. Well?'

She smiled a little. 'I'll tell you tomorrow. I must sleep on it.'

'Oh, very well, if you want it that way. I thought you were a sensible girl.'

'I am, that's why I have to think about it.'

There was a knock on the door and he opened it, glaring at the student nurse standing outside so that she sidled past him uneasily.

'It's all right, Nurse,' said Caro soothingly. 'What's the matter?'

'Mrs Skipton's dressing's down ready for you to see, Staff.'

'I'm coming now,' she smiled reassuringly, and the nurse retreated, casting an interested eye upon the Professor as she went—a remarkably handsome man even though he looked as black as a thundercloud.

He closed the door with a snap behind her and then stood in front of it so that although Caro had got to her feet she was forced to a halt before him. 'I do have to go,' she told him mildly.

He opened the door. 'I'll see you tomorrow, Caroline.'

She walked past him into the ward, looking as serene as she always did while her insides turned somersaults. The nurse who had been to the office rolled her eyes upwards and shrugged her shoulders for the benefit of the junior nurse with her. 'Poor old Staff,' she murmured, 'as prim as a maiden aunt even with that gorgeous man actually talking to her!'

'I'll have the forceps, Nurse,' said Caro briskly. She had seen the look and rightly guessed at the murmur. It would be fun, she mused as she deftly removed the rubber drain from Mrs Skipton's shrinking person, to see the girl's face when she announced her engagement to the Professor.

Because she was going to marry him, she had no doubts about that, and not for any of the reasons he had given her, either. He hadn't even thought of the only reason which mattered—that she loved him.

It was typical of the Professor not to mention when and where he would see her on the following day. Caroline spent the whole of it in a state of pleasurable excitement, one ear cocked for the telephone, and her eyes sliding to the ward door every time it opened. In the end she went off duty after tea, telling herself that he had forgotten all about her, thought better of it, or what seemed more likely, she had dreamed the whole thing. She explained this to Waterloo at some length as she gave him his supper and then went to peer into the cupboard and see what she could cook for her own meal. A tin of soup, she decided, and then a poached egg on toast with a pot of tea. And while she had it she would finish that interesting bit in Fodor's Guide about Friesland having its own national anthem. She knelt to light the gas fire, but before she could strike a match there was a knock on the door. Her heart shot into her mouth, but she ignored it; the Professor had no idea where she lived and she hoped and prayed that he never would. It would be her landlady, she supposed, and went to open the door.

She had supposed wrong. It was the Professor, looming large on the narrow landing. The sheer size of him forced her to retreat a few steps so that he was inside before she could say a word. He stood looking around him unhurriedly and asked: 'This is your flat?'

'Good evening,' said Caro, and didn't answer him.

He turned his eyes on to her then. 'I've annoyed you— probably you didn't wish me to know that you lived in a bedsitter in this truly deplorable neighbourhood.'

'It's convenient for Oliver's.' She added indignantly: 'It's my home.'

His eyes lighted on Waterloo, waiting impatiently for the fire to be lighted. 'Your cat?'

'Yes—Waterloo. I found him there when he was a kitten.'

'He will of course return with us to Huis Thoe.'

She had scrambled to her feet. 'But I haven't said I'd…
marry you.'

'Perhaps we might go somewhere and have dinner
and discuss it.'

She stared at him, wondering if there was another girl
in the world who had had such a dry-as-dust proposal.
Her first inclination was to refuse, but she was hungry
and soup and an egg weren't exactly gastronomic excite-
ments. 'I'll have to change,' she said.

'I will wait on the landing.' He opened the door and
a strong aroma of frying onions caused his winged nos-
trils to flare. He didn't speak, only gave her an eloquent
look as he closed it quietly.

There wasn't much choice in the rickety wardrobe,
but the few clothes she had were presentable although
the Professor had called them deplorable. How would he
know anyway, leading the life he did? Caroline put on
a plain wool dress of dark green, combed her hair, did
things to her face, found her good wool coat, her best
shoes, her only decent handbag, gave Waterloo a saucer
of food and assured him that she wouldn't be long, and
left the room. The Professor was standing quietly, but
giving the impression of an impatient man holding his
impatience in check with a great effort, and she could
hardly blame him; the smell of onions had got considerably worse.

They went down the narrow stairs and out into the
street where he took her by the arm and hurried her on to
the opposite pavement. 'The car is at Oliver's,' and at her
quick questioning glance, 'and if you are wondering why
I didn't go and fetch it while you were changing I will
admit to a fear that if I did so you might have changed
your mind and disappeared by the time I had got back.'

Caroline paused to stare up at him in the dusk. 'Well, really—is that your opinion of me? I would never dream of...'

'I am aware of that; it was merely a remarkably silly notion which entered my head.'

He wasn't going to say any more than that. They walked the short distance in silence and he opened the door of the Aston Martin for her. Settling himself beside her, he remarked: 'I've booked a table at the Savoy Grill Room.'

'Oh, no!' exclaimed Caro involuntarily. 'I'm not dressed...'

'The Grill Room,' he reminded her, and glanced sideways at her. 'You look all right to me.'

She had the idea that he hadn't the vaguest notion of what she was wearing; probably he never would have, for he never really looked at her for more than a few seconds at a time. If it came to that, very few did.

The Grill Room was full and she felt shy of her surroundings as they went in, but they were shown at once to their table and although she would have preferred one in a quiet corner where she could have been quite unnoticed, nothing could have bettered the attention they received.

She sipped at the sherry she had been given and studied the menu, mouthwateringly lengthy; she settled for salmon mousse, tournedos, sautéed straw potatoes and braised celery, and when it came ate it with appetite, replying politely to her companion's desultory conversation as he demolished a grilled steak. She enjoyed the Beaujolais he offered her too, but prudently refused a second glass, which was just as well, for the sherry trifle was deliciously rich. It was when the waiter had cleared the table and set coffee before them that the Professor abandoned his dinner table conversation and asked abruptly: 'Well, you've slept on it, Caroline, and now I should like your answer. Is it yes or no?'

She handed him his coffee cup without haste. He had asked a plain question, he was going to get a plain answer. 'Yes.'

She watched his face as she spoke and found it rather daunting to see his calm expression quite unchanged. 'Very well, we can now make plans for our marriage. As soon as possible, don't you think?'

'Very well, but I have to give in my resignation at Oliver's, Prof... What am I to call you?'

He smiled a little. 'Radinck. If you have no objection, I can arrange that you leave very shortly. We can be married here by special licence. Do you wish to invite anyone? Family? Friends?'

'I have an aunt—no one else—she's married now and I don't think she will want to come to the wedding. I expect some of my friends from the hospital would like to come to the church.'

'I'll see about it and let you know. Have you sufficient money to buy yourself some clothes?'

Caroline thought of her little nest egg, hoarded against a rainy day. 'Yes, thank you.'

He nodded. 'You can of course buy anything you want when we return, but I presume you will want something for the wedding.' His voice held a faint sneer.

'I won't disgrace you,' she told him quietly, and was pleased to see him look a little taken aback. If she hadn't loved him so much she would have been furious.

He begged her pardon stiffly and she said kindly: 'Oh, that's all right—it'll be super to have some decent clothes.' She wrinkled her forehead in thought. 'Something I can travel in and wear afterwards...'

He passed his cup for more coffee. 'Perhaps I should point out to you that you can buy all the clothes you want when you are my wife. I—we shall live comfortably enough.' He sat back in his chair. 'Now as to the actual wedding...'

He had thought of everything; the arrangements for her to leave, the obtaining of the marriage licence, giving up her bedsitter, a basket for Waterloo's comfortable transport to Holland. There would be no honeymoon, he told her, and that didn't surprise her at all, honeymoons were for two people in love, but she was surprised when he said: 'We will go tomorrow and buy the wedding rings and I will give you your engagement ring—I brought it over with me but forgot to bring it with me this evening.'

She didn't know whether to laugh or cry at that.

Radinck took her back to Meadow Road presently, waiting at her front door while she climbed the stairs and unlocked her own door. His goodnight had been casual and, to her ear, faintly impatient. Probably he found her boring company, but in that case why did he want to marry her? Probably he was tired. She got ready for bed, made a pot of tea because she was too excited to sleep and sat in front of the gas fire with Waterloo beside her, politely listening while she recounted the evening's happenings to him.

She was off in the evening again the next day and she supposed Radinck would meet her then; certainly there was no time to go buying wedding rings during the day—but apparently he thought differently.

Caroline had got well into the morning's routine when he came on to the ward with Sir Eustace, and Caro, hastily pulling down her sleeves, went down the ward to meet them, wondering which patient they wanted to see.

They wished her good morning and Sir Eustace said jovially: 'Well, Staff Nurse, I am delighted at the news that you are to marry. I haven't come to do a round, only to beg the pleasure of giving you away.'

Caro pinkened. 'Oh, would you? Would you really? I did wonder… I haven't got any relations…'

'I shall be delighted—Radinck will let me know the day when you've decided it.' He beamed at her. 'And now I must go to theatre—I'm already late.'

She escorted him to the door and went back to the Professor, who hadn't said a word after his good morning and in answer to her look of enquiry he observed: 'It is rather public here, perhaps we might go to the office for a minute.'

She led the way, offered him a seat which he declined and sat down at the desk. 'I will be outside at twelve o'clock,' he told her. 'You will go to your dinner then, I believe? We can go along to Apsleys and get the rings and have a quick lunch somewhere.'

'But I'll be in uniform—there's only an hour, you know—there'll never be time… I don't mind missing lunch.'

'Put a coat over your uniform. I'll see that you get back on duty on time.' He took a small box out of a pocket. 'This was my mother's—she had small hands, like yours, and I hope it will fit.'

He opened the box and took out a great sapphire ring set in a circle of rose diamonds and when she held out her hand, slipped it on to her finger. It fitted exactly. Caro, who was inclined to be superstitious, thought it was a good omen.

She thanked him for it and longed to throw her arms round him and kiss him, but instead she said: 'It's very beautiful: I'll take great care of it.'

He nodded carelessly. 'You will wish to get on with your work—I'll meet you at noon.'

He had gone before she could do more than nod.

It wasn't entirely satisfactory going out in her winter coat which was brown and didn't match her black duty shoes and stockings. She had made her hair tidy and powdered her nose, but rushing down to the front door of the hospital she thought crossly that all the girls she knew would have refused flatly to go out looking so ridiculous; but there again, she reminded herself, Radinck considered she dressed deplorably anyway; he wouldn't notice.

If he did he said nothing, merely stowed her in the car and drove smoothly to Apsleys where they must have expected him, for they were attended to immediately by a quiet-voiced elderly man, who said very little as he displayed rings of every variety before them.

The Professor gave them a cursory glance. 'Choose which you prefer, Caroline,' he suggested. He sounded bored, and just for a moment resentment at his lack of interest at what should be an important event to them both almost choked her, but her common sense came to her rescue; why should he be interested? Buying the ring was to him only a necessary part of getting married. She picked a perfectly plain gold one and the man measured her finger and found her one to fit it before doing the same for the Professor. While he was away wrapping them up, Radinck said quietly: 'You aren't wearing your ring.'

'It's in the box in my pocket. I haven't had a chance—I

mean, I can't wear it on duty and I forgot to wear it now—
I'm not used to it yet.'

'Will you put it on?'

She did so, and when the man came back he saw it
and smiled nicely at her. It made her feel much better
and almost happy.

It hadn't taken much time: there was more than half an
hour before she had to return to the ward, but when the
Professor turned the car back in the direction of Oliver's
she supposed that he had decided that there wasn't time
for even a snack lunch and in all fairness she had said
that she wouldn't mind missing her lunch. But in Cheap-
side he slowed the car, parked it and walked her into Le
Poulbot where it seemed they were expected.

'I took the liberty of ordering for you since we have
only a short time,' observed Radinck. 'Filets de sole Le-
onora and a glass of white wine to go with it, and perhaps a sorbet.'

She was surprised at his thoughtfulness and stammered her thanks. 'But it means you have to rush over
lunch too,' she pointed out.

'I'm not in the habit of sitting over my meals,' he observed. 'When one is by oneself it is a waste of time—
one gets into bad habits…'

Caroline resolved silently to get him out of them even
if it took her a lifetime and took care not to chat while
they ate. Actually she longed to talk; there was so much
she wanted to know, but she would have to wait; when
he had made all the arrangements he would doubtless
tell her. She was surprised when he asked: 'Which day
do you wish to choose for the wedding?'

She said with some asperity: 'Well, how can I choose

until I know when I'm to leave and when you want to go back to Holland?'

He waved aside the waiter and sat back to watch her eating her sorbet.

'Ah, yes—I saw your Senior Nursing Officer this morning. You may leave in five days' time—by then I shall have the licence, would any day after that suit you?'

She felt a surge of excitement at the very idea. 'That's…' she counted on her fingers, 'Sunday. Would Tuesday suit you? That would give me time to pack my things. Will you be here until then?'

He shook his head. 'I'm going back tomorrow—there are several patients I have to see. I'll come back on Sunday and see you then. Would you like to go to a hotel until the Tuesday?'

She was surprised again. 'That's very kind of you, but I'll stay in Meadow Road if you don't mind—Waterloo, you know.'

'Ah, yes, I had forgotten.' He glanced at his watch. 'We had better go.'

His leavetaking was casual. No one looking at the two of them, thought Caro, would have guessed that they were going to be married within a week. She watched him get into his car and drive away, her eyes filled with tears. She knew nothing about him; where he was staying, what he was doing in London, if he had friends… the only thing she was sure of was that she loved him enough to bear with his ways.

Chapter 4

Five days, Caro discovered, could last for ever, especially when one didn't know what was going to happen at the end of them. The Professor had said he was going to see her on Sunday, but once again he had forgotten to mention time or place. True, she had enjoyed several hours of shopping which had left her very satisfied and reduced her nest egg to a few paltry pounds, all the same she wished very much that Sunday would come.

And finally come it did and Caro, burdened with a variety of presents from her friends and fellow nurses, left Oliver's early in the afternoon. She had several hours of overtime due to her and Sister Pringle, generous after her holiday, had told her to go early rather than wait until six o'clock. She had been surprised to find her staff nurse engaged and on the point of leaving, but she had been pleased too; Caro got on well with everyone in her quiet way and she would be missed. She would miss her life at Oliver's too, she thought, as she crossed the busy street in front of the forbidding exterior and made her way to Meadow Road, but she wasn't daunted at the idea of living in another country; she would have lived wherever Radinck was and not complained.

She fed Waterloo, made herself a pot of tea and spread her packages on the bed—an early morning tea-set from Stacey, Miriam and Clare, a tea-cosy from the nurses on the ward, a bright pink bath towel from the ward maid and the orderlies and some handkerchiefs from Sister Pringle, and over and above these, a cut glass vase from all her friends. She admired them at length, for with no family of her own, presents had been few and far between. After she had had her tea she went to the wardrobe and looked at the new clothes hanging there. Her wedding outfit, covered in a plastic wrapper, took up most of the room; it was a rather plain fine wool dress in a warm amber colour which, if the weather should prove cold, would go very well under her winter coat. She had bought a small velvet hat to go with it, rather expensive shoes and gloves and a leather handbag. Not even the Professor would be able to find fault with them, she considered. She had bought a suit too, a multi-coloured tweed with a Marks and Spencer sweater to go with it, and more shoes, a sensible pair for walking in, and new undies and slacks. She would have liked some new luggage to pack them in, but her case, although shabby, was quite adequate and she wanted a few pounds in her purse; Radinck had talked about an allowance in a cool voice which had made her determined not to make use of it until she was forced to.

He arrived just as she was making toast for her tea.

The afternoon had turned wet and chilly and Caroline had drawn the curtains and got out the Fodor's Guide once more. She was sitting on the wool rug she had made for herself, the bread toasting on a fork, Waterloo sitting beside her, when Radinck thumped on the door. No one else thumped like that. She knew who it was and called to him to come in. She didn't get up but went on with her toast-making, saying merely: 'Hello, Radinck, would you like some tea? I'm just going to make it.'

'Thank you, that would be nice.' He took off his car coat and sat down in the shabby chair beside the fire.

'Have you just arrived?' she asked.

'Yes, they told me at Oliver's that you had left.' His eyes lighted on the presents still laid out on the divan and he looked a question.

'Wedding presents,' said Caro cheerfully, turning her toast. 'I've never had so many things all at once in my life.'

He said, 'Very nice,' and dismissed them. 'You are ready for Tuesday?'

'Yes, I think so.' She buttered the toast and got up to put the kettle on.

Radinck looked tired and even more severe than usual and so aloof that Caroline didn't dare to utter the words of sympathy crowding into her head. Instead she made the tea, poured him a cup and put it, with the toast, on a stool by his chair, and then set about making more toast.

Presently when he had drunk his tea and she had given him a second cup she asked in her soft voice: 'You haven't changed your mind? You really want me to marry you, Radinck? One often gets ideas that don't work out...'

'I still want to marry you, Caroline.' He had relaxed, leaning back eating his toast, stroking Waterloo who had got on to his knee. 'I thought that we might go out for dinner.'

'Thank you, that would be nice.'

'And tomorrow? I have to be at the hospital in the morning, but perhaps we might go out in the afternoon. You have finished your shopping?'

'Yes, thank you—I have only to pack.'

He nodded. 'They are all delighted at Huis Thoe. You realise that we have to return by the night boat on Tuesday?'

'Yes.' She bit into her toast, trying to think of something to add and couldn't. She was astonished when he asked:

'What is the colour of your dress?'

'The one I've bought for the wedding? I suppose you'd call it dark amber.' She took a sip of tea and went on: 'I know you aren't interested in what I wear, it's a very plain dress—quite nice, you know, but no one's likely to take a second look at me, if you see what I mean.'

He raised his thick eyebrows. 'And is that your ambition? I have always understood that women—especially young ones—like to be noticed.'

'Not with a face like mine, they wouldn't,' Caro assured him.

He eyed her gravely. 'Your figure is not displeasing,' he observed, and sounded almost as surprised at his words as she was.

He didn't have to wait on the landing this time. She had adopted the old-fashioned idea of wearing her best clothes on Sundays even if she wasn't going anywhere; it made the day seem a little different from all the others, so she was ready when Radinck suggested that they should go.

This time he took her to the Connaught Hotel Restaurant and because it was Sunday evening her green wool dress didn't seem too out of place, and she really wouldn't have minded; she had the sapphire on her finger, proclaiming that she had some sort of claim on her companion—although judging by the looks she received from some of the younger women sitting near them, it wasn't at all justified—besides, she was hungry. She did full justice to the cheese soufflé—as light as air, followed by filets de sole princesse and rounded off by millefeuille from the sweet trolley, all nicely helped down by the champagne the Professor had ordered. Caro wasn't very used to champagne; she wasn't sure if she liked it, but with the second glass she assured her companion that it was a drink which grew on one, and although she hadn't intended to make him laugh, he actually did.

She spent the next morning packing her clothes and putting her small treasures and ornaments, carefully wrapped, into a large cardboard box.

She was quite ready when Radinck called for her, dressed in the new suit, her face carefully made up. It was most gratifying when he remarked casually: 'You look nice—is that new?'

She told him yes, reflecting that it had been worth the scandalous price she had paid for it at Jaegers; a lukewarm compliment but still a compliment.

They went to the Connaught again and when she observed how very nice it was, the Professor agreed pleasantly enough. 'I stay here if I'm in England for a few days,' he told her, and she fell to wondering where he went if his stay was protracted. Her thoughts must have been mirrored on her face, for after a pause he said:

'I have a small house in Essex, but it is hardly worth going there unless I'm over for a week or more.'

'What exactly do you do?' she asked carefully. 'That's if you don't mind telling me.'

He didn't answer her at once but remarked testily: 'Why is it that so many remarks you make appear to put me in the wrong, Caroline?' and before she could deny this: 'I am a physician, specialising in heart conditions, and the various diseases consequent to them.'

'But you lecture?'

'Yes.'

'And of course you're a consultant as well. Do you travel a great deal?'

He frowned a little. 'What a great many questions, Caroline!'

She agreed cheerfully. 'But you see, Radinck, if I ask them now, you'll never have to answer them again, will you?'

'That is true. I hope you don't expect to travel with me? I'm used to being alone—I concentrate better.'

She eyed him with pity wringing her heart, but all she said was: 'Of course I don't—I haven't forgotten that I'm to be a sheet anchor.'

He gave her a hard suspicious look which she met with a clear friendly gaze.

She hadn't asked what they were doing with the rest of the afternoon. She expected to be taken to Meadow Road, but it seemed that Radinck had other plans, for after lunch he left the car at the hotel and hailed a taxi. It cost Caro a great effort not to ask him where they were going, but she guessed that he was waiting for her to do just that. In the taxi he said: 'I have a wedding gift for you, but I wish you to see it first—it may not please you.'

She would have been a moron not to have been
pleased, she thought presently, standing in front of the
triple mirror in an exclusive furrier's shop. Mink, no
less—ranch mink, he had carefully explained, because
he thought that a coat made from trapped animals might
distress her. It was a perfect fit, and when she remarked
upon this he had told her casually that Clare had very
kindly supplied her measurements.

She thanked him quietly and sincerely, careful to do
it while the sales lady wasn't there. 'I can wear it tomorrow,' she told him. 'I was going to wear my winter coat...'

She understood then that for his wife to return to Huis
Thoe in anything less than a mink coat would have upset
everyone's idea of the fitness of things. She reflected with
some excitement that she would be expected to dress
very well, go to the hairdressers too and use the kind of
make-up advertised so glossily in *Harpers* and *Vogue*.
It struck her then that she was going to be a baroness—
ridiculous but true. Just for a moment she quailed at the
thought, but then her sensible head told her that it didn't
matter what either of them were if they could love each
other—and she already did that; it was just a question of
getting Radinck to fall in love with her. She wasn't quite
sure how she was going to do it, but it would be done.

Leaving the shop Radinck observed: 'I hope you will
be pleased. I thought it would be pleasant if we gave a
small dinner party for your friends and Sir Eustace and
my best man this evening. At the hotel in my rooms there;
we shall have to leave directly after we have been married tomorrow, so there is no question of giving a lunch
party then.'

'How nice,' said Caro faintly. 'C-can I wear this dress?'

'Certainly not. It will be black ties—your three friends are wearing long dresses. Have you no evening gown?'

She shook her head. 'Well, no—you see I don't go out a great deal.' Not at all, she added silently, but pride stopped her from saying so aloud.

'In that case tell me where you would like to buy a dress and we'll go there now.'

'Oh, I couldn't...'

He said coolly: 'Don't be so old-fashioned, Caroline—it is perfectly permissible for a man to buy his future wife a dress should he wish to do so. We will go to Fortnum and Mason.'

Caro goggled at him. 'But I've never been there in my life—not to buy anything.'

'Then it's time you did.'

He was there and she was getting out of the car before she could think of any argument against this and was led unresisting to the Dress Department where the Professor, looking more severe than ever, was instantly attended to by the head sales lady.

Having made his wishes clear he took himself off to a comfortable chair and left Caro to be led away by the sales lady to go through a selection of dresses which were all so stunning that she had no idea what she wanted.

It was the sales lady who pointed out that green was a good colour for hazel eyes and furthermore she had just the thing to suit, and if that wasn't to madam's taste, there was a charming honey-coloured crêpe or a grey crêpe de Chine...

Caro, almost delirious with excitement, tried them all on in turn and settled for the green; organza over silk with full sleeves gathered into tight buttoned cuffs and a low ruffled neckline. And when the sales lady suggested that she might like some rather pretty sandals to go with it, she agreed recklessly. She told Radinck about the sandals as they left the shop. 'I had no evening shoes,' she explained gravely, 'so I hope you don't mind. They were rather expensive.'

She hadn't been able to discover the price of the dress; the sales lady had been vague and she had watched Radinck sign a cheque without showing any signs of shock. She hoped that it hadn't been too expensive, but it wasn't until later that evening while she was dressing that she saw its label; a couture garment, and her mind boggled at the cost.

They had tea presently in a tiny shop all gilt and white paint, with the most heavenly cakes Caro had ever eaten, and on the way back she thanked him fervently and then went scarlet when he said coldly: 'You have no need to be quite so fulsome in your thanks. I have hardly lavished a fortune upon you, Caroline.'

She turned her head and looked out of the car window, wanting to burst into tears; the last thing she must ever do before him. She said brightly, proud of her steady voice, 'How dark it grows in the afternoons—but I like winter, don't you?'

She didn't see his quick glance at her averted face. 'You will be able to skate on the canal near Huis Thoe if it freezes enough.' His voice was casual and quite different from the biting tones he had just used. Caroline supposed she would learn in time—not to mind when he snubbed her, not to mind when he was cold and distant; there would surely be times when they could talk together, get to know each other. It would take time, but after all, he had said that he liked her.

He had to go back to the hospital that evening. He left

her at Meadow Road, said that he would call for her at
half past seven and drove away, leaving her to tell Waterloo all about it, wash her hair, do her face and put on the
new dress. She had been ready and waiting half an hour
or more before he returned, pleased with her appearance
and hoping that he would be pleased too.

His cool 'very nice!' when he arrived was rather less
than she had hoped for and his further: 'The dress is
pretty,' although truthful, hardly flattered her, but she
thanked him politely, tucked Waterloo up in his box and
picked up the new fur coat. It was almost frightening
how the touch of his cool hands on her shoulders as he
held it for her sent her insides seesawing.

The evening was a great success; Clare, Miriam and
Stacey had been fetched by the best man whose name
Caro, in her excitement, didn't catch, although she remembered afterwards that he had said that he had an
English wife who had just had a baby, and Sir Eustace
and his wife arrived a few minutes after them. They all
looked very elegant, Caro considered, drinking champagne cocktails in the elegant room Radinck had taken
her to; her friends did credit to the occasion and sadly
seemed on better terms with their host than she did. Just
as he did with them. It was strange, she mused a little
cloudily because of the champagne, that he should want
to marry her when she never amused him, but there again,
she couldn't imagine any of them allowing him to lead
the quiet, studious life he seemed to enjoy. But her low
spirits didn't last for long; the ring was admired, as was
the coat, and her friends' pleasure at her change of fortune was genuine enough. And Lady Jenkins, under the
impression that it was a love match and knowing that
Caro had no parents, became quite motherly.

They dined late and at leisure at the round table set up in the Professor's sitting room at the hotel. Iced melon was followed by lobster thermidor and rounded off with ices, trifle and charlotte russe. They drank champagne and over coffee the Professor observed that it hardly seemed right to have a wedding cake before the wedding, but he had done his best to substitute that with petits fours, covered in white icing and decorated with silver leaves and flowers.

It was almost midnight when the party broke up and everyone went home, cracking jokes about seeing them at the church in the morning. When they had all gone, Caro put on her coat once more and was driven back to Meadow Road, making polite conversation all the way. She only stopped when Radinck remarked: 'You're very chatty—it must be the champagne.'

He didn't sound annoyed, though, only a little bored, so she said, 'Yes, I expect it is,' and lapsed into silence until they reached the house. He got out first, opened her door and went with her up the stairs, to take the key from her hand and open the door. The contrast after the spacious elegance of the hotel room was cruel, but he didn't say anything, only gave her back her key, cautioned her to be ready when he came for her in the morning and wished her goodnight.

'Goodnight,' said Caro hurriedly, because she hadn't thanked him yet and he seemed in a hurry to be gone. 'It was a delightful dinner party, thank you, Radinck.' And when he muttered something she added: 'I'll be ready when you come.'

She smiled at him and shut the door quite briskly, leaving him on the landing. She loved him so very much, but she mustn't let that weaken her resolve to alter his stern outlook on life. She suspected that he was a man who had always had his own way, even to shutting a door when he wanted to and not a moment before. A small beginning, but she had to start somewhere.

She slept dreamlessly with Waterloo curled up in a tight ball on her feet and was up much earlier than she needed to be, and true to her word, she was dressed and ready when Radinck came for her. Waterloo and her luggage were to be collected after the ceremony. Caroline cast a look round the little room and followed Radinck down the stairs to the car. The drive to the church was a short one and they hardly spoke. At the door she was handed over to Sir Eustace waiting in the porch and given a small bouquet of rich yellow roses which the Professor took from the back of the car. He nodded briefly at her and just for a moment she panicked, staring up at him with eyes full of doubt, and he must have seen that, for he smiled suddenly and she glimpsed the man under the calm mask and all her doubts went. If he could smile like that once, he could do it again, and she would make sure that he did. She took Sir Eustace's arm and walked firmly down the aisle to where Radinck, towering over everything in sight, waited for her.

She had no clear recollection of the ceremony. The best man had given her an encouraging smile as she reached Radinck's side, but the Professor didn't look at her at all. Indeed, he looked rather grim during the short service. Only as he put the ring on her finger he smiled slightly. She wanted to smile too, but she didn't; she would have to remember to remain friendly and undemanding quite without romantic feelings; he didn't hold with romance. That was something else which she had to alter.

There was to be no wedding breakfast. Everyone said

goodbye in the church porch and Caro got into the car beside Radinck, not feeling in the least married and resolved to change his life for him. Indeed when Clare put her head through the window and exclaimed: 'Good lord, you're a baroness now!' she started to deny it and then declared: 'I'd forgotten that— Oh, dear!' She looked so woebegone at the idea that Clare laughed at her.

The Professor didn't intend to waste time; Caro's luggage was put in the boot, Waterloo, in a travelling basket, was arranged on the back seat, and with a hurried word to Mrs Hodge, who looked aggrieved because it hadn't been a proper wedding at all, Caro settled herself tidily beside the Professor. Afterwards, she had no very clear recollection of the journey either. They travelled by Hovercraft from Dover and although they stopped for lunch and again for tea, she had no idea what they had talked about or what she had eaten. The Professor had laid himself out to be pleasant and she had been careful not to chat, answering him when he made some observation but refraining from discussing the morning's ceremony. It was he who asked her if she had been pleased with her wedding, in much the same manner as someone asking if she had enjoyed her lunch, and she told him yes, it had been very nice—a colourless statement, but she could think of nothing better to say. She did enquire the name of the best man and was told he was Tiele Raukema van den Eck, not long married to an English girl. 'You must meet her,' suggested the Professor casually. 'She's rather a nice little thing—they've just had a son.'

It seemed there was no more to be said on the subject. Caro sat quietly as they sped northward and wondered if Noakes and the other servants would be glad to see her. Radinck had said that they had missed her, but going back as the lady of the house was quite a different kettle of fish.

She need not have worried. They were greeted with wide smiles and a great deal of handshaking and when that was done, Noakes led them into the drawing room where, on a small circular table in the centre of the room, was a wedding cake. Caro stopped short and gave a delighted laugh. 'Radinck, how kind of you to think of…'

She looked at him, still laughing, and saw at once that she had been mistaken. He was as surprised as she was—it must have been Noakes.

He was standing in the doorway with Juffrouw Kropp and Marta and the others grouped around him, waiting to be praised like eager children. Caro hoped that they hadn't heard her speak to Radinck; she turned to them now. 'Noakes, all of you—what a wonderful surprise! We're both thrilled; it is the most beautiful cake. Thank you—all of you.' She went on recklessly: 'I'm going to cut it now and we'll all have a piece with some champagne. We were going to have the champagne anyway, weren't we, Radinck?'

She turned a smiling face towards him, her eyes beseeching him to act the part of a happy bridegroom. After all, it was only for once; every other night he could go to his study and spend the evenings with his books.

He met her look with a mocking smile she hoped no one else saw. 'But certainly we will drink champagne,' he agreed. 'Noakes, fetch up half a dozen bottles and get someone to set out the glasses. And thank you all for this magnificent cake.' He repeated it all in Dutch and there was handclapping and smiling and a good deal of bustling to and fro until the champagne had been brought and they went to cut the cake. Caroline, handed the knife by Noakes and alone with the Professor at the table for a moment, said softly; 'I'm afraid it's the custom for us both to hold the knife...'

His hand felt cool and quite impersonal and touched her only briefly. He was disliking the happy little ceremony very much, she knew that; perhaps it reminded him of his first wedding. He'd been in love then...

They ate the cake and drank the champagne and presently Juffrouw Kropp took Caroline upstairs to her room to tidy herself for dinner. It was a different bedroom this time; a vast apartment in the front of the house with an equally vast bed with a brocade coverlet to match the blue curtains and beautiful Hepplewhite furniture. A bathroom led from it and on the other side a dressing room, another bathroom and another bedroom, all leading one to another. Juffrouw Kropp beamed and smiled before she went away, and left alone, Caro explored more thoroughly; it was all very splendid but comfortable too. She tidied herself, did her hair and went downstairs again to join Radinck in the drawing-room, where they made conversation over their drinks before going in to dinner.

Marta had excelled herself with little spinach tarts, roast duckling with black cherries and a bombe surprise. Caro, desperately maintaining a conversation about nothing much, ate some of everything although she had no appetite, because Marta would be upset to see her lovely dishes returned to the kitchen half eaten, and she drank the hock Noakes poured for them, a little too much of it, which was a good thing because it made her feel falsely cheerful.

They had their coffee in the drawing-room and Noakes went away with a benign smile which drew down the corners of the Professor's mouth so that Caro, now valiant with too much drink, said cheerfully: 'You've hated every minute of it, haven't you, Radinck? But I'm going to my room in a few minutes, only before I go I'd like to thank you for giving me such a nice wedding.' She added kindly: 'It's only this one evening, you know, you won't have to do it ever again. You asked me not to disturb your life, and I won't, only they all expected...' She pinkened faintly. 'Well, they expected us to look—like...'

'Exactly, Caroline.' He had got to his feet. 'I'm only sorry that I didn't think of the wedding cake.' He smiled at her: it was a kind, gentle sort of smile and it held a touch of impatience. She said goodnight without fuss and didn't linger. She thought about that smile later, as she got ready for bed. It had been a glimpse of Radinck again, only next time, she promised herself, he would smile without impatience. It might take a long time, but that was something she had.

She woke early while it was still almost dark. She had opened the door to the verandah outside her room before she got into her enormous bed, and Waterloo, after a long sound sleep on his feet after his lengthy journey and hearty supper, was prowling up and down it, talking to her. She got up, put on her new quilted dressing gown and slippers and went to join him.

The sky was getting paler every minute, turning pink along the horizon; it was going to be a lovely November day, bright and frosty. Somewhere Caroline could hear Rex barking and the sound of horses' hooves and then Radinck's whistle to the dog. So that was what he did before breakfast. She vowed then and there to learn to ride.

One of the maids, Ilke, brought her her early morning tea presently, and told her smilingly that breakfast would be at half past eight, or would she rather have it in bed?

Caro elected to go downstairs. She had never had her breakfast in bed, for there had been no one to bring it to her, and the idea didn't appeal to her very much. She bathed and put on her suit and one of the Marks and Spencer sweaters and went down to the hall. It was absurd, but she wasn't sure where she was to breakfast. When she had been staying in the house she had seen only the library, the drawing-room and the dining-room, but there were several more doors and passages leading from the hall and she had no idea where they led. She need not have fussed; Noakes was waiting to conduct her to a small, cosy room leading off the hall, where there was a bright fire burning and a table laid ready for her. Of the Professor there was no sign and she thought it might sound silly if she asked Noakes where he was, so she bade him a smiling good morning, and while she made a good breakfast, listened to his carefully put advice.

'There's Juffrouw Kropp waiting ter show yer the 'ouse, ma'am, and then Marta 'opes yer'll go to the kitchens and take a look at the menu, and anything yer wants ter know yer just ask me. We're all that 'appy that yer're 'ere, ma'am.'

'Noakes, you're very kind to say so, and I'm happy too. When I've found my feet we must have some more singing—I still think we should do something about Christmas, don't you?' She remembered something. 'And, Noakes, I want your help. Is there someone who can teach me to ride? I—I want to surprise the Professor.'

His cheerful face spread into a vast smile. 'Now ain't that just the ticket—the Professor, 'e rides a treat, great big 'orse 'e's got, too, but there's a pony as is 'ardly used. Old Jan'll know—I'll get 'im to come and see yer and I'll come wiv 'im.'

'Thank you, Noakes—it must be a secret, though.' Caroline finished her coffee and got up from the table. 'I'm going to fetch Waterloo and take him round the house with Juffrouw Kropp, then he'll feel at home. Where's Rex?'

'Gone with the Professor. Most days 'e does, ma'am.'

It took all of two hours to go over the house. She hadn't realised quite how big it was, with a great many little passages leading to small rooms, and funny twisted stairs from one floor to the next as well as the massive front staircase. She would have got lost if it hadn't been for Juffrouw Kropp, leading her from one room to the next, waiting patiently while she examined its contents, and then explaining them in basic Dutch so that Caro had at least some idea of them. They were all beautifully furnished and well-kept, but as far as she could make out, never used. A house full of guests, she dreamed to herself, all laughing and talking and dancing in the evening in that lovely drawing-room and riding out in the mornings, with her riding even better than the best there. She sighed and Juffrouw Kropp asked her if she were tired, and when she shook her head in vigorous denial, preceded her downstairs to visit the glories on the ground floor.

The drawing-room she knew, also the library and the morning-room. Now she was conducted round a second sitting-room, furnished with deep armchairs, a work table from the Regency period, several lamp tables and two bow-fronted display cabinets. A lovely room, but not used, she felt sure. Well, she would use it. There was a billiard room too, a garden room and a small room furnished with a desk and chair and several filing cabinets—used by the secretary, Caroline supposed. There was a luxurious cloakroom too and a great many large cupboards as well as several rooms lined with shelves and a pantry or two.

She hoped she would remember where each of them was if ever she needed it, although she couldn't think why she should. The first floor had been easy enough; her own room and the adjoining ones took up half the front corridor and most of one side, and the half a dozen bedrooms and their bathrooms on that floor took up the rest of its space; the smaller rooms and passages she would have to explore later.

She drank her coffee presently, concentrating on what she had seen, reminding herself that it was hers now as well as Radinck's and he would expect her to be responsible for his home. She had no intention of usurping Juffrouw Kropp's position, but it was obvious that even that experienced lady expected her to give orders from time to time.

The kitchens she already knew, but now it was a question of poking her mousy head into all the cupboards and lobbies and dressers while it was explained to her what was in all of them and then, finally, she was given a seat at the kitchen table and offered the day's menu. Noakes translated it for her while Marta waited anxiously to see if she would approve, and when that had been done to everyone's satisfaction, Noakes led her back to the smaller sitting-room, where she had decided to spend her leisure and where after a few minutes Jan was admitted.

Noakes had to act as go-between, of course, but Jan agreed readily enough to teaching her. The pony, he agreed with Noakes, was just right since the Baroness was small and light. Caro, who had forgotten that she was a baroness, felt a little glow of pleasure at his words. They decided that she should begin the very next morning, and well pleased with herself, she got her coat and took herself off for a walk.

She lunched alone, since the Professor didn't come home, and in the afternoon she curled up in the library and had another go at her Dutch. She would have to have lessons, for she was determined to learn to speak it as quickly as possible, but in the meantime she could at least look up as many words as she could. She and Juffrouw Kropp were to go through the linen cupboard on the following morning. She would make her companion say everything in her own language and she would repeat it after her; she would learn a lot that way. And tomorrow she would get Noakes to drive her into Leeuwarden so that she could buy some wool and fill her time with knitting. More flowers about the house too, she decided, and an hour's practice at the piano each day. There was more than enough to keep her busy.

She went upstairs to change after her solitary tea; she put on her wedding dress again and then went to the drawing-room to wait for Radinck, taking a book with her so that it wouldn't look as though she had been there ages, expecting him.

When he did get home, only a short time before dinner, she wished him a cheerful good evening, volunteered no information as to her day, hoped that he had had a good one himself and took up her book again. He had stressed that she wasn't to interfere with his way of living and she would abide by it. She accepted a drink from him and when he excused himself on the plea of work to do before dinner, assured him that she didn't mind in the least.

They met at the dinner table presently and over an unhurried meal talked comfortably enough about this and that, and as they got up to go into the drawing-room for their coffee Caro said diffidently: 'Don't come into the drawing-room unless you want to, Radinck. I'll get Noakes to bring coffee to your study.'

He followed her into the room and closed the door. He said irritably: 'I'll take my coffee where I wish to, Caroline. I'm sure you mean well, but kindly don't interfere.' He glared down at her. 'I shall be going out very shortly.'

Her voice was quite serene. 'Yes, Radinck. Do you like your coffee black?' She poured it with a steady hand and went to sit down, telling herself she wasn't defeated, only discouraged.

Chapter 5

The days passed, piling themselves into a week. Caro, awake early as usual by reason of Waterloo's soliloquy as he paced the balcony, sat herself up against her lace-trimmed pillows and began to assess the progress she had made in that time. Nothing startling, she conceded, ticking off her small successes first: her riding lessons had proved well worth the effort. She had got on to Jemmy, the pony, each morning under Jan's eagle eye and done her best while her tutor muttered and tutted at her and occasionally took her to task in a respectful manner, while the faithful Noakes translated every word. And she had learned the geography of the house, having gone over it several times by herself and once or twice with Juffrouw Kropp, learning the names of the various pieces of furniture from that good lady.

She had applied herself to her Dutch too; even though

she had little idea how to converse in that language she had worried her way through a host of useful words. Besides all this, she had got Noakes to drive her to Leeuwarden, where she had bought wool and a pattern and started on a sweater for Radinck's Christmas present; probably he would never wear it, but she was getting a lot of pleasure from knitting it, although as the instructions were in Dutch she had had to guess at a good deal of the pattern and enlist Juffrouw Kropp's help over the more difficult bits.

Her eyes fell on Waterloo, who having finished his early morning exercise, was sitting in the doorway washing his elderly face; he at least was happy with the whole house to roam and a safe outdoors with no traffic threatening his safety, and she shared his opinion. The grounds round the house were large and beyond the red-brick wall which encompassed them were water meadows and quiet lanes and bridle paths. Caroline had roamed at will during the week, finding her way around, going to the village where she was surprised to be greeted by its inhabitants. She still found it strange to be addressed as Baroness and she had had a struggle to answer civilly in Dutch, but smiling and nodding went a long way towards establishing a sort of rapport.

But with Radinck she had made no progress at all. He was polite, remote and continued to live his own life, just as though she wasn't there. True, once or twice he had discussed some interesting point regarding his work with her, asked her casually if she had been to the village and informed her that now their marriage had been put in the *Haagsche Post* and *Elseviers* they might expect visitors and some invitations, and had gone on to suggest that she might like to go to Leeuwarden or Groningen and buy herself some clothes, and the following morning his secretary had given her a cheque book with a slip of paper inside it on which the Professor had scrawled: Your allowance will be paid into the bank quarterly. The sum he had written had left Caroline dumbfounded.

But it was early days yet, she reminded herself cheerfully. He would be surprised and, she hoped, delighted to discover that she could ride. The last thing she wanted to happen was for him to feel ashamed of her because of her social shortcomings, even if he didn't want her as a wife she would manage his home just as he wanted it, entertain his friends and learn to live his way of life. She owed him that, and never mind how impatient and irritable he became.

She drank her morning tea and presently went downstairs to her breakfast, to stop in the doorway of the breakfast room. Radinck was sitting at the table, a cup of coffee in one hand, a letter he was reading in the other.

He got up when he saw her, pulled out a chair and said politely: 'Do sit down; I forgot to tell you yesterday that I have given myself a day off. I thought we might go down to den Haag so that you can do some shopping. My mother always got her things from Le Bonneterie there—it's rather like a small Harrods, and you might possibly like it—if not, we can try somewhere else.'

Caroline didn't like to mention that she had never bought anything in Harrods. She agreed happily; a whole day in his company, even if he had nothing much to say to her, would be heaven, but here she was to be disappointed, for in the car, racing across the Afsluitdijk, he mentioned casually that he had a consultation at the Red Cross Hospital in den Haag and after leaving her at Le Bonneterie he would rejoin her there an hour or so later.

'I daresay it will take you that time to buy your clothes. I suggest that you get a sheepskin jacket and some boots—it can be cold once the winter comes.'

Caroline started doing sums in her head; her allowance was a generous one but she had no idea how much good clothes cost in Holland. She would need several dresses, she supposed, and more separates and some evening clothes.

'You're very silent,' remarked Radinck presently.

'Well, I was just thinking what I needed to buy. Would two evening dresses do?'

'Certainly not—there will be a hospital ball in Leeuwarden in a few weeks' time, and another one in Groningen and any number of private parties. At Christmas I invite a number of guests to the house, but before then we will have an evening reception so that you meet my friends.'

She had to get this straight. 'But you like to lead a quiet life; you told me so—you like to work and read in the evenings. You'll only be inviting them because of me.'

'That is so.' They were flying down the E-10 and there was plenty to capture her interest, only she had too much on her mind.

'Yes, but don't you see?' she persisted in her quiet voice, 'you're having to do something you don't want to do.' She went on quickly, looking straight ahead of her, 'You don't have to do it for me, you know. I'm—I'm very happy—besides, I'd feel scared at meeting so many strange people.'

'Once you have met them they won't be strange.' The calm logic of his voice made her want to stamp her feet with temper. 'And to revert to our discussion, I suggest that you buy several dresses of a similar sort to the one you wore at our wedding.' He glanced sideways at her. 'The suit you are wearing is nice, why not get another one like it? And some casual clothes, of course.'

Caroline said tartly: 'Do you want me to change my hairstyle too? It could be tinted and cut and permed and...'

'You will leave your hair exactly as it is.' He added stiffly, 'I like it the way you wear it.'

She was so surprised that she asked quite meekly: 'How much money am I to spend? I could get a great deal with about half of my allowance.' She frowned. 'And will they take my cheque? They don't know me from Adam.'

'I shall go with you. You will have no difficulty in writing cheques for anything you want, Caroline, but this time you will leave me to pay the bill when I come to fetch you.'

'Oh—all right, and I'll pay you back afterwards.'

'I do not wish to be repaid. Caroline, did I not tell you that I was a rich man?'

'No—at least I can't remember that you did. You did say that there was plenty of money, but I don't suppose that's the same as being rich, is it?'

A muscle twitched at the corner of the Professor's firm mouth. 'No,' he agreed quietly, 'it's not quite the same.'

They were in the heavily populated area of the country now, for he had turned away from Amsterdam and was working his way round the city to pick up the motorway to den Haag on its southern side. As they took the road past Leiden which would lead them to the heart of den Haag, Caro said: 'It's very pretty here and there are some beautiful houses, only I like yours much better.'

'Ours,' Radinck reminded her.

The city was full of traffic and people and a bewildering number of narrow streets. The Professor wove his way into the heart of the shopping centre and turned away down a side street to stop after a moment or two before a large shop with elegantly dressed windows. It was quiet there, the houses all round it were old and there were few people about, and Caro took a deep breath of pure pleasure at the thought of spending the next hour or two in the dignified building, spending money without having to count every penny before she did so.

The Professor was known there. An elderly woman with a kind face listened carefully to what he had to say, smiled and nodded and without giving Caro time to do more than say, 'Goodbye,' led her away.

The next hour or so was blissful: Caro, guided discreetly by the elderly lady, became the possessor of a sheepskin jacket because Radinck had told her to buy one, a suit—dogtooth check with a short jacket and a swinging pleated skirt—three Italian print dresses and a finely pleated georgette jersey two-piece because although she didn't think she needed it she couldn't bear not to have it, a dashing bolero and skirt with a silk blouse to go with them and four evening dresses: she would probably never wear more than one of them despite what Radinck had said, but it was hard to call a halt, especially with the elderly lady egging her on in her more than adequate English. And then there was the question of suitable shoes, stockings to go with them, gloves, a little mink hat to go with her coat, and since it seemed a shame not to buy them while she had the opportunity, undies. She was wandering back from that department and had stopped to examine the baby clothes in the children's department when Radinck joined her. She flushed under his mocking eyes and said defensively: 'I was on my way back. They're adding it up—the bill, I mean—I had a few minutes…'

She put down the muslin garment she had been admiring and walked past him. 'It's a lovely shop,' she told him chattily to cover her awkwardness. 'I've bought an awful lot. Did you have a successful consultation?'

He gave some non-committal answer, made some remark to the sales lady and then studied the bill. Caro, watching his face, was unable to discover his feelings about it. His expression gave nothing away, although the total was such that if it had been handed to her she would have screamed at the amount.

But he didn't mention it. The packages and boxes loaded into the boot, Caroline was invited to get into the car, and within ten minutes she found herself in a small, very smart restaurant, drinking a sherry and eyeing a menu with an appetite sharpened by its contents. And not only did Radinck not mention it, but he talked. He told her about the hospital where he had been that morning and the patients he had seen, he even discussed the conditions he had been asked to examine. Just for a while the bland mask slipped a little and Caro, always a good listener, became a perfect one, listening intelligently, asking the right question at the right moment and never once venturing an opinion of her own, and she got her reward, for presently he observed: 'You must forgive me, I am so used to being alone—I have been uttering my thoughts and you must have been bored.'

'No, I wasn't,' said Caro forthrightly. 'I'm interested— you forget that I'm a nurse, but there are bits I don't quite understand. You were telling me about Fröhlich's syndrome—I can't quite see how hypophosphatisia can't be medically treated—if it's just a question of calcium…'

The Professor put down his coffee cup. 'Well, it's like this…'

For a bridegroom of rather more than a week, his conversation was hardly flattering: she might have been sitting there, wearing a sack and a false nose, but to Caro, it was the thin—very thin—edge of the wedge.

Back home again she went straight to her room with one of the maids bearing her various parcels. Radinck was going out again and she hoped he might tell her where, but in this she was disappointed. He was leaving the house without a word before she had reached the top of the staircase. She consoled herself by trying on every single thing she had bought, and it was only as she took off the last of the evening dresses that she remembered her daydream—playing to Radinck in a lovely pink dress, and none of the dresses were pink; she would have to go to den Haag again and buy one. Meanwhile she might do a little practising while she waited for him to come back.

He wasn't coming. Noakes met her in the hall with the news that the Professor had just telephoned to say that he wouldn't be back for dinner, and Caroline, anxious to keep her end up, said airily: 'Oh, yes, Noakes, he did say he might have to stay. I'll have mine on a tray, please, and if none of you have anything better to do, shall we get together over those carols presently?'

She was so disappointed that she could eat hardly any of the delicious food Noakes brought presently, and even though she told herself she was a fool to have expected Radinck to have changed his ways all at once, she was hard put to it to preserve a cheerful face. It helped, of course, discussing the carols with Noakes and Marta and Juffrouw Kropp and the others. She sat at the piano, trying out the various tunes to find those they knew—and when they had, she was thrilled to discover that they sang rather well. With the aid of Noakes and her dictionary, she prevailed upon some of them to sing in harmony— it was a bit ragged, but there were several weeks to go to Christmas and if Radinck was going to be away most evenings, there was ample time to rehearse.

She made herself think about her new wardrobe and the carols as she got ready for bed, banishing Radinck from her mind. Easier said than done: he kept popping up all over the place.

It was after breakfast the following morning that he telephoned her to say that he was going to Brussels and wouldn't be back until the next day, late in the evening. 'So don't wait up for me,' his voice sounded cool over the wire. 'I haven't got Rex with me, so would you mind walking him—once a day will do, he is very adaptable.'

Caroline made her voice equally cool; rather like an efficient secretary's. 'Of course.' She wanted to tell him to take care of himself, to ask what he was going to do in Brussels, but she didn't; she said goodbye in a cheerful voice and rang off.

The day went by on leaden feet. Not even her riding lesson raised her spirits, although she was doing quite well now, trotting sedately round and round the field nearest the stables, with Rex keeping pace with Jemmy. He did the same thing again on the following morning, taking upon himself the role of companion and pace-maker, and because the weather was changing with thunderous skies swallowing the chilly blue, Caroline spent the afternoon in the library, conning her Dutch and knitting away at the sweater, with Waterloo and Rex for company, and because she had to keep up appearances, she changed into one of her new dresses that evening and

dined alone at the big table, feeling lost but not allowing that to show, and after an hour working away at the
carols again she went up to her room, meeting Noakes'
enquiry as to whether she knew at what time the Professor would be back with a serene: 'He said late, Noakes,
and I wasn't to wait up. I should lock up if he's not back
by eleven o'clock—ask Marta to leave a thermos jug of
coffee out, would you?'

It was long after midnight when the Professor returned. Caro, lying wide awake in her bed, heard the
gentle growl of the car and saw its lights flash past her
windows and presently her husband's firm tread coming up the stairs and going past her door. Only then did
she curl up into a ball with Waterloo as close as he could
get and sleep.

It was raining when she awoke, and cold and dark
as well. None of these mattered, though. Radinck was
home again and she might even see him before he left
the house—perhaps he would be at breakfast. She got
dressed in the new suit and the wildly expensive brogue
shoes she had bought to go with it, and went downstairs.

He wasn't there, and Noakes, remarking on her early
appearance, observed, 'Back late, wasn't 'e, ma'am? I
'eard him come in—ever so quiet.'

'Yes, I know, though I was still awake, Noakes.'

'Pity 'e 'ad ter go again so early—no proper rest. 'E
works too 'ard.'

'Yes, Noakes, I know he does.' She gave the elderly
face a sweet smile. 'Noakes, it's too wet for me to go riding, I suppose?'

'Lor', yes, ma'am—best stay indoors. Juffrouw Kropp
wanted to ask about some curtains that want renewing.'

'I'll see her after breakfast and then go to the kitchens.'

It was still only ten o'clock by the time she had ful-filled her household duties and the rain had lessened a little. 'I'm going for a walk,' she told Noakes. 'I won't take Rex with me and I won't go far—I just feel like some exercise.'

She put her new hooded raincoat on over the new suit, found her gloves and let herself out of a side door. The rain was falling steadily and there was a snarling wind, but they suited her mood. She walked briskly across the gardens, into the fields behind the wall, and joined the country lane, leading away to a village in the distance. She had walked barely half a mile when she saw a slow-moving group coming towards her—a cart drawn by a stout pony and surrounded by a family of tinkers. They were laughing and shouting to each other, not minding the weather, carefree and happy. Except for a small don-key tied to the back of the cart; it wasn't only wet, it was in a shocking condition, its ribs starting through its dirty matted coat, and it was heavily in foal. It was being ruth-lessly beaten with a switch wielded by a shambling youth, and Caro, now abreast of the whole party, cried 'Stop!' so furiously that they did. She took the switch from the youth and flung it into the canal by the side of the lane, then she mustered her Dutch. '*Hoeveel?*' she asked im-periously, pointing at the deplorable beast, and then with a flash of inspiration, she pointed to herself and added: 'Baroness Thoe van Erckelens.'

She was pleased to see that the name meant something to them. The leader of the party, a scruffy middle-aged man, gave her a respectful look, even if a bit doubtful. Caroline had to dispel the doubt; she turned and pointed again, this time towards Huis Thoe, just visible behind its high wall. While they were all staring at it she went

over to the dejected little beast and began to untie the
rope round its neck, and when they would have stopped
her, held up a firm little hand. '*Ik koop*,' she told them,
and waved towards the house, the rope in her hand, hoping that 'how much' and 'I'll buy' would be sufficient to
make them agree, for the life of her she couldn't think
of anything else to say to the point. Yes, one more word.
She ordered briskly '*Kom*' and had the satisfaction of
seeing them bunch together round the cart once more,
obviously waiting for her to lead the way.

She didn't know anything about donkeys, and she
prayed that this one would answer to the gentle tug she
gave its worn bridle. It did, and she made her way to the
front, not hurrying because the donkey's hooves were in
a frightful state. It took longer to go back too, because
she thought the tinkers might be more impressed if she
went in through the main gates, and every yard of the
way she was hiding panic that they might come to their
senses and make off with the donkey before she could
reach home. But the gates were reached at last and she
singled out the scruffy man, beckoning him to follow her,
leaving the rest of them grouped in the drive staring at
them. The man began to mutter to himself before they
reached the sweep before the house, but Caroline didn't
listen. She was planning what she would do; open the
door and shout for Noakes to mind the donkey and keep
an eye on the man while she fetched some money—and
that was another problem; how much did one pay for a
worn out starving animal? Perhaps Noakes would know.

The Professor, home early for his lunch and thus breaking a rule he had adhered to for years without knowing
quite why, was standing at the drawing-room windows,
staring out over the grounds, aware of disappointment

because Caro wasn't home. He frowned at the dripping landscape before him and then frowned again, staring even harder. Unless his splendid eyesight deceived him, his wife, a most disreputable man and a very battered donkey were coming up his drive, and what was more, there were people clustered round the gates, peering in. Something about the small resolute figure marching up to the front door sent him striding to open it and down the steps to meet her.

Caro, almost at the door and seeing her husband's vast form coming down the steps with deliberate speed, felt a wave of relief so strong that she could have burst into tears. She swallowed them back and cried: 'Oh, Radinck, I'm so glad you're home!' She had to raise her voice because he was barely within earshot. 'I've bought this poor little donkey, but I don't know how much to pay the man—I got him to come with me while I fetched the money. I thought Noakes would know, but now you're here you can tell me.' She looked up at him with complete confidence and added, just in case he didn't realise the urgency of the occasion: 'She's a jenny and she's going to foal soon; they were beating her, and just look at her hooves!'

The Professor looked, running a gentle hand over the bruised back, bending to examine each wretched neglected hoof, then he straightened up to tower over the tinker.

Caro couldn't understand a word he was saying. His voice was quiet and unhurried, but the tinker looked at first cowed and then downright scared. Finally, the Professor produced his notecase, selected what he wanted from its contents and handed them to the man, who grabbed them and, looking considerably shaken, made off as fast as his legs would carry him.

Caro watched him join his family at the gates and disappear. 'That was splendid of you, Radinck,' she said in deep satisfaction. 'I couldn't understand what you said, of course, but you scared him, didn't you? Oh, I'm so very glad you were here... I'll pay you back in a minute, but I ought to see to this poor thing first. What did you say to that horrid man?'

Her husband looked down at her, a half smile twitching his mouth. 'Enough to make him very careful how he treats any more animals he may own in future, and allow me to give her to you as a gift.' The half smile became a real one and she smiled back at him in delight. 'Tell me, how did you get him to come here?'

She told him and he laughed, a bellow of genuine amusement which set her hopeful heart racing, although all she said was, 'We ought to get in out of this rain. Where shall I take her?' And before he could answer: 'There's that barn next to the stables where the hay's kept...'

He gave her a questioning look. 'I didn't know you were interested in the stables—yes, the barn would do very well.'

Caroline began to lead the animal towards the back of the house. 'I'm not sure what donkeys eat. I'll ask Jan—he'll get me some carrots, though.'

Radinck gave her an amused glance. 'Jan too?' he asked, and then: 'She can go into the south field with the horses once she's rested.'

They were halfway there when Caro asked: 'What did you mean, "Jan too"?'

He answered her carelessly: 'Oh, you seem to have a way with people, don't you? The servants fall over themselves to please you and now Jan, who never does any-thing for anyone unless he wants to.'

'He's a dear old man,' declared Caro warmly, remem-bering Jan's deep elderly voice rumbling out the carols of an evening. 'He had a frightful cold, you know—I told him what to do for it.' She glanced sideways at him. 'I hope you don't mind?'

He sounded irritable. 'I don't suppose it would make any difference whether I minded or not. Give me that rope, and be good enough to go up to the house and ask Noakes to get Jan and young Willem, then telephone the vet and tell him to come out as soon as he can to exam-ine an ill-treated donkey in foal.'

'Yes, of course.' Caroline smiled happily at his rather irritable face. 'I'll go at once. Radinck, what shall we call her?'

He was staring at her with hard eyes as though he couldn't bear the sight of her. 'What could be more ap-propriate than Caro?' he wanted to know mockingly.

She hadn't taken a dozen steps before he was beside her, his hands on her shoulders so that she had to stop. 'I'm sorry, that was a rotten thing to say.'

She had gone a little white and the tears were thick in her throat, but she managed a smile. 'As a matter of fact it's a very good name for her.' She added earnestly: 'It doesn't matter, really it doesn't.'

'It does—you didn't deserve it, Caroline.' His voice was gentle. 'What shall we call her? We have a Waterloo and a Rex and the kitchen cat is called Anja—how about Queenie, and if the foal is a boy we can call him Prince.'

Caro had no doubt that he was trying to placate her hurt feelings, and although it wasn't much the tiny flame of hope she kept flickering deep down inside her brightened a little; at least he had realised that he had hurt her. She smiled at him a bit crookedly. 'That's a splendid name,' she agreed. 'I'll get Noakes.'

She slipped away before he could say anything else and took care not to return until she saw Jan and Willem going towards the stables.

Radinck had fetched a bucket of water and some oats while she had been gone and now the three men stood watching the donkey making a meal. She was still happily munching when Mijnheer Stagsma arrived. Radinck explained briefly what had happened, introduced Caro and waited patiently while the vet wished her happiness in her marriage, congratulated her on her rescue of the donkey, hoped that his wife would have the pleasure of calling on her soon and enquired how she liked her new home.

He was a youngish man with a friendly face. Caro would have enjoyed talking to him, but out of the corner of her eye she saw her husband's bland face watching them. He was growing impatient, so she brought their cheerful little talk to a friendly end and indicated the patient.

Mijnheer Stagsma took a long time, muttering to himself and occasionally saying something to the Professor. At length he came upright again.

'Nothing serious, I think—starved, of course, but that can be dealt with, and I'll deal with those hooves as soon as she's stronger. I should think she'll have the foal in a week or so—it's hard to tell in her present state. I'll give her a couple of injections and some ointment for those sores on her back. Who'll be looking after her?'

Caro, striving to understand what he said, looked at Radinck. He answered the vet, spoke to Willem who grinned and nodded and then turned to Caro, telling her what the vet had said.

'Oh, good—Willem doesn't mind feeding her? I don't…'

'No, not you, Caroline. You may visit her, of course, and take her out when she is better, but Willem will tend her and clean out the barn.'

She supposed that being a baroness barred her from such chores. 'If you say so,' she said happily, 'but I simply must learn Dutch as quickly as possible.'

The glimmer of a smile touched her husband's face. 'You seem to manage very well—but I'll arrange for you to have lessons.'

They wished the vet goodbye, standing together on the sweep as he drove down the drive and out of sight.

'Oh, dear—should I have asked him in for a drink?' asked Caro.

'I already did so, but he couldn't stop—he's a very busy man.'

'And nice—so friendly.' She didn't see the look her husband shot at her. 'May I go back and look at Queenie?'

He turned away to go into the house. 'There is no need to ask my permission, Caroline. I am not your gaoler—you are free to do exactly what you like as long as you don't interfere with my work.'

'Not your work,' said Caro, suddenly passionate, 'your life—and never fear, Radinck, I'll take care never to do that.'

She marched away, her chin in the air, in one of her rare tempers.

But her tempers didn't last long. Within half an hour they were lunching together and although she didn't apologise for her outburst she tried to be friendly. She supposed that it was for Noakes' benefit that Radinck met her conversational efforts more than halfway. It was a disappointment when he told her that he wouldn't be home for dinner. She spent her afternoon wrestling with an ever-lengthening list of Dutch words and the evening coaching her choir once again, and before she went to bed she went down to the stables to take a look at Queenie. The little donkey looked better already, she thought. She pulled the ragged ears gently, offered a carrot and went back to the house, where she mooned around for another hour or so before going to bed much later than usual, hoping that Radinck would come back before she did. But there was no sign of him. She fell asleep at last and didn't hear him return in the small hours of the morning.

She was up early and with Waterloo in attendance went down to see how Queenie had fared. Willem was already there, cleaning out the barn and feeding her, and Caro, trying out some of her carefully acquired Dutch, made out that the donkey had improved considerably, but Willem was busy and she didn't like to hinder him, so she wandered off again into the crisp morning—just right for a ride, she decided, and with Waterloo trotting beside her, hurried back for breakfast.

Jan was waiting for her when she got to the stables and Jemmy greeted her with a toss of the head and a playful nip. Caroline mounted his plump back and walked him out of the yard and into the field beyond. Walk round once, Jan had told her, then trot round once. She did so, watched by the old man, and then because she was feeling confident and enjoying herself she poked Jemmy's fat sides with her heels and started off again. Jemmy was enjoying himself too; his trot broke into a canter and Caro, her hair flying, let out a whoopee of delight. They were three quarters of the way round the field when she saw Radinck standing beside Jan.

Chapter 6

There was only one thing to do and that was to go on. Caroline finished circling the field and pulled up untidily in front of Radinck. Jan was standing beside him, but she couldn't tell from the craggy old face if anything had been said. To be on the safe side she leaned down from her saddle. 'Don't you dare be angry with Jan!' she hissed fiercely. 'I made him teach me—he thought I was doing it as a lovely surprise for you.'

'And were you?' It was impossible to tell if Radinck was angry or not.

'Well, yes—but not just for you. I thought that as you're a baron and have a lot of posh friends you might be ashamed of me if I couldn't do all the things they do...'

The gleam in Radinck's eyes became very pronounced, but he answered gravely: 'That was very thoughtful of you, Caroline. Were you going to use it as an argument in favour of inviting my—er—posh friends here?'

He was impossible! She looked away from him at the gentle countryside around them. 'No,' she said evenly, 'I promised that I wouldn't interfere with your life, didn't I? You seem to have forgotten that. It was only that I didn't want to let you down.'

'I beg your pardon, you are…' He stopped and started again. 'I should enjoy your company each morning before breakfast.'

'Would you really?' Her eyes searched his face. 'I saw you the first morning we were here, you know, that's when I made up my mind to learn to ride. But I'm not very good, it was lucky I didn't fall off just now.'

'Jan has taught you very well.' Radinck turned and spoke to the old man, who grinned at him and answered at some length, and then turned back to her. 'Jan says that all you need now is practice. It is a pity that I have an appointment this morning, otherwise I would have ridden with you.' His gaze swept over her. 'But I think you must have the right clothes. I'm free after lunch until the early evening. I'll take you into Leeuwarden and get you kitted up.'

Caro stammered a little. 'Oh, that would be s-super, but isn't it taking up your time? If you tell me where to go, I c-could go on my own.'

'We'll go together, Caroline,' and just as she was relishing this he added briskly: 'You would have no idea what to get, in the first place, and the shop is extremely hard to find.'

He was right about the shop; it was tucked away in a narrow street lined with old gabled houses, squeezed between a shirtmakers and a gentleman's hatters. Following Radinck inside, Caro wondered where on earth the customers went, and then discovered that the narrow little shop went back and back, one room opening into the next. The owner of the shop knew Radinck; he was ushered into a small room at the back, its walls lined with shelves stacked with cloth and boxes of riding boots and beautifully folded jodhpurs. Here he was given a chair while Caro was whisked into a still smaller room where, with an elderly lady to observe the conventions, she was fitted with boots, several white sweaters and shirts, a riding hat, a crop and a pair of jodhpurs, and finally the jacket. Looking at herself in the mirror she hardly recognised her image. 'Oh, very elegant,' she said out loud, and, obedient to the old tailor's beckoning finger, went rather shyly to show herself to Radinck. She stood quietly while he looked her over.

'Very nice, Caroline,' and then, to her surprise: 'What size are you?'

'In England I'm a size ten, I don't know what I am in Holland.' She was on the point of asking him why he wanted to know and then thought better of it; instead she said, 'Thank you very much, Radinck.'

He gave her a half smile. 'What else can you do, Caroline?'

She gave him a surprised look. 'Me? Well, nothing really—I can swim, but only just, if you know what I mean, and I can play the piano a bit and dance a bit...'

'You drive a car?'

She shook her head. 'No—I've never needed to, you see.'

'You shall have lessons and later on a car of your own. Tennis?'

'Well, yes.' She added waspishly: 'I hope I've passed.'

He turned away from her. 'You would have done that even if you could do none of these things. If you're quite

satisfied with the things we'll get them packed up and
I'll drive you back.'

She had deserved the snub, she supposed. She wondered for the hundredth time why Radinck had married
her; she hadn't been a very good bargain.

Fairmindedness made her stop there; he had wanted
a sheet anchor and she had said that she would be one.
She belonged in the background of his life, always there
when he wanted her, and it would be a good thing if she
remembered that more often.

On the way back she did her best. 'I expect,' she said
carefully, 'that now you've had time to think about it,
you'd rather I didn't ride with you in the mornings—
it's something you hadn't reckoned on, isn't it? And that
wasn't why I wanted to learn to ride,' she finished with
a rush.

He had turned off the motorway and had slowed the
pace a little, because the road was narrow. 'I didn't think
it was; shall we try it out for a day or two and see what
happens?'

Caroline agreed quietly and just as quietly wished
him goodbye presently. He had already told her that he
had an appointment and she forbore from asking him if
he would be home for dinner. She was surprised when
he told her that he would see her about seven o'clock.

She wore one of the new dresses, a silk jersey in old
rose with a demure stand-up collar and long sleeves,
and when he got back she was sitting by the fire in the
drawing-room engrossed in some tapestry work she had
bought as an alternative to the sweater. She wished him
a demure good evening and set a group of stitches with
care. There was a pleasantly excited glow under the new
dress, for Radinck had paused in the doorway and was

looking at her in a way he had never looked at her before. The stitches went all wrong, but this was no time to look anything but serene and casual. She went on stitching, the needle going in and out, just as though she knew what she was doing; there would be a lot of unpicking to do later. Radinck advanced into the room, offered her a drink and went to fetch it from the sofa table under the window. As he handed it to her he observed, with the air of a man trying out words he had almost forgotten: 'You look pretty, Caroline.'

The glow rushed to her cheeks, but she answered composedly: 'Thank you—this is one of my new dresses, it is charming, isn't it?'

'I was referring to you, Caroline.'

'Oh, how kind.' That sounded silly, so she added: 'The right clothes make such a difference, you know.'

She bent to scratch Rex's woolly ear and then offered the same service to Waterloo, sitting beside the dog. 'I went to see Queenie this evening,' she told him. 'It's a wonder how she's picked up, and Willem's done wonders with her coat already.'

'I've just come from there—she's reacting very nicely to the antibiotic.' Radinck sat down in the great winged chair opposite her, his long legs stretched out, his glass in his hand, and when she looked up briefly it was to find him staring at her again, his eyes very bright. It seemed a good idea to apply herself to her tapestry and by the time Noakes came to announce dinner was ready she had made a fine mess of it.

And to her surprised delight, after dinner, instead of going to his study or out again, Radinck followed her into the drawing-room and sat drinking his coffee, giving no sign of wanting to go anywhere else. Her fingers shook as she fell upon the tapestry once again, but her face was quiet enough as she gave him a quick peep. He had stretched himself out comfortably and was reading a newspaper—perhaps he had forgotten that she was there.

But he hadn't, and presently he began to talk; observations on the news, describing an interesting case he had had at the hospital that day and going on to ask her if she would like to start Dutch lessons straight away as he had found someone suitable to teach her.

She replied suitably to everything he said and presently, loath to do so, for she could have sat there for ever with him, she declared her intention of going to bed; it would never do for him to discover that she was eager for his company. She gave him a quiet goodnight and went to the door, aware as she went through it that he was looking at her again. She was halfway along the gallery above the hall when he called to her, and she stopped and leaned over the balustrade to ask 'Yes, Radinck?'

'You have forgotten that we are to ride together in the morning?'

'No, Radinck. Shall I meet you at the stables?'

'No, I shall be here at half past seven.' He said goodnight again as she turned away.

Contrary to her expectations Caroline slept dreamlessly until she was wakened by Ilke with her morning tea. She drank it while she dressed, afraid of being late. Actually she raced downstairs with a couple of minutes to spare, to find Radinck waiting for her. She thought he looked splendid in his riding kit and longed to tell him so. He wished her good morning and without wasting time they went to the stables. It was almost light with a clear sky and a cold wind and the grass was touched with frost.

'If it gets much colder you will have to stop riding—once the ground gets too hard there's more chance of a toss.'

She said, 'Yes, Radinck,' meekly. Frost or no frost, she would go on riding as long as he did.

The stables were lighted and Willem was there, busy with Jemmy and Rufus, Radinck's great bay horse. Caro, her fingers crossed, contrived to mount neatly and watched while Radinck swung himself into the saddle, whistled to Rex, and led the way out of the yard. He hadn't fussed over her at all, merely wanted to know if she were ready and carelessly told her to straighten her back. 'We'll go over the fields as far as the lane and go round the outside of the wall,' he told her. 'Don't trot Jemmy in the fields, but you may do so in the lane.'

Caro, completely overshadowed by man and horse, craned her neck to answer him. 'Yes, very well, but I expect you like a gallop, don't you?'

'Yes, I do—but not this morning. I must find a quiet little mare for you and then we can gallop together—it hardly seems fair to expect Jemmy to do more than trot.'

She patted the pony's neck. 'He's a darling—wouldn't he mind if I rode another horse?'

Radinck laughed. 'He's been here for years— he's quite elderly now, he'll be good company for Queenie and her foal.'

They reached the first field and once out of it started to trot, and presently when they reached the gate to the lane beyond Radinck said: 'Now try a canter, Caroline.'

She acquitted herself very well, although by the time they got back she was shaking with nerves, terrified that she would fall off or do something stupid, but she didn't, and had the pleasure of hearing her husband say as they went indoors: 'That went very well—do you care to ride each morning while the weather's fine?'

She tried not to sound eager. 'Oh, please, if you'd like to.'

He turned to give her a suddenly cool look. 'I should hardly have asked you if I hadn't wanted to, Caroline. Shall we have breakfast in fifteen minutes?'

'Yes, I'll tell Juffrouw Kropp.' She went along the passage to the kitchen, gave her message and went upstairs to shower and change, her feelings mixed. Radinck had seemed so friendly, then suddenly he had drawn back and looked at her as though he didn't like her after all. She was in two minds not to go down to breakfast, but if she didn't he might think that she minded being snubbed... She changed into a tweed skirt and sweater, tied her hair back and went to join him.

He was already at the table when she got downstairs, but he got up to draw out her chair, handed her her letters, and went back to reading his own. It was to be a silent meal, she guessed; for the time being she wasn't a sheet anchor at all, only a nuisance. She murmured a cheerful good morning to Noakes when he came with fresh coffee, and immersed herself in her post—a letter from Clare, excitedly telling her the news that she was engaged, one from her aunt, asking vaguely if she were happy and regretting that she hadn't been able to attend the wedding, and a card from Sister Pringle inviting her to her wedding in the New Year. Caroline was wondering what to do about it when Radinck leaned across and handed her a pile of opened letters. 'Invitations,' he told her. 'Will you answer them?'

She glanced through them and counted six and looked up in surprise. 'But Radinck, how strange! I mean, we've been here for almost two weeks and no one has even telephoned, and now all these on the same day.'

His smile mocked her. 'My dear girl, have you forgotten that we are supposed to be newlyweds? It would hardly have been decent to have called on us or invited us anywhere for at least a fortnight.' He tossed a letter across the table to her. 'Here's a letter from Rebecca—Tiele's wife. She wants us to go over for drinks soon—she will ring you some time today.'

'Am I to accept?'

He looked faintly surprised. 'Of course. Tiele is a close friend, and I hope you and Rebecca will be friends too. As for the others, if I tell Anna to type out the correct answer in Dutch perhaps you would copy it and get them sent off.'

Caroline glanced through them; three invitations to drinks, one to the burgermeester's reception in Leeuwarden and two for evening parties.

'But, Radinck—' she began, and stopped so he looked up rather impatiently.

'Well?'

'You don't like going out,' she observed, not mincing her words. 'You said so—you like peace and quiet and time to read and…'

'You do not need to remind me, my dear Caroline, I am aware of what I like. However, there are certain conventions which must be observed. We will accept the invitations we receive, and at Christmas I will—I beg your pardon—we will give a large party. By then you will have met everyone who is acquainted with me and we can revert to a normal life here. You will have had the opportunity of making any friends you wish and doubtless you will find life sufficiently entertaining.'

Words bubbled and boiled on Caro's tongue, and she went quite red in the face choking them back. The awful thought that she was fighting a losing battle assailed her, but not for long; she had had a glimpse just once or twice of Radinck's other self hidden away behind all that ill humour. She told herself that it needed patience and all the love she had for him, and she had plenty of both.

Rebecca telephoned later that morning and Caro liked her voice immediately. 'We're not far from you,' said Rebecca, 'and I've been dying to come and see you, but Tiele said you were entitled to a couple of weeks' peace and quiet together. Will you come over for drinks? Could Radinck manage tomorrow evening, do you think—I'm going to invite you to dinner too, but if he's got something on, ring me back, will you, and we'll be content with drinks. Have you settled down?'

'Yes, thank you, though I wish I could speak Dutch, but everyone's so kind.'

'Radinck told Tiele that you were managing very well—have you started lessons yet?'

'No, but Radinck said he'd found someone to teach me.'

Rebecca giggled. 'Well, you've not had much time to bother about lessons, have you?'

She rang off presently and Caro went to her room and looked through her wardrobe, wondering what she should wear. She came to the perfectly normal female conclusion that she hadn't anything, and then changed her mind. The rose pink jersey would do; it had had a good effect the other evening, and after all, it was Radinck she wanted to notice her, not Tiele and Rebecca.

She broached the subject of going to dinner when Radinck came home for lunch and managed not to show her disappointment when he said that it was quite impossible. He had a hospital governors' meeting to attend at eight o'clock; he would drive her back from the Raukema van den Ecks and go straight on to the hospital where he would get a meal later. He looked at her sharply as he said it, but she met the look calmly, remarking that it would be nice to meet another English girl. 'She sounded sweet,' she declared. 'Would you like your coffee here or in the drawing-room?'

'I'm due back in ten minutes—I won't wait. Don't wait dinner for me either, Caroline; I'll have some sandwiches when I get back.' He was at the door when he paused and asked: 'Will you come riding tomorrow morning?'

'Well, yes, I should like to. The same time?'

He nodded as he went out of the room.

Caroline didn't see him for the rest of that day, but he was waiting for her when she went downstairs the next morning. The weather was being kind, cold and windy but dry, and the skies were clear. She acquitted herself very well, although Radinck had very little to say as they rode across the fields and after a few remarks about Queenie and a request that she should be ready that evening by half past six he fell silent. It was when they had returned to the house and were crossing the hall that he observed that he would be unable to get home for lunch. He spoke in his usual austere way, but she thought that she detected regret and her spirits rose.

They stayed that way too. The morning filled with her visit to see Marta, a solemn consultation with Juffrouw Kropp about the renewal of some kitchen equipment, a visit to Queenie, now looking almost plump, and an hour at the piano. And the afternoon went quickly too. By half past five Caroline was upstairs in her room trying out

different hairstyles and making up her face. In the end
she toned down the make-up and decided to keep to her
usual hairstyle, partly because she was afraid that if she
attempted anything else it would disintegrate halfway
through the evening. The pink jersey dress was entirely
satisfactory, though. She gave a final long look in the pier
glass, and went down to the sitting-room.

It wasn't quite half past six and she hadn't expected
Radinck to be waiting for her, but he was, in an elegant
dark suit, looking as though he hadn't just done a day's
work at the hospital, only sat about in idleness. Caroline
wondered how he did it. He allowed himself very little recreation. One day, she thought with real terror, he
would have a coronary...

He got up as she went in, took her coat from her and
held it while she got into it and they went out together.
Beyond greeting her he had said nothing and nor had she,
but once on the sweep she was surprised into exclaiming: 'But where's the Aston Martin?'

There was another car standing there and she went
closer to see what it was. A Panther de Ville; she had
only seen one or two before. Now she admired the elegance and choked over its price. She hadn't quite believed Radinck when he had said that he was rich, now
she decided that she had been mistaken. Only someone
with a great deal of money could afford to buy, let alone
run such a motor car. 'What a lovely car,' she said faintly.
'Is it yours?'

'Yes.' He opened the door and she got in, cudgelling
her brains to find some way of making him say more than
yes or no. She was still worrying about it as he drove off
and since he had very little to say during the brief journey, she had time to worry some more. Perhaps it was a

good thing when they arrived and she had to empty her head of worries and respond to the friendly welcome from Tiele and his wife.

Rebecca, Caro was relieved to see, wasn't pretty; beautifully made up, exquisitely dressed, but not pretty, although it was apparent at once that her husband considered her the most beautiful woman in the world.

They took to each other at once and Caro was borne away to see the new baby before they had drinks. 'A darling,' declared Caro, and meant it.

'Yes, he is,' agreed his doting mother, 'but he keeps us busy, I can tell you, although we've got a marvellous nanny.' She giggled enchantingly. 'The poor dear doesn't get a look in!' She tucked an arm into Caro's as they went down the stairs. 'Tiele's a splendid father—he's a nice husband too. Radinck's a dear, isn't he? And that's a silly question!' They had reached the drawing-room and she laughingly repeated her remark to the men. 'As though Caro's going to admit anything!' she declared. Caro was glad to see that Radinck laughed too, although he didn't look at her, which was a good thing because she had got rather pink in the face.

There seemed to be a great deal to talk about and she found herself listening to Radinck's voice, warm and friendly, teasing Becky, exchanging views with Tiele, including her punctiliously in the talk so that they gave what she hoped was a splendid impression of a happily married couple. She was sorry to leave, but since they were to see each other again at the burgermeester's reception, she was able to echo her husband's '*Tot ziens*' cheerfully enough. But he showed no inclination to discuss their evening, indeed he didn't speak until they were almost halfway home.

'You enjoyed your evening?' he asked her. 'You liked Becky?'

'Very much; she's sweet, and such a darling little baby.'

Her husband grunted and she wished she hadn't said that; she hurried on to cover the little silence: 'It's nice that we shall see each other at the reception.'

'Yes. You will also meet a number of my friends there. You answered the invitations?'

'Yes, and three more came with the afternoon post.'

'Will you leave them on the hall table? I'll make sure they're friends and not just acquaintances.'

'You're not coming in before you go—wherever you're going?'

'I have no time.' She couldn't help but notice how cold his voice had become. She sighed very softly and didn't speak again until they reached the house, when she said hurriedly: 'No, don't get out, Radinck, I'm sure you're pressed for time.'

She jumped out of the car and ran up the steps where the watchful Noakes was already standing by the open door. 'We'll ride in the morning?' Radinck called after her. Caroline had been afraid he wasn't going to say that, so, careful not to sound eager, she said over her shoulder: 'I'll see you then,' and ran indoors.

She saw him much sooner than that, though. Left alone, she had whipped down to the stables to see how Queenie was, gone round the outside of the house with Rex, who was feeling hurt because Radinck had gone without him, had her dinner, conducted her choir and then gone upstairs to bed. She had been there two hours or more sitting up against her pillows reviewing her evening when she heard Queenie's voice—not loud, not nearly loud enough to rouse everyone else in the house, with their rooms right on the other side. Nor would Willem hear her, living as he did in a small cottage on the estate boundary with his mother. The noise came again and Caro got out of bed, put on her quilted dressing gown, whipped a pair of boots from the closet, and crept through the house. Radinck wasn't in and she had no idea when he would return. She could take a look at Queenie and if things weren't going right, she could get a message to Willem or old Jan, who would know what to do, and if necessary she could get Mijnheer Stagsma.

She let herself out of the side door nearest the stables, into the very cold, clear night, and, glad of her boots but wishing she had put on something thicker than a dressing gown, made her way to the yard. There was a light in the barn. She switched it on and went to peer at the donkey. Queenie looked back at her with gentle eyes. She was lying down on her bed of straw and even to Caro, who didn't know much about it, it was obvious that she was about to produce her foal. But whether she was in need of help was another thing. She might have been calling for company; after all, it was a lonely business, giving birth.

Caro knelt down by Queenie's head and rubbed the long furry ears; for the moment she wasn't sure what to do. 'I'll wait just for a few minutes,' she told Queenie, 'and if something doesn't start to happen by then I'll go and get help. It's a pity that Radinck isn't here, but even if he were, I wouldn't like to bother him. You see, Queenie, he doesn't…' Her soft voice spiralled into a small shriek as her husband spoke from the dimness of the door.

'I saw the light—it's Queenie, isn't it?' He came and stood beside the pair of them, and it was difficult to see his face clearly. Caroline nodded, her heart still thumping with fright, and he took off his car coat and his jacket, rolled up his shirt sleeves and knelt down to take a closer look at the donkey. 'Any minute now,' he pronounced. 'Everything looks fine. How long have you been here?'

'Ten minutes, perhaps a little longer.'

'Did she wake you up?'

She answered without much thought. 'No—I hadn't been to sleep.'

He had his head bent. 'It's almost two o'clock.' He turned to look at her then, a slow look taking in her tousled hair and the dressing gown. 'My dear good girl, it's winter! You should have put on something warmer than that.'

'I am wearing my boots,' Caro declared as though that was a sufficient answer, and added: 'I didn't want to waste time in case Queenie was ill.'

'And what did you intend to do?' he wanted to know.

'Well, I said I'd wait just a few minutes and then if she went on groaning and looking distressed I thought I'd go and get Jan up—only he's old, I didn't want to bother him.'

He put a gentle hand on the beast's heaving flanks. 'You didn't want to bother me either, Caroline.' His voice was quiet.

'No.' For something to do she ran her fingers through her untidy hair.

'Leave your hair.' He still spoke quietly and she dropped her hands in astonishment. After a moment he said: 'Look!'

The foal was enchanting. 'We shall be able to call him Prince,' observed Radinck as they watched him get to his wobbly legs and nuzzle his mother. 'Caroline, do you think you could make some hot mash? Willem should have it ready for the morning over in the far corner. There's a Primus—just warm it up, Queenie could do with it now. I'll stay here for a minute or two just to make sure everything's as it should be.'

Caroline went obediently, found the mash and the stove and waited while it heated, and presently went back with it to find that Radinck had fetched a bucket of water which Queenie was drinking thirstily. She gobbled down the mash too, standing between the pair of them. She was still far from being in the pink of condition, but she was clean and combed and content. Caro, sitting back on her heels so that she could see more of the foal, observed: 'Oh, isn't it lovely? She's so happy.' She caught her breath. 'What would have happened to her if we hadn't taken her in?'

'Oh, she would have been left in a field to fend for herself.' Radinck didn't add to that because Caro's eyes were filled with tears.

'In a couple of days she shall go out into the fields with the horses. She's almost strong enough—they like company, you know, and horses like them.'

Queenie finished her meal, arranged herself comfortably on the straw with the foal beside her and wagged her ears. 'She's telling us we can go,' said Radinck. 'She'll do very well until Willem comes.' He pulled Caro to her feet, draped his jacket round her and walked her back through the moonlight night to the side door. Inside she would have gone to bed, but he kept an arm round her shoulders. 'I have a fancy for a cup of tea,' he declared. 'Let's go to the kitchen and make one—it will warm you, too.'

He seemed to know where everything was. Caro, her arms in the sleeves of his jacket to make things a little easier, got mugs, sugar and milk while he fetched a teapot and a tea canister, found a loaf and some butter and put them on the table. 'Didn't you have any dinner?' asked Caro.

'Yes—only it was a very dainty one. I have been famished for the last hour.'

'Oh, that's a terrible feeling,' agreed Caro, 'and one always thinks of all the nicest things to eat. I've often…' She stopped herself just in time. He wouldn't want to know that she had sometimes been rather hungry; hospital meals cost money and although one could eat adequately enough if one were careful, there was never anything left over for chocolate clairs and steak and sole bonne femme.

'Well?' asked Radinck.

'Nothing.' She busied herself pouring the tea while he sliced bread and spread it lavishly with butter.

Caroline hadn't enjoyed a meal as much for a long time. It was as though Radinck was a different person. She wasn't just having a glimpse of him as he really was, he was letting her get to know him. She found herself talking to him as though she had known him all her life. She had forgotten to worry that he might, at any moment, revert to his normal severe manner. Everything was wonderful. She sat there, eating slices of bread and butter, oblivious of her tatty appearance, talking about Queenie, and her riding and how she was going to learn to speak Dutch and what fun it was to have found a friend in Becky. And Radinck did nothing to stop her— indeed, he encouraged her with cleverly put questions which she answered with all the spontaneous simplicity of a small girl. It was the old-fashioned wall clock striking a ponderous three which brought her up short. She began to collect up the mugs and plates, stammering a little. 'I'm sorry—I've kept you out of bed, I don't know what came over me.'

He took the things from her and put them back on the table. 'Leave those. Will you be too tired to ride in the morning?'

'Tired? Heavens, no, I wouldn't miss...' She stopped herself again. 'The mornings are lovely at this time of year,' she observed rather woodenly.

Radinck was staring down at her. 'I must agree with you, Caroline—the mornings are lovely.' He turned away abruptly and went over to the sink with the teapot and she watched him, idly sticking her hands into the pockets of his jacket which she still wore draped round her. There was something in one of them. She just had time to pull it almost out to look at it before he turned round; she only had a glimpse, but it was enough. It was a handkerchief—a woman's handkerchief, new but crumpled.

They walked out of the kitchen together and up the stairs, and all the way Caroline told herself that she had no reason to mind so much. She had taken her hands out of the pockets as though they were full of hot coals and handed him his jacket with a murmur of thanks, aware of a pain almost physical. If she was going to feel like this every time she encountered some small sign that she wasn't the only woman in his life, then she might just as well give up at once. Of course, the handkerchief could belong to an aunt or a cousin or...he had no relations living close by. It could belong, said a nasty little voice at the back of her head, to whoever it was he went to see almost every evening in the week. Then why had he married her? Couldn't the handkerchief's owner have been a sheet anchor too? She thought of herself as a shabby, reliable coat, always at hand hanging on the back door, necessary but never worn anywhere but in the back yard in bad weather, whereas a really smart coat would be taken from the closet with care and pride and displayed to one's friends.

At the top of the stairs she wished him goodnight and was quite unprepared for his sudden swoop and his hard, quick kiss. She turned without a word and fled into her room, aware that any other girl with her wits about her would have known how to deal with the situation.

Chapter 7

If Caro hadn't been so sleepy she might have lain awake and pondered Radinck's behaviour, but beyond a fleeting sense of elation mixed with a good deal of puzzlement, there was no time to think at all; she was asleep as her head touched the pillow. And in the morning there was no time for anything but getting dressed by half past seven. As she went downstairs she did wonder if she would feel awkward when she saw him, but that need not have worried her. He offered her a cool good morning, led her down to the stables, watched her mount, had a word with Willem about Queenie, and led the way into the fields. They rode in almost complete silence and on their return, even the sight of Queenie and her foal called forth no more than a further businesslike discussion with Willem as to their welfare. They were back to square one, thought Caro. Last night had been an episode to be forgotten or at least ignored. She remembered the hanky with a pang of sheer envy, subdued it with difficulty and loitered to add her own remarks to Willem, who, with the rest of the staff at Huis Thoe, made a point of understanding her peculiar Dutch.

By the time she got down to breakfast, Radinck was almost ready to leave. Caroline wasn't in the least surprised when he mentioned that he wouldn't be home for lunch. She was glad that there was so much to keep her occupied. It wasn't until after lunch that the wicked little thought that she might take another look at the handkerchief in Radinck's jacket pocket entered her head. The suit was to be sent to the cleaners, along with her dressing gown; they would be in one of the small rooms leading from the passage which led to the kitchen.

They were there all right. Feeling guilty, she searched every pocket and found the handkerchief gone. It must be something very precious to Radinck and it served her right for snooping. Feeling ashamed of herself, she put on her sheepskin jacket, pulled a woollen cap over her head and went to find Rex, prowling in discontent from room to room. He had been left behind again. They went a long way, indeed they were still only halfway home in the gathering dusk when Radinck opened his house door. He had a large box under one arm and went at once to the sitting-room where Caro liked to spend her leisure.

The room was empty of course, and in answer to his summons, Noakes informed him that the Baroness had gone out with Rex. 'Been gorn a long time, too,' observed Noakes. 'Great walker, she is too.' He turned to go, adding with a trusted old friend's freedom: 'Walking away from somethin', if yer ask me.'

His employer turned cold blue eyes on him. 'And what exactly does that mean?'

Noakes threw him a quick shrewd look. 'Just me opinion, Professor, take it or leave it, as you might say.'

'She's unhappy? The Baroness is unhappy?'

'Not ter say unhappy—always busy, she is, with this and that—flowers in the rooms and ordering stores and learning Dutch all by 'erself. 'Omesick, I've no doubt, Professor.' He added defiantly: 'She's on 'er own a lot.'

The master of the house looked coldly furious. 'I have my work, Noakes.'

'And now, beggin' yer pardon, Professor, you've got 'er as well.'

The Professor looked like a thundercloud. 'It is a good thing that we are old friends, Noakes…'

His faithful butler had a prudent hand on the door. 'Yes, Professor—I'd not 'ave said any of that if we 'adn't been.'

The austere lines of the Professor's face broke into a smile. 'I know that, Noakes, and I value your friendship.'

Caro walked in half an hour later, her cheeks glowing, her hair regrettably untidy. As she came into the hall from the garden door, Rex beside her, she saw Noakes on his stately way to the kitchen.

'Noakes!' she cried. 'We've had a lovely walk, I'm as warm as toast. And don't frown at me, I've wiped Rex's feet. I went to see Queenie too and she's fine.' She had thrown off her jacket and was pulling the cap off her head when the sitting-room door opened and she saw Radinck.

Her breath left her, as it always did when she saw him. After a little silence she said: 'Hullo, Radinck, I didn't know you'd be home early. I hope you've had tea—we went further than we meant to.'

He leaned against the wall, his bland face giving nothing away. 'I waited for you, Caroline.' He nodded at Noakes who hurried kitchenwards and held the door wide for her to go in. The room looked very welcoming; the fire burned brightly in the grate and Waterloo had made himself comfortable before it, joined, after he had made much of his master, by Rex. Caro sat down on the little armchair by the work table she had made her own, smoothed her hair without bothering much about it, and picked up her tapestry work. She had painstakingly unpicked it and now had the miserable task of working it again. She smiled across at her husband. 'I hope it's scones, I've been showing Marta how to make them.'

He said gravely: 'I look forward to them. Caroline, are you lonely?'

The question was so unexpected that she pricked her finger. She said rather loudly: 'Lonely? Why, of course not—there's so much to do, and now I'm going to start Dutch lessons, tomorrow, and Juffrouw Kropp is teaching me how to be a good housekeeper, and there are the animals...' She paused, seeking something to add to her meagre list of activities. 'Oh, and now there's Becky...'

Noakes brought in the tea tray then and she busied herself pouring it from the George the Second silver bullet teapot into the delicate cups. It wasn't being rich that mattered, she mused, it was possessing beautiful things, lovingly made and treasured and yet used each day...

'Queenie and Prince are doing very well,' remarked Radinck.

She passed him his cup and saucer. 'Yes, aren't they? I went to see them this morning—twice, in fact... Oh, and I asked Juffrouw Kropp to see that your suit went to the cleaners.'

'I imagined you might; I emptied the pockets.' He stared at her so hard that she began to pinken, and to cover her guilty feelings about looking for that hanky, bent to lift the lid of the dish holding the scones.

'Will you have a scone?' she asked. 'Marta's such a wonderful cook…'

'And your dressing gown? That was ruined, I imagine.'

'Well, yes, but I think it'll clean—it may need several…'

'I don't think I should bother, Caroline.' He bent down and took the box from the floor beside his chair. 'I hope this will do instead.'

Caroline gave him a surprised look, undid the beribboned box slowly and gently lifted aside the layers of tissue paper, to lift out a pale pink quilted satin robe, its high neck and long sleeves edged with chiffon frills; the kind of extravagant garment she had so often stared at through shop windows and never hoped to possess.

'It's absolutely gorgeous!' she exclaimed. 'I shall love wearing it. Thank you very much, Radinck, it was most kind of you.' She smiled at him and just for once he smiled back at her.

They had a pleasant tea after that, not talking about anything much until Caro reminded him that they were to go to the burgermeester's reception the following evening.

'You have a dress?' Radinck enquired idly, 'or do you want to go to den Haag shopping—Noakes can easily drive you there.'

'Oh, I have a dress, thank you. It's—it's rather grand.'

'Too grand for my wife?' He spoke mockingly, but she didn't notice for once.

'Oh, oh, no, but it's rather—there's not a great deal of top to it.' She eyed him anxiously.

The corners of Radinck's stern mouth twitched. 'It was my impression that—er—not a great deal of top for the evening was all the fashion this season.'

'Well, it is. The sales lady said it was quite suitable, but I—I haven't been to an evening party for some time and I'm not sure...'

'The sales lady looked very knowledgeable,' said Radinck kindly, and forbore from adding that she would know better than to sell the Baroness Thoe van Erckelens anything unsuitable. 'Supposing you put it on and I'll take a look at it before we leave tomorrow—just to reassure you.'

'Oh, would you? I wouldn't like people to stare.' Caroline added reluctantly: 'I don't think I'm much good at parties.'

'Neither am I, Caroline, but you don't need to worry. Everyone is eager to meet a bride, you know.' His voice held a faint sneer and she winced and was only partly comforted by his: 'I'm sure the dress will be most suitable.'

Caro repeated this comforting observation to herself while she examined herself in the long mirror in her bedroom, dressed ready for the reception. There was no doubt about it, it was a beautiful dress; a pale smoky grey chiffon over satin with a finely pleated frill round its hem and the bodice which was causing her so much doubt, finely pleated too.

She turned away from her reflection, caught up the mink and went quickly down the staircase before she lost her nerve.

The drawing-room door was half open and Noakes,

appearing from nowhere opened it wide for her to go through. Radinck was standing with his back to the hearth with Rex and Waterloo sitting at his feet enjoying the warmth. Caro nipped across the stretch of carpet and came to a breathless halt. 'Well?' she asked.

Radinck studied her leisurely. 'A charming dress,' he pronounced finally, 'exactly right for the occasion.'

She waited for him to say more, even a half-hearted compliment about herself would have been better than nothing at all, but he remained silent. And she had taken such pains with her face and hair and hands...

She said in a quiet little voice: 'I'm ready, Radinck,' and picked up her coat which Noakes had draped over a chair.

He didn't answer her but moved away from the fire to fetch something lying on one of the sofa tables. She thought how magnificent he looked in his tails and white tie, but if she told him so, he might think that she was wishing for a compliment in her turn.

He crossed the room to her, opened the case in his hand and took out its contents. 'This was my mother's,' he told her. 'I think it will go very well with this dress. Turn round while I fasten it for you.'

The touch of his fingers made her tremble although she stood obediently still, and then went to look in the great gilded mirror on one wall. The necklace was exquisite; sapphires linked by an intricate chain of diamonds, a dainty, costly trifle which went very well with her dress. She touched it lightly with a pretty hand, acknowledging its beauty and magnificence, while at the same time aware that if it had been a bead necklace from Woolworths given with all his love she would have worn it for ever and loved every bead.

She turned away from the mirror and got into the coat he was holding, picked up the grey satin purse which exactly matched her slippers and went with him to the car. On the way to Leeuwarden she asked: 'Is there anything special I should know about this evening?'

'I think not. I shall remain with you and see that you meet my friends, and once you have found your feet, I daresay you will like to talk to as many people as possible. It will be like any other party you have been to, Caroline.'

It was on the tip of her tongue to tell him that she had been to very few parties and certainly never to a grand reception, but pride curbed her tongue. She got out of the car presently, her determined little chin well up, and went up the steps to the burgermeester's front door, her skirts held daintily and with Radinck's hand under her elbow. She had a moment of panic in the enormous entrance hall as she was led away by a severe maid to remove her coat, and cast a longing look at the door—it was very close; she had only to turn and run...

'I shall be here waiting for you, Caroline,' said her husband quietly.

The reception rooms were on the first floor. Caroline went up the wide staircase, Radinck beside her, her heart beating fit to choke her. There were people all around them, murmuring and smiling, but Radinck didn't stop until they reached the big double doors opening on to the vast apartment where the burgermeester and his wife were receiving their guests. She had imagined that their host would be a large impressive man with a terrifying wife. He was nothing of the sort; of middle height and very stout, he had a fringe of grey hair and a round smiling face which beamed a welcome at her. She murmured politely in her carefully learned Dutch and was relieved when he addressed her in English.

'So, now I meet you, Baroness,' he chuckled, 'and how happy I am to do so. We will talk presently; I look forward to it.' He passed her on to his wife with a laughing remark to Radinck, who introduced her to a tall thin lady with a beaky nose and a sweet expression. Her English was fragmental and Caro, having repeated her few phrases, was relieved when Radinck took the conversation smoothly into his own hands before taking her arm and leading her into the room.

He seemed to know everyone there, and she shook hands and murmured, forgetting most of the names immediately until finally Radinck whisked her on to the floor to dance.

He danced well, but then so did she; not that she had had much chance to show her skill, but she had always loved dancing and it came naturally to her. She floated round in his arms, just for a little while a happy girl, although a peep at his face decided her not to talk. It was bland and faintly smiling, but the smile wasn't for her; she had the horrid feeling that he was doing his social duty without much pleasure. On the whole she was glad when the music stopped and Tiele and Becky joined them, and when the music started again it was Tiele who asked her to dance.

Unlike Radinck he chatted in an easy casual way, telling her how pretty she looked, how well she danced and wanting to know if she and Radinck would be at the hospital ball.

'Well, you know, I'm not sure about that—there were so many invitations...' And when her partner looked surprised: 'Does Radinck always go?'

Tiele studied her earnest face carefully. 'Oh, yes, though it's always been a bit of a duty for him—not much fun for a man on his own, you know. But you're sure to be there this year. We must join forces for the evening.'

He was rewarded by her smile. 'I'd like that—it's all rather strange, you know, and my Dutch isn't up to much.'

'Never mind that,' he told her kindly. 'You dance like a dream and everyone's saying that you're just right for Radinck.'

She blushed brightly. 'Oh, thank you—I hope you're right; I don't mind what people say really, only I do want Radinck to be proud of me.'

Tiele's eyes were thoughtful, but he said easily: 'He's that all right!'

And after that Caroline went from partner to partner. There seemed to be no end to them, and although she caught glimpses of Radinck from time to time he made no attempt to approach her. It wasn't until they all went down to supper that he appeared suddenly beside her, took her arm and found her a seat at a table for four, before going in search of food at the buffet. Becky and Tiele, following them in, hesitated about joining them until Becky said softly: 'Look, darling, he's only danced with her once this evening. If it had been you I'd have boxed your ears! Look at her sitting there—she's lonely.'

'I'd rather look at you, my darling, and I don't think Radinck would like his ears boxed.'

'Well, of course he wouldn't, and Caro's clever enough to know that.' Becky added darkly: 'He's been leading a bachelor life too long—she's such a dear, too.'

'Which allows us to hope that he will become a happily married man, my love.'

Caro had seen them. Becky gave her husband's arm

a wifely nip and obedient to this signal, they went to join her. Tiele said easily: 'Do you mind if we join you?' He settled his wife in a chair beside Caro. 'I suppose Radinck is battling his way towards the sandwiches— I'll join him.' He touched his wife lightly on her arm. 'Anything you fancy, darling?'

Becky thought briefly. 'Well, I like vol-au-vents, but only if they've got salmon in them, and those dear little cream puffs. What are you having, Caro?'

'I don't know.' Caro smiled brightly, wishing with all her heart that Radinck would call her darling in that kind of a voice and ask her what she would like, as though he really minded. Tiele, she felt sure, would bring back salmon vol-au-vents and cream puffs even if he had to go out and bake them himself.

But it seemed that these delicacies were readily obtainable, for he was back in no time at all with a tray of food and Radinck with him. Caro accepted the chicken patties he had brought for her, had her glass filled with champagne and declared herself delighted with everything. And Radinck seemed to be enjoying himself, laughing and talking with Tiele and teasing Becky and treating herself with charming politeness. Only she wondered how much of it was social good manners, hiding his impatience of the whole evening. It wasn't until Becky remarked: 'We shall all see each other at the hospital ball, shan't we? Can't we go together?' that Caro saw the bland look on his face again and heard the sudden coolness in his voice.

'I'm not certain if we shall be going—I've that seminar in Vienna.'

'Isn't that on the following day?' asked Tiele.

'Yes, but I've one or two committees—I thought I'd go

a day earlier and settle them first.' He glanced at Caro. 'I don't think Caroline will mind—we have so many parties during the next few weeks.'

Becky opened her mouth, caught her husband's quelling eye and closed it again, and Caro, anxious to do the right thing, observed with a cheerfulness she didn't feel that of course Radinck was quite right and she wouldn't mind missing the ball in the least.

'You could come with us,' suggested Becky, but was answered by Radinck's politely chilling:

'Might that not seem a little strange? We have been married for such a short time.'

'Oh, you mean that people might think you'd quarrelled or separated or something,' observed Becky forthrightly. 'Caro, let's go and tidy up for the second half,' and on their way: 'Caro, why don't you go to Vienna with Radinck?'

Caro tried to be nonchalant and failed utterly. 'Oh, he wouldn't want me around.' She went on quickly in case her companion got the wrong idea, 'He works so hard.' Which didn't quite seem adequate but was all she could think of.

Back on the dance floor, she almost gasped with relief when Radinck swept her into a waltz. She had been in a panic that he would introduce her to some dry-as-dust dignitary and leave her with him, or worse still, just leave her. They danced in silence for a few minutes before he asked her if she was enjoying herself.

'Yes, thank you,' said Caro. 'You have a great many friends, haven't you, and they are all very kind.'

'They have no reason to be otherwise.' He spoke so austerely that her champagne-induced pleasure dwindled away to nothing at all. She danced as she always

did, gracefully and without fault, but her heart wasn't in
it. Radinck was doing his duty again and not enjoying
it, although she had to admit that nothing of his feelings showed on his face. The dance finished and he re-
linquished her to another partner and she didn't see him
again until the last dance, when he swept her on to the
floor again—but only, she thought sadly, because it was
customary for the last dance to be enjoyed by married
couples and sweethearts together.

They left quickly, giving Caro barely time to say goodbye to Becky. 'I'll telephone,' cried Becky, 'and anyway we'll see each other at the Hakelsmas' drinks party,
won't we?'

Radinck maintained a steady flow of casual talk as
they drove home. Caro listened when it seemed necessary
and, once in the house, bade him a quiet goodnight and
started up the staircase. She was halted halfway up by
his query as to whether she wouldn't like a cup of coffee
with him, but she paused only long enough to shake her
head, glad that he was too far away to see the tears in her
eyes. The evening, despite the dress, had been a failure.
He had evinced no pleasure in her company and she had
no doubt at all that the moment she was out of sight he
would turn away with a sigh of thankfulness and go to
his study, to immerse himself in his books and papers.
She undressed very quickly and took off the necklace;
tomorrow she would return it to him.

Ilke, not having been told otherwise, woke her early
so that she might go riding, but she drank her tea slowly
and then lay, listening for the sound of Rufus's hooves
on the cobblestones. Presently, after they had died away,
she got up, bathed and dressed in her new suit, did her
face and hair and went down to her breakfast. Radinck

was back by then, already halfway through his own meal, and she said at once as she went in: 'Good morning—no, don't get up, I'm sure you have no time.'

She slipped into her chair and sipped the coffee Noakes had poured for her and took a slice of toast.

'You were too tired to ride,' stated Radinck.

'Me, tired? Not in the least.' She gave him a sunny smile and buttered her toast, and after a moment or two he picked up his letters again, tossing several over to her as he did so.

'Will you answer these? Drinks mostly, I think.'

'You want me to refuse them?'

He looked impatient. 'Certainly not. Why should you think that?'

Caroline didn't answer. After all, she had told him once; she wasn't going to keep on. Instead she got on with her breakfast and when Noakes went out of the room, she got up and put the necklace carefully beside her husband's plate.

'Thank you for letting me wear it,' she said.

He put down the letter he had been reading to stare at her down his handsome nose. 'My dear Caroline, I gave it to you.'

She opened her hazel eyes wide. 'Oh, did you? I thought you'd lent it to me just for the evening. How kind—but I can't accept it, you know.'

'Why not?' Radinck's brows were drawn together in an ominous frown.

She did her best to explain. 'Well, it's not like a present, is it? I mean, one gives a present because one wants to, but you gave me the necklace to wear because your wife would be expected to have the family jewels.'

Radinck crumpled up the letter in his hand and hurled it at the wastepaper basket.

'What an abominable girl you are, Caroline! As I said some time ago, you have this gift of putting me in the wrong.'

'I'm sorry if you're annoyed, but I can't possibly accept it, though I'll wear any jewellery you like when we go out together.'

He said silkily: 'Don't count on going out too often, Caroline, I'm a busy man.'

'Well, I wasn't going to.' She gave him a thoughtful look, and added kindly: 'You're very cross—I daresay you're tired. We should have left earlier last night.'

The silkiness was still there, tinged with ice now. 'When I wish you to organise my life, Caroline, I will say so. I am not yet so elderly that I cannot decide things for myself.'

'Oh, you're not elderly at all,' said Caro soothingly. 'You're not even middle-aged. How silly of you to think that; you must know that you're…' She stopped abruptly and he urged her blandly:

'Do go on.'

'No, I won't, you'll only bite my head off if I do.' She took a roll and spread it with butter and cheese. 'What time do you want to go to Mevrouw Hakelsma's party? Only so that I'll be ready on time,' she added hastily.

'It is for half past seven, isn't it? I should be home by six o'clock. Will you see that dinner is later?'

'Would half past eight suit you? I'll tell Juffrouw Kropp.'

He nodded. 'I should like to leave the Hakelsmas' place within an hour; I've a good deal of work waiting.'

Caro kept her face cheerful. 'Of course. Just nod and wink at me when you're ready to leave.'

Radinck got up from the table. 'I shall neither nod nor wink,' he told her cuttingly. 'You are my wife, not the dog.' He stalked to the door. 'I'll see you this evening.'

She said, 'Yes, Radinck,' so meekly that he shot her a suspicious look and paused to say:

'It will be short dresses this evening.'

She said 'Yes, Radinck,' again, still so meek that he exclaimed forcefully:

'I wish you would refrain from this continuous "Yes, Radinck," as though I were a tyrant!'

'Oh, but you're not,' Caro assured him warmly. 'That's the last thing you are; it's just that you've lived so long alone that you've forgotten how to talk. Never mind, you'll soon get into the habit again now that I'm here.' She gave him a limpid smile and he said something in a subdued roar, something nasty in his own language, she judged, as she watched him go.

She finished her breakfast, inspected more cupboards under Juffrouw Kropp's guidance, discussed the evening's dinner with Marta and then arranged the flowers, a task she enjoyed even though it took a long time, and then went down to see how Queenie was getting on. Willem was there and they stood admiring the little donkey and her son, carrying on a conversation, which, while completely ungrammatical on Caro's part, Willem understood very well. She had sugar for the horses too, and Jemmy whinnied when he saw her, looking at her so reproachfully that she changed after lunch and, with Jan keeping a watchful eye on her, rode round the fields. Which didn't leave her much time for anything else. She was ready, wearing one of her new dresses, pink silk jersey with a demure neck and long sleeves, well before six o'clock, and went to sit in the smaller of the sitting-rooms, industriously knitting. It was half past six when Noakes came to tell her that Radinck was on the telephone.

He sounded austere. 'I'm sorry, Caroline, but I shall be home later than I expected. Perhaps you could ring Mevrouw Hakelsma and say all the right things. I don't expect we can get there much before eight o'clock.'

She said, 'Yes, Radinck,' before she could stop herself, but what else was there to say? 'OK, darling,' wouldn't have pleased him at all. She went along to the kitchen and prudently arranged for dinner to be delayed, then went back to her knitting.

Radinck got home at half past seven, looking tired, which somehow made him more approachable.

Caro wished him a pleasant good evening. 'Would you like a sandwich before you go upstairs?' she asked.

He had gone to the sofa table where the tray of drinks was. 'Thank you, I should—I missed lunch. What will you drink?'

'Sherry, thank you.' She pressed the old-fashioned brass bell beside the hearth and when Noakes came asked for a plate of sandwiches.

Radinck was famished. He devoured the lot with his whisky, looking like a tired, very handsome wolf who hadn't had a square meal for days. Caro watching him, bursting with love, sighed soundlessly; he needed someone to look after him so badly.

He went away presently, to rejoin her in a little while looking immaculate in one of his beautifully cut dark suits. She got up at once, laid her knitting on the work table and went with him into the hall where Noakes was waiting with their coats. Radinck helped her into hers and shrugged on his own coat, and Caro, with a quick whisper to Noakes to be sure and have dinner ready to put on the table the moment they got back, followed Radinck out to the car.

The Hakelsmas lived on the outskirts of Leeuwarden, in a large red-brick villa full of heavy, comfortable furniture. Caro had already met them at the burgermeester's reception and liked them both—in their forties, jolly, plump and kind. They had a large family, and three of them were there helping to entertain the guests, of whom there seemed to be a great many.

Caro murmured her set piece to her host and hostess, accepted a glass of sherry and something called a *bitterbal* which she didn't like at all, and was swept away to go from one group to the other, careful never to lose sight of Radinck. He seemed very popular, laughing and talking as though he liked nothing better than standing about drinking sherry and making small talk, and some of the girls there were very pretty and he appeared to be on very good terms with them. Caro, swept by a wave of jealousy, tried not to look at him too much. She had never thought of him as being likely to fall in love with anyone else, but there was no earthly reason why he shouldn't. One couldn't help these things. Of course she had every intention of trying to make him fall in love with her, but she began to wonder if the competition was too keen. Her not very pleasant thoughts were interrupted by Becky's voice.

'Hullo—you're looking wistful. Why?' She beamed at Caro. 'You're late. Did Radinck get held up?'

'Yes. There are a lot of people here, aren't there? I expect I met most of them at the burgermeester's.'

'Don't worry, it took me months to remember everyone's name, but they're all very sweet about it, and we'll all be seeing each other quite a lot during the next few weeks. Radinck gave an enormous party last year—are you having one this year too?'

'I think so.'

'Well, I expect now he's got you, he'll go out more. He's always been a bit of a recluse—well, ever since...'

'His first wife died? That's understandable, isn't it?' Caro smiled at Becky and let her see that she knew all about the first wife and it didn't matter at all.

On their way home presently, she said carefully: 'Radinck, I don't a bit mind not going to all these parties if you don't want to. After all, everyone knows you're a very busy man—mind you,' she observed thoughtfully, 'I daresay you don't need to do as much work as you do, if you see what I mean. Becky said you didn't go out much before—before we got married, and I did promise you that I'd not interfere with your life...'

She couldn't see his face, but she could tell from his voice that he was frowning. 'I thought that I had made myself clear; we will attend as many of these parties as possible, give an evening party ourselves, and then I shall be able to return to what you call my life. For most of the year there is very little social life on a big scale, only just before Christmas and at the New Year. Once that is over...' He slowed the car a little and Caro, thankful for the chance to talk to him even if only for a brief while, said unhappily: 'You hate it, don't you? I'm glad it's only for a few weeks. What a pity I can't get 'flu or something, then we couldn't go...'

'That is a singularly foolish remark, Caroline. Of course you won't get anything of the sort.'

But just for once he, who was so often right, was

wrong. Caro woke up in the morning feeling faintly peculiar. She hadn't got a headache, but her head felt heavy,
and moreover, when she got out of bed her feet didn't
seem to touch the ground. She had no appetite for her
breakfast either, but as Radinck was reading his letters
and scanning the morning's papers, she didn't think that
mattered. He was never chatty over the meal; she took
some toast and crumbled it at intervals just in case he
should look up, and drank several cups of coffee which
revived her sufficiently to bid him goodbye in a perfectly
normal way. They weren't going anywhere that evening
and she would be able to go to bed early, as he so often
went straight to his study after dinner. She went through
her morning routine, visited Queenie and Prince, took
Waterloo for a brief walk in the gardens and retired to the
library to struggle with her Dutch. But she didn't seem
able to concentrate, not even with the help of several more
cups of coffee. She toyed with her lunch, which upset Noakes very much, and then went back to the sitting-room,
got out her knitting and curled up in Radinck's chair with
Waterloo on her lap. He was warm and comforting and
after a very short time she gave up trying to knit and
closed her eyes and dozed off into a troubled sleep, to be
wakened by a worried Noakes with the tea tray.

'Yer not yerself, ma'am,' he declared. 'Yer ought to
go ter bed.'

She eyed him hazily. 'Yes, I think I will when I've had
tea, Noakes. It's just a cold.'

She drank the teapot dry and went off to sleep again,
her cheeks flushed and her head heavy. She didn't wake
when Radinck, met at the door by an anxious Noakes,
came into the room.

Caro looked small and lonely and lost in his great

chair and he muttered something as he bent over her, a cool hand on her hot forehead. She woke up then, staring into the blue eyes so close to hers. 'I feel very grotty,' she mumbled. 'I meant to go to bed... I'll go now.'

She began to scramble out of the chair and he picked her up with Waterloo still in her arms. 'You should have gone hours ago,' he said almost angrily. 'You weren't well at breakfast—why didn't you say so then?'

He was mounting the staircase and she muttered: 'I can walk,' and then: 'I thought I'd feel better. Besides, I didn't think you noticed.'

Noakes had gone ahead to open the door and Radinck laid her on the bed, asked Noakes to fetch Juffrouw Kropp and then pulled the coverlet over Caro, who was beginning to shiver. 'So sorry,' she told him, 'such a nuisance for you. I'll be quite all right now.'

He didn't answer but waited until Juffrouw Kropp came into the room, spoke to her quietly and went away, while that lady undressed Caro as though she had been a baby, tucked her up in her bed and went to fetch Radinck, walking up and down the gallery outside. Caro, feeling so wretched by now that she didn't care about anything at all, put out her tongue, muttered and mumbled ninety-nine and then swallowed the pills she was given. She was asleep in five minutes.

She woke a couple of hours later, feeling very peculiar in the head, and found Radinck bending over her again. He looked large and solid and very dependable, and she sighed with relief because he was there.

'Now you won't have to go to the party tomorrow,' she told him, still half asleep, 'and there's a dinner party... when? Quite soon; we needn't go to that either.' She closed her eyes and then opened them wide again. 'I'm so glad, you can have peace and quiet again.'

She dropped off again, so that she didn't hear the words wrung so reluctantly from Radinck's lips. Which was a pity.

She felt a little better in the morning, but her recollection of the night was hazy; she had wakened several times and there had been a lamp by the bed, but the rest of the room had been in shadow. And once or twice someone had given her a drink, but she had been too tired to open her eyes and see who it was. Radinck came to see her at breakfast time, pronounced himself satisfied as to her progress and went away again, leaving her with Waterloo for company. Presently Juffrouw Kropp came and washed her face and hands, brushed her hair and then brought her a tray of tea—nice strong tea with a lot of milk, and paper-thin bread and butter.

Caro dozed through the day. Lovingly tended by Juffrouw Kropp, Marta and the maids, it seemed to her that each time she opened her eyes there was someone in the room looking anxiously at her. Towards teatime Noakes came in with a vase of autumn flowers and a message from Becky and Tiele, and that was followed by a succession of notes and several more flower arrangements.

'But I've only got 'flu,' said Caro. 'I mean, there's really no need…'

'Very well liked, yer are, ma'am,' said Noakes with deep satisfaction. 'The phone's bin going on and off all afternoon with messages.'

'But how did they all know?'

'The Professor will 'ave cancelled your engagements, ma'am.'

Caro nodded. She wasn't enjoying having 'flu, but at

least it was making Radinck happy. She drank her tea and after a struggle to keep awake, slept again.

She woke to find Radinck at the foot of the bed, looking at her, and she assured him before he could ask her that she was feeling a great deal better. She sat up against the pillows, happily unaware of her wan face and tousled hair. 'And look at all these flowers,' she begged him, 'and I'm not even ill. I feel a fraud!'

He said seriously: 'You have no need to—you have a quite violent virus infection of the respiratory system.'

It was silly to get upset, but somehow he had made her feel like a patient in a hospital bed; someone to be cured of an ailment with a completely impersonal care. Her eyes filled with tears until they dripped down her cheeks and although she put up an impatient hand to rub them away, there seemed no end to them. Radinck bent over her, a handkerchief in his hand, but she pushed it away. 'I'm perfectly all right,' she told him crossly. 'It's just that I don't feel quite the thing.' She added peevishly: 'I think I'd like to go to sleep.'

She closed her eyes so that he would see that she really meant that, and although the tears were still pouring from under her lids, she kept them shut. And after a minute or so she really did feel sleepy in a dreamy kind of way, so that the kiss on her cheek seemed part of the dream too. She woke much later and remembered it—it had been very pleasant; dreams could be delightful. She dismissed the idea that Radinck had kissed her as ridiculous and wept a little before she slept again.

Chapter 8

Two days later Caro was on her feet again. She had been coddled and mothered by Juffrouw and Marta, ably backed by the maids and old Jan who sent in flowers each day from his cherished hothouses, the whole team masterminded by Noakes. No one could have been kinder. Even Radinck, visiting her twice a day, had been meticulous in his attentions. Although that hadn't stopped him telling her that he would be going to Vienna that evening. 'You wouldn't wish to go to the hospital ball,' he pointed out with unescapable logic, 'and much though I regret having to leave you while you are feeling under the weather, my presence is hardly necessary to your recovery. My entire—I beg your pardon—our entire staff are falling over themselves to lavish attention upon you.' He gave her a mocking little smile. 'I leave you in the best of hands.'

Caro had agreed with him in a quiet little voice. Normally she wouldn't have allowed herself to feel crushed by his high-handedness, but she wasn't quite herself. Her chances of making him fall in love with her seemed so low they hardly bore contemplation. She wished him goodbye and hoped he would have a good trip and that the seminar would be interesting, and then, unable to think of anything else to say, sat up in bed just looking at him.

'Goodbye, Caroline,' said Radinck in a quite different voice, and bent and kissed her cheek. She didn't move for quite a while after he had gone, but presently when Waterloo jumped on to the bed and gave her an enquiring butt with his head, she scratched the top of it in an absent manner. 'I didn't dream it, then,' she told him. 'He kissed me then as well. Now, I wonder...'

It was probably a false hope, but at least she could work on it. She got bathed and dressed and went downstairs, to be fussed over by everyone in the house, and all of them remarked how much better she looked.

She felt better. Somewhere or other there was a chink in her husband's armour of cool aloofness; she would have to work on it. Much cheered by the thought, she spent her day catching up on her Dutch, knitting like a fury and entertaining Rex, who with his master gone, was feeling miserable.

'Well, I feel the same,' Caro told him, 'and at least he's glad to see you when he comes home.' She insisted on going to the servants' sitting-room to rehearse the carols after dinner too, although Noakes shook his head and said she ought to be in bed.

'Well, yes, I'm sure you're right,' Caro agreed, 'but Christmas is getting close and we do want to put on a perfect performance. I think that tomorrow evening we'd

better get together in the drawing-room so that you'll all
know where to stand and so on. The moment the Professor comes home on Christmas Eve, you can all file in
and take up your places and the minute he comes into
the room you can start. It should be a lovely surprise.'

She went to bed quite happy presently with Waterloo
to keep her company and Juffrouw Kropp coming in with
hot milk to sip so that she would sleep and strict instructions to ring if she wanted anything during the night.

They were all such dears, thought Caro, curled up cosily in the centre of the vast bed. Life could have been
wonderful if only Radinck had loved her even a little.
But that was no way to think, she scolded herself. 'Faint
heart never won Radinck,' she told Waterloo, on the edge
of sleep.

The weather was becoming very wintry. She woke
in the morning to grey, woolly clouds, heavy with snow
and the sound of the wind racing through the bare trees
near the house. But the great house was warm and very
comfortable and she spent her morning doing the flowers once again, with Jan bringing her armsful of them
from his hothouses. There was Marta to talk to about
the meals too; something special for dinner on the following day when Radinck would return. The day passed
quickly. Caroline ate her dinner with appetite with Noakes brooding over her in a fatherly way, then repaired
to the drawing-room.

They were all a little shy at first. The room was grand
and they felt stiff and awkward and out of place until
Caro said in her sparse, excruciating Dutch: 'Sing as
though you were in your own sitting-room—remember
it's to give the Professor pleasure and it's only because
this is the best place for him to hear you.'

They loosened up after that. They were well embarked on *Silent Night* with all the harmonies just right, when the Professor unlocked his own front door. No one heard him. Even Rex, dozing by the fire, was deafened by the choir. He stood for a moment in the centre of the hall and then walked very quietly to the drawing-room door, not quite closed. The room was in shadow with only a lamp by the piano and the sconces on either side of the fire-place alight. He pushed the door cautiously a few inches so that he could look in and no one saw him. They were grouped round Caro at the piano, her mousy head lighted by the lamp beside her, one hand beating time while the other thumped out the tune. Radinck closed the door gently again and retreated to where he had cast down his coat and bag and let himself out of the house again. The car's engine made no noise above the sighing and whis-tling of the wind. He drove back the way he had come, all the way to the airport on the outskirts of Leeuwarden where he parked the car, telephoned his home that he had returned earlier than he had expected, then got back into the car and, for the second time, drove himself home.

Caro had received the news of Radinck's unexpected return with outward calm. 'We'll find time to rehearse again tomorrow,' she told them all. 'Now I think if Marta would warm up some of that delicious soup just in case the Professor's cold and hungry…'

She closed the piano and went to sit in the sitting-room by the fire, her tapestry in her hands. She even had time to do a row or two before she heard Radinck open the door, speak to Noakes, on the watch for him, and cross the hall to open the sitting-room door.

'What a nice surprise!' she smiled as he came into

the room. 'Would you like dinner or just soup and sand-wiches?'

'Coffee will do, thank you, Caroline.' He sat down opposite her. 'You are feeling better, I can see that, and being sensible, sitting quietly here.'

'Oh, I've been very sensible,' she assured him. 'Would you like coffee in your study?'

He looked annoyed. 'My dear girl, I have just this minute returned home and here you are, banishing me to my study!'

Caro went red. 'I'm sorry, I didn't mean it like that, only you so often do go there—I thought you might rather be alone.'

'Very considerate of you; I prefer to remain here. What have you been doing with yourself?'

'Oh, almost nothing—the flowers and catching up with my Dutch, and showing Marta how to make mince pies…'

'I surprised you playing the piano before we married,' he said. 'Do you remember? Don't you play any more?'

Caro's red face went pale. 'Yes—well, sometimes I do.'

He sat back in his chair, relaxed and at ease, and watched while Noakes placed the coffee tray at Caro's elbow. 'Have you any plans for Christmas?' he asked idly.

She stammered a little. 'I understand from Noakes that you don't—that is, you prefer a quiet time.'

'I am afraid that over the years I have got into the habit of doing very little about entertaining—I did mention the party which I give, did I not? Is there anything special you would enjoy? A little music perhaps?'

'Music?' Caro's needle was working overtime, regard-less of wrong stitches. She took a deep breath. 'Oh, you mean going to concerts and that sort of thing; Becky was telling me…but you really don't have to bother. We did agree when we married that your life wasn't to be changed at all, but you've already had to go to these parties with me and you must have disliked them very much. I'm very happy, you know, I don't mind if I don't go out socially.'

'I thought girls liked dressing up and going out to parties.'

'Well, yes, of course, but you see I don't enjoy them if you don't.' She hadn't meant to say that. She stitched a whole row, her head bowed over her work, and wished fruitlessly that the floor would open and swallow her up.

'And what precisely do you mean by that?' asked Radinck blandly.

'Nothing, nothing at all.' And then, knowing that she wouldn't get away with that, she added: 'What I meant was that I feel guilty because you have to give up your evenings doing something you don't enjoy when you might be in your study reading…and writing.'

'Put like that I seem to be a very selfish man. I must endeavour to make amends.'

Caro gave him a surprised glance. He wasn't being sarcastic and his voice held a warm note she hadn't heard before.

'You're not selfish,' she told him in a motherly voice. 'No one would expect you to change your whole way of life, certainly I wouldn't. You've devoted yourself to your work and the staff adore you—so do the animals.'

'And what about you, Caroline?'

She took her time answering. 'You must know that I have a great regard for you, Radinck.' She looked across at him, her loving heart in her eyes and unaware of it.

'You have no need to reproach yourself; you made it very clear before we married that you didn't want to change your life, and I agreed to that. I'm very content.'

His eyes were searching. 'Are you? Perhaps I have done wrong in marrying you, Caroline—you might have found some younger man…'

'I wish you wouldn't keep harping on your great age!' declared Caro hotly. Suddenly she could stand no more of it. She threw down her embroidery carelessly, so that the wools flew in all directions, and hurried out of the room and up to her bedroom, where she burst into tears, making Waterloo's fur very damp while she hugged him. 'What am I going to do?' she asked him. 'One minute I think he likes me a little and then he says he regrets marrying me…' Which wasn't quite true, although that was how it seemed to her.

She went to bed because there was nothing else to do, but she didn't go to sleep; she lay listening to the now familiar sounds in the old house—the very faint clatter from the kitchens, Rex's occasional bark, the tread of Noakes' rather heavy feet crossing the hall, the subdued clang as he closed the gate leading to the garden from the side door, even faint horsey noises from the stables. It was a clear, cold night, and sounds carried. Presently she heard Noakes and Marta and the rest of them going up the back stairs at the end of the gallery on their way to bed, and after that the house was quiet save for the various clocks striking the hour, each in its own good time.

It was almost one o'clock and she was still awake when she heard cars travelling fast along the road at the end of the drive, and the next moment there was a kind of slow-motion crashing and banging and the sound of glass splintering and then distant faint cries. She was out of bed and pulling back the curtains within seconds and saw lights shine out as the front door was opened and Radinck went running down the drive, his bag in his hand. Caroline didn't stop to take off her nightie but pulled on a pair of slacks, bundled a sweater on top of them, and rushed downstairs in her bare feet. Her wellingtons were in one of the hall cupboards; she got into them just as Noakes came down the stairs with a dressing gown over his pyjamas.

'You'll need a coat, Noakes,' said Caro, 'and thick shoes, it's cold outside, then will you come to the gate and see if the Professor wants you to telephone.' She didn't wait for him to reply but opened the door and started down the drive. Something was on fire now, she could smell it and see the flickering of flames somewhere on the road to the left of the gates. But there were no cries any more, although she thought she could hear voices.

There were two cars, hopelessly entangled, and one was blazing with thick black smoke pouring from it. Well away from it there were people on the grass verge of the road, some sitting and two lying, and she could see Radinck bending over them. She fetched up beside him, took the torch he was holding from him and shone it on the man lying on the ground. 'Noakes is coming as soon as he's got his coat on,' she said quietly.

'Good girl!' He was on his knees now, opening the man's jacket. 'Shine the light here, will you? There are scissors in my bag, can you reach them?'

Noakes arrived then, out of breath but calmly dignified. He listened to what Radinck had to say and with a brisk: 'OK, Professor,' turned and went back again. 'And bring some blankets and towels with you!' shouted Radinck after him.

The man was unconscious with head injuries and a
fractured pelvis. They made him as comfortable as they
could and moved on to the other silent figure close by.
Head injuries again, and Radinck grunted as he bent to
examine him, but beyond telling Caro to wrap one of the
towels Noakes had brought back round the man's head
and covering him with a blanket he did nothing. There
were three people sitting on the frosty grass—an elderly
man, a woman of the same age and a girl. Radinck looked
at the older woman first, questioning her quietly as he did
so. 'Shock,' he said to Caro, 'and a fractured clavicle—
fix it with a towel, will you?' He moved on to the man,
examined him briefly, said, 'Shock and no injuries apparent,' and then bent over the girl.

The loveliest girl Caro had ever set eyes on; small and
fair with great blue eyes, and even with her hair all over
the place and a dirty face she was breathtaking. 'Were
you driving?' asked Radinck.

It was a pity that Caro's Dutch didn't stretch to understanding what the girl answered, nor, for that matter,
what Radinck said after that. She held the torch, handed
him what he wanted from his bag and wished with all
her heart that she was even half as lovely as the girl sitting between them. She had looked at Radinck's face just
once and although it wore the bland mask of his profession, she knew that he found the girl just as beautiful as
she did; he would have been a strange man if he hadn't.
The girl said something to him in a low voice and he answered her gently, putting an arm round her slim shoulders, smiling at her and then, to Caro's eyes at least,
getting to his feet with reluctance.

'Stay with them, will you, Caroline?—this poor girl's
had a bad shock, the others aren't too bad. I'll take a look

at the other two, though there's nothing much to be done until we get them to hospital.' He stood listening for a moment. 'There are the ambulances now.'

He went away then and presently as the two ambulances slowed to a halt, Caro saw him directing the loading of the two unconscious men. The first ambulance went away and he came over to where she was waiting with the other three casualties. 'Go back to the house,' he told her. 'There's nothing more you can do. Get a warm drink and go to bed. I'll follow these people in to the hospital, there may be something I can do.' She hesitated, suddenly feeling unwanted and longing for a reassuring word. He had spoken briskly, as he might have spoken to a casual stranger who had stopped to give a hand, only she felt sure that he would have added his thanks.

'Do as I say, Caroline!' and this time he sounded urgent and coldly angry. She turned without a word and went down the drive, her feet and hands numb with cold, and climbed the steps slowly to where Juffrouw Kropp was waiting, wrapped in a dressing gown, and any neglect she had suffered at her husband's hands was instantly made up for by the care and attention she now received. Hardly knowing what was happening, she was bustled upstairs and into bed where Juffrouw Kropp tucked her in as though she had been a small girl and Marta waited with a tray of hot drinks. Both ladies stood one each side of the bed, while she sipped hot milk and brandy, reassured themselves that she had come to no harm and then told her firmly to go to sleep and not to get up in the morning until one or both of them had been to see her.

'But I'm not ill,' protested Caro weakly.

'You have had the grippe,' Juffrouw Kropp pointed

out. 'The Professor will never forgive us if you are ill again.'

Caro searched her muddled head for the right words. 'He's gone to the hospital—he'll be late and cold...'

'Do not worry, Baroness, he will be cared for when he returns. Now you will sleep.'

'I ought to be there.' Caro spoke in English, not caring whether she was understood or not.

'No, no, he would not like that.'

She gave up and closed her eyes, not knowing that while Marta crept out with the tray, Juffrouw Kropp perched herself on the edge of a chair and waited until she was quite sure that Caro slept.

She wakened to find that lady standing at the foot of the bed, looking at her anxiously, but the anxious look went as Caroline sat up in bed and said good morning and then gave a small shriek when she saw the time.

'Ten o'clock?' she exclaimed, horrified. 'Why didn't someone call me? Is the Professor back?'

Juffrouw Kropp shook her head. 'He telephoned, Baroness. He will be back perhaps this afternoon, perhaps later.'

Caro plastered a cheerful smile on her face. 'Oh, yes, of course, he'll be busy. I'll get up.'

'Marta brings your breakfast at once—there is no need for you to get up, *mevrouw*, it will snow before long and it is very cold outside.'

Under Juffrouw Kropp's eagle eye Caro put her foot back in bed. 'Well, it would be nice,' she conceded. The housekeeper smiled in a satisfied way and shook up the pillows.

'There has been a telephone call for you—Baroness Raukema van den Eck—she heard about the accident. I

asked her to telephone later, Baroness. She hopes that
you are all right.'

It was nice to have a friend, reflected Caro, sitting
up in bed eating a splendid breakfast, someone who
wanted to know how you were and really minded. Not
like Radinck. She choked on a piece of toast and pushed
the tray away and got up.

It wasn't until the afternoon that Radinck telephoned,
and by then any number of people had rung up. Becky,
of course, wanting to know exactly what had happened,
asking if Caroline were quite better, did she need anything, would she like to go over and see them soon. 'Tiele
saw Radinck for a few minutes this morning,' went on
Becky. 'He was getting ready to drive one of the crash
people home—the girl who was driving. You'll know
that, of course. I must say it's pretty good of him to go
all the way to Dordrecht with her—let's hope the snow
doesn't get any worse.'

Caro had made some suitable reply and put down the
phone very thoughtfully. Of course, there might be some
very good reason why Radinck should take the girl back
home—something urgent—but there were trains, and
cars to hire and buses, and most people had friends or
family who rallied round at such a time. She did her best
to forget about it, answered suitably when a number of
other people she had met at the burgermeester's reception telephoned, took Rex for a quick walk in the garden, despite Juffrouw Kropp's protests that she would
catch her death of cold, and settled down by the fire to
con her Dutch lessons.

The weather worsened as the day wore on; it was
snowing hard by the time Radinck telephoned. He
sounded cool and rather casual and Caroline did her best

to be the same. 'I'm in Dordrecht,' he told her. 'I took Juffrouw van Doorn back to her home; she had no way of reaching it otherwise and her parents must stay in hospital for a few days. I shall do my best to get back this evening, but the weather isn't too good.'

'It's snowing hard here,' said Caro, anxious not to sound anxious. 'If you'd rather not drive back—I expect you can find a hotel or something.'

'Juffrouw van Doorn has offered me a bed for the night—probably I shall accept it. You're all right?'

'Perfectly, thank you.' And even if I weren't, she added silently, I wouldn't tell you. 'Do you want me to tell anyone? Have you any appointments for the morning?'

His low laugh came very clearly over the wire. 'Really, Caroline, you are becoming the perfect wife! No, there's no one you need telephone. I can do it all from here.'

'Very well—we'll expect you when we see you.'

'Caroline—about last night—'

She interrupted him ruthlessly. 'I'm sorry, I must go. Goodbye, Radinck.'

The rest of the day was a dead loss.

They were to go to a party the following evening. Becky had telephoned to know if they were going and Caro had improvised hurriedly and said that they expected to be there but Radinck would let her know the moment he could leave Dordrecht. 'The weather's awful there,' she invented, 'and I told him not to come home until the roads were clear.'

And Becky had said how wise she was and she hoped they'd see each other the next day.

There was no word from Radinck the next day. Caro ordered the meals as though he were expected home, took Rex for a snowy walk, rehearsed her choir and then tele-

phoned the people whose party they were to attend and made their excuses. She was on the rug before the fire in the sitting-room when Radinck walked in, with Waterloo purring beside her and Rex leaning heavily against her. He bounded to the door as Radinck came in and Caro looked round and then got slowly to her feet. 'You didn't telephone,' she observed, quite forgetting to say hullo.

'No, I'm sorry I couldn't get back sooner—the roads are bad.' He fended Rex off with a gentle hand and sat down. 'How quiet and peaceful you look, Caroline.'

Appearances can be deceptive, she thought. She wasn't either, inside her she boiled with rage and misery and jealousy and all the other things which were supposed to be so bad for one. 'I hope the trip wasn't too bad,' she remarked. 'Would you like some coffee?'

'Yes, thanks. Aren't we supposed to be going to the Laggemaats' this evening?'

'Yes, but I telephoned them about an hour ago and told them that as you weren't back we would probably not be able to go. I hope I did right.'

'Quite right. Did you not wonder where I was?'

She said evenly: 'When we married you particularly stressed the fact that that was something I was never to do.'

She poured the coffee Noakes had brought and handed Radinck a cup.

He said testily: 'You seem to have remembered every word I said and moreover, are determined to keep to it.'

Caroline didn't answer that but asked in her quiet little voice: 'How are the people who were hurt in the accident?'

'The first man is in intensive care, the second man died on the way to hospital—I think you may have guessed that; the two older people who were in the second car are to remain under observation for another day or so. Their daughter—Ilena—I drove home.'

Caro busied herself pouring a cup of coffee she didn't want. 'Oh, yes, Becky told me when she telephoned yesterday.' She was careful to keep all traces of reproach from her voice. 'I'm so glad she wasn't hurt; she was the loveliest girl I've ever seen.'

'Extraordinarily beautiful,' agreed Radinck blandly, 'and so young, too. She asked me to stay the night and I did.'

'Very sensible of you,' declared Caro calmly. 'Travelling back in all that snow would never have done.'

'What would you say if I told you that I've never allowed bad weather to interfere with my driving?'

She could say a great many things, thought Caro, and all of them very much to the point. She didn't utter any of them but said prudently: 'I think it was very wise of you to make an exception to your rule.'

She put down her coffee cup and picked up her work again, glad to be able to busy herself with something.

Radinck stretched out his legs and wedged his great shoulders deeply into his chair. 'Don't you want to know why I took Ilena home?'

'You must have had a good reason for doing so—I daresay she was badly shaken and not fit to travel on her own.'

'She was perfectly able to go on her own. I drove her because I wanted to prove something to myself.' He frowned. 'I seem to be in some confusion of mind—about you, Caroline.'

She looked up from her work, her eyes thoughtful as she studied his handsome and, at the moment, ill-tempered face. Her heart was thundering against her ribs. That he was about to say something important was evident, but what, exactly? She had promised herself that she would make him love her, but it seemed probable that she had failed and he was going to tell her so. She said steadily: 'If you want to talk about it I'm listening, Radinck.'

It was a pity that just at that moment the telephone on the table beside him should ring. He lifted the receiver and listened, frowning, and then embarked on what Caro took to be a list of instructions about a patient. The interruption gave her time to collect her thoughts, which were, however, instantly scattered by the entry of Noakes, announcing Tiele and Becky.

'We were on our way to the Laggemaats',' explained Becky, 'and Tiele thought it would be an idea to pop in and see how you were.'

She kissed Caro, offered a cheek to Radinck and perched herself on a chair close to Caro, spreading the skirts of her dress as she did so.

'That's pretty,' observed Caro. 'It's new, isn't it? I love the colour. I was going to wear a rather nice green...'

Tiele had bent to kiss her cheek and said laughingly: 'Oh, lord—clothes again! Radinck, take me to your study and show me that agenda for the seminar at Brussels. Are you going? We could go together—we need only be away for a couple of days.'

The two men went away and Becky, declining coffee, remarked: 'We weren't sure if Radinck would be back. The roads are very bad further south. He telephoned Tiele about some patient or other quite late last night—said he'd gone to a hotel in Dordrecht and planned to leave early this morning, but he got held up—you know all that, of course.' She ate one of the small biscuits on the coffee tray. 'He must have been glad to have handed that girl over to her aunt—a bit of a responsibility—supposing he'd got landed in a snowdrift!' She giggled engagingly.

Caro had listened to this artless information in surprise and a mounting excitement. If what Becky had told her was true, why had Radinck let her think that he'd stayed at the girl's house? Had he wanted to make her jealous? On the other hand, did he want her to believe that he had thought better of their dry-as-dust marriage and wanted to put an end to it? More likely the latter, she considered, although that was something she would have to find out. She wasn't sure how and she had a nasty feeling that whatever it was Radinck had been going to say wouldn't be said—at least not for the moment.

In this she was perfectly right. The van den Ecks went presently and Radinck went almost at once to his study with the observation that he had a good deal of paperwork to do. Which left Caro with nothing better to do than go to bed.

Chapter 9

The snow lay thick on the ground when Caro looked out of her windows in the morning. It was barely light and she could see Radinck, huge in a sheepskin jacket, striding down to the stables with Rex at his heels. He would be going to see how Queenie fared before walking Rex in the fields beyond. It would have been lovely to be with him, she thought, walking in the early morning cold, talking about his work and planning a pleasant evening together. Which reminded her that there was another party that evening and presumably they would be going: a doctor from the hospital and his wife—she searched her memory and came up with their name—ter Brink, youngish if she remembered aright and rather nice. She would have to ring Becky and ask what she should wear. She bathed and dressed and went downstairs and found Radinck already at the table.

It was hardly the time or place to expect him to disclose what he had intended to say to her, but she sat down hopefully and began her breakfast. But beyond a polite good morning, the hope that she had slept well, and could he pass her the toast, he had nothing to say, but became immersed in his letters once again. Caroline was glad that she had a modest pile of post beside her plate for once. It seemed to keep her occupied and by reading each letter two or three times, she spun out her interest in them until Radinck put his own mail down and got to his feet.

'You feel well enough to go to the ter Brinks' this evening?' he asked her pleasantly.

'Oh yes, thank you. Where do they live?'

'Groningen—not far. I should be home about tea-time and we shall need to leave here about half past six.' He paused on his way to the door. 'Be careful if you go out—it's very cold and treacherous underfoot.'

'Yes, Radinck.' She smiled at him as she spoke and he came back across the room and kissed her hard and quick. Caroline sat a long while after he had gone trying to decide whether he had meant it or whether he was feeling guilty; she remembered all the books she had read where the husband had tried to make amends to his wife when he had neglected her by being kind to her, only in books they sent flowers as well.

They arrived a few hours later—a great bouquet of fragrant spring flowers; lilac, and hyacinths, tulips and daffodils, exquisitely arranged in a paper-thin porcelain bowl. The card said merely: Flowers for Caroline, and he had written it himself and scrawled Radinck at the end. Caroline eyed them at first with delight and then with suspicion. Was he, like the guilty husbands in all the best novels, feeling guilty too? She was consumed with a desire to find out more about the beautiful girl in Dordrecht. She was a satisfyingly long way away, but absence made the heart grow fonder, didn't it?

Caro spent the whole day vacillating between hope and despair, so that by the time Radinck came home she was in a thoroughly muddled state of mind—made even more muddled by his unexpected friendly attitude towards her. He had always—well, almost always—treated her with punctilious politeness, but seldom with warmth. Now he launched into an account of his day, lounging back in his great chair, looking to be the epitome of a contented man and even addressing her as Caro, which seemed to her to be a great step forward in their relationship. She went up to change her dress presently; it was to be a long dress occasion and she chose one of the dresses she had bought in den Haag. A rose pink crêpe-de-Chine, patterned with deeper pink roses, it had a high neck and long tight sleeves and the bodice was finely tucked between lace insertions. She swept downstairs presently, her mink coat over her arm, and then stopped so suddenly that she very nearly tripped up. She had never thanked Radinck for his flowers.

A deep chuckle from the end of the hall made her look round. Radinck was sitting on a marble-topped side table, swinging his long legs, the picture of elegance. 'Such a magnificent entry!' he observed. 'Just like Cinderella at the ball—and then you stopped as though you'd been shot. What happened?'

'Oh, Radinck, I remembered—I'm so sorry, I never thanked you for the flowers, and they're so lovely. I hope you don't mind—I put them in my room, but I'll bring them downstairs tomorrow...'

'I'm glad they pleased you.' He swung himself off the

table and came towards her. 'That is a charming dress, and you look charming in it, Caro. I have something for you; I hope you will wear it.'

He took a box from a pocket and opened it and took out a brooch, a true lovers' knot of diamonds. 'May I put it on for you?'

He held the lovely thing in the palm of his hand and she put out a finger to touch it. 'It's magnificent!' she breathed. 'Was it your mother's?'

His hand had closed gently over the brooch and her fingers. 'No—I chose it yesterday as I came through den Haag on my way home. I want to give it to you, Caro, and I want you to wear it.'

She looked up into his face; his eyes were bright and searching and his brows were raised in a questioning arc.

'Why?' asked Caro, her head full of the girl in Dordrecht. Flowers, and now this heavenly brooch—it was even worse than she had thought, although Radinck didn't look in the least like a guilty husband.

'I'm afraid to answer that,' said Radinck surprisingly, and pinned the brooch into the lace at her neck with cool steady fingers.

And when he had done it: 'It's my turn to ask a question,' he smiled down at her. 'Why did you ask why, Caroline?'

Oh dear! thought Caro, now I'm Caroline again, and said carefully: 'Well, first you sent me those heavenly flowers and now you've given me this fabulous brooch, and you see, in books the husband is always extra nice to his wife when he's been neglecting her or—or falling in love with someone else—then he buys his wife presents because he feels guilty...'

He looked utterly bewildered. 'Guilty?' he considered it for a moment. 'Well, yes, I suppose you're right.'

Caro's heart dropped like a stone into her high-heeled, very expensive satin sandals. 'So there's no need to say any more, is there?' she asked unhappily.

Strangely, Radinck was smiling. 'Not just now, perhaps—I don't really think that we have the time—we are already a little late.'

She said yes, of course, in her quiet hesitant voice and got into her coat, then sat, for the most part silent, as he drove the Panther de Ville to Groningen, almost sixty kilometres away. The roads were icy under a bright moon, but Radinck drove with relaxed ease, carrying on a desultory conversation, not seeming to notice Caroline's quiet. He certainly didn't present the appearance of a guilty husband who had just been found out by his wife. Caro stirred in her seat, frowning. She could be wrong...

There wasn't much chance to find out anything more at the party. The ter Brinks were a youngish, rather serious-minded couple living in a large modern house on the outskirts of Groningen, and Caro found herself moving round their drawing-room, getting caught up in the highbrow conversations among their guests. She had met most of them already and almost all of them spoke excellent English, but—typical of her, she thought—she got pinned into a corner by an elderly gentleman, who insisted on speaking Dutch despite her denial of all knowledge of that language, so that all she could do was to look interested, say '*neen*' and '*ja*' every now and then and pray for someone to rescue her.

Which Radinck did, tucking a hand under her arm and engaging the elderly man in a pleasant conversation for a few minutes before drifting her away to the other end of the room.

'My goodness,' said Caro, when they were safely out of earshot, 'I only understood one word in a hundred—thank you for rescuing me, Radinck. What was he talking about?'

Her husband's firm mouth twitched. 'Nuclear warfare and the possibility of invasion from outer space,' he told her blandly.

'Oh, my goodness—and all I said was yes and no—Oh, and once I said *Niet waar* in a surprised sort of way.'

Radinck's shoulders shook, but he said seriously: 'A quite suitable remark, especially if you sounded astonished. "You don't say" is an encouraging remark to make—it sounds admiring as well as astonished, which after all was what Professor Vinke expected to hear.'

'Oh, good—I'd hate to let you down.'

He had guided her to another corner, standing in front of her so that she was shut off from the room. 'I believe you, Caroline. It is a pity that you cannot return my opinion.' He took her hand briefly. 'Caro, perhaps I'm going away for a day or two. Are you going to ask me where and why?'

She stared down at his fingers clasping hers. 'No, I don't break promises.'

He sighed. 'Perhaps the incentive isn't enough for you to do that...'

And after that there was no further chance to talk. They were joined by friends, and presently Tiele and Becky came across to talk to them and although they left soon afterwards they only discussed the party on their way home. They didn't talk about anything much at dinner either, and afterwards Radinck wished her a cool goodnight and went away to his study. And yet, thought Caro, left alone to drink her coffee by the fire in the drawing-room, he had looked at her very intently once or twice during the meal, just as though he was wanting to say something and didn't know how to start.

She went to bed presently and made a point of being down in time to share breakfast with Radinck the following morning. It was hardly the best time of the day to talk to him, but she didn't feel she could bear to go on much longer without asking more questions. When he had read his post she said abruptly: 'I'm going to break my promise after all. Are you going to Dordrecht?'

Radinck put his coffee cup down very slowly. 'Why should I wish to go to Dordrecht?' His eyes narrowed. 'Ah, now I see—the flowers and brooch were to cover my neglect, were they?' His voice held a sneer. 'You really believe that I would go tearing off after a girl young enough to be my daughter, just like your precious novels?' He got to his feet, looking to her nervous gaze to be twice his normal size and in a very bad temper indeed. 'Well, Caroline, you may think what you wish.'

'When are you going?' she asked, for there seemed no point in retreating now. 'And you needn't be so very bad-tempered; you wanted to know if I was going to ask you where you were going, and now I have you're quite peevish...'

He stopped on his way to the door. 'Peevish? Peevish? I am angry, Caroline.' He came back to tower over her, still sitting at the table.

'And why do you keep on calling me Caroline?' asked Caro. She had cooked her goose and it really didn't matter what she said now. 'And sometimes you say Caro.'

He said silkily: 'Because when I call you Caroline

I can try and believe that you are someone vague who has little to do with my life, only I find that I no longer can do that…'

'And what am I when I'm Caro?' she asked with interest.

'Soft and gentle and loving.' He bent and kissed her soundly. 'You have brought chaos to my life,' he told her austerely, and turned on his heel and went.

Caro sat very still after he had gone. Things, she told herself, had come to a head. It was time she did something about it. And he hadn't told her when he was going to Dordrecht, or even if he was going there. She poured herself more coffee and applied her wits to the problem.

She got up presently and went to the telephone. Radinck's secretary at his rooms was quite sure that he wasn't going anywhere, certainly not to Dordrecht, and at the hospital, in answer to her carefully worded enquiries, she was told that the Professor had a full day ahead of him. So he had been making it up…to annoy her? To get her interested in what he did? She wasn't sure, but his kiss had been, even in her inexperienced view, a very genuine one. Caroline nodded her mousy head and smiled a little, then went to the little davenport in the sitting-room and after a great deal of thought and several false starts, composed a letter. It was a nicely worded document, telling Radinck that since they didn't agree very well, perhaps it would be as well if she went away. She read it through, put it in its envelope and went in search of Willem, who, always willing, got out the Mini used by the staff for errands and rattled off to Leeuwarden, the letter in his pocket.

It was unfortunate that Radinck happened to be doing a round when Willem handed in his letter with the request that it should be delivered as soon as possible; the round took ages and it was well after lunch before a porter, tracking him down in the consultants' room, making a meal off sandwiches and beer, handed it to him. He read it quickly and then read it again, before reaching for the telephone. He had been a fool, he told himself savagely; Caro had believed that he had gone to Dordrecht because he had been attracted to that girl—and he shouldn't have let her believe that he had stayed there, either. He was too old to fall in love, he reminded himself sourly, but he had, and nothing would alter the fact that little Caro had become his world.

Noakes answered the phone and listened carefully to the Professor's instructions. The house was to be searched very thoroughly; he had reason to believe that the Baroness, who wasn't feeling quite herself, could be in one of its many rooms. Radinck himself would call at the most likely places where she might be and then come home.

He spent the rest of the afternoon going patiently from one friend's house to the next, calling at the shops he thought Caro might have visited and then finally, holding back his fear with an iron hand, going home.

Caro had been sitting working quite feverishly at her knitting for quite some time before she heard the car coming up the drive, the front door bang shut and Radinck's footsteps in the hall. It was a great pity that the speech she had prepared and rehearsed over and over again should now fly from her head, leaving it empty—not that it mattered. The door was flung open and her husband strode in, closing it quietly behind him and then leaning against it to stare across at her. Meeting his eyes, she realised that she had no need to say anything, a certainty confirmed by his: 'Caro, you baggage—how long have you been here?'

'Since—well, since Willem took my note.'

'The house was searched—where did you hide?'

'Behind the door.' She made her voice matter-of-fact, although her hands were shaking so much that stitches were being dropped right left and centre. She wished she could look away from him, but she seemed powerless to do so. Any minute now he would explode with rage, for he must be in a fine temper. His face was white and drawn and his eyes were glittering.

Caroline was completely disarmed when he said gently: 'I have been out of my mind with worry, my darling. I thought that you had left me and that I would never see you again. I wanted to kill myself for being such a fool. I had begun to think that you were beginning to love me a little and that if I had patience I could make you forget how badly I had treated you.' He smiled bleakly. 'I have just spent the worst two hours of my life...'

Caro's soft heart was wrung, but she went on ruining her knitting in what she hoped was a cool manner. 'I didn't mean you to be upset,' she explained gruffly. 'You see, I had to know...well, I thought that if you m-minded about me at all, you would look for me, but if you didn't then I'd know I had to go away.' She dropped three stitches one after the other and added mournfully: 'I haven't put it very clearly.' Not that it mattered now. He hadn't said that he loved her and everybody called everyone else darling these days.

Radinck crossed the room very fast indeed. 'Put that damned knitting down,' he commanded, 'you're hiding behind it.' She had it taken from her in a ruthless manner which completed the havoc she had already wrought, but it really didn't matter, for Radinck had wrapped her in his arms. 'To think that I had to wait half a lifetime to meet you and even then I fought against loving you, my darling Caro!' He put a finger under her chin and turned her face up to his. 'I think I fell in love with you when you told me to give you a needle and thread and you'd do it yourself...only I'd spent so many years alone and I didn't believe there was a girl like you left in the world.' He smiled a little. 'I carry one of your handkerchiefs, like a lovesick boy.'

He kissed her gently and then very hard so that she had no breath. 'My beautiful girl,' he told her, 'when I came in just now and saw you sitting there it was as though you'd been here all my life, waiting for me to come home.'

'Well, dear Radinck, that's just what I was doing.' Caroline's voice shook a little although she tried hard to sound normal. 'Only I didn't know if you would.'

He kissed her again. 'But I did, dear heart, and I shall always come home to you.'

She had a delightful picture of herself, with her delightful children, waiting in the hall for Radinck to come home...and now she would be able to wear the pink organza dress. She smiled enchantingly at the idea and Radinck smoothed the mousy hair back from her face and asked: 'Why do you smile, my love?'

She leaned up to kiss him. 'Because I'm happy and because I love you so much.'

A remark which could have only one answer.

* * * * *

FATE IS REMARKABLE

Chapter 1

It was quiet in the consulting room, if the difficult, rasping breaths of the patient were discounted. From somewhere behind the closed door came the steady, subdued roar of a great many people, interrupted at intervals by a nurse's voice calling the next in line. Sister Sarah Ann Dunn stood quietly, holding layers of woolly garments clear of the patient's shoulders, so that Dr van Elven could get at them in comfort. He was a large man, and very tall, and the patient was fat. He bent, his handsome grizzled head an inch or so from the starched bib of Sarah's apron, his grey eyes looking at nothing while he listened and tapped, then listened again. Presently he came upright with the deliberation which characterised all his movements, said, 'Thank you, Sister,' and turned his back, as he always did, while she dealt with hooks and eyes and zips. She fastened the last button, gave its owner a reassuring little pat and a friendly smile, and said, 'Mrs Brown is ready for you, sir.' It was one of the nice things about her, that she never forgot people's names, however hard pressed she was. Patients were still people to her, and entitled to be treated as such. Dr van Elven strolled back from the X-rays he had been studying, glanced at her briefly from eyes half shut, and nodded. It was her cue to leave him with his patient for a few minutes—an arrangement which suited her very well, for it gave her time to have a quick look round OPD and make sure that everything was going smoothly.

The hall was still quite full, for it was the orthopae-dic consultant's afternoon as well as the gynaecologist's clinic and the medical OP she was taking. Both staff nurses were busy, but she could only see one student nurse. She made her way along the benches and turned into the narrow passage leading to the testing room. There were two nurses in it, carrying on such an ani-mated conversation that they failed to see her for several seconds. When they did, they stopped in mid-sentence, their eyes upon her, presenting very much the same ap-pearance, she imagined, as she had done when she had been caught in a similar situation as a student nurse. She said now, half smiling:

'If you two don't do your work, we shall all be late off duty, and there's no point in that, is there? If you're not doing anything here, go back to Staff Nurse Moore, please.'

She didn't wait to hear their apologies, but gave them a little nod and went back the way she had come, hurrying a little in case Dr van Elven was waiting. All the same, she stopped for a brief word with several of the patients sitting on the benches, for after three years as OPD Sister, she was on friendly terms with a number of them.

Mrs Brown was on the point of going as she went into the consulting room, and the doctor said at once:

'Ah, Sister, I have been suggesting to Mrs Brown that she should come in for a short time, so that I can keep an eye on this chest of hers—I daresay you can fix a bed? In three or four days, I think; that will give her time to make arrangements at home.'

He was looking at her steadily as he spoke and she said immediately:

'Yes, of course, sir. I'll get someone to write and tell Mrs Brown which day to come.' She smiled at the elderly, rather grubby little woman sitting in front of the doctor's desk, but Mrs Brown didn't smile back.

'It's me cat,' she began. ''Oo's going ter look after 'im while I'm in?' She sat silent for a moment, then went on, 'I don't see as 'ow I can manage…'

'Perhaps the RSPCA?' suggested Sarah gently.

Mrs Brown shook her head in its shapeless hat. ''E'd pine. I'm sorry, doctor, for you've been ever so kind…'

He sat back in his chair, with the air of a man who had all day before him, and nothing to do. 'Supposing you allow me to—er—have your cat while you are in hospital, Mrs Brown? Do you feel you could trust him to my care?'

Mrs Brown's several chins wobbled while she strove for words. It was, to say the least, unusual for an important gentleman like a hospital specialist to bother about what became of her Timmy. She was still seeking words when he continued, 'You would be doing me a great favour—my housekeeper has just lost her cat after fifteen years, and is quite inconsolable. Perhaps looking after your Timmy for a week or so might help her to become more resigned.'

The old lady brightened. 'Oh, well now, that's different, doctor. If 'e's going ter make 'er 'appy, and it ain't no trouble...'

She got up, and he got to his feet too. 'No trouble—I'll see that your cat is collected just before you come in, Mrs Brown. Will that do?'

Sarah ushered her out, competently, but without haste, laid the next case history on the doctor's desk, put up the X-rays, and waited. He finished what he was writing, closed the folder and said in his rather pedantic English:

'A pity Mrs Brown wasn't referred to me earlier. There's very little to be done, I'm afraid. Chronic bronchitis, emphysema, and congestive heart failure, not to mention all the wrong diet for I don't know how many years.' He picked up the next folder, frowning. 'If her home conditions were not too bad, I could patch her up enough to get her back there for a little while...'

Sister Dunn said nothing, for she knew that nothing was expected of her. She had been working for Dr van Elven for a number of years now; he was rather a taciturn man, kind to his patients, considerate towards the nursing staff, and revealing on occasion an unexpected sense of humour. She was aware that he was not, in fact, addressing her, merely speaking his thoughts out loud. So she stood quietly, patiently waiting for him to rid his mind of Mrs Brown. The little pause in the day's work did not irk her in the least; indeed, it gave her the opportunity to decide which dress she would wear that evening for dinner with Steven—the newish black would have been nice, but she particularly wanted to look young and gay. It would have to be the turquoise crêpe again. He had seen it a good many times already, but it suited her and she thought he liked it. Besides, it made her look a lot younger than her twenty-eight years…she looked a little wistful for a moment, although there was not the slightest need, for she looked a lot younger anyway, and was possessed of a serene beauty which she would keep all her life.

Her face was oval, with wide grey eyes, extravagantly lashed by nature; she had a delicious nose, small and straight, and a soft curving mouth. Her hair curled a little and she wore it neatly pinned when she was in uniform, and loose in an unswept swirl around her neck when she was off duty. She had a pretty figure too, and a quiet, pleasant voice—everyone who knew her or had met her wondered how it was that she had reached the age of twenty-eight without getting married. She sometimes wondered herself; perhaps it was because she had been waiting for someone like Steven to come along—they had known each other for three years now, and for the last two she had taken it for granted that one day he would ask her to marry him. Only he hadn't—she knew that he wanted a senior post, and just lately he had been talking about a partnership. Last time they had been out together he had observed that there was no point in marrying until he was firmly established.

She frowned a little, remembering that last time had been more than a week ago. He had telephoned twice since then to cancel the meetings they had arranged. He was Surgical Registrar at St Edwin's, and she had always accepted the fact that his work came first and because of that she had made no demur and no effort to waylay him in the hospital; but tonight should really be all right— she hoped that they would go to that restaurant in Monmouth Street where the food was good and the company gay. She suddenly wanted to be gay.

She came out of her brown study with a start to find Dr van Elven staring at her with thoughtful eyes. She smiled.

'I'm sorry, sir,' she said. 'Do you want the next patient? It's old Mr Gregor.'

The doctor went on staring. 'Yes. I have studied his X-rays, and read his notes through twice, Sister.' His voice was dry.

She went faintly pink. She liked Dr van Elven very much; they got on well together, although she sometimes felt that she didn't know him at all. She knew from the hospital grapevine that he was unmarried, that he had had an unhappy love affair when he had been a young man, and that now, at forty, he was a prize any woman would be glad to win. Rumour had it that he had plenty of money, a flourishing practice in Harley Street, and a beautiful house in Richmond. Sarah considered privately that the reason that they got on so well was because they had no romantic interest in each other. But now she had annoyed him.

'I really am sorry, sir,' she said with a genuine humility, because his time was precious and she had been wasting it. 'I—I was thinking.'

'So I could see. If you would perhaps postpone your thoughts we could get finished and you will be free to enjoy your evening.'

The pink in her cheeks deepened. 'However did you know I was going out?' she demanded.

'I didn't,' he answered blandly. 'I was thought-reading. And now, Mr Gregor, please, Sister.'

The rest of the afternoon passed smoothly. The last patient came and went; Sarah started to pile X-rays and

Path. Lab. forms and notes in tidy heaps. Dr van Elven
rammed his papers untidily into his briefcase and stood
up. He was almost at the door when Sarah asked:

'Are you really going to look after Mrs Brown's cat,
sir?'

'You doubt my word, Sister?'

She looked shocked. 'My goodness, no. Only you don't
look as though you like cats…' She stopped, fidgeting
with the papers in her hands.

He said in surprise, 'Have you looked at me long
enough to form even that opinion of me?' He laughed in
genuine amusement, so she was able to laugh too.

'You look like a dog man,' she observed pleasantly.

'You're quite right, Sister. I have two dogs—it is my
housekeeper who is the cat-lover. But my dogs are well-
mannered enough to tolerate Mrs Brown's cat.' He turned
on his heel. 'Goodnight. I hope you have a pleasant evening.'

His remarks diverted her thoughts into happy chan-
nels. She hurried up with her work, sent the nurses off
duty and closed the department for the day. Tomorrow
they would be busy again, but now she was free. She
walked briskly across the courtyard in the direction of
the Nurses' Home, and halted halfway over to allow Dr
van Elven's car to pass her. It whispered past, as elegant
as its driver, who lifted a gloved hand in salute. She
watched it slide through the big double gates, and wondered for the hundredth time why the doctor should need
a car as powerful as an Iso Grigo to take him to and from
his work. Maybe he took long trips at weekends. She felt
suddenly rather sorry for him, because she was so happy
herself, with an evening in Steven's company before her,

while Dr van Elven had only a housekeeper to greet him when he got home.

When she went down to the Home entrance half an hour later, she could see Steven's car outside the gates. She had put on the blue crêpe and covered it with an off-white wool coat against the chilly March wind. She walked to the Mini Cooper, wondering why he hadn't come to the Home as usual; but when he opened the door for her to get in beside him, she forgot everything but the pleasure of seeing him again. She said, 'Hullo, Steven,' and he returned her smile briefly and greeted her even more briefly. She looked at his dark good-looking face and decided that he was probably tired; which was a pity, because she was looking forward to their evening out. He started the car and said with a cheerfulness which seemed a little forced:

'I thought we'd go to that place you like in Monmouth Street,' and before she could reply launched into an account of his day's work. When he had finished she made a soothing reply and then, thinking to amuse him, told him about Dr van Elven's offer to look after Mrs Brown's cat. He was amused, but not in the way she had intended, for he burst out laughing and said to shock her:

'Good lord, the man's a fool—bothering about some old biddy!'

Sarah breathed a little fast. 'No, he's not a fool—he's just a kind man, and Mrs Brown's going to die in a month or so. The cat's all she has!'

Steven glanced at her with impatience. 'Really, Sarah darling, you're just as much a fool as your precious old van Elven. You're not going to get very far if you're going to get sentimental over an old woman.'

He applied himself to his driving, and she sat silent,

biting back the sharp retort she would have liked to make. They had often argued before, but now it was almost as if he were trying to make her angry. He parked the car, and they walked the short distance to the restaurant, talking meanwhile, rather carefully, of completely impersonal things. It was warm in the small room but relaxing and carefree. They had a drink and ordered *entrecôte mon Plaisir,* which was delicious, and then cherry tart, and all the while they continued to talk about everything and everyone but themselves. They were drinking their coffee when Sarah said:

'I've got a week's holiday soon. I'm going home—I wondered if you'd like to drive me down and stay a couple of days,' and the moment she had said it, wished it unsaid, for she had seen the look on his face—irritation, annoyance and even a faint panic. He said far too quickly:

'I can't get away,' not quite meeting her eye, and she felt a cold hand clutch at her heart. There was an awkward silence until she said in a level voice, 'Steven, you're beating about the bush. Just tell me whatever it is—because that's why you brought me here, isn't it, to tell me something?'

He nodded. 'I feel a bit of a swine...' he began, and looked taken aback when she said briskly, 'I daresay you do, but you can hardly expect me to be sympathetic about it until I know what the reason for that is.'

She looked calm and a little pale; her hands were clenched tightly in her lap, out of sight. She knew, with awful clarity, that Steven was about to throw her over; a situation she had never envisaged—no, that wasn't quite correct, she told herself honestly. She had wondered a great deal lately why he never mentioned marriage any more.

He said sulkily, 'I'm going to be married. Old Binns' daughter.' Mr Binns was his chief. The sensible side of Sarah's brain applauded his wisdom—money, a partnership, all the right people for patients...

'Congratulations.' Her voice was cool, very composed. 'Have you known her long?'

He looked astonished, and she returned the look with calm dignity, the nails of one hand digging painfully into the palm of the other. If he was expecting her to make a fuss, then he was mistaken.

'About eighteen months.'

Her beautiful mouth opened on a gasp. 'Why didn't you tell me? Or was I being held as a second string?' she wanted to know in a kind of interested astonishment which made him say quickly:

'You don't understand, Sarah. We've had a lot of fun together, haven't we? But you always thought in terms of marriage, didn't you? You must see—you're not a child. If I want to get on—and I do—I must get some money and meet the right people.'

'Do you love her?' asked Sarah.

He blustered a little. 'I'm very fond of her.'

She looked down her exquisite nose and said with feeling, 'Oh, the poor girl! And now I should like to go back, please—I've a heavy morning tomorrow.'

On the way to the car, he asked in a surprised voice, 'Don't you mind?'

'That's a question you have no right to ask as it's of no consequence to you. In any case, I certainly don't intend answering you.'

'You're damned calm,' he answered on a sudden burst of anger. 'That's the trouble with you—calm and straitlaced; we could have had a grand time of it, if it hadn't been for your ridiculous moral upbringing!'

Sarah settled herself in the car. 'It's a good thing in the circumstances, isn't it?' she observed with icy sweetness.

But she wasn't icy when she got to her room. She went along for a bath, and exchanged the time of day with the other Sisters she met in the corridor, refusing a cup of tea on the plea of being tired, and finally shut her door so that at last she was alone and could cry her eyes out. She cried for loneliness and misery and the thought of the empty future and the wasted years, and, because she was a nice girl, she cried for Miss Binns.

The next day was nightmarish, made more so by the fact that it was Mr Binns' out-patients and Steven would be with him that afternoon. She went to her dinner, white-faced and heavy-eyed, and encouraged all those who asked in the belief that she was enduring a heavy cold. She allowed Mr Binns to think the same when he re-marked upon her jaded looks, carefully avoiding Steven's eye as she did so. She went about her work with her usual briskness, however, talking to Steven, when she had to, in her usual friendly manner and uttering calming plati-tudes to the patients as they came and went.

Mr Binns was a brilliant surgeon, but he was a thought too hearty in pronouncing judgment—no one likes being told that some vital organ is in need of repair—and Mr Binns, she suspected, tended to lose sight of the per-son in the patient. She wondered sometimes if he was quite so cheerfully abrupt with his private patients, and thought it unlikely. She studied him, sitting behind the desk, a shade pompous, faultlessly dressed and very sure of himself, and the unbidden thought streaked through her mind that in twenty years' time Steven would be just like him. This thought was closely followed by another one—most unexpectedly of Dr van Elven, who, although just as sure of himself and dressed, if anything, even more immaculately, had never yet shown himself to be pompous, and whose patients, however trying, he always treated as people.

The day ended at last. She went over to the Home, had a bath and changed out of uniform and went along to the Sisters' sitting room. As she went in, there was a sudden short silence, followed by a burst of chat. She smiled wryly. The grapevine was already at work; it was something she would have to face sooner or later. Luckily she knew everyone in the room very well indeed; she might as well get it over and done with. She caught Kate Spencer's eye—she had trained with Kate; they had been friends for a number of years now—and said cheerfully, 'I expect the grapevine has got all the details wrong— it always does, but the fact remains that Steven is going to marry Mr Binns' daughter. It isn't anyone's fault, just one of those things. Only it's a bit awkward.'

She sat down on one of the easy chairs scattered about the pleasant room and waited quietly for someone to say something. It was Kate who spoke.

'Of course it's Steven's fault. I bet,' she continued with her unerring habit of fastening on the truth, 'he's not in love with her. She's Dad's only daughter, isn't she? There'll be some money later on, and a partnership now.'

She glanced at Sarah's face, which was expressionless, and said with devastating candour, 'I'm right, aren't I? Sarah? Only you'll not admit it.'

She made a small snorting noise, indicative of indignation and echoed by everyone else in the room, because Sarah was liked and Steven had played her a rotten trick.

A small dark girl who had been curled up by the fire and had so far said nothing got to her feet.

'There's a new film on at the Leicester Square. Let's all go—if we're quick we can just manage it, and we can eat at Holy Joe's on the way back. It's only spaghetti for supper anyway.'

Her fortitudinous suggestion was received with a relief everyone did their best to conceal. They were all sorry for Sarah, but they knew her enough to know that the last thing she wanted from them was pity. They went in a body to the cinema, sweeping her along with them, and afterwards had a rather noisy supper at Joe's. It was after ten as they walked back through the mean little back streets of the East End to the hospital. It was a long walk, but they had agreed among themselves that it would be a good idea to tire Sarah out, so that she would sleep and not look quite so awful in the morning as she had done all day.

But she didn't sleep that night either—she still looked beautiful when she went on duty the next morning, but she had no colour at all, and her eyes were haggard. She would have to see Steven; work with him, talk to him until dinner time. It was Mr Peppard's surgical OP, and Steven would naturally be there too. She could of course tell one of the staff nurses to take the clinic and make herself scarce at the other end of the department, but pride forbade her. She did the usual round, making sure that patients were being weighed, tests done, X-rays fetched, and Path. Lab. forms collected. It was almost time for the clinic to open when she had done. She went into her office—she would have time to sketch out the off-duty rota before nine o'clock. She had barely sat down at her desk when Steven came in. Sarah looked up briefly, said

'Good morning' with quiet affability and went on with her writing. He stood awkwardly by the door, and when she didn't say anything else, said sulkily:

'I'm sorry, Sarah. I didn't know you were so serious about it all—I mean, we were only good pals, after all. I never said I'd marry you…'

Sarah put down her pen at that, gave him a haughty look, and said with deliberation, 'Aren't you being just a little conceited, Steven? No, you never asked me to marry you, so aren't you anticipating my answer? The one I might have made, that is. There's no point in raking over a dead fire, is there?' She had gone rather red in the face, and was regrettably aware that her lip was trembling. She went on sharply, 'Now do go away; I want to get this done before Mr Peppard comes.'

He went then, and she was left to sit alone, staring in front of her, the off-duty rota forgotten.

She went to first dinner, leaving Staff to finish Mr Peppard's clinic. Dr van Elven had his OP at one-thirty—he liked his patients ready and waiting when he arrived, and as he didn't keep other people waiting himself, Sarah did her best to achieve this state of affairs, although it often meant a wild race against time between the clinics. It was one of her lucky days, however. She was ready to start, with the first patient waiting in the little dressing room and the nurse outside already hovering over the second, and there were still five minutes to go. She had had no time to tidy herself. She began feverishly to do so now—showering powder over her pretty nose in a vain effort to cover its redness, and putting on far too much lipstick. She was tucking her hair into a neat pleat, her mouth full of pins, when Dr van Elven stalked in. He was never early—she was so surprised that she opened

her mouth and all the pins scattered on the floor. He put
down his case on the desk and went and picked them
up for her and handed them back gravely. He gave her a
quick, searching glance as he wished her good afternoon;
a look which she was convinced saw right through the
powder. She was annoyed to feel herself blushing—not
that it mattered, for he was standing, half turned away
from her, reading up the first patient's notes.

For some reason which she couldn't understand, she
didn't want him to know about Steven. Of course, in
time, he was bound to find out—news leaked through
even to the most exhalted of the senior staff. He had been
one of the first to know when she had started going out
with Steven; she remembered with awful clarity how
he had asked her lightly if she would like being a surgeon's wife. She thought that she had no more tears left,
but now, at this most awkward of moments, they rose in
a solid lump into her throat. She swallowed them back
resolutely and heard his calm voice asking her to fetch in
the first patient. He looked up as he spoke and gave her
a long steady look, and she was all at once aware that he
knew all about it. She lifted her chin and went past him
to the door to bring in his patient.

The clinic was a long one that afternoon. The medical
registrar was on holiday; it meant that one of the house
physicians was dealing with blood samples and blood
sugars and any of the various tests Dr van Elven wanted
done at once. He was nervous and therefore a little slow;
when they stopped for five minutes to snatch a cup of tea
cooling on its tray, there was still a formidable number
of patients to see. Of these, two had to be admitted immediately, and several were sent to X-Ray, which meant
that Dr van Elven had to sit patiently while the wet films

were fetched by a nurse. It was six o'clock by the time
the last patient had gone. Sarah had never known him to
be so late before, and even now he evinced no desire to
go home. He sat writing endless notes, and even a couple
of letters, because the secretary had gone at five-thirty.
Sarah cleared up the afternoon's litter around the department locking doors and inspecting sluices and making
sure that there were no patients lurking in the cubicles.
When she got back, he had apparently finished, for the
desk was cleared of papers, and his case was closed. He
got up as she went into the consulting room.

'Mrs Brown is to come in the day after tomorrow, I
believe, Sister?'

Sarah said yes, she was, and had he fetched the cat.

'Not yet,' he answered seriously. 'I wonder if you
would do me the favour of coming with me to Mrs
Brown's—er—home? It seems to me to be a good idea
if we were to take her to Richmond with the cat; she
could meet my housekeeper and then go on to hospital.
If you were there too… I believe that you are free on Saturday mornings?'

She was always free on Saturday mornings—she wondered why he asked, because after all these years he must
surely know. But she had nothing to do; it would fill the
hours before she came on duty after dinner. She replied:

'Yes, certainly, sir. Shall I meet you there?' She
thought a moment. 'Mrs Brown lives in Phipps Street,
doesn't she?'

The doctor nodded. 'Yes. But I will fetch you from
the Home. Would eleven o'clock suit you?'

He waited only long enough for her to murmur a rather
surprised Yes before he went, calling a brief goodnight
over his shoulder.

She went to the front door of the Home exactly on the hour on Saturday morning to find him waiting. The Iso Grigo looked sleek and powerful, and it was very comfortable. Dr van Elven got out and walked round and opened the door for her—something Steven had seldom done. Her spirits lifted a little, to drop to her shoes as the car slid to the gate and purred to a halt to allow Steven's Mini to pass them, going the other way. She had a glimpse of his face, gazing at her with a stunned surprise, then he had passed them and they themselves were out in the street. She remembered then that it was Steven's habit to play squash each Saturday and that he invariably returned at eleven. She wondered if the man beside her knew that, and decided that he didn't, but her flattened ego lifted a little—the small incident would give Steven something to think about.

She felt all of a sudden more cheerful and was able to utter a few pointless remarks about the weather, to which Dr van Elven made courteous replies in a casual voice. He was so relaxed himself that she began to relax too and even to feel pleased that she had dressed with such care. She had read once, a long time ago, when such advice seemed laughingly improbable, that it was of the utmost importance for a girl who had been jilted to take the greatest pains with her appearance. Well, she had. She had put on her new tweed suit—a rather dashing outfit in tobacco brown—and complemented it with brown calf shoes and handbag. She felt pleased that she had taken such sound advice, and pondered the advisability of getting a new hat until, obedient to the doctor's request, she peered out of the window to look for number 169. Phipps Street was endless, edged with smoke-grimed Victorian houses, the variety of whose curtains bore testimony to the number of people they sheltered; the pavements were crowded with children playing, housewives hurrying along with loaded baskets, and old men leaning against walls, doing nothing at all. Sarah said on a sigh, 'How drab it all is—how can they live here?'

The doctor eased the car past a coal cart. 'And yet you choose to work here.'

'Yes. But I go home three or four times a year—I can escape.' She broke off to point out the house they were making for, and he brought the car to halt between a milk float and an ice-cream van with a smooth action which earned her admiration. They had barely set foot upon the pavement before a small crowd had collected. The doctor smiled lightly at the curious faces around them and applied himself to the elderly knocker upon the front door. Several faces from various windows peered out, and after a good look, the windows were opened. The nearest framed a large man with a belligerent eye. ''Oo d'yer want?' he enquired without enthusiasm.

Dr van Elven said simply, 'Mrs Brown.'

'Ah,' said the man, and disappeared, to reappear a moment later at the door. 'You'll be the doctor,' he remarked importantly. 'Second floor back. Mind the stairs, there's a bit of rail missing.' He stared at them both and then stood back to let them pass him into the small dark hall. 'I'll keep an eye on that there car,' he offered.

'Thank you.' The doctor had produced some cigarettes from a pocket of his well-cut tweed suit and offered them silently. The man took one, said, 'Ta' and waved a muscled arm behind him. 'Up there.'

They mounted the stairs with a certain amount of caution, the doctor restraining her with a hand on her shoulder. She remembering the missing rail. They were on the first landing when Sarah said:

'You don't smoke cigarettes—only a pipe.'

He paused, a step ahead of her, and smiled over his shoulder.

'How—er—observant of you. They're useful to carry around in these parts; they smooth the way, I find.'

They went on climbing and she wondered why he talked as if he was in the habit of frequenting similar houses in similar streets. Most unlikely, she decided, when he lived in Richmond and had rooms in Harley Street and a large private practice to boot.

The second landing was smaller, darker, and smelled. The doctor's splendid nose flared fastidiously, but he said nothing. Sarah had wrinkled her own small nose too; it gave her the air of a rather choosy angel. The doctor glanced at her briefly, and then, as though unable to help himself, he looked again before he knocked on the door before them.

They entered in answer to Mrs Brown's voice, and found themselves in a small room, depressingly painted in tones of spinach green and margarine, and furnished with a bed, table and chairs which were much too big for it. Mrs Brown was sitting in one of the chairs and when she attempted to get up, said breathily, 'Well, well, this is nice and no mistake. I ain't 'ad visitors for I dunno 'ow long.' She beamed at them both. ''Ow about a nice cuppa?'

Rather to Sarah's surprise, the doctor said that yes, he could just do with one, and drew forward an uncomfortable chair and invited her to sit in it. The twinkle in his eye was kindly but so pronounced that she said hastily, 'May I get the tea while you and Mrs Brown talk?' and left him to lower himself cautiously on to the chair, which creaked in protest under his not inconsiderable weight.

Making the tea was quite a complicated business, for it involved going out on to the landing and filling the kettle from the tap there, which presumably everyone adjacent to it shared, and setting it on the solitary gas ring in a corner of the room. She found teapot, cups and sugar, and was hunting for the milk when Mrs Brown broke off her conversation to say:

'In a tin, Sister dear, under the shelf. I can't get down to the milkman all that easy, and tinned milk makes a good cuppa tea, I always says.'

The tea was rich and brown and syrupy. Sarah sat in the chair which the doctor had vacated and inquired for Timmy.

Mrs Brown put down her cup. 'Bless 'im, 'e knows I'm going.' Her elderly voice shook and Sarah made haste to say kindly, 'Only for a week or so, Mrs Brown, and you'll soon feel so much better.'

'That's as may be,' Mrs Brown replied darkly. 'I wouldn't go to no 'ospital for no one but Doc 'ere.' She drew a wheezy breath. 'Timmy, come on out ter yer mum!'

Timmy came from under the bed—an elderly, lean cat with battle-scarred ears and magnificent whiskers. He climbed into the old lady's lap, butted her gently with his bullet head, and purred.

'Nice, ain't 'e?' his owner asked. 'Pals, we are—don't know as 'ow I wants ter go…'

Dr van Elven turned from his contemplation of the neighbouring chimney pots. His voice was gentle.

'Mrs Brown, if you will consent to go to hospital now, and stay for two weeks, there will be no chance of you waking up one morning and not feeling well enough to

get out of bed. You remember I explained that to you.
What would happen to Timmy then? Surely it is better
to know that he is safe and cared for now than run the
risk of not being able to look after him?' He picked up
her coat from the bed. 'Shall we go? You will be able to
see where he will be and who will be looking after him.'

He sounded persuasive and kind and quite sure of what
he was talking about. The old lady got up, and allowed
herself to be helped into her coat, put on the shapeless
hat with a fine disregard as to her appearance, and pronounced herself ready. When they reached the pavement,
the small crowd was still there, kept firmly under control by the man who had opened the door to them. He
accepted the remainder of the cigarettes from the doctor,
shut the car doors firmly upon them and saluted smartly.

''E's me landlord,' Mrs Brown informed them from
the back of the car. 'Real gent 'e is. Let me orf me rent.'
She settled back, Timmy perched on her lap, apparently
unimpressed by his surroundings. Sarah didn't look at
the doctor, but she had the feeling that they were thinking
the same thing. She was proved right when he murmured:

'Bis dat qui cito dat.'

She said. 'Oh, Latin. Something about giving, isn't it?'

The man beside her chuckled. 'He who gives quickly,
gives twice.'

'That's what I thought too, only in English. He didn't
look as though he'd give a crumb to a bird, and I don't
suppose he could really afford to lose the rent, even for
a couple of weeks.'

Dr van Elven said briefly, 'No,' then glanced at his
watch. 'You're on at half past one, are you not? It's just gone
half past eleven. Time enough; we'll go by the back ways.'

He knew his London, that was evident; he didn't hesitate once, but wove his way in and out of streets which all looked alike, until she wasn't at all sure where they were. It was a surprise when they crossed the river, and she recognised Putney Bridge. They turned into Upper Richmond Road very shortly after, then into Richmond itself and so to the river. The doctor's house was one of a row of Georgian bow-fronted houses set well back from the road, with their own private thoroughfare and an oblique view of the water, which was only a couple of hundred yards away. It was surprisingly peaceful. Sarah got out of the car and looked around her while the doctor helped Mrs Brown to get out. It would be nice to live in such a spot, she thought, only a few miles from the hospital, but as far removed from it as if they were upon another planet.

The doctor unlocked the front door with its gleaming knocker and beautiful fanlight and stood aside for them to go in. The hall was a great deal larger than she had thought from the outside, and was square with a polished floor and some lovely rugs. There was a satin-striped wallpaper upon which were a great many pictures, and the furniture was, she thought, early Regency—probably Sheraton. The baize door at the back of the hall opened and a woman came towards them. She was tall and bony and middle-aged, with dark brown eyes and pepper-and-salt hair; she had the nicest smile Sarah had seen for a long time. The doctor shut the door and said easily:

'Ah, there you are, Alice.' He glanced at Sarah and said, 'This is my good friend and housekeeper, Alice Miller. Alice, this is Sister Dunn from the hospital, and this is Mrs Brown, of whom I told you, and Timmy.' He threw his gloves on to a marble-topped wall table. 'Supposing you take Mrs Brown with you and show her where Timmy will live, and discuss his diet?'

Sarah watched the two women disappear through the door to the kitchen and looked rather shyly at Dr van Elven.

'Come and see the splendid view from the sitting room,' he invited, and led the way to one of the doors opening into the hall. The room was at the back of the house, and from its window there was indeed an excellent view of the river with a stretch of green beyond. It was almost country, and the illusion was heightened by the small garden, which was a mass of primulas and daffodils and grape hyacinths backed by trees and shrubs. There was a white-painted table and several chairs in one corner, sheltered by a box hedge; it would be pleasant to sit there on a summer morning. She said so, and he replied, 'It is indeed. I breakfast there when it's fine, for it is difficult for me to get out of doors at all on a busy day.'

She didn't reply. She was picturing him sitting there, reading the morning paper and his post—she wondered if he had any family to write to him. She hoped so; he was so nice. He had gone to the ground-length window and opened it to let in two dogs, a basset hound and a Jack Russell, whom he introduced as Edward and Albert. They pranced to meet her, greeted her politely and then went back to stand by their master.

He said, 'Do sit down, won't you? We'll give them ten minutes to get to know each other. There are cigarettes beside you if you care to smoke.'

She shook her head. 'No thanks. I only smoke at parties when I want something to do with my hands.'

He smiled. 'You won't mind if I light my pipe?'

'Please do. What will you do about Mrs Brown, sir?'

'What I said. Pull her together as far as we can in hospital and then let her go home.'

Sarah looked horrified. 'Not back to Phipps Street?'

He raised his brows. 'Phipps Street is her home,' he said coolly. 'She has lived there for so long, it would be cruel to take her away, especially as she has only a little of life left. I shall arrange for someone to go in daily and do everything necessary, and I think the landlord could be persuaded to clean up the room and perhaps paint it while she is away.'

Sarah nodded, highly approving. 'That would be nice. Yes, you're right, of course. She'd be lost anywhere else.'

He had lighted his pipe; now he stood up. He said, quite without sarcasm, 'I'm glad you approve. I'm going to fetch Mrs Brown—will you wait here? I shan't be long.'

When he had gone, she got up and began an inspection of the room. It was comfortable and lived-in, with leather armchairs and an enormous couch drawn up before the beautiful marble fireplace. The floor was polished and covered with the same beautiful rugs as there were in the hall. There was a sofa table behind the couch and a scattering of small drum tables around the room, and a marquetry William and Mary china cabinet against one of the walls. A davenport under one of the windows would make letter writing very pleasant…it had a small button-backed chair to partner it; Sarah went and sat down, feeling soothed and calmer than she had felt for the last two days or so. She realised that she hadn't thought of Steven for several hours; she had been so occupied with Mrs Brown and the ridiculous Timmy—it had been pure coincidence, of course, that Dr van Elven should have asked for her help; all the same she felt grateful to him.

He couldn't have done more to distract her thoughts even if she had told him about the whole sorry business.

Her gratitude coloured her goodbyes when they parted in the hospital entrance hall, he to go off to some business of his own, she to take Mrs Brown to Women's Medical. But if he was surprised by the fervour of her thanks, he gave no sign. It was only later, when she was sitting in the lonely isolation of OPD that the first faint doubts as to whether it had been coincidence crept into her mind. She brushed them aside as absurd at first, but they persisted, and the annoying thing was that she wasn't sure if she minded or not. There was no way of finding out either, short of asking Dr van Elven to his face, something she didn't care to do; for if she was mistaken, she could imagine only too vividly, the look of bland amusement on his face. The amusement would be kindly, and that would make it worse, because it would mean that he pitied her, a fact, which for some reason or other, she could not bear to contemplate.

She drew the laundry book towards her, resolutely emptying her mind of anything but the number of towels and pillow cases she could expect back on Monday.

Chapter 2

Sarah went to see Mrs Brown on Sunday. She went delib-erately during the visiting hour in the afternoon, because she thought it unlikely that the old lady would have any visitors. She was right; Mrs Brown was sitting up in bed in a hospital nightie several sizes too large for her, looking very clean, her hair surprisingly white after its washing—a nurse had pinned it up and tied a pink bow in it as well.

'How nice you look, Mrs Brown—I like that ribbon.' Sarah drew up a chair and sat down, aware of the glances Mrs Brown was casting left and right to her neighbours as if to say 'I told you so'. She made a resolve then and there to pop in and see her whenever she could spare a minute, and enquired after the old lady's health.

Mrs Brown brushed this aside. ''E sent a message,' she stated. 'Timmy's 'ad a good sleep, 'e said, and eaten for two.' She fidgeted around in the bed and all the pillows fell down, so that Sarah had to get up and rearrange them. 'One of them young doctors told me this morning.' She frowned reflectively. 'They knows what they're doing, I suppose? Them young ones?'

'Yes, Mrs Brown.' Sarah sounded very positive. 'They're all qualified doctors and they're here to carry out the consultant's wishes.'

'So all them things 'e did to me 'e was told ter do by the doc?'

Sarah nodded. 'That's right. Now is there anything I can do for you while you're here? Was anyone going to get your room ready for you to go back?'

The old lady looked astonished. 'Lor', no, ducks. 'Oo'd 'ave the time? Though I daresay someone'll pop in and do me bed and get me in some stuff.'

Sarah made a noncommittal reply to this remark, and made a mental note to go round to Phipps Street one evening and make sure that there really was someone.

She didn't see Steven again until Tuesday morning, when Mr Binns had an extra OP clinic. They had barely exchanged cool good mornings, when he was called away to the wards, and didn't return until all but two of the patients had gone. It was already past twelve, and they were behind time. Dr van Elven had a vast clinic at one-thirty. For once she was glad of Mr Binns' briskness; he took no time at all over the last patient—a post-operative check-up—thanked Sarah with faint pomposity, and hurried away with Steven beside him. She sent the nurses to dinner, had a few words with Staff, who had come on duty to take the gynae clinic, and then got on with the business of substituting Dr Binns' paraphernalia for that of Dr van Elven. She had almost finished when Steven returned.

He said abruptly as he came in, 'Where the hell were you going on Saturday with old van Elven?'

Sarah's heart gave an excited jump. So he minded! She stacked the case notes neatly and consulted her long list of names before she replied, in a calm voice she hardly recognised as her own:

'Is it any business of yours? And if you refer to Dr van Elven, he's not at all old, you know.'

He gave an ugly laugh. 'You're a sly one—pretending to be such a little puritan and playing the hurt madam with me! How long have you been leading him by the nose? He's quite a catch.'

He was standing quite near her. She put down her list and slapped his face hard, and in the act saw Dr van Elven standing at the doorway. As he came into the room he said quietly, 'Get out.' His voice had the menace of a knife, although his face was impassive.

Sarah watched Steven standing irresolute, one hand to a reddened cheek, the look of surprise still on his face, and then turn on his heel and go. She had never expected him to brazen it out anyway. Dr van Elven was the senior consultant at St Edwin's, and could, if he so wished, use his authority. She didn't look at him now, but mumbled, 'I'm late for dinner...'

'Sit down,' he said placidly, and she obeyed him weakly. She had gone very white; now her face flamed with humiliation and temper—mostly temper. She shook with it, and gripped her hands together in her lap to keep them steady. Dr van Elven went over to the desk in a leisurely fashion and put down his case. He said, not looking at her, in a most reasonable voice:

'You can't possibly go to the dining room in such a towering rage.'

He was right, of course. Sarah stared at her hands and essayed to speak.

'You know about me and Steven.'

'Yes. But I see no need to enlarge upon what must be a painful subject.'

Sarah choked on a watery chuckle, 'I'm behaving like a heroine in a Victorian novel, aren't I?' She gave him a sudden waspish look. 'I'm furious!' she snapped, as though he hadn't commented upon her feelings already. He said 'Yes,' again and gave her a half smile, then bent over his desk, leaving her to pull herself together. Presently he remarked:

'That's better. We have a large clinic, I believe. How fortunate—there's nothing like hard work for calming the nerves. Might I suggest that you go to your dinner now? I should like to start punctually.'

She got up at once, unconsciously obedient to his quietly compelling voice. 'Yes, of course, sir. I've been wasting time.'

She fled through the door, feeling that somehow or other he had contrived to make the whole episode not worth bothering about. She even ate her dinner, aware that he would ask her if she had done so when she got back and would expect a truthful answer.

There was not time to ask her anything, however. When she returned the benches were overflowing. The air rang with a variety of coughs, and as it was raining outside, the same air was heavy with the damp from wet coats and the redolence of sopping garments which those who had arrived first had had the forethought to dry out upon the radiators. Sarah went swiftly into the consultants' room, saw that Dr van Elven was already sitting

at his desk, adjusted her cuffs and said in her usual serene tones:

'Shall I fetch in the first one, sir? Mr Jenkins—
check-up after three weeks as in-patient.'

He gave her a brief, impersonal glance, nodded and
returned to his writing. 'I've seen his X-rays—I'll want
some blood though. Will you get Dr Coles on to it?'

She fetched in Mr Jenkins, waited just long enough to
make sure that she wouldn't be wanted for a moment, and
flew to find the Medical Registrar. Dr Coles was tucked
away in the little room near the sluice, going through
Path. Lab. forms and various reports, so that later, when
Dr van Elven wanted to know some detail about one of
his patients, he would know the answer. He looked up as
she went in and said pleasantly:

'Hullo, Sarah. Is the chief already here? I'm still choking down facts and figures.' He grinned and she smiled at
him warmly. He was a nice man, not young any more, and
apparently not ambitious, for he seemed content to stay
where he was, working in hospital. He got on well with
the consultant staff and was utterly reliable and invariably
good-natured. He was reputed to be very happily married
and was apt to talk at length about his children, of whom
he was very proud. He got up now and followed her back
past the rows of patients. Mr Jenkins was still describing
the nasty pain that caught him right in the stomach, and
Dr van Elven was listening to him with the whole of his
attention. When the old man paused for breath, though,
the doctor said, 'Hullo, Dick', and smiled at his Registrar. 'What did you make of Mr Jenkins when he was in?'

The two men became immersed in their patient, leaving her free to make sure that the one to follow was ready

and waiting in the dressing room, and that everything that Dr van Elven might want was to hand.

The afternoon wore on, the small room gradually acquiring the same damp atmosphere as the waiting hall. Sarah switched on the electric fan, which stirred up the air without noticeable improvement. She switched it off again and Dr van Elven said:

'Don't worry, Sister,' and then, surprisingly, 'I am a little ashamed that I can drive myself home, warm, and dry for I imagine, from their appearance, that quite a number of my patients haven't even the price of a bus fare, and even if they have, won't be able to get on a bus.' He caught her eye and smiled. 'How about tea?'

Over their brief cup, the men discussed the next case and Dr Coles told them about his eldest son, who was doing rather well at school. It was while Sarah was piling their cups and saucers on to a tray that Dr van Elven remarked quietly, 'Mrs Brown tells me that you visit her regularly, Sister. That is good of you.'

Sarah whipped the next patient's notes before him and said in a matter-of-fact voice, 'Well, I don't think she has any relations or friends to come and see her, sir. And you know how awful it is for a patient to be the only one in the ward without visitors.'

He eyed her thoughtfully. 'I imagine it must be a miserable experience. She is responding very well, you know. I must see about getting her home.'

Sarah was on the way to the door. She paused and looked back at him.

'How's Timmy?' she asked.

'The perfect guest—his manners, contrary to his appearance, are charming.'

They finished at last—she sent the student nurses off

duty, left Staff to clear up the gynae clinic on the other side of the department, and began her own clearing up. Dr Coles had gone to answer a call from one of the wards, and she was alone with Dr van Elven, who was sitting back in his chair, presumably deep in thought. She bustled about the little room putting it to rights and piling the case notes ready to take back to the office. She was trying not to remember that it was just a week since she had gone out to dinner with Steven, but her thoughts, now that she was free to think again after the afternoon's rush, kept returning to the same unhappy theme. She had quite forgotten the man sitting so quietly at the desk. When he spoke she jumped visibly and said hurriedly:

'I'm sorry, sir, I didn't hear what you were saying.'

He withdrew an abstracted gaze from the ceiling, stared at her from under half-closed lids, and got up. At the door he said quietly:

'It gets easier as the days go by—especially if there is plenty of work to do. Good night, Sister Dunn.'

Sarah stood staring, her mouth open. He was well out of earshot when she at length said 'Good night' in reply.

There was a message for her when she got over to the Home, from Steven, saying that he had to see her, and would she be outside at seven o'clock. To apologise, she surmised; but he could have done that in his note, and she had no intention of running to his least word. She changed rapidly; she had a good excuse to go out, and was glad of it. She would go and see about Mrs Brown's room. There was actually plenty of time, but as Dr van Elven had said, being busy helped.

Phipps Street looked depressing; the rain had stopped, but the wind was fresh and the evening sky unfriendly. Sarah banged on the front door and the same man opened it to her. He looked at her suspiciously at first, perhaps because she was in a raincoat and a headscarf and looked different, but when he saw who she was he opened the door wide.

'It's you again, miss. Thought you'd be along. Come to 'ave a look, I suppose, and do a bit o' choosing. 'Ow's the old girl?'

Sarah edged past him. 'She's fine—and settled in very nicely, though of course she's longing to come home.'

He lumbered ahead of her up the miserable staircase.

'Well, o'course. 'Oo wants ter stay in 'ospital when they got a good 'ome?'

They had reached the little landing and he flung open Mrs Brown's door with something of a flourish. It was empty of furniture—of everything, she noted with mounting astonishment. Two men were painting the woodwork; one of them turned round as she went in, greeted her civilly and asked if she had come to choose the wallpaper. Her grey eyes opened wide and she turned to the landlord. 'But surely you want to decide that?' she wanted to know.

'Lor' luv yer, miss, no. What should I know about fancy wallpaper?' He let out a great bellow of laughter and went out, shutting the door behind him. Sarah looked around her. The room was being redecorated quite lavishly. The hideous piping which probably had something to do with the water tap on the landing had been cased in: one of the men was fitting a new sash-cord to the elderly window frame he was painting. The paintwork was grey, the walls, stripped of several layers of paper, looked terrible. There were several books of wallpaper patterns in the centre of the room, on the bare floor. After an undecided moment, Sarah knelt down and opened the first of them. The man at the window said:

'That's right, ducks, you choose something you like; we'll be ready to 'ang it soon as the paint's dry.'

She gave him a puzzled look. 'Well, if there's no one else.'

She was contemplating a design of pink cabbage roses when she heard someone running upstairs and the door was opened by Dr van Elven. He nodded to the two men, and if he was surprised to see Sarah, she had to admit that he didn't show it. He said, 'Hullo. What a relief to see you—now you can choose the wallpaper.'

She had to laugh. 'It's like a conspiracy—when I got here the landlord seemed to think that was why I had come, and so did this painter. I really only came to see if there was any cleaning to do before Mrs Brown came home.'

'Not for ten days at least.' His tone was dry.

She was annoyed to feel her cheeks warming. 'Well, I wanted to get away from the hospital.' She turned back to the pattern book, determined not to say more, and was relieved when he said casually:

'That's splendid. Have you seen anything you like?'

'Mrs Brown likes pink,' she said slowly, and frowned. 'Surely if the landlord is having this done, he should choose?' She looked up enquiringly, saw his face and said instantly: 'You're doing it.' She added, 'Sir.'

'My name is Hugo,' he said pleasantly. 'You are, of course, aware of that. I think that after three years we might dispense with sir and Sister, unless we are actually—er—at work. I hope you agree?'

She was a little startled and uncertain what to say,

but it seemed it was of no consequence, for he continued without waiting for her reply:

'Good, that's settled. Now, shall we get this vexed question of wallpaper dealt with?'

He got down beside her as he spoke, and opened a second book of patterns, and they spent a pleasant half hour admiring and criticising in a lighthearted fashion until finally Sarah said:

'I think Mrs Brown would like the roses. They're very large and pink, aren't they, and they'll make the room look even smaller than it is, but they're pretty—I mean for someone who's lived for years with green paint and margarine walls, they're pretty.'

The man beside her uncoiled himself and came to his feet with the agility of a much younger man. 'Right. Roses it shall be. Now, furniture—nothing too modern, I think, but small—I had the idea of looking around one or two of those second-hand places to try and find similar stuff. Perhaps you would come with me, Sarah. Curtains too—I've no idea...'

He contrived to look so helpless that she agreed at once.

'Would eleven o'clock on Saturday suit you?' he asked. She gave him a swift suspicious glance, which he returned with a look of such innocent blandness that she was instantly ashamed of her thoughts. She got to her feet and said that yes, that would do very well, and waited while he talked to the two men. When he had finished she said a little awkwardly:

'Well, I think I'll go now. Goodnight, everyone.'

The two workmen chorused a cheerful, ''Night, ducks,' but the doctor followed her out. On the stairs he remarked mildly:

'What a shy young woman you are!' and then, 'Let me go first, this staircase is a death-trap.'

With his broad back to her, she found the courage to say, 'I know I'm shy—it's stupid in a woman of my age, isn't it? I try very hard not to be; it's all right while I'm working. I—I thought I'd got over it, but now I seem worse than ever.'

Her voice tailed away, as she remembered Steven. They had reached the landing and he paused and turned round to look at her. 'My dear girl, being shy doesn't matter in the least; didn't you know that? It can be positively restful in this day and age.'

They went on down to the little hall and Sarah felt warmed by the comfort of his words; it was extraordinary how he put her at her ease, almost as though they were friends of a lifetime. She stood by the door, while he, in a most affable manner, pointed out to Mr Ives, the landlord, the iniquity of having a staircase in the house that would most certainly be the death of someone, including himself, unless he did something about it very soon. Mr Ives saw them to the door, and stood on the pavement while the doctor opened the car door for Sarah to get in. It was only when they were on their way back to St Edwin's that she realised that there had been nothing said about taking her back. The doctor had ushered her into his car, and she had got in without protest.

She hoped he didn't think she'd been angling for a lift. 'I could have walked.' She spoke her thoughts out loud. 'You're going out of your way…'

She looked at him, watching the corners of his eyes crinkle as he smiled.

'So you could. I'm afraid that I gave you no opportunity—you don't mind?'

She said no, she didn't mind, and plunged, rather self-consciously, into aimless chatter, in which he took but a minimal part. At the hospital, she thanked him for the lift.

'I could have easily walked...' she began, and stopped when she saw Steven standing outside the Home entrance. The doctor saw him too; he got out of the car in a leisurely way, and strolled to the door with her; giving Steven a pleasant good evening as they passed him. He opened the door, said 'Good night, Sarah' in an imperturbable voice, urged her gently inside and shut the door upon her.

Steven wasn't at the surgical clinic the following day. Mr Binns had the assistance of Jimmy Dean, one of the house surgeons; he and Kate were in love, but he had no prospects and neither of them had any money. It would be providential if Steven left when he married Mr Binns' daughter, so that Jimmy could at least apply for the post. He was good at his job, though a little slow, but Sarah liked him. But Steven was with Mr Peppard when he arrived to take his clinic on Thursday morning—and as soon as opportunity offered, he asked shortly:

'Why didn't you answer my note—or wasn't I supposed to know that you had a date with van Elven?'

Sarah picked out the X-ray she was looking for. She said in a voice it was a little hard to keep steady because he was so near, 'I had arranged to go out; not, as you suppose, with Dr van Elven—and anyway, what would be the purpose of meeting you?'

She walked briskly to the desk, and remained, quite unnecessarily, throughout the patient's interview. She was careful not to give Steven the opportunity to waylay her again, a resolve made easier by the unexpected absence of a part-time staff nurse who usually took the ear, nose and throat clinic. She put a student nurse in her place because there was no one else, which gave her a good excuse for spending the greater part of the morning making sure that the nurse could manage. Mr Peppard went at last, with Steven trailing behind him. He gave her a look of frustrated rage as he went, which, while gratifying her ego, did nothing to lessen her unhappiness.

It was a relief to see Dr van Elven's placid face when she came back from dinner. His 'Good afternoon, Sister' was uttered with his usual gravity, but she detected a twinkle in his grey eyes as he said it. Perhaps he was remembering that the last time they had seen each other, they had been kneeling side by side on a dusty floor, deciding that pink cabbage roses would be just the thing… but if he was thinking of it too, his manner betrayed no sign of it.

The clinic went smoothly, without one single reference to Mrs Brown or her rooms; it was as if none of it had happened. And he didn't mention Saturday at all. Sarah decided several times during Friday, not to go at all, and indeed, thought about it so much that Mr Bunn, the gynaecologist, had to ask her twice for the instruments he required on more than one occasion—such a rare happening that he wanted to know if she was sickening for something.

She was still feeling uncertain when she left the Nurses' Home the next morning—supposing Dr van Elven had forgotten—worse, not meant what he had said? But he hadn't; he was waiting just outside the door. He ushered her into the Iso Grigo, and she settled back into its expensive comfort, glad that she was wearing the brown suit again.

He said, 'Hullo, Sarah. I'm glad you decided to come.'
'But I said I would.'

He smiled. 'You have had time enough to change your mind…even to wonder if I would come.'

It was disconcerting to have her thoughts read so accurately. She went pink.

'Well, as a matter of fact, I did wonder if you might forget, or—or change your mind.' She added hastily, 'That sounds rude; I didn't mean it to be, only I feel a little uncertain about—well, everything.'

He sat relaxed behind the wheel. 'That's natural, but it won't last.' His mouth curved in a smile. 'You look nice.'

Her spirits rose; she smiled widely and never noticed Steven's Mini as it passed them. She had forgotten all about him, for the moment, at least.

The morning was fun. They chose the furniture for Mrs Brown with care, going from one dealer to the other, until it only remained for them to buy curtains and carpets. They stood outside the rather seedy little shop where Sarah had happily bargained for the sort of easy chair she knew Mrs Brown would like.

'We'll go to Harrods,' said the doctor.

She looked at him with pitying horror. 'Harrods? Don't you know that it's a most expensive shop? Anyway, it'll be shut today. There's a shop in the Commercial Road…'

Mindful of the doctor's pocket, she bought pink material for the curtains, and because it was quite cheap, some extra material for a tablecloth. She bought a grey carpet too, although she thought it far too expensive and said so, but apparently Dr van Elven had set his heart on it. When they were back in the car she pointed out to him that he had spent a great deal of money.

'How much?' he queried lazily.

She did some mental sums. 'A hundred and eighty-two pounds, forty-eight pence. If it hadn't been for the carpet...'

He said gravely, 'I think I can manage that—who will make the curtains?'

'I'll do those—I can borrow Kate's machine and run them up in an hour or so. They cost a great deal to have made, you know.' She paused. 'Dr van Elven...'

'Hugo.'

'Well, Hugo—it's quite a lot of money. I'd like—that is, do you suppose...'

He had drawn up at traffic lights. 'No, I don't suppose anything of the sort, Sarah.'

She subsided, feeling awkward, and looked out of the window, to say in some surprise, 'This is Newgate Street, isn't it? We can't get back to St Edwin's this way, can we?'

His reply was calm. 'We aren't going back at the moment. I have only just realised that you'll miss first dinner and not have time for second. I thought we might have something quick to eat, and I'll take you back afterwards. That is, if you would like that?'

She felt that same flash of surprise again, but answered composedly.

'Thank you, that would be nice. I'm on at two today—I had some time owing.'

They went down Holborn and New Oxford Street and then cut across to Regent Street, and stopped at the Café Royal. Sarah had often passed it and wondered, a little enviously, what it was like inside; it seemed she was to have the opportunity to find out. They went to the Grill Room, and she wasn't disappointed; it was pretty and the mirrors were charming if a trifle disconcerting. The doctor had said 'something quick'; she had envisaged something on toast, but on looking round her she deduced that the only thing she would get on toast would be caviare. She studied the menu card and wondered what on earth to order.

'Something cold, I think,' her glance flew to her watch, 'and quick.'

Quick wasn't quite the word to use in such surroundings, where luncheon was something to be taken in a leisurely fashion. She caught her companion's eye and saw the gleam in its depths, but all he said was:

'How about a crab mousse and a Bombe Pralinée after?' He gave the order and asked, 'Shall we have a Pernod, or is there anything else you prefer?'

'Pernod would be lovely.' She smiled suddenly, wrinkling her beautiful nose in the endearing and unconscious manner of a child.

'What a pity that we haven't hours and hours to spend over lunch.' She stopped, vexed at the pinkening of her cheeks under his amused look. 'What I mean is,' she said austerely, 'it's the kind of place where you dawdle, with no other prospect than a little light shopping or a walk in the park before taking a taxi home.'

'You tempt me to telephone Matron and ask her to let you have the afternoon off.'

He spoke lightly and Sarah felt a surprising regret that he couldn't possibly mean it. 'That sort of thing happens in novels, never in real life. I can imagine Matron's feelings!'

They raised their glasses to Mrs Brown's recovery, and over their drinks fell to discussing her refurbished room, which topic somehow led to a variety of subjects, which lasted right through the delicious food and coffee as well, until Sarah glanced at her watch again and said:

'Oh, my goodness! I simply must go—the time's gone so quickly.'

The doctor paid the bill and said comfortably:

'Don't worry—you won't be late.' And just for a moment she remembered Steven, who was inclined to fuss about getting back long before it was necessary. Dr van Elven didn't appear to fuss at all—as little, in fact, as he did in hospital. She felt completely at ease with him, but then, her practical mind interposed, so she should; they had worked together for several years now.

They didn't talk much going back to the hospital, but the silence was a friendly one; he wasn't the kind of man one needed to chat to incessantly. There wasn't much time to thank him when they arrived at the Nurses' Home, but though of necessity brief, her thanks were none the less sincere; she really had enjoyed herself. He listened to her with a half smile and said, 'I'm glad. I enjoyed it too. I hope I'm not trespassing too much on your good nature if I ask you to accompany Mrs Brown when I take her home.' He saw her look and said smoothly, 'Yes, I know she could quite well go by ambulance, but I have to return Timmy, so I can just as well call for her on my way. Would ten o'clock suit you? And by the way, I've found a very good woman who will go every day.'

Sarah said how nice and yes, ten o'clock would do very well, and felt a pang of disappointment that once Mrs Brown was home again there would be no need for her to give Dr van Elven the benefit of her advice any more. She stifled the thought at once; it smacked of disloyalty to Steven, even though he didn't love her any more. She said goodbye in a sober voice, and later on, sitting in the hollow stillness of OPD, tried to pretend to herself that any minute now Steven would appear and tell her that it was all a mistake and he wasn't going to marry Anne Binns after all. But he didn't come—no one came at all.

The week flew by. She saw Steven several times, but never alone; she took care of that—although she thought it likely that he didn't want to speak to her anyway. Perhaps, she thought hopefully, he was ashamed of himself, although there was no evidence of it in his face. She went out a great deal in her off-duty too—her friends saw to that; someone always seemed to be at hand to suggest the cinema or supper at Holy Joe's. She made the curtains and the tablecloth too, and took them round on Friday evening. Hugo van Elven had said nothing to her about Mrs Brown or her room—indeed, upon reflection, she could not remember him saying anything at all that wasn't to do with work.

Mr Ives let her in with a friendly, ''Ullo, ducks.' Sarah responded suitably and was led up the stairs, pausing on the way to admire the repair work he had done. When they reached the top landing he opened Mrs Brown's door with something of a flourish and stood back, beaming.

'Nice little 'ome, eh?' he remarked with satisfaction. Sarah agreed; despite the pink roses, which seemed to crowd in on her the moment she set foot inside the room, and the superfluity of furniture, it was just what she was sure Mrs Brown would like. She undid her parcel and spread the cloth on the table, and gallantly helped by Mr Ives, hung the curtains. She had been to visit Mrs Brown several times during the week and had contrived to bring the conversation round to the subject of colours. Mrs Brown had been quite lyrical about pink. Sarah stood back and surveyed her handiwork and thought that it was a good thing that she was, because there was pink enough and to spare. Mr Ives obviously had no such qualms.

'Nice taste that doc's got—couldn't 'ave chosen better meself.'

She agreed faintly, thinking of the gracious house at Richmond with its subdued colours and beautiful furniture. She told Mr Ives the time they expected to arrive and he nodded, already knowing it.

'Doc told me last night when 'e was 'ere. Brought a bottle of the best with 'im too.' He saw Sarah's look of enquiry. 'Brandy,' he explained, 'I'm ter keep it safe and give Mrs Brown a taste now and then like; just a teaspoon in 'er tea. Brought me a bottle for meself too. I'll keep an eye on the old gal like I promised; I got Doc's phone number, case 'e's wanted.'

He led the way down the stairs again and bade her goodbye after offering to escort her back to St Edwin's. 'Don't know as 'ow the doc would like yer out at night,' he observed seriously.

Sarah, a little overcome by such solicitude, observed in her turn that it was highly unlikely that the doctor would care a row of pins what she did with her free time, and in any case, it was barely nine o'clock in the evening. She spoke briskly, but Mr Ives was not to be deterred.

'I dunno about that,' he said in a rather grumbling voice, 'but I knows I'd rather not be on the wrong side of the doc. Still, if yer won't yer won't. I'll stand 'ere till yer get ter the end of the street—yer can wave under the lamppost there so's I can see yer.'

Sarah did as she was told. She had a sneaking feeling that she would prefer to keep on the right side of the 'doc' too.

Mrs Brown was sitting in a wheelchair in the ward, waiting for her when she went along to collect her on Saturday. She looked better, but thinner too—probably worry about Timmy and her little home and all the other small things that were important to old people living alone. Sarah sighed with relief to think that the old lady would have a nice surprise when she got home. Dr van Elven greeted them briefly at the entrance, stowed Mrs Brown in the back of the car, motioned Sarah to get in the front and released Timmy from his basket. Neither he nor Sarah looked round as he drove to Phipps Street. Mrs Brown's happiness was a private thing into which they had no intention of prying.

There were several neighbours hanging around when they arrived, and it took a few minutes to get into the house. The doctor, without speaking, scooped up the old lady, trembling with delight and excitement, and trod carefully upstairs, leaving Sarah and Timmy and Mr Ives to follow in his wake. On the landing he nodded to Sarah to open the door.

Mrs Brown didn't quite grasp what had happened at first, and when she did she burst into tears. It seemed the right moment to make a cup of tea. Sarah bustled around while Mrs Brown composed herself and began incoherent thanks which only ended when she sat in her new armchair with a cup and saucer in her hand. She had calmed down considerably by the time the door opened and a pleasant-faced, middle-aged woman with a cheerful cockney voice came in. Sarah had no difficulty in recognising her as the 'very good woman' the doctor had found, and it was obvious before very long that his choice had been a happy one; the two ladies were going to get on splendidly. They got up to go presently, and Dr van Elven drove Sarah back to the hospital, saw her to the door of the Home, thanked her politely and drove away again. It was barely twelve o'clock. Sarah went up to her room; a faint stirring of disappointment deep inside her which she refused to acknowledge as regret because he hadn't asked her out to lunch.

She saw Steven on Monday—he came in at the end of Dr MacFee's diabetic clinic. Dr MacFee had just gone, and the place was more or less empty when Steven walked in, taking her quite by surprise. She stood looking at him, waiting for him to speak first, and was inwardly surprised to find that the sight of him, though painful, was bearable.

'I suppose you expect me to apologise,' he began. 'Well, I don't intend to. All I can say is, I'm glad we split up before I found out what a…'

He caught her belligerent eye. 'A what?' she enquired with icy calm. 'I should be careful what you say, Steven—I'll not hesitate to slap you again!'

He flung away. 'I wish you joy, that's all I can say!' he shouted, as he strode through the empty waiting hall. She watched him go. He was very good-looking, and when he wasn't angry, charming too. She sighed and went to her dinner, wondering why he should wish her joy.

Dr van Elven's clinic was, as usual, splitting at the seams. Sarah, nipping from one patient to the other, weighing them, taking them to the Path. Lab., to X-ray, helping them in and out of endless garments, wished that he wasn't quite such a glutton for work. She'd had to send two of her nurses up to the wards for the afternoon because a number of the staff were off with 'flu. Now and again, when she made a sortie into the waiting hall for another patient, she glimpsed Staff at the other end with the one junior nurse they had been left with; they were busy in Gynae too. She went back into the consulting room to find Dr van Elven dealing, with commendable calm, with the attack of hysterics which his patient had sprung on him.

Dick Coles went as soon as they had finished and Sarah began to tidy up, although she longed for tea. It would be too late to go to the Sisters' sitting room; she would have to make her own when she got to her room.

The doctor was sitting at the desk, absorbed in something or other. Sarah supposed that he was in no hurry to go home—it wasn't as if there was a wife waiting for him... She finished at length, picked up the pile of notes she intended dropping into the office on her way, and went to the door. When she reached it she said, 'Good night, sir,' then stopped short when he said 'Come back here, Sarah, and sit down. I want to talk to you.'

She did as she was asked, because when he spoke in that quiet voice she found it prudent to obey him. She sat in the chair facing him, the notes piled on her lap; she was tired and thirsty and a little untidy, but her face was serene. She looked at him across the desk, smiling a little, because in the last few days she had come to regard him as a friend.

He sat back, meeting and holding her glance with his own, but without the smile. He said, 'Sarah, will you marry me?'

Chapter 3

His words shocked the breath out of her; she gaped at him until he said with a touch of impatience, 'Why are you so surprised? We're well suited, you know. You have lost your heart to Steven; I—I lost mine many years ago. We both need companionship and roots. Many marriages succeed very well on mutual respect and liking—and I ask no more than that of you, Sarah—at least until such time as you might feel you have more to offer.'

She said bluntly, her grey eyes candid, but still round with astonishment:

'You don't want my love? Even if I didn't love someone else?'

He settled back in his chair, his eyes half closed so that she had no idea of what he was thinking.

'I want your friendship,' he answered blandly, 'I enjoy your company; you're restful and beautiful to look at and intelligent. I think that on the important aspects of life we agree. If you could accept me on those terms, I think I can promise you that we shall be happy together. I'm forty, Sarah, established in my work. I can offer you a comfortable life, and I should like to share it with you… and you—you are twenty-eight; not a young girl to fall in and out of love every few months.'

He got up and came round the desk to stand beside her and she frowned a little, because it was annoying to be told that she was twenty-eight. The frown deepened. He had implied that she was too old to fall in love! As though she had spoken her thoughts aloud he said gently:

'Forgive me if I sounded practical, but I imagine you are in no mood for sentiment, but I hope very much that you will say yes. I shall be away next week—perhaps it will be easier for you to decide if we don't see each other.'

She got up slowly to face him, forgetful of the case notes, which slid in a kind of slow motion to the ground, shedding doctors' letters, Path. Lab. reports, X-ray forms and his own multitudinous notes in an untidy litter around their feet.

'You're going away?' Even to her own ears her voice sounded foolishly lorn. She tried again and said with determined imperturbability:

'I'll think about it. I'm rather surprised—you must know that, but I promise you I'll think about it.'

The words sounded, to say the least, inadequate. She looked at him helplessly and he took a step towards her through the papery confusion at their feet and looked down. He said on a laugh, 'My God! It looks as though we're going to spend this evening together anyway!'

* * *

It was surprising how much she missed him, which on the face of things was absurd, for she had rarely seen him more than twice or three times a week in the clinics. She had always been aware of her liking for him, but hadn't realised until now how strong that liking was. Perhaps it was because she had always felt she could be completely natural with him. She had lain awake a long time that first night, remembering how he had got down on his knees beside her and spent more than an hour helping her to sort out the chaos on the floor, without once referring to their conversation. She was forced to smile at the memory and went to sleep eventually on the pleasant thought that he considered her beautiful.

She had little time to ponder her problems during the days which followed. The clinics were full and she didn't allow her thoughts to wander. Steven came and went with Mr Binns and Mr Peppard and Sarah steeled herself to be casually friendly with him. Mr Coles, who took Dr van Elven's clinic in his absence, was of course quite a different matter; there was no need to be on her guard with him. He worked for two, taking it for granted that she would keep up with him, and still contrived to talk about his family. There was another baby on the way, and he was so obviously pleased about it that Sarah felt pleased too.

'How many's that?' she enquired. 'There are Paul and Mary and Sue and Richard...'

He interrupted her with a chuckle. 'Don't forget the current baby—Mike. Hugo's already staked his claim as godfather—that makes the round half dozen. He never forgets their birthdays and Christmas. We have to warn the children, otherwise he goes out and buys them anything they ask for. Pity he's not married himself…it's at least fifteen years since that girl threw him over.' He shrugged his shoulders. 'He deserves the best, and I hope he gets it one day.'

She visited Mrs Brown too, and found her happy and content, sitting by the new electric fire with Timmy on her lap. Sarah made tea for both and listened while Mrs Brown sang the praises of her daily helper.

'A gem,' she declared, 'and it don't cost me a farthing to 'ave 'er.' Sarah agreed that it was a splendid arrangement and wondered if the doctor had had a hand in that as well. It was surprising and rather disconcerting to find that she knew so little about him…less, apparently, than her hostess, who disclosed during the course of conversation that he had been in to see her, and that now he had gone to Scotland. 'It's ever so far away,' she confided to an attentive Sarah. 'Up in the 'ills, and 'e can see the sea. 'E's got a little 'ouse and 'e does the garden and goes fishin' and walks miles.' She chuckled richly. 'Good luck to 'im, I says; nicer man never walked.' She stroked Timmy. 'Do with a few more like 'im.'

Sarah agreed with a fervour which surprised her even more than it surprised Mrs Brown, although upon reflection she was forced to admit to herself that 'nice' was a completely inadequate word with which to describe Hugo van Elven. She found herself beginning to count the days until his return, which wouldn't be until the Friday afternoon clinic. Once or twice, she thought of writing to her mother and asking her advice, but how could she seek advice from someone who had never met Hugo; someone, moreover, who still thought that she would one day marry Steven? It was something she would have to decide for herself, but it wasn't until Thursday night that she admitted to herself that she had made the decision already. Hugo van Elven represented a quiet haven after the turbulence of the last few weeks; she believed they had a very good chance of being happy together; she felt completely at ease with him, and now that she thought about it, she always had done, and she was aware, without conceit that he liked her. He needed a wife to run his home and entertain for him, and bear him company—she thought that she could do those things quite satisfactorily. It worried her that there was no love between them, but Hugo had said that companionship should suffice, and it seemed to be all that he wished for. Perhaps, later on, their deep liking for each other might turn to affection.

She went to sleep on that thought, and when she woke in the morning, she knew that her mind was made up. Any small doubts still lurking, she resolutely ignored, firmly telling herself that they were unimportant.

She knew she had been right when he walked in. He said 'Good afternoon, Sister,' in a perfectly ordinary voice and gave her the briefest smile, then turned to the pile of notes on his desk and said resignedly, 'Oh, lord, I wonder where they all come from!'

Sarah was putting out wooden spatulas. ''Flu,' she said, and gave his downbent head a grateful look. She had been nervous, almost shy at the idea of seeing him again, trying to imagine what they would say, and he was making it all very easy. She went on, 'They go on working, or take someone's cough cure because they don't like to bother the doctor, and then he sees them and sends them to you with bronchitis. Did you have a pleasant holiday?'

He nodded absently, not looking at her. 'Delightful, thank you. First one in when you're ready, Sister.'

She was actually on the point of leaving after the clinic

was finished, when he came back. He and Dick Coles had gone away together, leaving her to clear up—and without him saying a word! She felt deflated; she hadn't expected him to overwhelm her with questions when they met, because he wasn't that kind of man, but she had expected him to ask her if she had made up her mind. She turned to switch off the desk light, and found him at the door.

He asked abruptly, 'Are you tired?' And when she said 'No,' he went on briskly, 'Good. May I take you out to dinner?' His mouth curved in a faint smile. 'I've been wanting to ask you that all the afternoon, but each time I was on the point of doing so, you either confronted me with another patient or waved a bunch of notes under my nose.' He was still smiling, but his eyes searched her keenly. 'Shall we be celebrating, Sarah?'

At that she smiled too and the cold lump of unhappiness she had been carrying around somewhere deep inside her warmed a little. They might not be able to give each other love, but there were other things—understanding and friendship and shared pleasure in shared interests; they each had a great deal to offer. She turned out the light and went past him into the waiting hall where the cleaners were swabbing the floor under the harsh lights, because the daylight, however bright, rarely penetrated its vastness. She looked up at him, her smile widening, and said:

'Yes, Hugo, we'll be celebrating. What time shall I be ready?'

The expression on his face was hard to read. 'Seventhirty? Wear something pretty, we'll go to Parkes'.'

Sarah went over to her room, tea forgotten, her mind a jumble of thoughts, the chief of which was what she should wear. She was rummaging through her wardrobe when Kate appeared in the doorway of her room. She leant against the wall, swinging her cap.

'What are you doing?' she wanted to know. 'Surely you're not going to spend the evening tidying clothes? A pity I'm not off duty, there's that marvellous film I wanted to see and Jimmy's on duty until Sunday.' She strolled over to the bed and eyed the jumble of dresses upon it. 'That pink thing looks nice,' she commented. 'Isn't that the one you bought…' her voice tailed off, because she had remembered that Sarah had bought it to go out with Steven.

Sarah was tearing off her apron. 'Yes—I'm going to wear it tonight.'

Her friend eyed her with interest. 'Sarah! You're never…?'

Sarah was wriggling out of her dark blue cotton dress. 'I'm going out to dinner with Hugo van Elven, and don't you dare tell a soul, Kate.'

Kate whistled piercingly, 'Cross my heart,' she promised, 'though you're making history, ducky. He's never so much as lifted an eyebrow at a female creature within these walls.' She went reluctantly to the door. 'I'm late. Come and see me when you get in. I'll stay awake.' She started to run along the corridor towards the stairs. 'Have fun!' she called as she went.

Sarah had almost reached the bottom of the stairs when the doubt suddenly beset her that perhaps she was making a mistake. She was actually on the point of turning round and going back to her room when she saw Hugo standing in the hall, looking elegant in his black tie and very much at ease. He was talking to Home Sister, of all people, one of the most dedicated gossips the hospital had ever known. Sarah greeted him briefly under that lady's interested eye and they went out to the car together, leaving her to gaze after them, already rehearsing her bit of news ready for the supper table.

Sarah arranged herself carefully, with an eye to the pink dress.

'Of course we would have to meet Sister Wilkes! She—she talks rather a lot, you know. She'll put two and two together and make ten.'

Hugo idled the car out of the hospital forecourt. 'Do you mind? Everyone will know soon enough, I imagine. They'll see the announcement in the paper. In any case, I should have cause to be grateful to her.'

'Whatever for?'

'Because if I hadn't waited inside instead of out in the car, and if she hadn't been there, I think you would most probably have changed your mind and disappeared on the staircase like Cinderella.'

Sarah stole a look at his profile to see if he was smiling. He wasn't.

'You're rather disconcerting,' she said at last. 'How could you possibly know that—that... Oh, dear! Did you feel like that too?'

This time he did smile. 'No. I have no doubts, and I hope that you will have none either.'

He didn't give her a chance to answer, but began a rambling sort of conversation which lasted until they reached the restaurant, where it was supplanted by a leisurely discussion as to what they should eat. They decided on *quenelles* in lobster sauce with *feuilleté de poulet à la reine* and then *Monte Bianco* because Sarah confessed to a passion for chestnuts. The waiter was barely out of earshot when Hugo spoke.

'Will you marry me, Sarah?' His voice was friendly

and almost casual, and she was conscious of a vague disappointment until he smiled—a warm smile, compelling her to smile in return. She said, a little shyly:

'Yes, Hugo, I'll marry you.' Her voice was steady, as was her gaze as their eyes met across the elegantly appointed table. The pleasant feeling of warmth she had felt before returned and strengthened at the admiration in his. He lifted his glass in a toast, and for the first time in several weeks, she felt almost happy. Perhaps it was because of this that she realised, some two hours later, that not only had she helped Hugo to compose an announcement of their engagement, she had also accepted his offer to drive her down to her home when she went on holiday, and what was more, had invited him to stay the weekend. And, last but not least, she had agreed most readily to marry him in exactly one month's time.

They had parted on the steps of the Nurses' Home and she had enjoyed it when he kissed her lightly on one cheek before opening the door for her. She crept to her room, so that Kate should not hear, and undressed with haste. In bed, thinking about it, she decided she had probably had a little too much champagne, so that Steven's image had become dulled enough to allow her to find pleasure in Hugo's kiss, even though she was aware that he could have done a lot better.

When he came to fetch her on Sunday morning, however, he contented himself with a cheerful 'Hullo there,' stowed her cases in the boot, herself into the seat beside him, and then, with a wave to the various faces watching them from a variety of windows, drove the Iso unhurriedly through the gates. It was still early—barely nine o'clock. London was comparatively free of traffic and it was a mild spring day. Sarah had put on a knitted dress the colour of the April sky above them. She settled into her seat, confident that she had made the most of herself, looking forward to her holiday.

She had telephoned her mother the previous evening, so that by the time they arrived she hoped that her parents' natural surprise would have been tempered to a mildness that wouldn't be too obvious. Her father, a retired colonel, was inclined to be peppery and speak his mind. Her mother was sweet and a little vague, but occasionally disconcerted those around her by being devastatingly candid. She said rather uncertainly:

'I hope you'll like my mother and father, Hugo.'

He allowed the Iso to ooze past a dawdling taxi. 'I see no reason why I shouldn't…it's much more likely that they won't like me, you know. I am, after all, a usurper—' he glanced at her and went on deliberately, 'They must have supposed that you and Steven would marry.'

Sarah stared ahead of her. She said carefully, 'Yes, I think they did, though we never discussed it. They…they teased me sometimes about it. They only met him twice, when he took me down, and then he didn't stay. They were surprised when I told them yesterday—about us, I mean, but I'm not a young girl to be rash.'

He agreed with her gravely and without looking at her so that she failed to see the gleam in his eyes.

'No, I should hardly call you rash. But you are a beautiful young woman, Sarah. I shall be proud of my wife.'

She blushed. 'I hope you always will be.' She added without guile, 'You're very good-looking too, although I don't suppose you like to be told that.'

He chuckled. 'No. But I'll let it pass this once. After all, we must be frank with each other, must we not?'

They were on the A30 now. Hugo passed three crawling cars and raced ahead of them down the empty road. He sat relaxed at the wheel, checked the car's controlled rush momentarily at a crossroads, gave her head once more and glanced at Sarah. 'Do you drive, Sarah?' he asked.

'Yes, at home—a little. I think I should be scared in London.'

'I've a Rover TC 2000. You shall try it out, and if you like it you shall have it for your own use—you'll need a car, you know. I'm almost never home during the day and you'll want to get out and about.'

He spoke carelessly and Sarah was conscious of a faint chill, but before she had time to think about it, he went on, 'Another thing. I've a small cottage in the north-western Highlands; I wondered if you would like to go there for a week or two after we're married—it's very quiet and remote and the scenery is magnificent.'

She was grateful he hadn't said honeymoon. 'Mrs Brown told me you had a house in Scotland. Yes, I'd like that very much—it sounds delightful. What do you do there? Fish?'

'Yes—and walk, and there's a garden I work in, although a man in the village below looks after it—his wife sees to the house.'

'Where is it?' she wanted to know.

'Wester Ross, overlooking Loch Duich. It's about forty miles from Inverness. The cottage is perched on the hillside. There's a tiny village—I suppose you would call it a hamlet—a mile below and a small place called Dornie four or five miles away.'

'I shall like it,' Sarah declared positively. 'Now I know why you've got an Iso Grigo. It must be five hundred miles.'

'Five hundred and seventy-two. Sometimes in the summer I do the through trip.'

She made a small protesting sound and he laughed.

'Oh, it's not as bad as it sounds, because I stop to rest and eat. But we'll take two days over it when we go and stop the night somewhere this side of the border.'

They were beginning to leave the spreading fingers of London behind them now. It wouldn't be long before they were in Basingstoke.

'There's a good road through Laverstock to Andover,' she offered, 'and you can turn off at the crossroads before you reach the town and take the Salisbury road.'

He nodded. 'We'll do that—we can stop at Overton and have coffee at the White Hart.'

'Oh, you've been this way before.'

'Yes, years ago.' He spoke shortly, and she knew with the same certainty as though he had told her that he had been with the girl he had wanted to marry. Impulsively she said:

'Hugo, I don't mean to pry, but if you want to—to talk about her—the girl you loved—love, I won't mind; it helps to talk about such things, and I think I know how you feel.'

There was a small tremor in his voice when he answered; she thought it was emotion. 'Thank you, Sarah. I think perhaps I shall tell you about her, but not, I think, until we have been married for a while and have a complete understanding of each other.'

It wasn't quite a snub, but she coloured a little none the less because there were other questions, and perhaps he was a man who didn't brook questioning. She asked in a dogged voice:

'May I know something about your family? Mother is

bound to ask...' she hesitated. 'Of course, I know what the grapevine says about you, but that isn't always very accurate.'

He said on a laugh, 'I should imagine not, although I think you must know that I'm not English. That at least is true.' He glanced sideways at her and she nodded. 'My parents live in Holland, north of Arnhem. My father is a retired doctor. I have three sisters, they're ten years or more younger than I—they're all married with children. Two of them live in Holland, my youngest sister lives in France. There are cousins and aunts and uncles, of course, though I see very little of them, save for three aunts who live together in Alkmaar.'

'You don't want to live in Holland?'

'Not at present—maybe, when I retire, I would go back, but that would depend on your wishes too. My father came to England in the twenties; he had a Leiden degree—he took a degree at Cambridge too. He met my mother here—she was visiting her grandparents, as her mother was an Englishwoman. They married and returned to Holland where I was born. I followed my father's pattern—Leiden and then Cambridge. It was there that I met Janet and I decided to stay in England. I had inherited the house at Richmond and it was already a second home to me. Even when there was no reason for me to remain there any longer, I had my work and friends in England, and Holland is near enough for me to go over whenever I wish.' He paused and went on in a lighter tone, 'I think we must go there in the late summer so that you may be welcomed into the family.' He was silent for a moment, then enquired blandly, 'Is there anything else you would like to know?'

She heard the blandness so that her voice was stiff.

'No. Thank you for telling me what you have. Please understand that I have no intention of being inquisitive, but if I'm to marry you I must know the—the bare bones of your life. I can assure you,' she went on, getting haughtier with each breath, 'I'll not trouble you with any unnecessary questions.'

He didn't answer, but to her surprise pulled the car on to the side of the road and stopped. He looked serious enough, but she had the suspicion that he was secretly laughing at her.

'I'm not sure what I have said, that you should be so high and mighty. My dear girl, you may ask as many questions as you wish and I'll engage to answer them as truthfully as I am able—and if I don't wish to give you an answer, I shall say so, and I hope you will do the same. And there is no question of your inquisitiveness or any other such nonsense, so let us have no bees in our bonnets on that score.'

Sarah saw him smile. His large hand covered hers for a moment. She stared at it; it was a nice hand, cool and firm and reassuring. She said a little awkwardly, 'I expect I shall say a great many silly things until I...' she paused. 'If you'll bear with me—you see I can't help thinking that I...' she stopped.

'Will be jilted again?' He asked the question cheerfully. 'That is something I can promise you won't happen—I can give you proof of that.' He searched through his pockets and eventually found a small box. There was a ring inside—a magnificent diamond in an old-fashioned setting. He picked up her left hand and fitted it on. 'There,' he said, 'now you have the token of my firm intention to marry you.'

She was a little breathless. 'It's beautiful,' she managed at length. 'How extraordinary that it fits—is it old?'

'It's been in the family for two hundred years or so—and it's not at all surprising that it should fit. There is a legend that it fits only upon the finger of the woman destined to be a van Elven bride.'

Sarah was holding her hand up the better to admire the ring. 'I feel like Cinderella. Thank you very much, Hugo—I'll wear it with pride.' She said, giving him a quick glance through her lashes, 'I'm sorry I was silly just now.'

He bent his head and kissed her on the cheek—a casual friendly salute that made no demands of her, and started the car again. 'Never silly,' he stated positively. 'And now what about that cup of coffee?'

Sarah found the rest of the trip delightful; she had always thought Hugo to be taciturn, but now, away from his work, she realised how mistaken she had been. He was amusing and considerate and restful. She had never met a man who was so completely untroubled. By the time that they had reached Salisbury they were on the best possible terms with each other. He skirted the town and took the Blandford road, and after about ten miles, she said, 'You turn right at Sixpenny Handley, then right again after a mile.'

The very small village was tucked away between the folds of the hills. There was a large church, a small pub, a manor house, a scattering of cottages and a handful of pleasant houses standing on their own. They had to go through the village before they reached Sarah's home; it stood back from the lane, its grey stonework brightened by the spring flowers which filled its garden. Hugo turned in at the propped-open gate and drew up at the front door which was immediately opened by Sarah's mother, a woman in her fifties and still wearing the traces of a beauty as splendid as her daughter's. She was beautifully groomed and well dressed. She was clasping a knife and a cauliflower closely to her. Sarah embraced her warmly, took the knife and the cauliflower from her with an air of having done it before, and introduced Hugo. Mrs Dunn shook hands, studying him in a manner which might have shaken a lesser man and then said sweetly:

'So much better than Steven, darling.' She smiled at them both. 'Come inside, my dears. Your father is in the sitting room.'

They followed her, and as they went Sarah felt the pressure of Hugo's hand on hers. It was surprising, but she was sure that he was more at ease than she herself was. Her father was sitting behind the *Sunday Times* which he put down as they entered. He kissed her heartily and stared at Hugo as she introduced him. Apparently he liked what he saw, for after a series of polite but guarded questions, answered equally politely, he felt free to pour the sherry.

As the day wore on, it was obvious to Sarah that her parents found Hugo an acceptable son-in-law. It was a pity that she had no opportunity to have five minutes alone with him, in order to find out what he thought of them. When she and her mother at length went up to bed, leaving the two men to talk, he went to the door with them and after ushering her mother through it, put out a detaining hand.

'Do you take the dogs out before breakfast?' he asked quietly, 'because if you do, I should like to come with you.'

'Half past seven—in the kitchen,' Sarah said promptly,

so glad that he wanted to be alone with her that she smiled widely, so that the dimple in her cheek made her look like a little girl again. 'Good night, Hugo.'

She went to sleep almost at once, thinking with pleasure of the morning.

She was down first and had made the tea when he arrived. They sat in the deep window seat drinking it, while the dogs whimpered with impatience at their feet. It was a lovely morning, with a clear blue sky and almost no wind, nor any sound other than the birds singing and someone a long way off, calling the cows. Sarah had put on an oatmeal-coloured skirt and a matching silk shirt-blouse, and had slung a vivid pink cardigan across her shoulders. She tried not to notice Hugo studying her over his mug of tea and was pleased out of all proportion when he remarked:

'You look nice, Sarah. I like the way you dress—you even wear your uniform with *éclat*.' He added speculatively, 'I wonder who I shall get in your place?'

Sarah felt a sudden vague surprise that she hadn't thought of that at all, and now that she did, the idea of another girl taking her place at Hugo's clinic didn't please her at all. She looked thoughtful without being aware of it and was secretly delighted when he observed:

'Someone like Sister Evans would do nicely.'

Sister Evans was fiftyish, homely in appearance and cosy in manner—and she was happily married. Sarah looked at him to see if he was joking, but although his grey eyes were alight with laughter he went on soberly enough: 'Not even the grapevine could do much about her, could it?' He put down his cup. 'I must see what I can do.'

They went out of the back door, the Colonel's two labradors and Sarah's mother's corgi circling around in a very frenzy of excitement. They went through the kitchen garden and opened the little arched door in its wall and so into a lane that presently became a path which wound up the bare hill before them. At the top they paused to admire the view.

'Magnificent, isn't it?' Sarah remarked. 'When I feel miserable sometimes, I think of this view.'

'And have you felt miserable, Sarah?'

'You know I have. Oh, not only just these last few weeks—I think I knew in my heart that Steven wouldn't marry me, only I pretended to myself that he would. I know now that I've been pretending for almost three years. I suppose I shall get over it—perhaps I don't love him as you've loved your Janet, because I believe I shall recover, and you never have, have you?'

He had bent to pat one of the dogs so that she couldn't see his face.

'I gather the grapevine has you very well informed,' was all he said.

On the way back, he caught her hand and held it lightly as they walked and told her a little of his work. He was a busy man; it seemed that she would see very little of him during the week. She remarked upon this in a rather wistful voice, to have it pointed out to her bracingly that they would spend most of their evenings together and that weekends were usually free. She agreed and on a happy thought, enquired if he took his dogs for a walk each morning.

'Yes, always. Would you come with me? It would be pleasant and give us time to talk, just as we have been talking this morning.' He stopped and turned her round to face him. 'No regrets?' he asked.

'No, none. It's funny, but you don't seem strange—I mean, it's as though I've known you for a long time.'

He smiled down at her. 'But, my dear girl, you have—three years, is it not? One gets to know someone very well indeed when one works with them.'

They started to walk again. 'What will you do with Mrs Brown?' asked Sarah.

'Leave her where she is for as long as possible. In fact, I think she would prefer to die there rather than go back into hospital—I should imagine that she has a couple of months—maybe less.'

'You won't mind if I go and see her sometimes? And do you suppose we could find a home for Timmy?'

He said at once. 'Of course you can go and see her when you like. I shall have to visit her when we get back; her own doctor is away ill and I suggested I took her over until he is back again. As for Timmy, he can come to us—Alice will be delighted.'

It wasn't until they were in the kitchen garden again that she asked:

'Do you like Mother and Father, Hugo?'

'Very much,' he replied promptly. 'And I'm sure they will get on excellently with my parents. Your mother wasn't disappointed that we want to be married quietly?'

Sarah smiled. 'Yes, she was really. I suppose mothers always want their daughters to wear white satin and a veil.'

'Do you want to wear white satin, Sarah? We could easily arrange…'

She sounded quite apprehensive. 'Oh, no. I'd like it to be just us and our mothers and fathers.'

His voice was smooth. 'Would you have worn white satin if you had married Steven?'

She was a truthful girl. 'Yes. I used to think about it sometimes—girls do, you know. But that isn't the reason why I want a quiet wedding with you. That sounds silly because I'm not sure what the reason is; but when I am, I'll tell you.'

He loosed her hand, and put a great arm around her shoulders.

'You're a nice girl, Sarah,' he said placidly. He somehow made it sound like a delightful compliment.

She was sorry to see him go that evening, at the end of a day which had seemed too short. They had been to see the vicar about the wedding, and on the way home had sat on a fallen tree trunk in the warm sunshine and talked like old friends. They parted like old friends too, although he hadn't kissed her, but taken her hand and said in a casual manner:

'I'll be back at the weekend, Sarah. Enjoy your holiday.'

And he had gone, leaving her with the feeling that she would have liked to have gone back with him.

But the week went quickly. Her mother, showing an unexpectedly practical turn, whisked her off to Salisbury to buy clothes, an undertaking much enhanced by the size of the cheque which her father had given her. Moreover, the village sheltered among its inhabitants a dressmaker of incredible skill; a retiring, middle-aged little woman, who on casual acquaintance looked incapable of hemming a duster, but who in the privacy of her Edwardian front parlour became a kind of *haute couture* fairy godmother. Sarah spent a sizeable part of each day closeted with this paragon, listening to her soft country voice discussing patterns and materials, and later to stand, more or less patiently, to be pinned and fitted...but whenever she could escape the mild hubbub of a quiet country wedding, she took the dogs and wandered for miles, thinking about Hugo, and regrettably, of Steven.

If her parents thought of Steven, though, they gave no sign of it, nor, she was glad to discover, did they talk incessantly of Hugo—it seemed that they had accepted him and were content. Just as she would be content, she told herself with a rather painstaking frequency, once she could forget Steven.

There were flowers for her mother during the week, with a correct note from Hugo and a letter for herself—a brief letter written in his small, almost unreadable handwriting. It was the kind of friendly note she occasionally had from her brother. She read it several times, but by no flight of imagination could it be altered into anything else. She sighed without knowing it, and put the letter in the frivolous beribboned sachet which held her handkerchiefs, telling herself that that was what she wanted anyway—what he had promised to be—a friend and companion, who would maybe, over the years, develop an affection for her as she would for him—once she had Steven out of her system.

He had said that he would arrive in time for lunch on Saturday. It was a glorious warm morning; even after she had done a few chores around the house and arranged the flowers, and done her hair and then done it again, there were a couple of hours to spare. She whistled up the dogs and strolled away, up the hill behind the house. She was lying on her back in the short springy grass, with a fine disregard for her twice-done hair, when Hugo sat down beside her. Sarah sat up at once.

'Hugo! I was going to be home, waiting for you.' She put a questing hand up to her flyaway hair. 'I'm all untidy.'

He studied her with deliberation. 'I like it like that—have you had a pleasant week?'

She told him. 'And you?'

'Busy—busier than I need have been without your capable help.'

Sarah paused in her half-hearted efforts to tidy her hair. 'Oh, Hugo, how nice of you to say so.'

'Not only I but Peppard and Binns—they wanted to know if you would continue to work after we were married.'

Her grey eyes were enquiring. 'What did you say?'

'An emphatic no. My dear girl, there's no need for you to work, and think how my practice would suffer if it got about that my wife went to work!'

He was smiling and she knew that he was joking, but not altogether.

'Yes, of course. But I'd work willingly if you ever needed help... I mean with money.' She glanced at him, but his face was inscrutable. He chose a blade of grass with care and began to chew it.

'Thank you, Sarah. Spoken like a true friend. As a matter of fact I wanted to talk to you about money. I've plenty—a good income from the practice and enough of my own to be independent. Later, when we're married, I'll take you to old Simms, my lawyer, and we'll have everything in writing. In the meantime there will be a quarterly allowance for you—paid in on our wedding day.' He mentioned a sum which made her sit up very straight indeed.

'All that? For me? Just for three months? It's enough for a year!' She had an enlightening thought. 'Of course, that's the housekeeping as well.'

He laughed. 'No, it's not. You run the house as you think fit and give me the bills each month—if you're too extravagant I'll tell you. And if you ever need money, Sarah, you are to ask me for it.'

She said obediently. 'Yes, Hugo,' although she couldn't see how she could possibly spend all that money. Her voice must have betrayed her doubts, for he said with firmness:

'Leave me to worry about it, Sarah.' He chose another blade of grass. 'I've letters from my mother and father for you—would you like to read them now?'

He lay stretched out beside her while she read them. They were kindly letters, a little formal perhaps, but then they had never seen her, while Hugo was their son and they must have known about Janet. She wondered what they were really like—she would know, of course, on her wedding day.

Hugo's placid voice interrupted her thoughts. 'Should we be going back?' he asked. 'Your mother mentioned one o'clock.'

They were within sight of the little door in the wall of the kitchen garden when he stopped. 'Sarah, I have an engagement present for you.'

He put a small box into her hand and she opened it, conscious of delight that he should have thought of it, and caught her breath at the diamond and pearl earrings in it. She said, a little breathless:

'Hugo, they're superb! I love them. They're marvellous, only I—you…' She stopped and started again, her voice very level. 'Don't you see, Hugo? They're so lovely, such a magnificent gift… I don't deserve them. I don't expect you can understand…'

He interrupted coolly, 'You mean because we're not in love? Don't be a goose, Sarah.' He gave her a half-mocking, wholly friendly smile. 'I came down in the

Rover; she's yours too—you shall drive her back to-morrow.'

She said in a shaky voice, 'Hugo, you're too good to me,' and stretched up and kissed him on one cheek, just above his jaw, because she couldn't reach any higher.

'Thank you very much. I've never had anything quite as beautiful, and they match perfectly with my ring.' She touched the earrings gently with a forefinger, her beautiful head full of half realised thoughts which she shrugged aside to say, 'I'll try and be a perfect driver, too.'

He laughed gently. 'I'll answer that when we get to London tomorrow.'

The journey back went well, despite the fact that Sarah made the initial mistake of going into reverse, and had on several separate occasions clashed the gears in a manner which caused her to flush most becomingly. Hugo, how-ever, ignored these small mishaps and kept up a sooth-ing flow of small talk which restored her confidence, so that she drew up before the house in Richmond with something of a flourish, to be rewarded with his quiet:

'You'll do, my girl. Just a little more practice.'

Sarah went pink with pleasure; she would have minded very much if he had levelled criticism at her, although she was aware that she had merited it. Somehow, his good opinion of her mattered a great deal. It was there-fore in a mood of relaxed content that she accompanied him into the house, to eat the delicious supper Alice had prepared for them, and afterwards to inspect her future home. They wandered around the rooms, quietly content with each other's company.

It was a lovely house; the furniture, although antique, had a pleasantly used air about it; the chairs were com-fortable, the colours subdued. She approved of everything and roundly declared that she had no wish to alter any of it. Presently they went upstairs and she looked with something like awe at the beautiful room which was to be hers. It was at the back of the house and had a little iron balcony overlooking the garden. The furniture was Sheraton and the floor-length curtains chintz in muted pinks and blues, colours which were echoed in the carpet and bed coverlet. There was a bathroom leading off on one side, and a dressing room on the other side of the room, and Hugo said easily:

'My room is in the front of the house, so you can spread yourself as much as you like.'

His own room was smaller, and although the furniture was just as beautiful, it looked cold. Sarah decided that she would make sure that there were always flowers there. There were more bedrooms, all equally charming; even the small attic rooms had been furnished with care. On their way downstairs again, she paused by a big door at the back of the landing; she had seen it as they had gone up, but Hugo had walked straight past it.

'Where does this door lead to?' she wanted to know, and was chilled when he said, 'Nowhere in particular.' Which was nonsense, of course—he didn't want her to know. She promised herself that she would find out as soon as she was able. Meanwhile: 'The house is charmingly furnished,' she remarked lightly. 'Who did it?'

Hugo said rather shortly, 'I did, a long time ago. Nothing's been changed, merely replaced from time to time.'

He led the way downstairs, and Sarah followed him, digesting the unpleasant thought that probably he had done it all for Janet. A little subdued, she suggested that perhaps she should be getting back to St Edwin's.

* * *

It seemed strange to be back in uniform again and to see Hugo when he came to take his clinics. He addressed her with his usual polite formality, and at the end of the first one went away with Dick Coles, to reappear after ten minutes.

'It's fortunate that this state of affairs will only last for another week or so,' he observed from the door, 'for I find it both ridiculous and difficult to address you as Sister.'

Sarah giggled. 'I thought you'd gone,' she said, and was conscious of a surge of relief. 'I know it's silly, but you're—different here, you know. It seems as though none of it is true.' She picked up a pile of papers and prepared to go.

'In that case, I had better make it true, had I not, Sarah?' He had come to stand near her. 'How long will it take you to change?'

'Ten minutes—no fifteen.' She stood looking at him, the pile of notes clasped to her apron bib, her lovely face aglow. She hoped suddenly that he would kiss her. He did—a light, unhurried kiss on her mouth, the effect of which was entirely spoilt by his saying prosaically:

'I'll wait outside the Home. Don't dress up—we'll go and see Mrs Brown and then find somewhere quiet to eat.'

It was to be the forerunner of many such evenings— sometimes spent at Richmond, dining alone in the quiet dining room and sitting afterwards, talking—there was so much to say; Sarah found the time too short. Twice they went to the theatre and once to the Mirabelle because Hugo thought that she should have the opportunity to wear the earrings. Then again to Mrs Brown's rose-decked room, to drink strong tea and receive a wedding gift—a knitted teacosy of a breathtaking red, which its donor declared would go very well with a nice brown tea-pot. Sarah thought of the delicate silver Queen Anne tea-pot which was in Hugo's house and agreed with her, vowing silently that she would use it on her early morning tea-tray whether it matched the china or not.

She had had a wedding present from her friends in the hospital too, and spent her last evening there going from ward to ward, wishing them goodbye. It was on her way over to the surgical block to see the night Sisters that she met Steven. She would have passed him, but he stopped her with an outflung hand.

'I suppose you expect me to wish you happiness, Sarah. Well, I don't. You're a fool; van Elven's not the man for you—he's still wrapped up in his first love, and you're still mourning me...'

Sarah dragged her arm free and said furiously, 'That's a lie!' then stopped to fight the tears of rage which choked her. Hugo's voice behind her, quiet as always, but full of chilling menace, said:

'My friend, it seems I must tell you to get out yet again—and I should go if I were you, otherwise I might be tempted to use persuasion.'

She began to cry as Steven turned on his heel, and as he went she found herself swept into Hugo's arms to be comforted. After a minute or two of snivelling she was able to raise a tear-stained face and say in a furious voice:

'I'm so ashamed of myself, Hugo. And I'm not crying because I'm unhappy; I'm so—so angry.'

She dragged the back of her hand across her eyes like a child and accepted his proffered handkerchief. Presently she smiled at him in a watery fashion. 'Whatever do you think of me?' she asked.

Hugo put the damp handkerchief into a pocket, still holding her with one arm. 'Remind me to tell you some time— Where were you going? I know we had agreed not to go out tonight, but when I got home I changed my mind and came back to see if you would come out after all. You see how I have got used to your company... We can have supper somewhere.'

'I'd like that very much—I missed you too. I must just say goodbye to Sister Hallett and Sister Moore—I can do the rest of my packing in the morning. We're not going until ten, are we?' She hesitated. 'You wouldn't like to come with me? They'll be in the duty room on Surgical.'

He didn't answer, only took her arm and walked with her down the long, deserted corridor, waited while she said her goodbyes, and then walked back to the Home with her. It was a lovely May evening. They lingered a moment outside the door and he said:

'Wear that blue thing with the pleats. We'll go to a place I know of in Jermyn Street.' She nodded and before she went inside said on an impulsive rush, 'Hugo, you're so nice—I wish...'

His voice sounded curt. 'What do you wish?' he asked.

She heard the curtness. 'Oh, nothing.' She paused, feverishly trying to think of the right thing to say. 'I expect we shall be a great comfort to each other,' she achieved finally. Up in her room, changing rapidly, she paused to laugh ruefully. Her well-meant remark had been a stupid one, but it had been impossible to put her thoughts into words, especially as she wasn't sure what those thoughts were.

She was thinking about it when she sat beside him in the Iso Grigo, driving away from her parents' home after the wedding. He was nice, and he was a comfort; it was as though he had known of the last-minute uncertainty which assailed her. She had got up early and taken the dogs for a walk, and halfway up the hill Hugo had been waiting for her. He was wearing an open-necked shirt and elderly flannels, and she had put on an old cotton frock and hadn't bothered with her hair. All he had said was:

'No one would ever think to see us now that we'll be getting married in an hour or so,' and then had gone on to talk about everything else under the sun. By the time they had got back to the house, getting married to him had seemed a perfectly sensible and ordinary thing to do.

She had liked his parents too—they had been kind, and charming to her mother and father as well. If they had felt any doubts about their son's marriage, they had given no sign. Her dress had been a success too, and although Hugo had had no time to tell her so, she was aware that he had liked it. The white ribbed silk, made up into the elegantly simple pattern she had chosen, had been just right for the lovely weather, and the little hat she hadn't been quite certain about had been the right choice after all. She glanced down at the plain gold ring on her finger, and then looked sideways at Hugo's hand on the wheel. She had been diffident about asking him if she might give him a ring too, and had been surprised when he had agreed without demur. He had put the heavy signet ring he always wore on the other hand. He interrupted her thoughts:

'You made a delightful bride, Sarah—I don't think I realised how beautiful you are.' He smiled fleetingly. 'I enjoyed my wedding.'

She smiled back at him, and settled back beside him as he sent the car speeding on the first stage of their journey to the cottage in Wester Ross.

Chapter 4

It was barely half past one, for they had married at the early hour of half past ten. The day was bright and warm and the country looked fresh and green. Hugo had told her that they were to spend the night at Windermere, a journey of almost two hundred and fifty miles—a distance, Sarah realised, of no consequence to the Iso Grigo, nor for its driver, who drove with the casual air of a man taking his wife to do the shopping. But she had travelled enough with him by now to know that the casual air was deceptive. He said now:

'And did you enjoy your wedding too, Sarah?'

It surprised her that upon reflection, she had. Wedded friends had told her that they had scarcely realised that they were being married, what with worrying about their veils and the bridesmaids and whether the best man had the ring. But she had had no veil and no bridesmaids, and the best man, a cousin of Hugo's who had flown over from Holland just for the ceremony, evinced no nervous fumbling at the last minute; he had been as calm as the bridegroom, who had been very calm indeed. She had been free to think her own thoughts, knowing that anything that needed taking care of would be dealt with by Hugo without fuss. She answered reflectively:

'Yes, I did—very much.'

He glanced at her briefly and smiled and she thought that he was on the point of speaking, but when he didn't she went on:

'I like your mother and father, Hugo.'

'And they liked you. I've promised we will go over before the summer is over, so that you can get to know each other. I can show you something of Holland at the same time.'

'Tell me about them—and about Holland too?' she invited.

She listened happily to his quiet deep voice, marvelling at the stupid idea she had always entertained that he was taciturn. When he chose to talk he had a dry wit which was never unkind, and an amusing way of describing things and people. She pondered the strange fact that although her heart was broken, she could so enjoy Hugo's company. They reached Tewkesbury and the M5 without her having solved the problem.

'Dull, but quick,' was Hugo's comment as he allowed the car to run up to seventy and then kept her there. But it wasn't dull at all. Sarah forgot her problems; she felt happy and content, and delighted with her companion—it was like being with a life-long friend to whom she could voice her thoughts; she amended that to almost all her thoughts. They had talked frankly about their future together and Hugo had made it plain in the nicest possible way that he was content to wait indefinitely until such time as she felt that Steven no longer mattered quite as much—he had said it in such a way that she had gathered the impression that he didn't care overmuch, and had felt unreasonably hurt, only to chide herself for being foolish, for if Hugo had told her that he loved her, she would have refused him out of hand. To marry someone who loved you when you yourself were in love with someone else seemed to her to be a towering wickedness. As it was, she and Hugo had a deep regard for each other and nothing more, and upon that they would build their marriage.

Just before they reached Manchester he turned off the motorway into Knutsford where they had a rather late tea. Sarah, who was hungry, ate her way through an assortment of sandwiches, an odd scone or two and a variety of cakes with an unselfconscious pleasure, for, as she remarked to Hugo, she had been much too nervous to eat her breakfast and too excited to do more than nibble at the delicious titbits which her mother had provided for the wedding breakfast. She beamed at him across the table.

'You weren't nervous at all, were you, Hugo—or excited?' She drew in a breath. 'Of course, it isn't quite—quite...well, I suppose you feel different if you love someone very much.'

She had gone a little pink, but made no attempt to evade his gaze.

He said, with the merest hint of a smile, 'So I am led to believe—but I am neither nervous nor excitable by nature. Shall we go? It's roughly seventy-five miles to Windermere; we should arrive in good time for a late dinner. The food's rather good, I believe.'

She got up. 'Oh, I'm so glad.' She looked at him doubtfully. 'I don't mean to sound greedy—only I'm mostly hungry, especially now I shall have time to eat. In hospital one eats fast, either because one has to be on duty in a few minutes, or because one is off duty and doesn't want to miss a minute of it. It's ruinous to a proper appreciation of food.'

They were walking back to the car and Hugo took her arm and said:

'The first time I took you out, you begged for something quick.'

'And such a gorgeous place too!' she sighed, and he answered quickly:

'We'll go there again soon, and you shall take as long as you like.'

He was fastening her seat belt. She said to his downbent head, 'You don't mind—I mean, that I like food?'

He laughed, looking all at once much younger. 'I find it delightful to be with someone who enjoys herself—quite a lot of women pretend not to be interested in what they eat; which is nonsense, of course.' He started the car and said, smiling, 'There's some quite good scenery presently; that should give you an appetite.'

The hotel was old and rambling and lay, delightfully, by the lake. Their rooms overlooked the water and the fells beyond; the slow falling sun touched everything in sight with gold; the water of the lake looked like smooth shot silk. Sarah flung her hat on the bed and ran on to the balcony in order to have a better look, and found Hugo on the balcony alongside. 'It's lovely,' she cried enthusiastically. 'I've never seen anything like it.'

'Wait until you see the cottage,' was all Hugo would say, and 'I'm coming for you in five minutes.'

She was ready, with her bright hair brushed and a

face nicely powdered and lipsticked. They went down, arm in arm, to the almost empty dining room and ate *filet de sole Grand Duc* and *chicken Marengo* and drank champagne, then Sarah found room for a water ice while Hugo watched her lazily over his coffee. Afterwards they strolled along the road beside the lake, it was almost dark, although the sky was still a deep turquoise in the west. Everything around them smelled delicately sweet and they hardly spoke until Sarah asked, 'What time do we go tomorrow?'

'We've about three hundred and thirty miles to go—if we leave at nine, allowing stops for lunch and tea and the condition of the roads, which will slow us down a little, we should get there about six. Are you tired?'

'No, not really.' She said with quick intuition, 'Shall we go for a walk before breakfast—would there be time?'

'Yes, if you don't mind getting up early... I'll ask them to call you at seven.'

The morning was even more beautiful than the evening had been. They walked in the opposite direction this time and discussed the pleasures of getting up early, something they were both used to, as their jobs demanded it. The sun struck warm upon them, early though it was, and Hugo looked up at it and murmured, '"Busie old foole, unruly Sunne," although perhaps that's a little out of context.'

'John Donne,' said Sarah, pleased that she knew what he was talking about, 'and most inappropriate, if I remember the rest of the poem.'

He burst out laughing and caught her by the hand. 'You know, Sarah,' he said, 'I think that we are going to enjoy life together.'

They stopped for lunch at Crianlarich, with Ben More

and Ben Lui looming majestically on either side of them, and arrived in Inverness after a journey through scenery which had left Sarah speechless and round-eyed. Its grandeur, however, had by no means detracted from her enjoyment of her tea, although she found so much to talk about that Hugo had to press her to try a second slice of fruit cake. She took it absently.

'How many years have you had the cottage?'

He thought. 'Five—no, six; I come up twice a year, and when I can manage it, a third time as well.'

'Shall we—that is, shall I come with you?'

He raised surprised eyebrows. 'My dear girl, of course, unless there is anything else you would prefer to do.'

Sarah shook her head. 'I can hardly wait to get there.' The road ran along the edge of Loch Ness, but at Invermoriston Hugo turned away from it on to a narrow road and slowed the car's pace.

'We're almost there,' he said, and she could hear the happiness in his voice.

'It's beautiful and lonely and makes everything else seem unreal.' She craned her neck in order to see as much as possible of the grandeur around them and then stole a glance at him. 'Aren't you tired?'

'Not really. I enjoy it too much. I know the road quite well now, you see, which helps considerably.'

Sarah said, 'Only the direst of circumstances would make me drive all this way; I should be terrified by myself. Supposing I got a puncture, or ran out of petrol?'

Hugo laughed and said in a comfortable reassuring voice:

'The country looks empty, doesn't it? But you're far less likely to be overlooked here than in London. Would you really not drive up here?'

'No—at least, only if I were desperate.'

Loch Duich looked at its loveliest in the early evening light. The mountains of Kintail hung in the near distance, looking like some splendid, gigantic backdrop to a natural stage scenery of incredible beauty. A couple of miles along the loch's edge, and Hugo turned the car again, up a winding little road which appeared to go nowhere but presently unravelled itself into a tiny huddle of cottages, pressed against the side of the hill. He stopped the car at the last cottage and got out and knocked on its stout door. He had told Sarah that Mrs MacFee was one of the most remarkable women he had ever met, and when she had asked why, he had said:

'She's forty, sandy-haired and plain-faced and beautiful. She has a brood of children like angels and a husband who is the best shepherd in the district. She's completely content with her lot—so is he. Each time I meet them I'm cut down to size.'

Sarah knew exactly what he had meant when the door opened and Mrs MacFee appeared. She had no beauty at all, and yet she appeared beautiful. She went straight to the car and spoke to Sarah in her soft Highland voice, then gave Hugo a large old-fashioned key, and stood waving as they drove on up the hill.

'I usually leave the key under the water-butt,' Hugo explained, 'and so does Mrs MacFee, but I guessed she would have it with her today.' He gave her a wicked look. 'Everyone loves a bride, even in these lonely parts.'

Sarah giggled. 'You've got it wrong—that only applies to arriving at the church, all dressed up.'

'Which reminds me—your dress was quite perfect, Sarah, so was that ridiculous hat. You looked quite beautiful.'

She said, 'Thank you, Hugo,' in a demure voice and went on, 'Mrs MacFee is exactly as you described her, and I see what you mean. How do you manage about food?'

'Over the years we've worked out a very good system. When I leave, Mrs MacFee goes up to the cottage and re-stocks the cupboard, gets in coal for the Aga, makes up the beds, scrubs and polishes and so forth and leaves everything in apple-pie order—in fact, she leaves it so that if I were to arrive unexpectedly, I could walk straight in and live in comfort for at least a month. MacFee grows vegetables in the garden—and there's a potato clamp, and apples and onions in the shed. What more could I want?'

The last few yards were steep, and he slowed the car to walking pace and turned it sharply between the gate-posts set in the old stone wall bordering the lane. The cottage stood a little way back; it was whitewashed, with a grey slate roof and small windows either side of its door. It was alone in the little lane, but Sarah had no feeling of loneliness as she inspected it. It was cosy and solid and looked as though it had grown out of the mountains all around it. The front door opened directly into a minute lobby and thence to the living room, which held a pleasant clutter of furniture—comfortable chairs, several small tables, well-filled bookshelves flanking a stone fireplace, and a variety of oddments conducive to comfort, all so well arranged that the small room looked larger than it was. The floor was wooden, covered to a large extent by thick handmade rugs. The crimson serge curtains and the brass oil lamp on the table beside the easy chair drawn up to the fireplace added a colourful little glow to the room, so that she sensed how pleasant it would be to draw the curtains against a cold evening and light the lamp. The kitchen was beyond—small, expertly planned, and equipped down to the last saltspoon. There was a scrubbed table against one wall, partnered by two rush-bottomed chairs and crowned by a bowl of fruit, witness of Mrs MacFee's thoughtfulness. The Aga took up most of the opposite wall, with the stairs, neatly hidden behind a narrow arched door, beside it.

'Go on up,' suggested Hugo, 'while I fetch the cases in.'

There were two small bedrooms upstairs, divided by a bathroom. The whole floor was carpeted by a pale amber which showed up the white-painted furniture very well. The curtains at the small windows were blue and white chintz with splashes of yellow. There were fitted cupboards cleverly built into the unequal angles of the walls and some beautiful candlesticks; pewter and old, each with its snuffer. The front room was the larger of the two, with a small Pembroke table under the window, bearing a shieldback mirror, a fine linen runner, exquisitely embroidered, and a little vase of garden flowers— Mrs MacFee again. She thought that the room would be hers, and Hugo confirmed this when she went downstairs to the kitchen. He had lighted the Aga, and the fresh aromatic tang of pine as the kindling blazed, filled the small room. He had taken off his jacket and was leaning against the wall, waiting to replenish the stove. He looked content, as though he had come home…for a second, Sarah had the feeling that she didn't know him at all. He looked so very different from the rather silent, immaculate doctor she had worked for. Then he glanced up and she knew that he wasn't changed in the least; it was she who was seeing him as he really was. They smiled at each other.

'Come up to the end of the garden and see the view,' he invited. The garden was long and narrow, with a path running up its centre to the boundary hedge—the village, a tiny cluster of rooftops, lay a mile or so below them, and lower still and further away was the road running alongside Loch Duich.

'We'll unpack, shall we? And then go down to Dornie for a meal. There's a splendid little hotel there.'

Sarah was disappointed; she was as good a cook as she was nurse; she was anxious to display her talents, but she said nothing. After all, they would be at the cottage for two weeks at least; plenty of time to demonstrate her ability to cook.

The days passed—long slow days of lovely weather, made longer because they got up early. It was the new Hugo Sarah was still learning to know who got up just after six and made tea and brought her up a cup. He was dressed and out in the garden by the time she got down to get breakfast; chopping wood or weeding or cutting back a hedge—he had a boundless energy which she had never suspected of him. At breakfast, that first morning, she had said, 'You're so different. I'd never thought of you as someone who could be so—so practical—chopping wood, and washing up and gardening and making tea in the morning.'

She caught his mocking eye and blushed brightly.

'My poor Sarah, have you been disillusioned? Perhaps I have the best of the bargain, for you are a famous cook.'

She had laughed then, and they had left the little house in Mrs MacFee's capable hands and packed a picnic basket and roamed the lower slopes of the mountains until the early evening, when they went back to the cottage and Sarah surpassed herself in the roasting of a superb joint of Angus beef.

They went somewhere different each day; sometimes

to spend hours fishing, a sport at which Hugo excelled, but which Sarah didn't much care for because of taking out the hook, but she was content to sit as still as a mouse while he went after his trout. He took her to Inverness one day, and she bought a quantity of wool to knit him an Aran sweater. This, together with an assortment of books from the sitting room, kept her contentedly occupied while Hugo fished. They might not speak for an hour, for she knew better than to start up a conversation, but that didn't matter, for her sense of companionship had deepened with the days. There was no need to talk, but it was pleasant to look up from time to time and see him, pipe in mouth, standing motionless and enormous in his waders, and to be ready with a wifely word of praise at the right moment.

But it wasn't all fishing—they went to Skye, taking the car with them, and spent the night at Portree, so that Sarah might have a chance to see as much of the island as possible. And he took her along the coast road too, north to Lochinver, and then inland to Lairg, where they lunched and then on to Dingwall and Loch Garve, where they left the car to allow Sarah to stare spellbound at the Falls of Rogie. She gazed in silence, and presently put out a hand and slipped it into Hugo's. After a minute, he loosed it gently and put an arm around her shoulders and drew her close, and for all that his touch was casual, Sarah felt a small thrill at it, instantly dispelled by his placid voice bringing her down to earth again with some rather prosaic facts and figures.

They went on to Achnasheen after that, where they had tea at a hotel overlooking Strath Bran, and then on to the Strome Ferry, and so home. After their meal they sat in the small living room, still light with the late sun of an early summer evening, and later, when she was in bed, Sarah couldn't remember what they had talked about, only wonder at the endless things they had to say to each other. She thought, fleetingly, of Steven and wondered if Hugo thought of Janet, and hoped, hazily and half asleep, that he didn't. She yawned, listening to Hugo walking about downstairs, shutting doors and seeing to the Aga, and, lulled by these homely sounds, she went to sleep.

They stayed just over two weeks at the cottage, and when they finally locked its door and put the key under the water-butt in the garden, Sarah felt as though she had turned the last page of a particularly delightful book. They had said goodbye to Mrs MacFee the day before, but all the same, she was at her cottage door to wave to them as they went past early in the morning.

It was glorious weather. They lunched in Edinburgh and stopped briefly in York, then went on to Monk Fryston, a village to the south of the city where there was a hotel which had once been a twelfth-century manor house. It was set in idyllic surroundings, and was, Sarah considered, a most romantic place. Her bedroom was vast and luxurious, with a bathroom which could have done justice to one of the glossy magazines. Influenced by her surroundings, she changed for dinner, and put on a straight little dress in pale coffee silk, one of the village paragon's masterpieces. She added the earrings which Hugo had given her for good measure, and was rewarded for her pains when Hugo tapped on her door and then stopped short as he entered. He said at once:

'How pretty you look, Sarah—that dress is perfect with your tan.' He raised quizzical eyebrows. 'And the earrings.'

She went a little pink under his admiring eye. 'Well,

it's such a lovely place I felt I should try and do it justice.' She twiddled an earring absently. 'Hugo, do you always stay in this kind of luxury?' She stopped and frowned, then tried again. 'Is it because we're on holiday?' It still wasn't quite what she had meant to say; she had sounded rude. She peeped at him to see if he was offended. Apparently not. He leaned easily against the door, his hands in his pockets. He looked well turned out, idle and completely assured.

He said silkily, 'My dear good girl, I like comfort and the good things of life, and I shouldn't dream of offering you anything less than that—you are my wife.'

He was smiling, but he was also, she saw, annoyed. She took a step towards him and said contritely, 'There, I knew it sounded wrong when I said it—I didn't mean to criticise you, you know. I love having b-bathrooms all to myself and champagne at dinner, only what I meant was—I don't mind if I don't—I'm happy without them.' She added, still trying desperately to make herself clear, 'The cottage was perfect.'

She had a sudden vivid memory of standing at the stove in the early morning, frying bacon and eggs, watching Hugo through the open door, chopping wood in old corduroys and an open-necked shirt. She raised troubled eyes to his and said baldly, 'I didn't know you were so—so—rich—this sort of rich.' She waved an expressive arm around her. It was a relief to see that he was no longer annoyed. He left the door and came across the room to her and she felt the firm touch of his hands on her shoulders. He said gently as though he were talking to a child:

'My dear, you are surprisingly naïve, and it's refreshing. My money isn't important. I have a good deal more than most people, perhaps, and I use it how and when I wish...'

She interrupted, 'Oh, Hugo, I do beg your pardon! I'm sure you use your money wisely and you're not in the least selfish—no one else would have bothered with Mrs Brown, and I expect there are quite a number of Mrs Browns you've helped, and Dick Coles told me that you're godfather to all his children and that you're always buying them presents...and Kate's Jimmy told her you gave Matron bottles and bottles of super sherry for the nurses' dance and didn't tell a soul...' She paused, a little incoherent and out of breath, to see laughter surging over him. She said crossly, 'What's so funny about that?' then smiled, albeit reluctantly because he was smiling at her—not laughing any more; staring at her in an odd speculative way. 'Am I a disappointment to you?' she asked slowly.

She felt his fingers bite into her flesh. 'On the contrary, my dear Sarah—you have been in many ways a delightful surprise.'

'Because I can cook?' she queried practically. 'People seem to think that if one is a nurse, one is incapable of doing anything else.'

He took his hands from her shoulders and said lightly, 'I believe you to be capable of anything, Sarah. And now shall we go down to dinner?'

They reached Richmond the following evening, and getting out of the car, Sarah thought what a lovely house Hugo's was. There were Bourbon roses out in the front garden, and the soft pink of a New Dawn climber mingled with the rich mauve of wisteria on the house walls. They went inside, to be welcomed by Alice's quiet warmth and to sit by candlelight in the dining room eating lobster Thermidor and the strawberries and cream she had served after it. Afterwards they sat in Hugo's study; he at his desk, reading a pile of correspondence, while she, having devoured the few letters which were hers, sat quietly doing nothing at all. There had been a letter from Kate, written in haste and excitement because Jimmy had got the Surgical Registrar's job—for Steven would be leaving when he married Anne Binns. The news was heavily underlined and surrounded with exclamation marks, then lost in a pageful of wedding plans. Sarah had put the letter aside, resolving to ask Kate over for the day. It would be nice to hear all the news, although hospital life had never seemed so remote. There were letters from her mother and father too, and her brother, who had flown over from his regiment in Germany for the wedding and to have a brief glimpse of the bride and groom. Apparently he thoroughly approved of Hugo and was looking forward to seeing them both again on his next leave.

Hugo's voice cut through her vague thoughts. 'Anything in your letters?' he enquired idly.

She told him about Kate, and about Steven too, and he said:

'Ah, yes. I'm glad Jim got the job—I had a word with Binns about him.'

She exclaimed warmly, 'How kind of you, Hugo—what a dear you are!'

She was sitting in a leather easy chair within the soft glow of a red-shaded lamp. She smiled at him, unaware of the beautiful picture she made. He glanced up briefly and then down again to his letters. When he spoke it was about quite another matter.

'We're bidden to a cocktail party to celebrate Anne

Binns' engagement—er—Thursday week. Will you accept?'

She looked at him anxiously. 'If you were alone—I mean before we married, you'd have gone, wouldn't you? So we'll go—only don't leave me alone, Hugo.'

He put his letters down and sat back. 'No, I'll not do that, Sarah—but it's a good idea to plunge in at the deep end, however cold the water.'

He got up and pulled up a chair to sit beside her. 'I've not opened these yet. They'll be invitations of one sort or another—shall we look at them together, and decide about them? There's a letter from my mother too, and my sisters,' he tossed them into her lap, 'and there's this.'

He handed her a card. It had a drawing of an unlikely-looking bride and groom standing under an archway of horseshoes, any available spaces being filled with cherubs and rosebuds.

'Mrs Brown,' said Sarah instantly. 'Bless her shaky old heart!'

The verse inside was as unlikely as the cover, and underneath it Mrs Brown had written in a careful, spidery hand:

'To dear Dr and Sister, knowing you'll be Happy.'

Sarah avoided her husband's eye. 'I suppose she doesn't think of us as Mr and Mrs.'

'Do you?' His question was unexpected.

She answered him, a little flustered, 'I don't know... I'd like to go and see her one day soon.'

'That's easily arranged. Come up to town with me in the morning. I'll drop you off somewhere and you can shop if you wish and we'll meet for lunch. While I'm at the clinic you can sit and drink tea with her. I want to have a look at her anyway.'

The morning sun was glorious. Sarah took advantage of it to wear one of her new dresses—a shirtwaister of silver grey lawn, cunningly pleated and tucked. She was aware how nice she looked as they strolled along Cholmondley Walk. There were few people about, the dogs had the place to themselves, and when Hugo whistled them to heel they obeyed him rather huffily, implying in a doggish manner that it was a day to spend out of doors.

Hugo dropped her outside Fortnum and Mason's. She watched him drive away feeling a little lost, then turned to examine the tempting displays in the windows. He had bidden a cheerful goodbye and urged her to buy whatever she pleased and charge it to his account, and when she demurred on the grounds that no one in the shop would know her, informed her placidly that he had already taken care of that contingency. It was still barely half past nine. Sarah wandered round the food department, then found her way to the cosmetic counters where she spent a pleasant half hour choosing some new lipsticks. They weren't a great deal of money and she had several pounds of her own in her handbag—she opened it and found a small roll of notes neatly ringed with a rubber band and bearing a message in Hugo's awful handwriting that it was an advance on her allowance.

She counted it stealthily while she had coffee—for an advance it seemed a lot of money, but presently she was rather glad, because she saw just the scarf her mother had been wanting for some time, and then exactly the gloves she had been searching for. She strolled up Regent Street and on an impulse purchased all that was necessary for the making of a *gros-point* chair cover, and was appalled at its cost, but it would take a long time to stitch and it would be pleasant to do when they were home in the

evenings. All the same she was secretly a little appalled
at her extravagance as she made her way to St George's
Hotel where Hugo had said he would meet her at half past
twelve. He was waiting for her, although she had taken
care to be punctual, and took her up to the bar, where she
admired the view while they drank their sherry and he
talked of nothing in particular in his pleasant way. Sarah
looked around while she sipped, and was glad she was
wearing the shirtwaister and the white straw hat with
its grey ribbon—it was a pert little hat and the ribbon
matched her eyes as well as the dress.

She ate *sole el Mansour* because Hugo had suggested
that she might like it. It was as delicious as he had said it
would be; so were the raspberries and cream which followed it. They were drinking their coffee when he said
reluctantly, 'We must go, Sarah, or my new OPD Sister
is going to hate me for evermore.'

They both laughed because he had already told her
that Sister Vines was exactly what he had wished for—
middle-aged and married and pleasantly dowdy, poor
fodder for the hospital grapevine.

He had left Sarah in Phipps Street, waiting patiently
in the car until Mr Ives had opened the door and ushered
her inside the dark little hall. She had turned to wave, and
he had lifted a casual hand in farewell and driven away.

Mrs Brown was delighted to see her, but her delight
didn't quite mask the fact that she wasn't well. Her elderly
face was too pale and lined; her ankles, Sarah noted with
a nurse's eye, were badly swollen. She had been twice to
the hospital, she informed Sarah, driven there by someone whom she described as 'a kind old geezer in a bowler
'at', who Sarah guessed was a member of the hospital car
service…and Dr Coles had seen her and suggested that

she should go back into hospital, but she had refused. She ate a chocolate from the box Sarah had brought with her and enquired about the honeymoon. Over tea, Sarah told her about the cottage, and when Mrs Brown observed, rather wistfully, that it sounded rather like Hyde Park, she found herself fighting a ridiculous desire to cry...but Mrs Brown, for all the fact that she was making no progress at all, seemed happy. She welcomed Hugo when he arrived, submitted cheerfully to a lengthy examination and then sat, Timmy once more on her lap, answering a great many questions. When he had at length finished she said comfortably, 'I ain't so well, Doctor dear, and it's no use you telling me to go into 'ospital again, for it's of no use, and I'd rather be 'ere with Timmy.'

Hugo was sitting on the side of the bed, his stethoscope swinging from one hand. He said kindly, 'Then, you shall stay here, Mrs Brown. Your own doctor—Dr Bright, isn't it?—is back again. I'll ask him to visit you and our good friend Mrs Crews will perhaps pop in rather more frequently.'

He smiled and got to his feet, and Sarah, who had been quietly watching him, was aware that if ever she was ill she would want Hugo to look after her and no one else. His glance flickered over her and she got to her feet and said goodbye. Mrs Brown looked from one to other of them.

'It's nice ter see yer so 'appy,' she said. 'Come again, Sister dear, and you too, Doc.'

On the way home Sarah asked, 'Is Mrs Brown going to die soon?'

'Yes—within a few weeks. We could keep her alive a little longer in hospital, but she would hate every minute of it. I'll see that Mrs Crews understands the position.'

She said diffidently, 'I should like to go and see her—you don't mind?'

They had stopped at the traffic lights; he turned and looked at her coolly.

'My dear girl, why should I object? I'm your husband, not your keeper. Did you enjoy your shopping?'

She felt snubbed and she wasn't sure why; perhaps he didn't like her being inquisitive about Mrs Brown, but after all, she had known the old lady for a year or more when she had been in OPD. She replied in a subdued voice that yes, she had had a very pleasant morning, and remembered the money she had found in her handbag. It didn't seem quite the moment to mention it, but she said a little stiffly:

'Thank you for my allowance. It was thoughtful of you, Hugo.'

He didn't answer and after a pause she asked, 'Did you have a busy clinic?' With this remark she had better luck. He told her about it with no sign of ill-humour, so that she began to think that she had imagined it all. They stayed at home that evening, talking shop in a relaxed way for a good part of the time, and Sarah got out her *gros-point* and sat by the open window, and presently the talk turned to the garden and the house, and small everyday matters, so that she felt like a real wife.

The days passed quickly and smoothly. Sarah settled into a gentle routine which she found she enjoyed very much. She had thought that she would miss the busy life of hospital, but this was not so. Alice had proved herself to be a gem, handing over the reins of housekeeping without withholding her support, so that within a week Sarah was beginning to feel her feet. She took over the flowers for the house and a few odd dusting jobs and busied herself inspecting drawers and cupboards, and twice a week, when Alice was free, she cooked.

She took the Rover out several times and found that she wasn't as nervous as she had expected to be. Greatly daring, she drove to St Edwin's and brought Kate back to Richmond on her day off. Her friend had a great deal to say about everyone in the hospital, with the notable exception of Steven, so that when Sarah asked, with no sign of emotion, when he was leaving, Kate stared at her in surprise. 'Sarah,' she exclaimed, 'you aren't—you don't still...' She caught Sarah's eye. 'No, you couldn't possibly. Your Hugo's marvellous—you're the envy of every female at St Edwin's. Are you happy?' she demanded.

'Very,' said Sarah, very quickly and not giving herself time to think about it. 'I only asked because Hugo and I are going to Steven's and Anne's engagement party next week.'

Kate was all attention. 'What will you wear?' she wanted to know. It was an interesting topic of conversation and lasted them until it was time for her to go back to meet her Jimmy. Sarah drove her to the hospital very carefully, mindful of the rush hour, and on the return journey so busy with her thoughts that its terrors were quite dimmed. Hugo wouldn't be home for dinner, so there was no need for her to hurry. Alice was out too; she would have the house to herself for the whole evening. Hugo hadn't been home for dinner on Tuesday evening either; he had said he had work to do. She wondered what that work was, and thought wistfully that although they were such excellent friends, she didn't like to ask. She supposed that when one was married—really married, and loving one other—one didn't need to ask what the other one was doing, because life would be shared anyway. She sighed, deep in thought, and stalled the engine, and an irate taxi-driver leaned out of his cab to tell her what he thought of her, looked at her lovely, unhappy face and shouted instead:

'Hard luck, miss!' and waited patiently while she got noisily into gear.

The house was quiet when she got in. She went into the garden with the dogs, then went to the kitchen and made a sandwich because she couldn't be bothered to cook anything, and when she had tidied everything away, she roamed the house, looking at the portraits on the walls, and examining the china and silver, of which Hugo had a small but choice collection. In the end, she went to bed with a book, and read the same page over and over again before she shut it, turned out the light and lay awake listening for Hugo. When he came at last, she heard him pause at her door and call a soft good night, but she didn't answer.

Chapter 5

She overslept the next morning. It was Saturday and Hugo was free all day. Alice had called her, for her morning tea-tray was in its usual place beside the bed—she must have gone to sleep again. When she got downstairs Hugo was in the garden, reading his post. He looked up briefly and said pleasantly, 'Good morning, Sarah.' He smiled. 'Lazy-bones! It was barely eleven when I got in and you must have been asleep when I called goodnight.' His grey eyes were suddenly raised to hers. 'You weren't asleep, perhaps?'

She evaded a direct answer. 'I must have been tired—I expect it was the result of driving to St Edwin's twice in one day.'

'Did you? Good girl! Just for that I'll take you to the theatre and supper afterwards…the Mirabelle. I've got tickets for that show at the Comedy.' He tucked an arm into hers. 'Come and have breakfast—I'm famished.'

Sarah, dressing for her evening out, surveyed her person in the long mirror in her bedroom and decided that she didn't look bad at all. She had bought the dress in Salisbury with part of her father's cheque, and now she was glad that she had; it was sugar-pink organza with a scooped-out neck and long sleeves caught into a tight buttoned cuff—it looked faintly Regency, and she had dressed her hair to match it in a honey bun. The earrings looked fabulous with it too. She turned from admiring them as there was a tap on the door and Hugo came in. She caught up her purse and said, 'I'm ready—will I do?' in a happy, excited voice.

She revolved slowly, so that the dress blew out in soft folds around her, and stopped to face him. He was standing with his back to the door, with his hands behind him. He said gravely:

'You look like a fairy princess—I only hope you won't disappear during the evening.' He left the door and she saw the velvet case he was holding. 'You should have had this when we were married, but I had no opportunity to get it from the bank. It was my grandmother's—a gift from my grandfather when she was his bride, just as it is now a gift from me to my bride.'

There were pearls inside—a double string with a diamond clasp. She held them in her hands and said, breathless with delight, 'They're gorgeous—fabulous!' She gave him a long look, trying to read the expression on his face. But it wasn't for her to read; she gave up after a moment and said in a small voice, 'Thank you, Hugo—will you put them on for me, please?'

She felt his cool fingers on her neck, and then, hands resting lightly upon her shoulders, he turned her round to face him again. He put a finger under her chin and stood staring down at her, then released her and said lightly, 'Are you ready? Will you need a wrap?—it's a warm night.'

She answered him, not really aware of what she said; she had thought for one moment that he was going to kiss her, but he hadn't. And she was disappointed.

The evening was magic; the play was excellent and the Mirabelle a fitting background for the pearls. She hardly noticed what she ate, and they danced, not talking. They got back home at three o'clock and he kissed her lightly on her cheek and said, 'Up to bed with you.'

Sarah was suddenly petulant. She wasn't a little girl, to be told when to go to bed! 'I'm not sleepy,' she said slowly.

He turned from locking the door behind them. 'Well, I am,' he said mildly, and she turned without a word and went upstairs to her room, only pausing at the door to say, 'Thank you for a lovely evening, Hugo. I enjoyed it.' She waited a moment hopefully, but all he said was, 'Good. Sleep well.'

She lay seething with a rage she didn't understand, and her last waking thought was that never—never would she wear the pink organza again. She was vague as to the reason for this momentous decision and she was suddenly too sleepy to bother, anyway.

It was on Tuesday again that Hugo called over his shoulder as he left the house that he wouldn't be back until after nine at the earliest, and would she mind being on her own. Before Sarah could utter the sharp observation which sprang to her lips, he had gone. She watched the car slide away with a smouldering eye, then tried to forget about it. But she thought about it a good deal dur-

ing the day. Perhaps he went to his club, or visited an old
friend—a cold reasoning voice at the back of her head
asked what kind of friend, and she decided against pur-
suing this dangerous train of thought. One day, when the
occasion was right, she would mention it. She had other
things to occupy her mind, she told herself stoutly. There
was the matter of a new dress for Mr Binns' party—she
had several in the cupboard which would do very well,
but there was no harm in looking around. She had a game
with the dogs, talked house with Alice and then went to
Harrods, where she found a very simple and consequently
very expensive dress in honey-coloured silk jersey—it
would be exactly right for the pearls. She bought it, and
because the day stretched before her into a lonely evening, took a taxi to Phipps Street.

Mrs Brown was glad to see her—she was also very
much worse, although she made no mention of this,
merely asking Sarah in a small, breathless voice if she
would make tea for them both. Sarah had brought her a
bedjacket, a frivolous thing, pink and frilly. They admired it together and drank their tea, then Sarah, on
the pretext of talking to Mr Ives, went in search of Mrs
Crews and arranged for that good soul to let her know
immediately if Mrs Brown should become worse. She
went back to Mrs Brown and stayed another half hour
or so before taking her leave. It was only four o'clock—
she went home and took the dogs for a long walk, then
went to bed early after a lengthy talk with her mother
on the telephone, in which she gave a somewhat inaccu-
rate account of life in Richmond in a voice which was a
little too cheerful.

She was glad about the new dress when they arrived at
Mr Binns' home, which was a splendid house in Hamp-

stead, furnished to the last inch by a well-known decorator. It was like walking through the pages of *Ideal Home* but far less interesting, for nothing had been left to individual choice. Mrs Binns had obviously submitted to the dictates of the current fashion in furniture. Sarah, studying a peculiar chair as they crossed the imposing entrance hall, hoped that she was happy with it.

The rooms were full, but she knew a great many of the people there—Matron, the consultants, members of the Hospital Committee—she had an acquaintance with them all. There was a number of younger men and women too, friends of Anne Binns, she supposed. Sarah said the right things to Anne and thought she looked rather pretty in a mousy sort of way. Her dress was quite lovely, and a good thing too, thought Sarah waspishly; with a figure like that... Meeting Steven wasn't as bad as she had thought it would be; perhaps it was the new dress and the pearls, or the gentle pressure of Hugo's hand under her elbow, which made it possible for her to greet him so easily and congratulate him with every sign of sincerity. She had expected that the pain of meeting him again in such circumstances would be acute, but she felt nothing at all except a well-concealed embarrassment; perhaps that was what being numb with pain meant—probably she would feel dreadful later on. She went around the room greeting those she knew and receiving a great many good wishes in the process; it was probably coincidental that Steven joined the group she found herself with. She knew none of the people in it very well, some not at all. They went away one by one, leaving her with Steven.

He said rapidly, 'I want to talk to you, Sarah.'

She gave a polite smile. 'But I don't want to talk to you,' she said coldly. She glanced round the room as she spoke; Hugo wasn't to be seen, unless he was behind her, and she couldn't very well turn round and look.

'You're not in love with him,' Steven said roughly, 'you married him to spite me.' His eyes fell on the pearls, and he gave a sneering little laugh, so that Sarah felt rage bubble up into her throat. She went white, swallowed the rage and said softly, 'How dare you, and how insufferably conceited you are!'

This time she did turn round. Hugo was at the other end of the room, talking to Matron. With the most casual air in the world he strolled across the space between them, bringing Matron with him. He ignored Steven and said pleasantly, 'Darling, I've just been telling Miss Good what a phenomenal cook you are.' His manner was placid, but she caught the gleam in his eyes as he smiled down at her. She didn't stop to think what the gleam might be, but returned his smile with one of pure relief and said gaily, 'Oh, Hugo, have you been puffing me up?'

She transferred her smile to Matron, who said comfortably, 'And why not? And what is more, your husband has invited me to dinner on the strength of it.'

By some means, she wasn't sure how, Hugo had got between her and Steven. He stood close to her and had caught her hand in his and held it lightly while he asked Steven in a polite voice which wholly covered his dislike of him what his plans were for the future. Sarah felt they must present a picture of perfect wedded bliss, but the glow of satisfaction the thought had engendered faded into a peculiar hollow feeling that it was only a picture. She arranged a date with Matron, and when Mr Peppard joined them, answered his fatherly jokes with just the right amount of pertness, and presently, having bidden her hostess goodbye with the gentle good manners Hugo deserved of her, went home with him.

He hardly spoke on the short journey save for trivialities about the evening, but when they were home, sitting over a leisurely meal, he asked:

'What did Steven say to make you angry, Sarah?'

She hesitated, then, 'He was offensive.'

Hugo selected a peach from the dish before him and asked, 'Shall I peel it for you?' and proceeded to do so. After a moment he said gently, 'I am aware that he was offensive. I thought you would hit him.' He smiled briefly and his grey eyes, very compelling, met hers across the table. 'What did he say, Sarah?'

She said miserably, 'It doesn't matter, does it?'

'Not in the least. That's why I can see no reason why you shouldn't tell me.'

She looked at him with a smouldering eye, annoyed at his bland persistence, and said clearly, 'He said I wasn't in love with you and that I had married you to spite him.'

She hadn't known what he would say, she only knew that she was put out when he chuckled dryly. 'Conceited fool!' was all he said. He passed her a plate with the peach on it, and took one for himself. 'By the way, I shan't be in tomorrow evening, Sarah—perhaps you would like Kate or some other friend to come to dinner and spend an hour or two.'

She put down her fruit knife with a hand which shook ever so slightly.

She spoke with a certain amount of violence. 'No, I would not! You...on Tuesdays and Fridays you come home late!'

He glanced up with raised eyebrows, there was the hint of a smile at the corners of his mouth. 'Yes, I do, don't

I?' he agreed imperturbably. Sarah waited for him to say something—anything, but he didn't. It was like having a door shut quietly in her face. She put her napkin down on the table and got up and ran from the room and upstairs, where, to her own amazement, she burst into tears. She felt better afterwards—probably it was the result of seeing Steven again—she thought about him, and was surprised to find the process rather dull. She gave up after a time and had a bath and went to bed. She heard Hugo go out with the dogs and then lock up for the night, but he didn't come upstairs. She guessed he had gone to his study; it was past midnight when she heard his quiet step pass her door and cross the landing to his room.

She felt foolish and self-conscious when she woke up the next morning, but when she went downstairs at her usual time it was to find Hugo waiting as though nothing unusual had occurred. It was a breathless day, the sun already brassy in a thunderous sky, the river reflected the dull clouds, making it look like sluggish oil. They strolled along by the water and she talked a little wildly of anything that came to mind, jumping from one subject to the next with a fine disregard for context. When she at last paused for breath, Hugo enquired, 'Are you going to visit Mrs Brown today?'

She hadn't thought to do so, but now that he had put the idea in her head she said yes, she rather thought she might.

'May I suggest that you don't take the car? I think we're in for a storm, and driving in blinding rain can be unpleasant. Take a taxi up after lunch.'

They turned for home and she answered meekly, 'Very well, Hugo,' secretly relieved because she hated thunderstorms anyway. She remembered then that Alice would be out that evening, and hoped it would have cleared away by the time she got home. She said so to him, then went scarlet, because it sounded as though she was getting at him because he wouldn't be home. He didn't answer, though, and after a minute she concluded that he hadn't been paying attention to what she had been saying.

It was raining by the time she reached Phipps Street. The taxi-driver looked at her curiously when she paid him outside the shabby little house, and when Mr Ives appeared in the doorway, scowling horribly, Sarah made haste to assure the man that there was no need for him to wait. She soothed Mr Ives, whose scowl was due to anxiety over Mrs Brown, and went upstairs to greet the invalid and arrange the flowers she had brought with her in a dreadful china vase with 'A present from Southend' written in gold across its front. It was one of Mrs Brown's treasures and the sight of it led the old lady to a series of reminiscences about day trips to that popular resort. It worried Sarah to see that she was in bed, sitting comfortably enough, it was true, with Timmy under the quilt, and her new bedjacket on. Doc, she assured Sarah, had told her it would be a good idea if she stayed in bed until her dinner, so after Mrs Crews had been to tidy her up, she popped back in. That it was now almost four o'clock in the afternoon seemed to have escaped her notice, and Sarah saw no point in telling her. They had tea, and she produced the chocolate cake Mrs Brown was partial to, then sat listening to the old lady's snatches of talk. Every now and then Mrs Brown dropped off into a light nap, and woke up apparently refreshed, to continue where she had left off.

Sarah hadn't meant to stay so long, but Mrs Crews would be coming at five, and it seemed a shame to leave

Mrs Brown by herself. Thunder had been rumbling for
the last hour or so; now there were fitful flashes of lightning; she wondered uneasily if she would be able to get a
taxi. She was washing the tea things when Hugo walked
in. He smiled and nodded at his patient and said to Sarah,
'I counted on you staying until Mrs Crews got here,' and
proceeded to examine Mrs Brown in a casual fashion
which didn't deceive Sarah at all. He hadn't quite finished when Mrs Crews arrived and without looking up
he said quietly, 'Don't go, Sarah.'

So she stayed, standing with her back to the window
so that she shouldn't see the lightning. He gave Mrs
Crews some instructions and said goodbye, then waited
while Sarah made her farewells and then followed her
downstairs to where Mr Ives was waiting. She stood
while the men talked, only half listening, but when they
were at length on the pavement she stood stubbornly
where she was.

'Jump in,' said Hugo cheerfully, but Sarah stayed
where she was. 'I shall take a taxi, thank you,' she said
with an hauteur which was spoiled by an ear-splitting
crash of thunder. He looked up and down the empty
street.

'Don't be mulish, Sarah. Taxis seldom come along
here, you know.'

'If you think you have to come home with me,' she
burst out, 'just because I said I didn't like thunderstorms—there's no need. I—I was joking.'

'You're a shocking liar, Sarah.' He laughed softly. 'I'm
not taking you home, anyway. There's something I want
you to see.'

She eyed him uncertainly. He looked quite serious.

'Get in, my girl. There's no time to explain now—I'm late already.'

She got in at that, and Hugo started the car at once without saying any more. The journey wasn't a long one; he picked his way through the maze of small streets between Bethnal Green and the Whitechapel Road and eventually turned into a drab street improbably called Rose Road, and stopped before a two-storied house, one of a row; and distinguished from its neighbours by the fact that its lower windows were painted white with the words *Surgery. Dr John Bright* written upon them in large black letters. Sarah let out a slow breath and turned to Hugo, but he said quickly:

'Not now, Sarah—come inside.'

She did as she was bid, following him meekly through the ramshackle door which led directly into a bare waiting room very full of people, all talking at the tops of their voices. They stopped as Hugo entered, however, and rather raggedly chorused a 'Good evening, Doctor' and stared at Sarah. Hugo paused on his way to one of the doors at the back of the room, drawing her to a standstill too. 'My wife,' he said to the room at large. 'She is a trained nurse and has come to help this evening.' There was a murmur of interest and Sarah smiled uncertainly, then coloured when a voice said, 'Cor, Doc, you got yerself the fairy orf the Christmas tree and no mistake!'

There was a little ripple of good-natured mirth in which Hugo joined before he took her by the arm again and ushered her into one of the rooms at the back. There was an elderly man there, going bald and stooping. He had rugged features and bright, dark eyes; they searched Sarah's face as she went in and he straightened up. Hugo said easily, 'Hullo, John. I've brought my wife—Sarah, this is John Bright who runs the practice. He's kind enough to let me come along and help twice a week.'

The smile he gave her was wholly friendly, which did nothing to lessen her feeling of guilt. She had thought… Heaven knows what she had thought… She raised troubled eyes to his, but Dr Bright was speaking.

'I'm delighted to meet you, Mrs van Elven. Hugo has told me so much about you; and don't believe a word he says—he keeps this place going. I'd never manage on my own, and well he knows it.' He paused. 'There's a room next door where Sandra, our clerk, sits. Would you like to sit with her?'

Sarah put her gloves and handbag down on the hideous little mantelshelf. 'I'd like to help,' she said simply. She looked at Hugo as she spoke. He was smiling. 'Why not? Heaven knows we can do with it, eh, John? Come and meet Sandra—I daresay she's got some sort of white coat you can wear.'

Sandra was young and blonde and mini-skirted and patently pleased to see a fresh face. She pinned Sarah into a white overall, very starched and much too large, and confided that the sight of blood fair turned her up, and they'd get on a fair treat with another pair of hands.

By the end of the evening Sarah wondered how they had managed with only the three of them; she undressed babies and struggled with small children wearing clothes which were a little too small for them and therefore not at all easy to peel off, let alone put on again; she tested urine and took temperatures and did a few simple dressings, and cleaned the dirt from hands and faces and feet—good honest dirt from good honest workers who told her sheepishly that they hadn't had time to clean up before surgery hours.

The last patient went just after nine o'clock and Sandra, with a cheerful, 'So long', followed him. The doctors lighted their pipes and settled down to notes and forms. Sarah tidied up, turned off the gas from under the old-fashioned sterilizer and then sat down on the hard wooden chair in the tiny room used by Hugo. He looked up briefly, smiled and went on with his writing. She sat quietly, watching him, until Dr Bright put his head round the door and said, 'There you are, how about coffee in my flat?'

He looked a little wistful. She peeped at Hugo who wasn't looking at her and said at once, 'There's nothing I'd like better—I'm exhausted after all that hard work!'

She smiled at Dr Bright, looking, for an exhausted person, remarkably pretty and lively. Hugo hadn't looked up, but she sensed that he was pleased with her answer—perhaps they always had coffee after the surgery had closed.

Dr Bright lived alone on the second floor. He had a daily woman, he explained to her, who cooked and cleaned. He added stiffly that his wife had died several years ago and that he had a son, running a hospital in Mombasa. He led the way into a comfortable sitting room, very much cluttered up with books and papers and old copies of *The Lancet;* he swept a pile of them off a shabby but enormous armchair and invited her to sit down. Instead, she asked tentatively, 'Would you let me make coffee? I'm sure you and Hugo don't get much time for a good talk.'

She listened to the steady rumble of their voices as she boiled milk and found mugs, and then, inspired by a sudden idea, she put her head round the door.

'Are you hungry? How about some sandwiches, or have you had a meal?'

They hadn't, nor for that matter had she. The fridge yielded a surprising hoard of comestibles. She took in the coffee, and then, preceded by a delicious smell, omelettes stuffed with bacon and tomatoes and mushrooms. When she returned with her own, they had already demolished theirs.

'I told you she was a good cook,' Hugo commented as he got up to replenish their coffee mugs. While he was in the kitchen, Sarah said quickly:

'Would I really be a help if I came every week? Twice a week, isn't it?—with Hugo. I don't want to be in the way...'

Dr Bright looked at her over the heavy rims of his glasses.

'My dear Mrs van Elven, of course you will be of help—we need someone desperately, but I can't afford an assistant and I'll not let Hugo put his hand deeper into his pocket than he has done already.' He smiled. 'The omelette was delicious.'

She laughed. 'I'll make a cheese soufflée next time—only it'll take a little longer.' She broke off as Hugo came back. He said nothing, only smiled, so presently Sarah cleared the dishes away and went back into the kitchen, and when she had tidied up, got ready to go home.

In the car, on the way to Richmond, she said half defiantly:

'I told Dr Bright I'd come with you to help,' then added hastily, because she had sounded overbearing, 'That is, if you don't mind. It would be nice to have a little job... not that I'm bored or anything like that. I can always find lots to do at home, and there's the garden—and the dogs; but there's still time over...'

'You don't need to make excuses,' Hugo replied shortly. 'We shall be glad of your help. It's a busy practice,' and added as an afterthought, 'John and I have known each other for years.' And that was all he said. After a short silence, she began to talk, rather aimlessly, about the weather, hardly noticing that he did no more than make polite comments from time to time, because she was busy with her own thoughts.

Inside the house, in the dim-lit hall, he said almost curtly: 'I expect you're tired—I'll say goodnight. There's some reading I must do.' He took a handful of letters from the marble-topped side table and walked away from her to his study, went inside and shut the door with quiet emphasis. Sarah started up the stairs, getting slower and slower, until half way up she stopped, turned round, and ran down again and across the hall to the study door and went in before she could change her mind. Hugo was standing with his back to her, looking out of the open window, the dogs beside him, but he turned round as she went in and took a couple of steps towards her, saying, 'Sarah, is anything the matter?'

She stayed by the door. 'Yes, there is. I had no business to suggest to Dr Bright that I should work for you both— not without asking you first.' She sought for words. 'I thought you would be glad,' she said woodenly, 'but you're not. I—I pried into something private you didn't want me to know about. I'll write to Dr Bright and make some excuse...'

She turned to go, to be checked by his quiet, 'Just a minute, Sarah.' She turned to face him and he went on, 'If you choose to remember, it was I who—er—put the idea into your head to visit Mrs Brown.' She blinked and then nodded. 'I also suggested that you should not take the Rover.' She nodded again. 'And I counted on you— being you—staying with Mrs Brown until five o'clock when Mrs Crews arrived. I knew that if I left the last two or three cases to Coles I should find you still at Phipps Street.' He paused, staring at her. 'I could have brought you home even then, if I had wanted to.'

She gasped. 'You didn't mind me going to Rose Road.' Her voice rose a little. 'You wanted me to…' She frowned heavily and looked magnificent, but she gave no thought to that. 'Why couldn't you have just said so?' she demanded.

He said blandly, 'I should prefer you to—er—like me for myself, not for what I do.'

Sarah digested this in silence, understanding very well what he meant. It was romantic, even a little dramatic, that a successful Harley Street specialist, presenting an immaculate person to his own world, should choose to help out in a scruffy little surgery near the Whitechapel Road. It would impress any girl less level-headed than herself. She twiddled her wedding ring, admitting to herself that, level-headed or not, she was impressed too. She glanced up and found his grey eyes upon her.

'I see you understand me,' he remarked smoothly.

She said at once, 'Oh, yes. But you see, you need not have kept it a secret, because I like you already, and I can't imagine anything you might do making any difference to that…even though I don't know you very well.' She sounded forlorn, but only for a brief second, for she went on briskly: 'Why were you angry coming home just now?'

'Not angry,' he corrected her patiently. 'I was uncertain as to whether I had done the right thing after all. Rose Road is hard work, and dirty and smelly—far worse than OPD. I realised that perhaps I had let you in for a worse job than you had had before we married.'

Her ill-humour and unease quite evaporated. She smiled widely and asked, 'Was that all it was? But I shall like it very much, really I shall, and it's only twice a week.' She added with unconscious candour, 'I shall be with you too.'

There was no expression on his face, nor in his voice.

'Er—yes, so you will. I didn't realise you would wonder where I was.'

'Hugo, how ridiculous you are!' she remarked roundly. 'Of course I wondered! I even thought that you—you wanted to get away from me or—or something…'

He said gravely, 'Never that, I promise you, Sarah.' His voice sounded strange, but she couldn't see his face clearly, because he had his back to the light. She said with relief, 'Oh, good! I'm glad we're friends again—I don't like it at all when we fall out; now I'm going to bed, for you must be wanting to be by yourself.' He didn't answer this, but gave a half-smile as she went to him and reached up and kissed his cheek. 'Goodnight.'

It was several days later that Mrs Crews telephoned. Sarah had just finished arranging a bowl of flowers on the dining table—it had taken her a long time to do, but was, she considered, well worth the trouble she had taken. The telephone cut across her gentle thoughts and she went into the sitting room to answer it. Ten minutes later she was in the car, thankful that the morning rush hour was over as she made her unhindered way to Phipps Street.

Mrs Brown was in bed, the awful pallor of her pinched

little face in cruel contrast to the pink bedjacket. She said in a thin, cheerful voice, ''Ullo, ducks. Funny, I was just thinking about you and the doc.'

Sarah smiled warmly at her. 'Now, isn't that funny,' she remarked cheerfully. 'Because I told the doctor that I was coming to see you today and he said he'd pop in later and take a look at you before we go home.'

Mrs Crews was at the sink, placidly preparing a dinner Mrs Brown wasn't going to eat. Sarah caught her eye.

'If you'd like to do your shopping, Mrs Crews, I shall be here for an hour or so.' They exchanged an understanding look. 'I'll come down to the car with you, there's something I have to bring up.' They went down together and at the door Sarah said, 'I've not had time to let my husband know... Did you get a message to Dr Bright?'

'Yes, 'fore I rang you, ma'am. He's out on a baby case—Sandra said twins.'

Sarah dug into her handbag, wrote a number on a leaf of her notebook, tore it out, and gave it to her companion. 'Dr van Elven will be at St Edwin's by now—it's getting on for two o'clock. Will you ring this number and give him a message from me? That Mrs Brown is very poorly and would he please come here when his clinic is finished.' She paused, frowning. 'There's nothing more to be done, you know. Mrs Brown doesn't want to go into hospital and there's nothing more to do for her. I'll be quite all right here, so don't rush too much.'

'You're alone in the 'ouse until four o'clock,' said Mrs Crews doubtfully. 'I'll pop in about three to see 'ow things are. It ain't right you should be on yer own.'

She trotted off, and Sarah went back upstairs, carefully carrying something she had taken from the car. She deposited it on the small table drawn up to Mrs

Brown's bed and saw Mrs Brown's face light up. There had been no time to gather flowers from the garden— she had picked up her floral masterpiece from the table, and brought it with her, bowl and all. Mrs Brown gazed at it with pleasure. 'Cor!' she said in a whispering voice. 'All them lovely flowers—you shouldn't 'ave, Sister dear.' She stroked Timmy, lying under her hand. ''Ow about a cuppa?'

Sarah made tea and they drank it together, and Mrs Brown talked a great deal about everything under the sun in a voice which rapidly became more breathless, until she said, 'I think I'll 'ave a little nap.'

When she was asleep Sarah felt her pulse—it was almost imperceptible, as were the shallow breaths. The old lady's face was very pinched and very tranquil. Sarah looked at her watch; it was a little after three—an afternoon had never seemed so long. She thought about Hugo, and longed for him to come.

Mrs Brown opened her eyes when Mrs Crews came softly in and they all had tea again, only this time Mrs Brown only took a sip or two, lifted carefully against her pillows by Sarah, who said comfortably:

'The doctor will be here presently.' There was no need for her to say more, because Mrs Brown had gone to sleep again, and Mrs Crews, after performing a soundless pantomime to show that she would be back again, crept away.

The old lady still slept when Hugo came quietly into the room. He stood in the doorway and gave Sarah a swift all-seeing glance before he turned his attention to his patient. He put his case down on the table in the middle of the cluttered little room and took his stethoscope from it and asked quietly, 'Where's John Bright?'

Sarah was still sitting by the bed, Mrs Brown's hand

in hers. She looked at Hugo with eyes shining with relief. He seemed to fill the room; she was conscious of
the confidence and calm and gentleness he had brought
with him. Just for a moment her lip quivered, but her soft
voice was steady.

'Mrs Crews tried to get him. He's out on a midder
case—twins.'

He nodded and bent over the bed to put a large cool
hand over Mrs Brown's and Sarah's as well. His touch
was very reassuring but brief. He straightened up again
and looked at her with the careful noncommittal mask
of his profession upon his handsome face. She asked
worriedly:

'Did I do right? Should I have got an ambulance?'

He shook his head. 'Perfectly right, my dear. No point.'
His eyes left hers and studied Mrs Brown, who opened
her eyes with the abruptness of a small child and said
breathily, 'There you are.'

He lowered himself carefully on to the side of the bed.

'Hullo, Mrs Brown,' he said, and frowned with mock
severity. 'What have you been doing the moment my
back is turned?'

She managed a faint chuckle. 'Don't you be bamboo-
zling me, Doctor dear.' She paused to get her breath. 'Because it ain't no use, for all you're a good kind man.' She
closed her eyes and then opened them again. 'Thanks fer
all yer've done—and ducks 'ere. Them flowers...'

Her glance invited Hugo to admire them, and he did
so, concealing his astonishment at the sight of his highly
valuable and prized Rockingham flower bowl gracing
her bedside table, he murmured, 'Delightful,' and Mrs
Brown said, 'Timmy—yer'll give 'im an 'ome?'

'Certainly—you can be sure that he will be happy and cared for.'

She sighed and slept again, to wake presently and fix Sarah with a tired eye. 'Me name's Rosemary—it's a nice name for a little girl.'

Sarah, knowing what she meant, said cheerfully, 'It's a lovely name. When—when we have a little daughter, she shall have your name.' She didn't look at Hugo as she spoke, but she didn't think he would mind her saying that, it was so obviously what the old lady wanted to hear. It was a harmless lie that would hurt no one—that wasn't true; she was conscious of her own deep hurt even as she smiled at Mrs Brown, who gave the ghost of a chuckle and closed her eyes and didn't open them again.

There were things to do, of course, and presently Mrs Crews came and Hugo said, 'Come along, Sarah,' and she found herself outside on the landing with him. It smelled of fish and chips and hot vinegar, and the tap over the sink in the corner was dripping steadily. She choked on a sob she was trying to suppress and found herself in Hugo's arms, crying into his waistcoat. She heard him say, 'My poor darling, you have had a bad day,' and accepted the handkerchief he offered, mopped her face and blew her beautiful nose with resolution and said in a watery voice:

'I feel better now, thank you. So silly of me!'

He still held her in a comfortable, impersonal grip. 'No,' he said in a kind voice. 'Not silly. I'm only sorry I couldn't leave the clinic and come to you at once.'

She looked at him in genuine astonishment. 'But of course you couldn't—all those people waiting for you.'

He looked as though he was going to say something at that, but instead he bent and kissed her gently, then led

her downstairs where Mr Ives was waiting by the door.
Hugo kept his arm about her while he spoke briefly to
him, and she stood quietly within its comfort, not listening. When they reached the pavement she said helplessly,
'Oh—two cars,' and stood staring at the Iso in a helpless
way until Hugo took her handbag and got the keys before opening the Rover door and pushing her gently on
to the seat. He got in beside her, started up the engine
and said matter-of-factly:

'We'll leave the Rover at St Edwin's for the night—
perhaps you would come up tomorrow morning and drive
it back. We'll pick up a taxi and come back here and go
home in the Iso.'

When they got back again to Phipps Street, he put
her firmly in the car and said firmly, 'Stay there, Sarah,
I shan't be long,' and went into the house. Presently he
came out again with the Rockingham bowl under one
arm and Timmy under the other. He was followed by
Mr Ives, who came across to peer at her through the car
window. He said hoarsely:

'I'll miss yer, Sister.' He put out a hand and shook hers
solemnly. 'Be seeing yer,' he said.

They were halfway home when she roused herself to
speak. She stared at Timmy, sitting on her lap, and asked,
'Who's going to see to…?'

'I've arranged things with Ives and Mrs Crews. Don't
worry about it, Sarah.'

His voice was calm and very kind; she found that she
wasn't worrying for the simple reason that he had told
her not to.

Inside the house, she took Timmy to Alice and went
back to the hall in time to meet Hugo coming in with

the Rockingham bowl. She followed him into the dining room and watched him put it back on the table.

'I hope you didn't mind me taking it, Hugo; there wasn't time to pick anything—I was in a hurry, and I'd just arranged the flowers in it—it looked gorgeous.' She stopped, appalled to find her voice wobbling. 'I—I was going to wear my jersey dress when you came home because it matched so well...'

He was standing in the shadow, so she was unable to see his face very well. 'How delightful of you,' he said after a pause, 'although you look charming in that dress.'

She looked surprised. 'This one? Why, it's that old cotton thing I wore when I was at Mother's.'

'Yes, I remember.'

She found herself blushing and didn't know why. 'I'll run upstairs and change,' she said. 'I shan't be more than ten minutes.'

He talked about Mrs Brown during dinner, gently at first, then with a cheerful matter-of-factness, and presently led the conversation to other things. 'I think,' he said, as they drank their coffee, 'we might have a few people to dinner, don't you? We owe one or two already, don't we? Shall we have the Coles and Kate and Jim to start with, and then something more ambitious with the Binns and Peppards and Matron?'

'Black tie?' Sarah asked anxiously.

'Oh, yes, I think so, don't you? It will give you an opportunity of wearing one of your pretty dresses...the pink fairy-tale princess would be nice. There are plenty of roses in the garden to match it—you could do another centrepiece.'

She agreed, not sure if he was teasing and then sure he was when he asked:

'Not scared? You shouldn't be, you know. A colonel's daughter...'

She got up and said hotly, 'I'm not a colonel's daughter any more, but a doctor's wife—and proud of it!'

Her own words had surprised her; she had really no idea of saying them. To cover her confusion she went over to the piano and started to play. She played well, but with a regrettable lack of attention, for her thoughts were confused and needed sorting out. After a while she jumped up and said:

'I think I'll go to bed.' It was barely nine o'clock, but Hugo got out of his chair and went to the door with her without mentioning this fact. She stared up at him as they said goodnight, trying to read she knew not what into his placid, gently smiling face. She went upstairs, feeling confused.

Chapter 6

During the next few weeks, Sarah found herself wondering about the state of her own feelings. For a few days Mrs Brown's death had occupied her thoughts to a certain extent. She had gone to the funeral with Hugo and Dr Bright and an astonishing number of people from Phipps Street. They had been bidden to the room on the top landing afterwards, where Mrs Ives dispensed strong tea, fish-paste sandwiches and slab cake stuffed with unlikely-looking cherries, and everybody had congratulated everybody else on the success of the whole undertaking. Dr Bright had seen her astonished look and explained, 'This is exactly what Mrs Brown would have wanted—I can think of no better memorial to her.'

She looked across the stuffy little room to where Hugo was talking to Mr Ives and the funny little man who lived on the landing below. He appeared completely at ease—

she suddenly wanted to be beside him, sharing his feelings and thoughts. She turned back to Dr Bright, looking unhappy, but unaware of it, and he said briskly:

'You'll be along this evening, I hope, Sarah? It's such a luxury to have you to do the bandaging and cope with the babies—you're not sorry you started?'

She smiled. 'No—I like it very much, and I see more of Hugo.'

She enjoyed the sessions at Rose Road. She had bought herself some white overalls which fitted her, and called Hugo 'Doctor' in front of the patients, and if they exchanged half a dozen words of a personal nature during the evening, that was a rarity; yet they were together and she felt as though she was sharing at least part of his life, albeit a very small part. About his practice in Harley Street she knew very little indeed, and when, one day, she had made the suggestion that she should call upon him there, he had discouraged her, though in the kindest possible way. They walked the dogs each morning, it was true, but that was only half an hour at the most, and although he had never once given her the smallest hint that he preferred to be alone, she wished he would suggest that she sat with him in his study while he read his post, just as she had done that first evening. He was the pleasantest of companions, kind and considerate, and amusing too…she wondered if it was she who had changed, and had she really been content to see so little of him when they first married? And yet they enjoyed each other's company. They went out together frequently; she had everything she could wish for. He was generous to a fault. He had taken her down to spend a Sunday with her parents, and she hoped he would suggest a walk; but he didn't, preferring to discuss world politics with her father. And yet he had been quite delightful on their way home, although when she had thought about it afterwards, his conversation had been quite impersonal. The ugly little idea that he was beginning to regret their marriage crossed her mind and she suppressed it sternly as being unworthy of him; but it was there, all the same, to worry her in an unguarded moment. Sometimes, when she awoke in the night, she wondered if he still thought of Janet, and greatly daring, she essayed to bring her name into conversation, only to be quietly checked by Hugo, firmly introducing another topic.

It was during their first dinner party that she made an interesting discovery about herself. They had invited Matron and John Bright, as well as the Coles and Kate and Jimmy Dean. She sat opposite Hugo, well satisfied with the elegantly appointed table, with its silver and crystal and the Worcester dinner service—she had conjured up a flower arrangement almost exactly the same as the one she had taken to Mrs Brown, and had put on the honey-coloured dress and the earrings and pearls. Their glances met for a moment and she felt a thrill of pleasure at the pride and admiration in his eyes. She had spent a long time in the kitchen with Alice, enjoying the planning of the menu. They had come up with artichoke soup, followed by roast beef with one of Alice's superb Yorkshire puddings, the whole rounded off by *fraises Empress* with a *sauce sabayon*. Now she watched the results of their labours being eaten with every sign of enjoyment by their guests. Hugo was a good host; the wine was excellent; the company were enjoying themselves. She was roused from her pleasant domestic thoughts by Kate, who asked her if she had heard the news that Steven was to marry Anne Binns in October. Sarah stared at her, struck dumb by the sudden awareness of a total lack of interest in Steven. She hadn't thought about him for days—weeks; she saw no reason ever to think of him again. She went on looking rather vacantly at Kate until Hugo's voice bridged the awkward little pause. 'There you are, darling, A chance to buy a magnificent hat!'

She turned her fine eyes upon him, still looking astonished at her discovery, and said on a happy sigh, 'Yes, Hugo,' thinking how marvellous it was when he called her darling, although it was only because they had guests. She gave him a dazzling smile, and mindful of her duties, pressed Matron to try a little more of the *fraises Empress*.

When the last of their guests had gone, she wandered back to the drawing room and began to plump up the cushions, while Hugo, who had lingered to let the dogs into the garden, stood in the doorway watching her. She peeped at him once and saw that he was smiling.

'Congratulations, Sarah. A most successful evening— it seems that I have a wife who is a first-rate hostess as well as a beautiful woman.'

She gave him a smile and began to rearrange the flowers in their vases. Surely he would mention Steven's marriage, then it would be easy to tell him. She started on the cushions once more, but when at last he said, half laughing, 'Did you want to tell me something, Sarah?' she said immediately and pettishly, 'No, I don't.'

She went up to bed soon after that, and cried herself to sleep without knowing why. She woke up during the night with the thought very clear in her mind that of course she couldn't tell Hugo that she no longer loved Steven—it would create an impossible situation: living with a man you loved and who loved another woman, even if that woman was a memory. Only if, by some miracle, he fell out of love with his Janet would she be able to tell him. She sat up in bed, made aware of what she had been thinking—it wasn't Steven she had loved at all, it was Hugo. It had always been Hugo, and like a stupid blind fool she hadn't known. And now that she knew, what was she to do about it? Impossible to tell him. She lay down again, telling herself to be thankful that at least he liked her enough to have made her his wife—perhaps in time he might love her. She went to sleep on the thought.

He was in the hall when she went downstairs in the morning. He had his back to her, bent over the morning papers. The sunlight shone on his grizzled head; he looked distinguished and elegant and very large. He turned his head and smiled at her and her heart thumped against her ribs in a way that it had never thumped before. She stopped on the stairs, quelling an urgent desire to fling herself into his arms and forcing himself to move across the hall towards him and wish him a good morning in her usual voice. She had the peculiar sensation that her feet weren't quite touching the ground, and when they left the house and he took her arm with his usual friendliness, she shook with excitement and happiness so that he asked her in some astonishment if she was cold. It was indeed a cool morning, but not sufficiently so to warrant a shiver.

She said lightly, 'It must be a goose on my grave,' which sounded so nonsensical that they both laughed, but she missed the penetrating look he gave her; only when she glanced up, she thought how happy he looked. They had crossed the river and were strolling along the Promenade, the dogs racing up and down, playing their own particular games.

'I think we might go to Holland in a week or so,' Hugo remarked. 'September's a good month for a holiday, don't you agree? I think I can manage the last ten days or so—if this weather holds, it will be delightful. We'll take the car—Holland's a small country, I can show you quite a lot of it in that time. We can visit my family too, but I think we will stay on our own, don't you? There's a good hotel at a small place called Vierhouten, not so very far from my parents, and within easy reach of Hasselt and Wassenaar where my sisters live. Gemma, my youngest sister, lives at Nîmes—we could drive down from Holland, and spend the night somewhere on the way, stay a couple of days at Avignon and visit her from there and return along the west coast to one of the Channel ports.'

Sarah agreed that it sounded delightful. He must have thought about it a good deal; no one could reel off a trip like that without having made a few plans first.

'What about your aunts in Alkmaar—the three old ladies?' she asked.

'Ah, yes. We must try and spend a few hours with them…it won't be too much of a rush for you?'

They were nearly home. She went through the gate ahead of him, her head full of the delightful prospect of having him all to herself for two weeks. 'I shall love it, Hugo. How marvellous to have two holidays in one year!'

He laughed, looking surprised. 'Well, I usually manage to get away several times. It's difficult to take more than two weeks at a time, otherwise it's merely a question of fitting appointments…have you enough money to buy any clothes you want?'

They were in the dining room, facing each other across the table. Sarah poured his coffee and as she passed it to him said in a wifely voice, 'You've only got ten minutes. I've still got some money left from my allowance.'

'Then you had better spend it, as your quarterly allowance was paid in at the beginning of the month; we've been married three months now, three months and ten days, to be exact.'

She went pink. 'Oh, do you remember it too?' The pink deepened, for she hadn't meant to tell him that she knew, almost to the hour, how long they had been married. He had gone over to the sideboard, and looked at her over his shoulder. 'I have a businesslike mind,' he observed. 'Would you like two eggs or one?'

She had no appetite. 'I'll just have toast,' she said, and saw his brows lift and heard the faint mockery in his voice.

'Slimming? I can assure you there is no need.' She shook her head as he came back to the table, to subject her to a bright searching look as he sat down. 'Feel all right?'

She said a little vaguely, 'Yes, thank you,' wishing with all her heart that she could tell him just how she felt. Instead she drank her coffee and broke her toast into small pieces, not eating any of it.

After he had gone, she wandered into the garden and then back into the house again, where she did a little desultory dusting and made out a list of groceries with Alice before getting her shopping basket. She enjoyed her visits to the grocer and the time spent choosing vegetables and fruit, and discussing cuts of meat with the butcher. She enjoyed, too, being addressed as Mrs van Elven. She mooned along the streets, savouring the delightful fact that she bore Hugo's name. It was strange that until that moment she hadn't thought very much about it, but now, because she loved him, everything was different.

It wasn't until after lunch, while she was pottering in the garden, that common sense once more took possession of her mind, reminding her that she had been living in a dream world all the morning, in which Hugo had most conveniently fallen in love with her. She had been aware of the foolishness of her thoughts and brushed the awareness aside because they had been so delightful, but now she sat down on the grass and began to tidy away the bits and pieces of her dreams—it wouldn't help at all to allow them full rein. She would have to be constantly on her guard with Hugo, so that he would never know. They had been happy so far; she had done her best to be the sort of wife he apparently wanted, she hoped with some success, although she was uneasily aware that she hadn't penetrated his deep reserve. Perhaps she never would. Janet would have been the only one to do that.

She got to her feet and started to garden with a furious energy which strove to overcome the sudden despair for the future. Her eyes blurred with stupid tears; it was only when she stopped to blow her pretty, reddened nose and wipe her eyes that she became aware that she had uprooted a flourishing colony of carnation cuttings. She planted them carefully once more, sniffing prodigiously as she did so.

She went by bus to Harley Street, and found Hugo waiting for her in the car. At the sight of him, misery and love and delight at seeing him again caused her to look so peculiar that he asked for a second time that day if she was feeling all right. As she got into the car he watched her with an expression she was unable to read, but mindful of her good resolutions, she said cheerfully that yes, she was feeling marvellous, and told him what she had done with her day and then enquired with a somewhat overpowering brightness if he had been busy. He gave her another look before he replied, a thoughtful, frowning one, and began to tell her, rather abruptly, about a chance meeting with an old colleague.

Rose Road looked dingy and forlorn despite the children playing on its pavements, and the dogs running to and fro between the idlers who had stopped for a gossip and the hurrying figures intent on getting home or round to the pub. The waiting room was full too. Sarah said hullo to Dr Bright and went to put on her overall in Sandra's slip of a room, and then, armed with notebook and pencil, began to sort out the patients. There were more than usual for Hugo that evening, and several new ones as well as the hard core of bronchitics and arthritics and stomach ulcers. Sarah knew the regulars by name as well as by sight now, and exchanged a word with each of them as she made her way round the packed room. They called her 'missus' or 'luv' and occasionally gave her a peppermint to suck or a banana. She, in her turn, kept the vase on the centre table filled with flowers from the Richmond garden. She was gradually replenishing the vintage magazines too, although no one read very much, preferring to talk. The first once or twice she had been there, they had gossiped unhappily in church voices, glancing at her uneasily, but now she was accepted. She moved to and fro, making sure that they had their turns right, unruffled by the cheerful four-letter words which flew around her ears. A few of the words she had never heard before, and since that occasion when she had asked Hugo to explain one of them to her, and he had looked at her with outrage and told her that he would be damned if he would, she had thought it best not to bother about them.

The waiting room emptied slowly; there were still half

a dozen people left in it when three youths came in and sat down together. They didn't speak at all but stared around them at the other patients, who glanced at them quickly and then looked the other way. Sarah, coming in from Dr Bright's surgery, sensed uneasiness in the air; she also smelled their cigarettes.

'No smoking here, please. If you want to finish your cigarettes, you can go outside. You won't be going in to doctor yet—I'll call you.' She smiled at them impartially. 'Names?'

The boy in the middle spoke. 'We don't want ter wait—we'll go in next.'

She looked at him coolly. 'People take turns here,' she said reasonably. 'And put out those cigarettes.'

They laughed and blew smoke in her face, and were disconcerted when she took no notice at all, merely asking, 'Which of you is the patient? And who is your doctor?'

They didn't answer. Sarah put her notebook back in her pocket and said, hiding a fast rising irritation, 'I suggest you go—you're wasting my time.' Before she could say anything else, the boy in the middle caught her by the wrist—not painfully, but she would have had to struggle to release herself. She stood still, annoyed but not particularly frightened. The boys were young and silly and inclined to bully. Out of the corner of her eye she saw the patient nearest Hugo's surgery door get up and go through. He was elderly and slow, but the boys didn't notice. Seconds later, the same door was flung open, and Hugo, looking very large indeed in the bare room, had reached her in a couple of hurried strides.

He put an arm across her shoulders and the boy dropped her wrist, as though it had burned him. Hugo spoke without raising his voice, but it cracked around the boys' heads like a whip.

'You lay one finger on my wife and I'll thrash the three of you!' He inspected them deliberately down his patrician nose, while his fingers exerted a reassuring pressure upon her shoulder. The boys had drawn together. They threw their cigarettes on to the floor and ground them out hastily, while the youngest and cleanest made haste to say:

'Hey, doc, we didn't know she was yer wife—honest we didn't.' His companions joined in, all talking together. 'It was jist a joke—we 'adn't got nothing to do—we didn't do no 'arm.'

'Quite true,' agreed Sarah, still incensed, but fair by nature. 'They were only being annoying.' She took a quick look at Hugo. His face was stern and there was a gleam in his eyes which boded ill for the culprits. She added hastily, 'I'll accept their apologies if they'll offer them.'

She caught an unexpected sparkle of laughter in Hugo's look—but whatever he intended to say was drowned in a chorus of, 'Sorry, missus,' and, 'No 'ard feelings, lady.' The three of them began to edge towards the door, and almost reached it when Hugo said, 'Wait! Why did you come in here? And don't put me off with a lot of lies…there's nothing wrong with you except idleness. Bored stiff, I suppose?'

They shuffled their feet in deplorable shoes, shrugging their shoulders, and looking helplessly at him. Unwillingly they nodded and the boy who had held Sarah's wrist grinned sheepishly at her.

'You're none of you worth a brass button,' remarked Hugo almost lazily, 'and I don't suppose you know what work is. Come along next week. We could use some extra help—and don't expect to get paid for it!' They looked surprised, suspicious and eventually, pleased. When he said. 'Now—out!' in a manner conducive to obedience, they went.

When they had gone he looked down at Sarah, still held fast against him. 'I'm sorry, Sarah—did they scare you?' His tone was so light that she instantly took exception to it. She had secretly been just a little alarmed, but now nothing would induce her to say so. She said crossly, and decidedly loftily, 'Of course not. I'm not easily scared.'

He might at least have asked her if she felt faint or upset or something…instead, he said shortly, 'No, I imagine you aren't,' then took his arm away from her shoulders and went back to his surgery without another word, leaving her to smoulder.

Five minutes later she was required to bandage a septic finger he had just incised. She did it with an efficient calmness which covered the riotous tumult going on beneath the starch of her overall, and was on the point of slipping out after the patient when he leaned forward and caught her by the arm and said slowly, 'I should never have brought you here in the first place.'

The tumult exploded into a spreading wave of happiness. He hadn't been angry with her at all—only with himself. She gave him a glorious smile, and was shaken when he said silkily, 'You smile—perhaps you will tell me why?'

She gave him a puzzled look. 'Well, I thought just now that you were angry with me, and then I thought it was all right because you were angry with yourself—and now you're angry with me again.' She paused. 'And I'm not sure why,' she finished a little uncertainly.

They stared at each other for a long moment, then he let go of her arm and said in an exasperated voice, 'Oh, my dear girl...' and kissed her swiftly and brusquely on the mouth. He drew away from her almost at once. 'That mustn't happen again.' He spoke in his usual voice, calm, almost casual. She thought he was referring to the three boys, and tried not to think about the kiss, for she felt that it had been given by way of an apology.

Ten days later they gave their second dinner party. Sarah, who had enjoyed the first one enormously, wasn't quite so sure about this one; for one thing she didn't know the people who were coming very well, and they were all a good deal older than she was. But they were Hugo's colleagues, if not his chosen friends, and she quite saw that a certain amount of entertaining was obligatory. He had a great many friends, she was beginning to discover—young married couples, and some who had been married for some years and had children at school, and a handful of rather vague professors who, surprisingly, fitted in with everyone else.

She was beginning to realise too that he had been very considerate when they had first married, introducing her into his life gradually, so that she had never, at any one time, felt surprise at the number of people who made up his circle of friends. Now they were beginning to drop in informally from time to time for drinks in the evening, and occasionally an impromptu supper, and she and Hugo returned the visits. His friends had made her very welcome, and life was altogether enjoyable. That it could be a great deal more enjoyable was something which she steadfastly shut her eyes to, although she had the good sense to know that sooner or later she would give herself away, or worse, blurt everything out to Hugo.

She and Alice had spent a long time over the menu—they were to have *tournedos* with oysters, preceded by flamenco eggs and followed by grilled fresh peaches accompanied by whorls of Chantilly cream. She decorated the table with late pink roses and geraniums and verbena, and wore the pink dress, quite forgetful of her vow never to wear it again. Hugo was late home and she was already downstairs, putting the last-minute touches to the table, when he got in. She went to meet him as he opened the door and was halfway across the hall as he tossed his bag on to one of the wall tables and came to meet her. He stopped an arm's length away and studied her. 'I was beginning to think I should never see you in this dress again,' he said. 'I'm glad you're wearing it tonight—it's most becoming.'

She smiled with pleasure and thought how tired and strained he looked. They would be going on holiday the following week and he looked as though he needed it. She said now, 'Shall I get you a drink before you go up? I put everything ready—I thought it might save you a few minutes.'

He said briefly, 'Good girl. I'll change first and we'll have a drink together before they arrive.'

He went upstairs and Sarah went to the kitchen to make sure that Mrs Biggs had arrived to give Alice a hand, and found that she had. Alice as usual was in calm control of the culinary arrangements; there was nothing for Sarah to do but to stroll back into the dining room and then into the drawing room to switch on some of the lamps there. The room looked quite beautiful. She stood in its centre, loving it, and presently, because there was nothing further to do, sat down at the piano.

She was thundering through the noisier passages of a Beethoven sonata when Hugo joined her. She stopped as abruptly as she had begun and he fetched their drinks with the remark, 'You were playing as though you were running away from something, Sarah.' He gave her a piercing look. 'Are you nervous about this evening? You don't need to be, you know—it's bound to be a success.' She didn't answer, and he went on, 'I've got the tickets for next week—the midday ferry from Dover. I think it will be best if we spend a night in Amsterdam on the way to Vierhouten. I telephoned for rooms this morning.'

She said, 'That sounds very nice, Hugo. I'm looking forward to it.' She smiled fleetingly and went over to the window to let in Timmy and the dogs, then stayed there, looking out into the garden. She felt lonely, even though Hugo was standing, tall and handsome and self-assured, on the other side of the room. Only suddenly he wasn't on the other side of the room at all, but beside her, and before she could draw another breath he was holding her close, smiling down at her with a look which made her heart stop and race on again wildly. He said quietly, 'Sarah, there is something...' and was interrupted by the clanging of the front door knocker. He released her at once, said something forceful in his own language, and then, mildly, 'Our guests, I imagine.'

It was the Sopers, a pleasant couple in their thirties, who lived close by. John Soper was something in the City and had known Hugo for years. Sarah liked him; she liked Margery Soper too—a small, dark woman, good-natured and lively and kind. The Peppards followed hard on their heels, and lastly, the Binns. Sarah greeted them all with a serenity which successfully hid her annoyance. Hugo had been going to say—what? She thought she would never know now, for he hadn't meant to speak; the words had been wrung from his lips—unpremeditated. She thought that whatever he had been going to say would never be said.

Then she dismissed the thought with an effort and concentrated on her role of hostess with such success that after dinner the ladies retired to the drawing room full of praise at her good management, leaving the men to talk around the dining table. 'And let's hope they won't be too long,' remarked Sarah, as she arranged her guests comfortably around the log fire. It hadn't been really necessary to light it, indeed all the windows were open to the quiet September evening, but the room looked so lovely with the firelight flickering and one or two lamps alight. Alice had brought in the coffee tray, and Sarah busied herself with the delicate little cups and saucers, to be surprised when the men joined them almost at once, and then covered in confusion when Mr Peppard said loudly:

'I saw no point in sitting around talking about politics and antibiotics and such dreary stuff when I could be here with you, Sarah, I shall sit beside you and you shall tell me what you thought of Scotland.' He drew up a chair and continued, 'There's an advantage in being elderly, my dear. One can do as one wishes and merely be labelled eccentric instead of ill-mannered.'

Sarah poured the coffee amid the ensuing laughter and then, obedient to Mr Peppard's whim, entertained him with her views on Scotland. But presently the conversation became general and she was free to look around her. Hugo was at the other end of the room, talking to Margery Soper, when Mrs Binns took advantage of a pause to enquire archly, 'I suppose this house contains some splendid nurseries—after all, it was built in a period when large families were the thing. I expect they're on the top floor.' She looked at Sarah. 'Will you use them?'

With admirable composure Sarah smiled at the wretched woman. She was aware that Hugo, as well as everyone else, was listening. She said evenly, 'As a matter of fact, there are some super nurseries on the first floor. They're separated from the front landing by a soundproofed door—such a sensible precaution, don't you think?'

Hugo's voice came pleasantly across the room. 'I've some happy memories of the nurseries in the house—it's virtually sound-proof, as Sarah has said. My sisters and I could quarrel to our heart's content while some poor housemaid acted as an uneasy referee…my grandmother was a little deaf, and my mother in a perpetual state of apprehension as to what we would do next.'

Margery Soper spoke quickly, as though she were picking up a cue.

'Do tell us—do you still quarrel with your sisters? I can't imagine you doing any such thing with anyone. I think you just go on getting your own way!'

Everyone laughed, although Mrs Binns' laugh was half-hearted—she wanted to know more about the nurseries. She knew, as everyone else present knew, that Sarah and Steven had been, at some time or another, in love with each other. It had been providential that Hugo had married her, leaving the way clear for dear Anne…and while she had no doubt that Sarah was happy, there was no avoiding the fact that she was a striking-looking girl and attractive to men. A baby—several babies—would keep her nicely occupied. She decided to pop in for tea one afternoon and ask a few tactful questions…

The last of the guests had gone by eleven o'clock. Sarah preceded Hugo into the hall from the front door. The evening had gone very well—at least, she thought so. Hugo said just behind her, 'Thank you, Sarah. Another feather in your cap…the evening was delightful.'

She stood still and he came and stood beside her in the dim-lit hall.

'I don't remember telling you about the nurseries when we went over the house.' His voice was bland, and although it wasn't a question, she was aware that he expected an answer.

'No,' she answered, her voice very matter-of-fact, 'you didn't. Alice told me, because I asked her. You—you didn't want me to know, did you?' She turned round to face him. 'But I love this house—all of it. I wanted to see all of it, so I asked Alice. You don't mind?'

He said shortly, 'I should have preferred it if you had asked me.'

'Oh, I thought—as you hadn't mentioned it…'

His voice was all silk. 'I had forgotten your discretion, Sarah.'

She said nothing, for there was nothing to say—nothing, that was, that could penetrate the aloofness of his manner. She watched him walk past her into the drawing room and put the guard before the still smouldering fire. He said over one shoulder:

'Would you like to go to your parents on Sunday? It's rather short notice, but perhaps they would have us for luncheon.'

'I'd like that—and of course Mother won't mind short notice. Shall I telephone her tomorrow?'

He strolled back, hands in pockets. 'Yes, will you?' He smiled down at her charming and elegant and infuriatingly good-natured. Sarah's heart bounced against her ribs because he was near and at the same time she felt rage snatch at her good sense. She said with almost painful clarity, 'I wasn't being discreet, I was being kind—at least I thought I was. It must be—painful for you to talk about the nursery wing. It's empty; it could have had yours and Janet's children in it.'

She met his thunderous, astounded look briefly. 'Goodnight.'

She swept past him and started up the stairs. By the time she had reached her bedroom she had regretted every word.

She would have apologised the next morning, but he gave her no chance—there was nothing in his manner to indicate his true feelings. He discussed their forthcoming holiday and wanted to know if she could spare the time to go to Rose Road that evening, and presently left for his consulting rooms, leaving her to wonder if he had heard her at all.

Sarah arrived a little early at St Edwin's and went to sit in the car to wait for him. When he came through the gloomy archway which led from Outpatients, he had Dick Coles and Kate's Jimmy with him. They were deep in discussion, and once they all stopped and bent their heads over the papers he was holding. Watching him standing there, Sarah felt quite light-headed at the sight of him. But the face she lifted to his presently was calmly welcoming, and she greeted the three of them with a mild pleasure which gave no hint of the commotion going on inside her. It was quickly apparent that she was to be given no chance to apologise. Hugo, during the short drive to Rose

Road, began a dissertation on a case of phaeochromo-cytoma which had been referred to him that afternoon. Sarah agreed politely with his deliberations over irregular cardiac rhythm, and marvelled silently that he found so much to say about it.

It was a relief to get to Rose Road and plunge into the cheerful hubbub of the waiting room. Sandra was on her summer holiday, but she had the somewhat erratic help of Shorty and Lefty and Tom, who, true to their promise, had indeed turned up to make themselves useful at the surgery. She had despaired of them on their first evening, but now that they had been several times, they were beginning to be of help. Tonight she set them collecting names, so that she could get the cards from the filing cabinet…but there were several patients with dressings to be taken down and re-done, and any number of specimens to be tested. She began to wonder if half the residents in the area suffered from diabetes.

They were down to their last two patients when the door was flung open and a young woman carrying a bundle rushed in. She thrust it at Sarah, her face parchment white, struggling for words although she made no sound. But she had no need to speak, for the bundle was a very small baby. From the state of the charred tatters around it, it had been very severely burned. It was alive; Sarah thanked heaven for its faint wailing voice even as she winced for its pain. She went straight to Hugo's little surgery and put her bundle on the couch, indicated the mother and set about wringing out a sheet in saline solution. She had it ready as Hugo asked, 'Have you got…?' then stopped because she was already wrapping the mite very gently in it. He said then, 'Hospital—you take the baby, the mother can sit behind. I'll tell John.'

She sat beside him, her pathetic burden in her arms while he drove through the crowded streets. It was the only time she had seen him with his hand on the horn... Casualty were ready for them, because of course John Bright would have telephoned. She handed her tiny patient to a waiting nurse, then took the girl into one of the cubicles and gave her tea while she gently wormed from her all the information the hospital had to have. It seemed a long time that they sat there, though in reality it wasn't above an hour and at the end of that time Night Sister came to say that the baby had a fair chance and that the mother could stay the night in the hospital if she wished. The girl went with her, her face empty with shock. Sarah thought it probable that she didn't realise where she was. Dr Bright would have contacted her husband by now; perhaps when he came she would draw comfort from him.

There was no sign of Hugo. Sarah tidied the cubicle and took the tea cup to the sink and washed it, then started to clear the small cluttered treatment room. She was only half done when she heard a car stop outside and a moment later Dr Bright and a short, thick-set young man came in.

Dr Bright wasted no words. 'Where is she?'

'Children's—Special unit. I'll take Mr McClough up.' She started for the door, the pale-faced young man keeping pace with her. 'Will it be too late for us to come back to you?' she asked as she went.

John Bright was on his way out. 'Of course not—I'll be waiting.'

Children's was quiet, deceptively so, for there was subdued activity in the glass-walled cubicle at the end of the wide corridor. The cot was in the centre of the small room; she could see the plasma drip on its stand

and Night Sister fiddling with it...and Hugo straightening his long back to speak to the Registrar. There was a nurse there too, and the baby's mother. She looked up and saw them coming and rushed out to meet them, not stopping to take off the white gown they had put her into. She hurtled through the door like a small whirlwind and hurled herself into her husband's arms. He held her close and despite his pallor said bracingly, 'Or'right, me darlin', 'ere I am, so yer don't need ter worry no more.'

He gave her a smacking kiss and Sarah half turned away, horrified at the envy she felt for the girl—to envy a woman so unhappy, because her husband loved her! She closed her eyes for a second and when she opened them Hugo had come out into the corridor too and was standing watching her. She turned and went back to Casualty then; there was nothing more to do but wait for him. He came presently, quite unhurried and said mildly:

'I'm sorry you had to wait, Sarah.'

They sat silent as they went back through the late evening. Lefty was hanging about outside the surgery. Sarah saw his quick glance before he looked away with studied indifference. She got out of the car and said, 'Hullo, Lefty, thanks for your help—we couldn't have managed without you.' Which wasn't quite true, although they were improving.

He grinned. 'Garn, missus! 'Ow's the baby?' His narrow chest swelled. 'I fetched 'er dad.'

Hugo joined them. 'I told you you'd be useful if you hung round here long enough. The baby will be all right—we hope.' He took something from his pocket. 'Split that with your pals.'

Lefty took a look at what he had been offered and gave

a shrill whistle. 'Cor! Ta, Doc. You're OK.' He grinned. 'Missus 'ere, she's OK too.'

Inside, John Bright was waiting for them. He had made coffee and while they drank it Sarah made sandwiches, then took them into the sitting room, where Dr Bright said, 'What a woman you are, Sarah! I can think of quite a few women who would be sitting back complaining that they were tired or upset.'

She smiled gently at him. 'I hate to disillusion you; I'm both—but I'm hungry too.' She bit into a sandwich and said, 'I hope the baby does.'

'She's got a good chance, I hear. You looked very— lonely—when we got to Casualty this evening.' He looked at Hugo. 'You have a wonderful wife, Hugo.'

She tried not to look at Hugo, but it was impossible not to do so. He was staring at her very hard and half smiling. After a little pause he said, 'Yes, John, I have.'

She was disappointed. He could have thanked her on their way back from the hospital; he could have told her she was beautiful, and wonderful too, never mind if it were true or not. She remembered then how horrible she had been about Janet and the nurseries and conceded that it had been generous of him, in the circumstances, to agree with Dr Bright. She got up and collected the cups and plates and, refusing help, washed them up with a cheerful clatter.

They spoke very little on the way back to Richmond. Sarah could have told him how sorry she was a dozen times, but, sadly, she couldn't find the words.

It wasn't until Sunday after lunch with her parents, when she elected to take the dogs for a walk and Hugo unexpectedly joined her, that she plucked up her courage. They had reached the top of the hill and had paused to admire the sweep of country around them. She spoke quickly before she could change her mind.

'I'm sorry I was beastly the other evening, Hugo—it was a rotten thing to say. I beg your pardon, and if Janet were here, I'd beg hers too.'

He gave a rumble of laughter. 'If Janet were here your—er—regrettable words wouldn't have been uttered.'

She had been taken aback by his laughter until she realised that of course he was hiding his true feelings. She encountered the mockery of his smile as he observed, 'You know, Sarah, I can't remember feeling hurt. Should I have been?'

She went an indignant pink. 'Please don't joke, Hugo. You told me before we married how you felt about Janet...' She was very earnest.

He stopped smiling and stood staring at her with an expressionless face, his grey eyes a little bleak. He said at last, 'My dear, I'm sorry. I didn't realise that you had so much thought for my happiness. Shall we cry quits?'

He kissed her briefly and she managed a very credible smile, and presently began to talk about their holidays, resolutely ignoring her aching heart.

Chapter 7

They arrived in Amsterdam in a wet dusk. The weather had been pleasant enough when they had landed at Zeebrugge—they had followed the coast road as far as Le Zoute and had tea there and then gone on to catch the ferry at Vlissingen. It was crowded with enormous lorries and long-distance transports, standing nose to tail, hedging them in on all sides. Hugo eased the car between them and they climbed the iron steps to the deck. Sarah had been momentarily taken aback to hear Hugo speaking Dutch to one of the drivers. When they were leaning on the rail watching the grey water of the Scheldt, she said:

'You know, I'd almost forgotten that you're Dutch. Your English is so perfect—well, nearly perfect.'

He smiled lazily. 'Dear me, do I drop my H's?'

'Don't be ridiculous! I didn't mean your grammar—it's just your accent; but only now and then.' She frowned.

'I wish I spoke Dutch—even a modicum. I suppose you couldn't teach me a few words?'

'Perhaps—a word here and there as you need it. My family speak English so you will have no difficulty there.'

She watched Vlissingen advancing towards them across the wide river's mouth; it looked grey and disappointing until she saw the row of houses along its sea boulevard. 'When we go home,' she said, 'perhaps I could find someone to teach me Dutch.'

Hugo laughed. 'Am I to take that as an invitation?'

She gave him a quick sidelong glance to see if he was serious. She was unable to tell. 'You would never have time,' she said flatly, and then, in case she had sounded ungracious, 'Thank you just the same.'

They had said no more on the subject, as it was time to go ashore, and later, when they were crossing the flat countryside towards Bergen-op-Zoom, their talk was of the country around them. The road was good and fast, running through endless fields, showing a vista of villages and tall church spires under a wide sky, into whose empty blue bowl clouds were beginning to pour. They skirted Breda—a tantalising view of churches and steeples, gone in a flash, and then on to the Moordijk bridge crossing the Hollandsche Diep, worthy of a long explanation from Hugo.

Rotterdam was, to her, a jungle of flyovers and bridges and traffic coming at them from all sides. She hadn't quite got used to travelling on the other side of the road for a start, a fact which didn't seem to worry Hugo at all for he drove steadily through the confusion without hesitation, commenting upon the interesting aspects of the city as he did so. It was pleasant to leave the city behind at last, and the motorway with it. It was beginning to drizzle, but the country was pretty now, with small villages whose houses might have come from Brueghel's brush. As they slowed to go through Alpen-aan-der-Rijn, Hugo told her about the International Bird Park. 'If you like,' he said, 'we'll come over one evening for dinner. There's an excellent restaurant and the lighting is rather special, I think you might enjoy it.'

Sarah replied warmly, 'Oh, please, yes—I'd love it. How interesting it all is!' More than interesting—she was just beginning to realise that they would be together for two weeks or more. It hadn't seemed quite true; the idea was so delightful that her heart began to hurry. She was unaware that she was smiling until Hugo's hand came down on her own two hands clasped on her knee. 'Why do you smile like that?' he asked quietly. 'Are you happy?'

He had withdrawn his hand, but she still felt its warmth. He had never asked her if she was happy. She said now, 'Yes, I am—I haven't been so happy...' she paused, for she had been on the verge of saying since she discovered that she didn't love Steven; but of course she couldn't say that. 'For a long time,' she ended rather lamely, then added:

'That sounds as though I haven't been happy, but I have—I like being married.' It sounded naïve, but it was the truth anyway; as much as she would be able to tell him.

He said, his deep voice thoughtful, 'Thank you, Sarah. I believe that we—er—suit each other admirably.'

After that they drove in a companionable silence until he suggested that as they were nearing Amsterdam, she might like to study the map.

They were on the motorway again, passing Schiphol. She stared at it for as long as she was able, then applied herself to the map of Amsterdam.

'It looks like a spider's web,' she said, to be told that she was a clever girl because that was exactly what Amsterdam was. He sent the car racing past an articulated lorry to join the steady fast-moving stream of traffic making for the city's heart. 'Our hotel is in the heart of Amsterdam,' he explained. 'A pity we aren't staying longer, but next time we'll spend a week here—or we can fly over for a weekend.'

They were in the city now. Sarah peered out at the tall thin, quaint houses and the multitude of shops and the ever-recurring canals, and thought privately how nice it was to be able to take casual weekends whenever one felt like it. Her own family weren't poor, but more than one holiday a year would strain the finances. It seemed that Hugo hadn't exaggerated when he had told her not to worry about money. It was a pleasing thought.

Hugo had slowed down. The street they were in was lined with shops and she craned her neck to look at them until Hugo said cheerfully:

'I can see we shall have to have a quick look round before we leave tomorrow—as a matter of fact, we don't need to get to Vierhouten until the evening, that will give us the whole day here.'

She said hastily, 'Oh, I don't mind—really. Only it's all strange and foreign and I'm as curious as a cat.'

He laughed. 'Well, we're almost there. Here's the *Munttoren;* the hotel's across the bridge.'

The hotel was delightfully situated close to a canal and inside it proved to be quietly and comfortably luxurious. Moreover, Hugo had been there before and was remembered. Sarah, standing beside him while he signed the register, wished that she understood even a little of what was being said, and even as she thought this, he remarked in English, 'Forgive me speaking Dutch, Sarah. You'll find the staff speak English—they'll get you anything you want.'

Her room was pretty and very comfortable and had a view of the canal. She stared out of the wide window for a few minutes, then wandered through the intervening bathroom to Hugo's room. He looked up as she went in through its open door.

'Will dinner in half an hour suit you? You can have the bathroom first.'

She nodded. She wanted very much to unpack for him and talk, but there was an air of aloofness about him which prevented her from suggesting it. She went back to her own room and presently, dressed in a silk jersey dress printed in a glorious mixture of pink and cream, accompanied him down to dinner. That her appearance drew a number of admiring glances mattered not at all to her. What did matter was Hugo's pleasant, 'How charming you look, Sarah!'

She ate her dinner with an excellent appetite and in a warm glow of content, and when they had finished their meal, accompanied him on a stroll through the nearby streets. The Rokin housed some mouth-watering antique shops, and although she wasn't very knowledgeable about such things, she knew enough to appreciate the treasures he pointed out to her. There was some particularly fine Friesian silverware, and a variety of golden trinkets which, he explained carefully, probably constituted part of the dowry of some wealthy farmer's daughter two hundred or more years ago.

They parted in the hotel presently, he to read the papers, she to go to her bed, armed with a guide to Amsterdam and the latest Paris edition of *Vogue* which he had conjured from thin air for her delectation. Leafing through it, she decided that one of the many reasons why she loved Hugo was because he was untiringly considerate of her without once drawing attention to that fact.

She was busy with her hair when he knocked on the door in the morning, and although she called a muffled 'Come in' through a mouthful of pins, he merely opened the door a couple of inches and after enquiring if she had slept well, asked her if she would make her own way down to breakfast when she was ready and he would meet her at table. It was another ten minutes before she was ready. She was wearing a new suit for the first time— a toffee-and-white tweed with a silk blouse beneath its jacket. It had swinging pleats and rather nice buttons. Sarah had been horrified when she had asked its price, but it had suited her when she tried it on, and now, taking a long careful look at herself, she had to admit that she had done well to buy it.

Hugo was waiting for her, leaning against the table, reading *De Telegraaf.* He looked up as she approached and said to please her mightily, 'That's new—I like it.'

She sat down, a little pink with pleasure, and at once perceived the small package by her plate. She looked at it and then at Hugo, who said, 'Go on, open it—it's for you, Sarah.'

It was an old Friesian watch chain which she had admired the previous evening, remarking that it would make a gorgeous bracelet. She took it from its box exclaiming, 'Oh, Hugo, it's lovely! How kind of you, and thank you!' She studied his face across the table; perhaps she would see something more than his habitual calm expression. She didn't.

'A trifle to remind you of Amsterdam,' he observed,

and took the chain from her and wound it round her wrist. 'I'm glad you like it.' He smiled then—the kind of smile, she told herself hopelessly, that her brother might have given her; mildly affectionate and good-natured.

They had almost finished their breakfast when Hugo was hailed by a man who had just entered. He made his way rapidly towards their table and Sarah had time to observe that he was as tall as Hugo, although of a heavier build and about his age. Hugo held out a welcoming hand.

'Jan, how delightful! What are you doing here? You must meet my wife.' He looked at Sarah. 'Sara, I must introduce you to one of my oldest friends in Holland— we went to school together. Jan Denekamp.'

She shook hands and smiled delightedly when the big man said:

'I've been wanting to meet you, Sarah—I may call you Sarah? We have all heard such tales of Hugo's bride— all of which are understatements.' He laughed, a deep, jovial rumble, and Hugo said, 'We've almost finished, but do have breakfast.'

His friend sat down at once, but declined his offer. 'I breakfasted hours ago—saw you as I passed. I'm on my way to meet Jacoba and the children.' He turned to Sarah. 'You must meet my wife, and if you can bear the idea, my six children.' He gave her no chance to do more than nod, but rattled on, 'What do you think of Amsterdam? Do you stay long? You will visit Hugo's family, I suppose.'

Sarah said quickly before he could start again, 'We arrived yesterday evening…'

'And leave today,' interposed Hugo. 'I want to show Sarah something of Holland, and we plan to visit Gemma.'

Jan raised his thick brow. 'Quite a trip! I take it you've

got the Iso Grigo with you. Do you like fast driving, Sarah?'

'With Hugo, yes, I do,' she answered promptly, and was rewarded by the look on Hugo's face. Jan Denekamp rumbled pleasantly, 'There speaks a good wife! But there, you have a good husband, unless he's changed in the last year.'

In another five minutes he took his leave, repeating his invitation to visit his home when they had the opportunity. 'Next time you come, eh?' he queried genially. 'Now it would not be kind to ask you, for you are not long married and you wish to be together.'

During the morning she asked Hugo if Jan was a doctor too—a question which made him laugh very much. 'Heaven forbid!' he replied. 'He's in shipping. Do you like him?'

'Yes, very much. Does he ever come to England? I should like to meet his wife.'

'They usually come over for a few days or so before Christmas. We could have them to stay—you'll like Jacoba.'

'And the six children?'

'You'll like them too. I daresay we can find room for them all, could we not?' He added, 'Jan and Jacoba are devoted to each other.'

She said slowly, 'Yes, I thought perhaps they were. I mean, you can tell…the way he said her name.' She paused. 'Anyway, you can tell,' she reiterated defiantly, just as though he had contradicted her, which he had made no attempt to do, saying merely, 'Yes, I daresay you are right.'

She had the absurd suspicion that he was secretly amused, but when she stole a look at him, he was contemplating a somewhat way-out trouser suit in the boutique window she had stopped to study; his eyes were half shut and there was no expression upon his face.

They lunched at *De Borderij*—they had chicken on the spit and an excellent burgundy which she found a trifle heady, and then, because it looked so delicious, she ate trifle piled with whipped cream, remarking happily as she did so that it was fortunate that such things made no difference to her weight. Hugo, who had chosen cheese, agreed with her, pointing out with a twinkle that, under such a happy circumstance, she would be able to eat all the whipped cream she wished to—she had merely to ask.

After lunch, he took her along the *Nieuwe Spiegelstraat,* which, Sarah was quick to point out, was not in the least new, its houses having been built a good two hundred years previously although they were now, almost all of them, antique shops. They strolled along its length and Hugo obligingly purchased her a carved *koekeplank* because she thought it might look rather sweet in the kitchen at Richmond. From there, the shops in the Singel were but a step, and in one of them, Sarah having been much taken with some old Dutch prints in its window, Hugo waited patiently while she chose a selection of them. While they were being wrapped and paid for, she prowled off on her own and when he joined her she was standing before a small bowl—a creamy porcelain, painted exquisitely with puce and pink flowers, touched with green and blue and yellow. When he enquired whether she liked it she said guardedly that yes, it was charming. She loved it, in fact, but if she said so, Hugo would buy it. 'Where does it come from?' she wanted to know. 'I've not seen anything quite like it.'

'Weesp,' said Hugo knowledgeably. 'Some time in the eighteenth century. It's charming.'

She forgot to be guarded. 'It's absolutely gorgeous!' She moved away. 'Hugo, I should like to give you a present too. Is there something you like, something you could use or—or look at every day?'

He said immediately, 'Yes, there is. A pewter inkstand in the window, for my desk.' He smiled at her charmingly. 'Shall I leave you to buy it?'

'Well—yes. Shall I be able to speak English?'

'Certainly—and I'm here to help.'

The inkstand was nice. Sarah bought it and opened her purse to pay, then asked, 'Hugo, can I pay with English money?'

'Of course. Presumably you have a good reason, for I seem to remember that you had a considerable amount of Dutch money with you.'

She counted out her English pounds and while the dealer dealt with change she said, 'Oh, yes, I have. It's a silly reason. I want to pay for your present with my own money—money I earned. I had some left. You don't mind?'

'It makes it twice as acceptable, Sarah. Thank you.' He strolled away to talk to the shop owner and presently she saw him handing over some money—probably, she surmised, paying for the prints.

They left the hotel after tea. Vierhouten was some sixty miles away, but the late afternoon was pleasant and there was no hurry. Hugo forsook the motorway as soon as they had left Amsterdam behind them and took the road through Hilversum and Weesp, then turned into the small byroads which he seemed to know so well. The country was well wooded and the small towns looked prosperous, with villas set in neat gardens and here and there a solid, square house standing well back from the road, half screened by trees. At Soestdijk, Hugo drew up obligingly so that Sarah could take her fill of the royal palace, at the same time furnishing her with a concise history of the House of Orange, then circled away again, back to the country roads through the Veluwe, until they reached the hotel. It sat delightfully in a pocket of woodland—not large as hotels went, perhaps, but comfortable to the point of luxury. Sarah, changing her dress, looked round her room and reflected that Hugo was a man who expected, and obtained, the best things of life.

Later, as they sat over dinner, he asked, 'You like this place, I hope, Sarah? I have always found it pleasant. It has only been reopened for a couple of years, but it's comfortable and the food is good.'

She was eating smoked eel by way of a starter.

'It's delightful. Tell me, Hugo, do you know all the best hotels in Europe?'

'Oh, my dear girl, you credit me with too much,' he answered carelessly. 'And to be honest, I have never found anything better than my—our home.'

'The cottage?' she asked, and saw his eyes smile.

'Ah, the cottage—my bolthole, shall we say? Or rather, our bolthole now, isn't it? Each time I go there, I have the feeling that something wonderful will happen.'

'Perhaps it will,' said Sarah, forgetting to be nonchalant. Her grey eyes stared into his, momentarily lost in a dream world which held her and Hugo and the cottage.

'Don't you feel like it anywhere else?' Her voice was eager, and he gave her a brief, bright glance before replying. 'Now you mention it,' he answered blandly, 'I have recently experienced the feeling on several occasions—

and what is more, I have—er—no doubt that sooner or later that same feeling will become substance.'

Sarah fell silent. Surely he wasn't expecting to meet Janet again, not after all those years? She opened her mouth, intent on asking him, when he said quickly, 'You were asking me about the Veluwe—let me explain...'

The explanation lasted for the rest of the meal, and continued throughout the stroll they took afterwards. Presently Sarah went to bed, stuffed with useful information, and quite out of humour.

They spent the following day doing nothing because Hugo had said that she needed a quiet day before embarking on a round of visits. They walked in the countryside in the morning, and in the afternoon played tennis. Sarah, who was rather proud of her game, was soundly beaten, but consoled herself with the knowledge that Hugo had paid her the compliment of playing his usual game. She was consoled still further in the evening by being taken to dine at *De Ouwe Stee*—a restaurant housed in an eighteenth-century farm. Its interior was exactly what Sarah had been led to expect from her perusal of Old Dutch interiors, and she quite forgot her dinner while she stared around her, asking a great many questions which Hugo answered with competent brevity. Finally he said on a laugh, 'Look, my girl, if I promise to bring you here again, may we dine now?'

She smiled enchantingly, showing a dimple in one cheek which he hadn't previously noticed, and answered him saucily, filled with a reckless desire to egg him on. She knew that she looked nice—she was wearing the pink patterned jersey again, and the soft lighting was most helpful. She allowed her long curly lashes to sweep her cheeks, and allowed the dimple to appear once more. She asked demurely:

'Have you been here before?'

'Oh, yes, several times. With Jan.'

'Just the two of you?' she wanted to know.

He began to smile. 'Naturally Jacoba was with Jan; did I not tell you that they were a devoted couple?'

Sarah studied the fine diamond of her engagement ring as though she had only just recognised its magnificence. 'Oh? Three's such an awkward number.'

'I must agree with you,' he answered in a hatefully bland voice. 'But of course we were a foursome.'

She poked at the *poulet Grand'mère* on her plate with a pettish fork wishing with all her heart that she had never begun the silly conversation. As though she minded with whom he had been! And if he was going to be secretive about it, she couldn't care less...

Hugo chuckled. 'Do ask,' he invited.

She gave him a fleeting, fuming glance. 'Ask what?' she demanded.

'Don't you want to know about the girls I brought here?'

She raised her eyebrows in what she hoped was a dignified surprise, and then, because she couldn't help it, met his amused look.

'I don't care,' she said crossly, and was dumbfounded when he said instantly and with an air of patience:

'Why, Sarah, of course and quite rightly, you don't care. That's why our marriage is so—er—rational. We are, after all, two level-headed and mature people, not young things whose good sense is blinded by our emotions.' He smiled blandly at her and she wished rebelliously that she was a young thing, and not a mature woman whose emotions didn't seem to take age into account. She heard him say:

'I can recommend the ice pudding—would you care for some?'

She said 'No, thank you—just coffee' in a politely wooden voice which barely concealed curiosity and rage and frustration, but he didn't appear to notice but beckoned the waiter and gave the order, and went on talking as though she had never interrupted him.

'The first time I came here I brought a—let me see— yes, she was blonde, tall and handsome.' He frowned in thought. 'And for the life of me I cannot recall her name. No matter. She ate a great deal—no, don't look like that, Sarah—you appreciate your food as you appreciate everything else in life. She had no interest in anything else.' He sighed. 'She was a dead loss.'

Sarah stifled a giggle and then looked severe, but he went on, undeterred, 'We came again a year or so ago. I brought Elsa—a charming redhead, very small and dainty; she had a dainty appetite too because she was dieting—she ate almost nothing and we, perforce, with her. I remember when I had taken her home, I returned for Jan and Jacoba and we went to a village café and ate *Kaas Broodjes* and *Patat Frit* and washed them down with Pils. Jacoba was charming about it, but she is a charming woman.'

Sarah stirred her coffee and observed with a faint choke in her voice:

'How unfortunate you were in the choice of companions.'

He nodded cheerfully. 'Yes, wasn't I? But third time lucky, as they say. Perfection, my dear Sarah—the right size, the right shape, beautiful, intelligent—a charming voice, a healthy appetite…'

'How nice for you!' Sarah spoke with asperity, giving him a smouldering look. He was lounging back in his chair, his gaze intent, his eyes puckered in a smile which brought the colour to her face. She said rather feebly, 'Oh!' and then, because she wasn't much good at dissembling, 'You mean me?'

He said gently, 'I mean you, Sarah. I suppose you cannot object to a husband, however rational, paying his wife a compliment?'

Her heart was in her throat, she swallowed it back to its rightful place before replying. 'Of course not. Thank you—I don't deserve it after being so inquisitive.'

Her heart was still being troublesome. It would perhaps be a good idea to change the conversation. She asked presently, 'What time do we leave in the morning? Are we expected for lunch?'

She didn't know whether to be pleased or sorry that he seemed quite willing to follow her lead.

Before she went to sleep that night, Sarah had promised herself that she would never again give way to the childish impulse to know more about Hugo's life before they met, for even when her curiosity was satisfied, her peace of mind suffered.

Hugo's home proved to be a fair-sized square house, with a pointed scalloped roof, cut square on top, standing in its own grounds well back from the quiet country road. The village was only a mile or so away—nearer, perhaps, but the thickly wooded country around it made it appear more isolated than it was. It had an iron railing fencing it in, a low stone balustrade enclosing a formal garden in the front of the house, and a pair of formidable gates which stood invitingly open.

Hugo said nothing as they mounted the short double step to the front door, and Sarah was glad because she was a little disappointed with the house. From its exterior, she fancied it would be filled with late Victorian furniture of a particularly repulsive sort, and a good deal of red plush. They were admitted by an elderly maid, who exclaimed at some length over Hugo and would doubtless have done the same over Sarah if they could have understood each other. As it was, she uttered a terrifyingly long word in her own language and clasped Sarah's hand. Hugo said gently, 'Mien is congratulating us upon our marriage,' then looked pleased at Sarah's careful, '*Dank je.*'

Mien looked pleased too as she threw the inner door of the entrance lobby with something of a flourish, so that they might enter. Sarah, completely taken by surprise, stopped short, and said, 'Oh!' She had been utterly mistaken. It wasn't Victorian at all, but pure Old Dutch—there were the black and white tiles, the carved staircase, the white plaster walls above shoulder-high panelling, the great Delft plates separating groups of dim family portraits. There was a scattering of tables along the walls and one or two outsize William-and-Mary chairs and an enormous stone chimneypiece.

'Rather unexpected?' asked Hugo from behind her. 'The ancestor who built this house owned a fleet of East Indiamen and made a fortune. He collected his furniture over the years, but refused to part with the furniture he had inherited, so the place is a kind of museum—a very comfortable one, mind you, and if one is born here, as I was, one loves it. I hope you will come to love it too.'

They had crossed the hall as he was speaking and
Mien opened the door into what Sarah rightly supposed
was the drawing room. She had time to see that it was
large and lofty, that its windows were vast and draped
with floor-length curtains, and that the walls were white-
painted wood picked out with gold leaf; then Hugo's hand
under her elbow urged her gently towards the marble
fireplace, flanked by two enormous chesterfields and
several comfortable easy-chairs, from two of which Mijnheer and Mevrouw van Elven rose to greet them with
a warmth which put Sarah entirely at her ease within a
couple of minutes.

They lunched in comfortable state in a dining room
which she judged to be furnished in the French Empire
style; the chairs were heavy and leather-covered, the side
table ornately elegant—she wasn't sure if she liked it, but
perhaps it would grow on her; in any case, she wasn't
going to let it spoil her appetite. She had been a little
nervous of visiting Hugo's family, but now she found
that she was enjoying herself. It was strange and a little
disturbing to see this new aspect of Hugo. In hospital he
had seemed remote, all-sufficient—or so she had thought
during the years she had worked for him. She had obeyed
his requests there without question, and seldom thought
of him as a person…and now, because she loved him,
she could never learn enough about him.

After lunch, Hugo and his father retired to the latter's
study to discuss what his mother called family matters,
but which she informed Sarah as they started on a tour of
the house, would be disposed of in so many minutes, so
that they could enjoy a comfortable dissertation on their
shared love of medicine. As they climbed the staircase
together, her mother-in-law said kindly:

'We are so glad to welcome you into the family, Sarah. You are so right for Hugo; you understand his work and will be such a help to him. He told us how you go with him to Rose Road. How pleased he must be about that, and how you must enjoy working together—such a worthwhile job, my dear. Of course, when the children come, it won't be easy for you.'

Sarah, behind her hostess, and thankful for it, murmured suitably, fiercely dispelling a pleasant vision of a bunch of children, all bearing a marked resemblance to Hugo, trooping upstairs in the wake of a loving Dutch Oma. It didn't bear thinking about. She concentrated upon the portraits lining the walls of the corridor they were traversing and presently recovered her spirits sufficiently to take a real interest in the various rooms they inspected, wandering in and out in a leisurely way while Mevrouw van Elven kept up a gentle flow of small talk.

'Next time you come, my dear,' she said, 'you must stay here with us. We quite understood when Hugo told us that he intended to show you something of Holland in the week or so that you are here, and it is easier for you to stay in hotels instead of coming back here each evening. But he usually comes over several times in the year even if it is only for a couple of days, so we hope to see you very soon.'

Presently they went back to the drawing room and in a little while tea was brought in, followed by the men. They had finished tea and were preparing to go when Hugo's father got up from his chair and came over to sit by Sarah. He gave her a half smiling look which made him look very like his son, and said:

'Sarah, there is something we wish to give you—we were unable to bring it with us to your wedding, and you must forgive us for that, but now you shall have it, as Hugo can arrange things with the Customs.' He put a small velvet box into her hand. 'It is old, you understand, two hundred years old, and now that you are one of the family we wish you to have it. When Hugo inherits'—he waved an arm—'you will of course have what jewels there are, for then they will be yours by right. This little trifle is their forerunner.'

Sarah opened the box. The 'little trifle' was a diamond crescent brooch of a splendour which would bear comparison with her ring and earrings.

'It's beautiful! Thank you both, and thank you for wanting to give it to me. I'll treasure it, but I'll wear it too, because it's too lovely to keep hidden away.'

She bent forward and kissed him on one cheek, then kissed her mother-in-law as well, feeling a little overcome. She was grateful to Hugo when he caught her hand and drew her to stand beside him. 'We'll go somewhere special so that you can wear it,' he promised lightly. 'And now fetch your things, my dear girl—I'll take you out to dinner...'

They were to go again within the week, and still again for the family dinner party Hugo's mother had arranged. In the car she said:

'How lucky I am! Your mother and father might have disliked me.'

Hugo was driving slowly, sitting relaxed behind the wheel. 'Not very likely, I fancy. You're my wife, Sarah, and as a family we share the same tastes and views about the more important things in life.'

Her heartbeats deafened her. 'Am I important?' she asked. He glanced at her, his eyes sharp. 'Of course; I'm old enough to regard a wife as a vital as well as a permanent part of a man's life.'

She swallowed; perhaps this would be the right moment to try and tell him. She drew a steadying breath, but before she could speak, he remarked, 'It was a good day, don't you think? You like my home?'

She swallowed disappointment with resignation. 'Very much, only I didn't know it was going to be quite so— so grand.'

He looked incredulous. 'It doesn't seem grand to any of us, and it won't to you when you know it better. We shall come over quite often, you know. When my father dies, and I hope that won't be for many years yet, and I inherit the house—could you consider living there?'

Sarah didn't need to think. She said at once, 'Oh yes, of course! I should like it very much. Did you think I shouldn't?'

'No. I think I know your likes and dislikes, Sarah, but if you had set your face against it, then we would have dropped the whole idea.'

She digested this in silence. 'You consider me too much, Hugo. I don't expect you to alter your whole life to please me.'

She heard the laugh in his voice as he answered. 'My dear Sarah, let me be the judge of that.'

They did a great deal during the next week. They explored the Veluwe thoroughly; they dined, as Hugo had promised, at the Avifauna's attractive restaurant; they visited Arnhem, where Sarah spent a couple of enthralled hours in the open-air museum and shopped for presents to take home; they went back to Amsterdam so that she might enjoy a trip along its canals, and a brief glimpse of its museums. He took her to lunch at the Hotel de Nederland near Hilversum, and to Alkmaar to see his aunts, three dear old ladies who lived in a house which must have rivalled any museum she had yet seen. They adored Hugo and were prepared to adore her too and made her promise, with a gentle persistence there was no gainsaying, to return soon and spend a few days. She heard Hugo agree to visit them again in the early spring, and bring her with him.

They went to Hasselt too, to spend the day with his sister, Joanna. The September sun shone on the small, partly medieval town, lying, peaceful and old-fashioned, so unexpectedly near the main road. Joanna lived on the very edge of the town, with her husband—the local doctor— and her four children. The children fell upon their uncle once they had offered a polite hand to Sarah, and he had at once disappeared with them to examine a boat they had just acquired. Their father came in from his rounds presently—a rather silent man who obviously adored his wife. The three of them sat over coffee, and Sarah decided very quickly that she liked them both immensely. By the time Hugo had returned with the children, she was firm friends with Joanna, and from the shrewd look he gave them both as he entered the room, Sarah deduced that he had made himself scarce deliberately.

He did the same thing at Wassenaar, romping with lazy good nature with his two small nephews while his sister Catherina and Sarah got to know each other. Catherina was younger than Joanna and pretty, with Hugo's grey eyes and quiet manner. She took Sarah over the house—a large thatched cottage in one of the leafy lanes of Wassenaar. It was delightfully furnished; it must have taken time and thought and money too; but Hugo had said

that her husband was a highly successful solicitor. Sarah
met him at lunch, and was surprised to find him a quiet,
unassuming man with the kind of face she could easily
forget. She tried to get Hugo to talk about the children on
their way back to the hotel, he was so obviously devoted
to them, but he rebuffed her gently, and she went to her
room thinking with something like panic that life was
by no means the simple clear-cut affair she had imagined when they had married. But then she hadn't been
in love with him.

They spent a day in the Noordoost Polder, because
Hugo said it was a miracle of reclamation. Sarah found it
flat and bleak, even though she could appreciate the mag-
nitude of the task the Dutch had performed. She listened
with interest while he explained what had been done.

'We spend our lives keeping our country from slipping back into the sea,' he remarked finally.

Sarah stared at him. She said after a pause, 'It's
strange, in England I never thought of you as anything
but English—Oh, I know from time to time your accent
betrays you, but here you're all Dutch, even while you
speak English to me.'

He began to laugh. 'You know, Sarah, I begin to wonder if you gave enough serious thought to marrying me.'
He was still laughing, but his eyes studied hers intently
so that she flushed and said hastily:

'Oh, but I did—at least I wasn't quite sure at first. It
was…that is…' she faltered a little before his bright stare,
and he caught her by the arm and said, with a return of
his usual placid manner:

'Poor Sarah! I'm only teasing. Let's go to Kampen and
have lunch and then go and see Mother.'

The rest of the day was perfect. Hugo's parents made

much of her over a lively tea and the talk was of the Richmond house, and Scotland, and the possibility of a visit to London later on. 'Come for Christmas,' invited Hugo, 'and perhaps we can persuade Sarah's mother and father to come up at the same time. Would you like that, Sarah?' He turned to smile at her, looking handsomer than ever, so that just looking at him sent her off into a daydream in which he suddenly and overwhelmingly fell in love with her. When he said 'Darling?' in a gentle questioning voice, it seemed, for one blissful moment, part of the dream which had somehow come true.

She caught her mother-in-law's smiling eye and went scarlet, saying hastily, 'That would be marvellous, Hugo,' and was relieved to feel the blush subsiding even though her heart was bouncing against her ribs. She would have to learn not to blush—it was too ridiculous. Apparently Mevrouw van Elven didn't share her view; for she nodded approvingly and said, to no one in particular:

'A lot of girls would give their eye teeth to colour up so prettily.'

Sarah said miserably, 'Would they? But I'm not a girl—I'm twenty-eight.'

She heard her father-in-law chuckle from the depths of his chair.

'I should have said that you are very much a girl, my dear. And if you're still uncertain, why, you can ask Hugo when there's no one else about.'

This remark almost had the same effect of making Sarah blush all over again. She was saved by Hugo, making some trivial remark which turned the attention on to himself. She gave him a grateful look which he acknowledged with a faint smile and a twinkle which had a bad effect on her pulse again. She turned from him with res-

olution and applied herself to taking her mother-in-law's
advice about Dutch cooking.

Two days later, they were back again—this time for
the dinner party. Sarah dressed with care in the honey
crêpe, because the diamonds needed something simple.
She was standing with the pearls in her hands when Hugo
came in. 'Will I look gaudy?' she asked anxiously. 'I did
want to wear everything.'

He studied her carefully and at leisure. 'That dress
is very plain and a lovely colour; you won't look in the
least gaudy.'

He took the necklace from her and fastened it, then
turned her around to face him. 'You look very beautiful, Sarah,' he said. She thought he was going to kiss
her, but he took his hands from her shoulders and said
lightly, 'Shall we go? We don't want to be too late leaving Mother's. If we get away by nine tomorrow we should
make Nevers in time for dinner.'

They were the last to arrive, although not late, and
were immediately engulfed by the family. Sarah found
herself talking to Catherina's husband, Franz, and discovered that his nondescript face covered a quick wit and
a sense of humour she hadn't expected. She sat next to
Huib, Joanna's husband, at dinner, and he was nice too,
although neither of them could hold a candle to Hugo.
He was at the other end of the table on the opposite side,
and although he gave her an occasional smile they had no
chance to speak, and when they all went into the drawing room he went and sat with his mother, apparently
content to see Sarah talking to Joanna. She felt resent-
ful and neglected, and although she knew she was being
silly, she contrived to turn her back. Which was a pity,
because he stared at her most of the evening.

She had recovered her temper by the time they were ready to drive back to the hotel. They chatted about the evening and his family until she asked, 'Hugo, I thought your sister was called Joanna, but Huib called her something quite different. It sounded like Shot.'

She felt him laugh in the dimness beside her. 'I think you mean *Schat*. It's a term of endearment—er—treasure. It's used a good deal between mothers and children and husbands and wives.'

'Is that the only word—what do they say for darling?'

'We don't use darling as the English do—everyone is darling, are they not? Go to any party in London, and the air rings with the word. We say *lieveling*, but not very often in public—and *liefje*—little love. Perhaps we don't use endearments as much—I don't know. What I do know is that when we say them we mean them.'

They had arrived back at the hotel, which Sarah found annoying, for the conversation was promising. She waited while he put the car away, hoping that he would continue. Evidently he considered there was no more to be said on the interesting subject. He reminded her kindly that she would have to be up early in the morning, and wished her a good night.

They left on time. Sarah, who had spent some time looking at a map before breakfast, was secretly appalled at the distance Hugo intended to cover. The car was a fast one and supremely comfortable, but by her reckoning it was a distance of almost five hundred miles. Over their coffee she mentioned this fact to Hugo. He passed his cup to be filled again and enquired in an irritatingly bland voice:

'Nervous, Sarah?'

'No,' said Sarah snappishly, 'I'm not. Won't you get tired?'

He raised a derisive eyebrow. 'No, I seldom get tired driving. I know the road; the car can more than hold her own. Besides, there are long stretches of motorway where there is no speed limit.' He took some toast and buttered it lavishly. 'Still,' he continued, 'we can easily take another day over the trip and spend another night on the way.' His tone was gentle and mocking. Sarah choked on her coffee.

'Look,' she said, being sweetly reasonable with an effort, 'I told your friend Jan that I liked driving fast with you. Not driving fast, full stop. With Father or—or anyone else I can think of, I might be scared, but not with you. And I really was worried about you getting tired.' She added with a little burst of temper, 'Did you think I was pretending when I told Jan I liked travelling fast with you?' She frowned severely at him across the table. She looked delightful.

Hugo stared at her for a long moment and said suddenly, 'Dishy—that's the word I want.'

She stared at him open-mouthed. 'What do you mean?' she demanded, 'and have you heard a word I've been saying?'

'You're dishy,' he said deliberately, 'decidedly dishy, despite the fact that you're as cross as two sticks...and I heard every word you said.'

Sarah put down her cup and strove for dignity. 'I'll get my coat,' she began, and spoilt it by giggling. 'This is the silliest conversation!' she remarked, suddenly good-tempered again, then caught her breath as he stretched an arm across the table and caught her hand.

'May I not call my wife dishy if I wish?' he asked. There was something in his voice which made her look at him. He was smiling, but there was no mockery this time, and his eyes were bright. For a brief moment she thought she saw something in his face which she had never hoped to see, and then it was gone. Probably wishful thinking, she thought, allowing common sense to take over. All the same, when she went upstairs to collect her things, her heart sang...

They lunched, rather late, in Arras, then sped south for Paris. At Bapaume they joined the motorway, and then after half an hour Sarah remarked, 'I used to wonder why you drove an Iso Grigo; now I know.'

He kept his eyes on the road ahead. 'Did you wonder about me, Sarah? I always had the impression that although we were good friends you barely knew what I looked like.'

She gave a little gurgle of laughter. 'Don't be absurd, Hugo! And anyway, you must know that you're one of the most discussed consultants at St Edwin's.'

'Not any more. You forget, I'm now a married man. Which reminds me, I must send a picture card to OPD. We'll stop for a cup of tea in Fontainebleau and buy one.'

They had tea as he had promised, and, also as he had promised, they drew up before their hotel in Nevers as the September dusk was falling, apparently as fresh as when they had set out that morning. They set out again the following morning after a breakfast of coffee and croissants. It was a mere two hundred and twenty miles to go, as Hugo said, and Sarah, hypnotised by yesterday's speed, found herself agreeing cheerfully that they would be in Avignon for tea. They were to stay there, so that she might see something of the old town and go over to Nîmes to visit Gemma. Hugo turned off the N7 at Lyon, on to a quieter road running more or less parallel with it, then beyond Valence turned off again to eat lunch at a restaurant in Privas. He had been there before, he explained, and the food was good. Sarah, eating what was set before her with a healthy appetite, thought how nice it was that Hugo always seemed to know where to go and how to get there, and did so without the least fuss. She supposed that if he were to find himself in Siberia or Brazil or some other far-flung spot, he would still contrive to get the best of what was to be had in that particular region.

The walled city of Avignon charmed her. Over tea in their hotel, she asked, rather doubtfully, if there would be time to see the Papal Palace.

'Of course there will,' Hugo replied promptly. 'We'll go and dance on the Pont d'Avignon, too.' He smiled nicely at her. 'Tomorrow morning—before we go over to Gemma's. She won't expect us before noon. Now let's take a look round the town, shall we?'

She was almost happy. They walked arm-in-arm, looking in shop windows, and after a while sat at a table outside one of the cafés in a square, and drank Pernod. 'The first drink we had together,' Hugo remarked as he gave the order. On the way back to the hotel he asked for the second time in a few weeks, 'Are you happy, Sarah?'

She stopped in the narrow street and looked up at him. 'Yes, Hugo. Happy and spoiled too—I haven't lifted a finger since we started out, and we've been to the loveliest places and you bought me that bracelet and the prints and...'

He stopped her laughingly. 'You're not in the least spoiled, and I'm enjoying myself just as much as you are.'

'I'm glad; and it's fun, being together.' When she had said it she went pink because she hadn't meant to sound so enthusiastic, but he didn't seem to notice—so she went on quickly to cover her slight confusion, 'I am a fool—you know, I can't remember the name of our hotel.' She started to walk on. 'I must be in a dream.'

He gave her a keen look. 'Yes, I think perhaps you are. It's the Europe—easy enough to remember if you should get lost. But there's not the remotest chance of that, because I shan't let you out of my sight.'

They dined gaily and grandly from the *menu gastronomique*—scrambled eggs with truffles, fillet steak *aux moelles* with baby courgettes and *pommes mousselines* and to follow this richness, Carlsbad plums with thick cream, the whole washed down with Chambéry. It seemed wise, for the sake of their digestions, to go for another stroll in the still, warm darkness, talking, as they always did when they were together, about everything under the sun.

It was overcast the next morning, but still bright enough for Sarah to look across the Rhone to the distant Alpilles. She danced a few steps on the old bridge, as unselfconscious as a child, influenced by her surroundings and the memory of the old French song. She had put on yet another new dress—a Givenchy model in white Crimplene with short sleeves and a little collar. It was tied with inspired simplicity by a chocolate brown leather belt, exactly matching her buckled shoes. It was just right for the weather, which was warmer than it had been in Holland. They walked back to the hotel, turning their backs on the four remaining arches of the bridge, followed the path outside the walls of the little city, and presently entered it again by the massive gate, and so to the Papal Palace, which she found awe-inspiring, towering out of the rock, shading the town beneath it. She found it gloomy too, and was glad that they didn't stay very long.

Hugo's sister lived in one of the old houses lining the road which led through Nîmes to its famous gardens and the Tour Magne. They were admitted into a narrow hall and then into a small salon, overlooking the canal running down the centre of the road, but the view from the windows was restricted by reason of their narrowness. The room was very French, its treasures screened from the passerby by heavy brocade curtains. Not that Sarah fancied any of the furniture with which it was adorned; indeed, she doubted if any of the fragile-looking chairs would bear Hugo's weight. She was unable to test this interesting theory, however, because the door was flung open and Gemma burst in, to fling herself at Hugo and hug him violently, and then to embrace Sarah with an equally sincere warmth. She was small and pretty, and younger than Sarah, and it was obvious that Hugo loved her very much. She spoke a jumble of English and Dutch and French, and said at once, 'Come away from this awful little room—we never use it—only to receive visitors we do not like.' She twinkled at Sarah with Hugo's eyes, and slipped an arm through hers.

'I've been longing to meet you, Sarah. Hugo told me that you were beautiful, but of course you are so much more pretty than he described. I am so glad to have you in the family.'

As she spoke, she led them upstairs to a large comfortable room at the back of the house, with wide windows overlooking a small garden. There was a baby lying on its stomach in a playpen in the centre of the carpet, and a very small boy rolling on the floor with a spaniel.

Gemma waved at them airily. 'Hugo, here is your new niece, Simone. Pierre, come and say hullo to your Uncle Hugo.'

They sat talking, the baby sitting plump and roundeyed on Sarah's lap, while Pierre climbed on to Hugo's knee to examine his watch and cuff links and waistcoat buttons while his uncle imperturbably drank sherry. When Gemma's husband joined them, tall and slim and dark, and speaking excellent English, Sarah felt no surprise to hear that he, too, was a doctor.

The children were whisked away, and they lunched in an increasingly friendly atmosphere, afterwards going into the garden, leaving the men to talk over their coffee. Sarah sat beside her hostess, and talked about clothes and children and housekeeping, and presently Gemma said:

'Hugo is a good husband.'

Sarah smiled at her widely. 'Marvellous. There isn't anyone like him.'

Gemma nodded in agreement. 'He's a dear. You know about Janet, of course. He would never have married you without telling.'

Sarah replied composedly, 'Yes, I know about Janet,' and Gemma went on, 'Then we do not need to talk about the tiresome woman, eh? I was a little girl, you know, and then I was not able to understand how he felt, and of course he told me nothing... Come, we will go for a little walk in the gardens while the children sleep and the men talk.' She got up. 'Doctors!' she uttered in disgust. 'When two of them get together!' She threw up her hands in mock horror. 'They have no need of us.'

They looked at the Tour Magne and the Temple of Diana, then went into the town to inspect the Amphitheatre and the Maison Carrée and a few of the shops, and in one of them Sarah bought a leather pocket book for Hugo—he had one already, but she was filled with an urge to give him something.

They left after tea, with the promise that Gemma and Pierre would dine with them the following evening at their hotel in Avignon. Sarah spent the first ten minutes of the journey in silence, deciding what to wear. Gemma had been beautifully dressed; she would doubtless be rather eyecatching.

'A penny for them,' said Hugo idly.

'Not worth it,' she replied. 'Just wondering what I shall wear…'

'That's easy. We'll go out tomorrow and buy something.'

She shot him a horrified look. 'But, Hugo, I've several dresses.'

He shook his head. 'Nothing pink. I like you in pink—there are some good shops in Avignon.'

They found the pink dress—a finely pleated silk in pale rose. Its astronomical price had no visible effect upon Hugo, although Sarah was shattered by it. As they left the shop he looked at her face and said briskly, 'My dear girl, if you disapprove so much, I shall give it to Gemma.'

She whirled round on him so suddenly that she almost overbalanced.

'You wouldn't! My lovely dress! I—I don't disapprove.'

He took her arm in a firm grip and steered her to one of the little tables outside one of the cafés in the square they were crossing. When he had ordered their drinks, he leaned back dangerously in the flimsy chair and said mildly, 'Well, my dear?'

She had recovered herself very nicely by then. 'Hugo, please understand. You give me such lovely things—not just now and then, but all the time…'

'And shall continue to do so,' he interrupted her. 'I

should warn you Sarah, that I am a man who likes his own way.'

He smiled at her, and her heart jumped because she saw that same look on his face again—at least, she couldn't be quite sure, for it had gone again. She said breathlessly, 'I did warn you that I might say some silly things...'

His hand reached for hers; his eyes puckered in a smile.

'Sarah, did I not once say "never silly"? I'll say it again—and remember this; you are being all, and more, than I asked of you.' He crossed his long legs and the chair creaked under him. 'And now, what shall we drink? A long one, I think, don't you? Will a Dubonnet suit you?'

She nodded and smiled a little uncertainly, and said almost in a whisper, 'It's a gorgeous dress, Hugo. I didn't mean to be ungrateful. Thank you very much—I'm looking forward to this evening.'

'Good. I'm told that there will be dancing at the hotel. Do you want to do anything special today?' And when she shook her head, 'Shall I take you to the Pont du Gard? It's not far, and the scenery is well worth the trip—we can have a meal at the hotel there.'

They went back to their own hotel and she hung up the new dress with care and then went down to join Hugo in the car, and after a pleasant drive was suitably awed by the magnificence of the Roman aqueduct.

They waited for Gemma and Pierre in the hotel bar, and when they arrived Sarah was instantly glad that she had on the pink dress, because it competed so successfully with Gemma's pale green gown. They complimented each other happily upon their appearances, and well satisfied, enjoyed their drinks, conscious that they were attracting admiring glances from most of the men present. Gemma, settling down beside Sarah, blew her

brother a kiss and said pertly, 'Do we not look nice together? It is to be hoped that our husbands realise how
very pretty we are. I shall enjoy myself.'

They all enjoyed themselves. The evening, after a leisurely dinner, passed all too quickly. They danced, and
presently Pierre asked:

'Dance with me, Sarah? I am but a poor substitute for
Hugo, I know…'

Sarah disclaimed this remark charmingly, while
secretly agreeing with him. Hugo was dancing with
Gemma—she watched them across the dance floor;
Gemma seemed to have a great deal to say, and Hugo
was listening very intently. Pierre saw her look.

'I think that my dear little Gemma is telling Hugo
what a wonderful wife he has found for himself. I imagine he knows that already!'

They had a last drink together and after Gemma and
Pierre had gone, Hugo suggested, 'One more dance, shall
we?' and whirled Sarah away for a blissful five minutes,
during which there was no past and no future—only a
delightful present.

They left early next morning, going via Le Puy and
stopping to lunch at a village inn a few miles short of
Clermont-Ferrand. The inn was small, but the cooking
was superb. They ate breast of chicken with a mushroom
sauce, which Sarah followed by a chocolate soufflée,
thoughtfully ordered for her by Hugo, before they had
their coffee and Courvoisier. There was still more than
two hundred miles to go, for he intended to spend the
night at Tours; but she found it no distance at all. There
was so much to talk about, that she found herself wishing that it had been twice that distance, and that Hugo
would drive more slowly…

She wanted the day to go on for ever. All too soon they were in Tours; tomorrow they would be back in England, and back, too, to the brief glimpses of Hugo before he left for his consulting rooms or the hospital. There was still Rose Road, of course, and she thanked heaven for that—and the weekends although she suspected that with the oncoming winter they would entertain and be entertained more frequently, which would mean less time together and a consequent withdrawal of the intimacy they had discovered while they had been on holiday. Perhaps if she could be patient until they went to the cottage in the spring…she went to sleep on that resolve.

England welcomed them with a soft grey October sky and a fine rain as Hugo took the road out of Southampton, but the weather had no effect upon their good spirits. The journey from Tours had been, from necessity, fast, but the crossing had been smooth and they had walked the deck, talking endlessly. True, upon reflection Sarah realised that she had done most of the talking, with Hugo contributing a quiet word from time to time; but he appeared to have enjoyed her company as much as she had enjoyed his.

The house at Richmond looked very pleasant as they stopped before its door. Alice was waiting for them, with Edward and Albert and Timmy. There were flowers in the hall, and soft lamplight. Sarah stood in the doorway, glad to be home. She said so to Hugo as they went inside. He was bending over the dogs, making much of them, and didn't look up when she spoke.

He said quietly, 'I'm glad of that, Sarah.'

When she came downstairs again from taking off her things, he was still in the hall, and on one of the wall tables stood the porcelain bowl she had so much admired in Amsterdam.

Chapter 8

It was a few days after their return, while they were sitting at breakfast, that Hugo asked:

'Will you meet me in town this morning, Sarah? I'm free after eleven-thirty until the clinic…we might lunch together.'

Sarah looked up from the letter she was reading, to find him watching her intently. She put the letter down and said at once and happily:

'Oh, yes, lovely! Shall I come to your rooms?' But to her disappointment he said, as he always said, 'Well, no, I think not. Let me see—could you manage New Bond Street—er—somewhere we can't miss each other? How about Asprey's? Take a taxi—I daresay you can fill in the afternoon, can't you? If you don't feel like coming to St Edwin's, I'll pick you up.'

'Gracious, there's not the least need of that.' She

looked quite shocked. 'I'll be there as usual and wait in the car. Dr Bright said on the phone that he expected a crowd this evening, and you won't want to be held up.' She poured more coffee for them both, and greatly daring, tried again. 'You're sure you don't want me to come to Harley Street? I'll have loads of time.'

It was no good; he countered her request with a smiling blandness which was nevertheless as definite as if he had said a bald 'no', and presently he got up to go, leaving her sitting at the table, a prey to a number of unhappy thoughts, not the least of which was the possibility that his receptionist was some lovely curvaceous blonde. She pondered about this for quite a few minutes, then, having made up her mind, went to find Alice, before she could change it again.

She got to Harley Street just about eleven. She had dressed carefully in the new suit, and had complemented it with her Jourdan shoes and a matching calf handbag and gloves, and had crowned her lovely head with a wide-brimmed hat which gave her a decidedly dashing air.

Hugo's rooms were on the first floor, according to the neat, impeccably shining plate upon the discreet front door. The door stood open; Sarah went inside and up the stairs and walked in through another door which invited her to enter. The room was discreetly comfortable and very restful, and save for the woman sitting behind a large desk in one corner, was empty. She was a round, cosy person with a sweet face, and, Sarah noted with soaring spirits, unmistakably middle-aged. She went across the room to her, her smile dazzling in its relief.

'Forgive me for just walking in. I'm Mrs van Elven—you must be my husband's receptionist. I'm so glad to meet you.' She held out a hand. 'Miss Trevor—have I got it right?'

Miss Trevor got up, beaming with pleasure. 'Well,' she said, 'I am glad to meet you, Mrs van Elven—I'll tell the doctor you're here.' She glanced at the clock. 'He's got one more patient to see—she telephoned to say that she would be a little late…' She looked at Sarah enquiringly.

'Don't tell the doctor I'm here—I'll surprise him.' Sarah smiled again and put her hand on the door handle, which rattled slightly because her hand was shaking.

Hugo was at his desk, writing. It was a large desk, and for a doctor, very tidy. He got to his feet when he saw her and said with his usual air of calm, 'Sarah, this is a surprise.' He didn't look in the least surprised, however, but then he was adept at concealing his feelings. It was impossible, looking at him, to have the least idea as to his reaction to her sudden appearance; probably he was annoyed.

She advanced a few steps into the room. 'I was early,' she explained. 'You don't mind if I wait for you here? Miss Trevor says you have one more patient—I could sit in the waiting room, if you don't mind?'

He was lounging against the desk, his hands in his pockets, staring at her. 'No, I don't mind. That's a fetching hat.'

She went a little pink and a dimple appeared for a devastating moment.

'Oh—well, yes.' She sounded guilty and he said gravely, his eyes dancing, 'I wonder what you have done to make you look so apprehensive. Spent all my money?'

She gave him a swift look and smiled. 'No—I've not had time to…' she stopped and felt her cheeks getting red. She had been on the point of telling him that there had been no time to even look at shops, otherwise she would never have got to Harley Street in time. She peeped at him between her lashes. He was looking down at his desk and she couldn't see his face; perhaps he hadn't noticed. She said chattily:

'What a nice room this is—so restful.'

'Naturally,' he agreed amicably, 'I endeavour to exercise a calming influence.'

He was still standing by the desk, screening something she had seen as soon as she entered the room. Her eyes, unbidden, lighted upon it once more, although there was only very little of it to be seen. A photo frame—a rather old-fashioned one, she thought, probably silver. It was a pity she couldn't see it—perhaps Hugo didn't want her to. Her heart plummeted into her fashionable shoes. Perhaps this was why he had never encouraged her to come; perhaps Janet's photo was on his desk—after all, he couldn't very well have it at home. Impelled by some strong feeling she didn't stop to analyse, she whisked past him to have a look. She had been right about the frame, it was silver shell-back, a riot of cherubs' heads and true lovers' knots and roses; it housed two photos, and she had been wrong about those—they were of herself. One, a coloured snapshot her brother had taken the previous summer—she was standing in the garden with her hair hanging round her shoulders, laughing; the other was a portrait she had had taken to please her mother, very serious in her sister's uniform. She stared at them foolishly and then said in a small voice:

'Oh, it's me!'

Hugo was no longer lounging by the desk. He asked, at his most urbane:

'Why are you surprised? Whom did you expect to see, Sarah?'

She was for once, speechless, and even if she could have thought of something to say, she couldn't have said it, by reason of a lack of breath. Hugo laughed and took a purposeful step towards her, and then stopped as the buzzer on his desk broke the silence. He stopped short and said softly, 'Damn—my patient!' and Sarah, who wasn't at all sure what he had been going to do, added an unspoken swearword of her own and said out loud, 'Yes, of course, I'll go,' and slipped through the door he had gone to open for her. A bony old lady was talking to Miss Trevor. She gave Sarah an appraising stare as she swept past to where Hugo was waiting and broke into immediate speech, cut short, to Sarah's regret, by the gentle shutting of the door. She would have liked a little time to think, but Miss Trevor evidently thought that it was her duty to engage her employer's wife in small talk, and Sarah was too kind-hearted to do anything else but carry on her side of the conversation, trivial though it was.

The old lady reappeared after ten minutes or so to be ushered firmly to the door by Hugo, when he said, 'Five minutes, Sarah,' and disappeared into his consulting room again, but it was less than that and she had had no time to sort out her thoughts, and because he seemed disposed to be silent, she felt it incumbent upon her to talk, although she had very little idea of what she was saying. They took a taxi, and because she thought that she had been curious enough for one morning, she forbore from asking where they were bound for. When they alighted halfway down Bond Street and were on the point of entering a famous furriers, she stopped in its entrance. 'Why are we here?' she wanted to know.

Hugo was opening the door, a firm hand urging her gently forward.

'A winter coat...' was all he said, and then when she stopped again, 'Don't worry, Sarah, I know your views about wild animals being slaughtered for furs. You'll be shown only ranch mink.'

She tried on several, uncertain which to choose, because Hugo hadn't mentioned price, and nor, for that matter, had the saleslady. She decided at length looking a little anxiously at Hugo, who smiled blandly back at her. When the saleslady took it from her, remarking, 'A lovely coat, madam, and an investment, if I might say so—real value for nine hundred guineas.'

She sailed away and Sarah made a terrible face at Hugo and said in a small voice, 'Hugo, it's nine hundred guineas,' to be stopped by his calm, 'And very good value for the money, I imagine. I'll tell them to send it, shall I?'

She tried to thank him as they walked to Claridges for lunch, but it was difficult in the street, so she made another attempt when they were seated in the Buttery, only to be firmly but kindly discouraged.

'My dear Sarah,' said Hugo, 'must I remind you that you are my wife and as such can expect to be the recipient of an occasional gift from me?' Sarah, spearing hors d'oeuvres, lifted her awed gaze to his as he continued. 'And if that high-flown speech had no effect upon you, I assure you that I can think up half a dozen more as good or even better.'

He smiled, his eyes twinkling and she gave a gurgle of laughter.

'Hugo, you sounded like a Church elder—a very nice one, of course! I could wear it to—to Anne's wedding, couldn't I? And Kate's. I shall need a new hat.' She contemplated an olive, lost in thought, and was taken aback when Hugo laughed.

'Now what have I said?' she asked. 'And that reminds me—shall I get Kate's present today? I could bring it with me and give it to her before I meet you at St Edwin's.'

'An admirable idea,' agreed Hugo, 'provided it's of a carryable nature. What had you in mind?'

'Well, they won't have an awful lot of money—I thought table linen or a great many towels.'

'An excellent choice,' he agreed, 'though I doubt if young Dean will be very enthusiastic. I think I'll send him half a dozen bottles of claret…just for himself, you know.'

'Well, how horrid!' protested Sarah. 'He's going to share the towels and things with Kate, so he'll have to share the claret with her too.' She caught his eye across the table; he was laughing at her silently. She said hastily, 'I shall go to the White House this afternoon.'

She waited until the waiter had substituted *poulet demi-deuil* for the remains of the hors d'oeuvres and said with commendable tenacity:

'I don't know how to thank you properly for my lovely coat.'

Hugo put down his knife and fork. He said gently, 'What a persistent woman you are, Sarah! I thought I had made myself clear.'

He gave her a mocking smile; his voice had an edge to it. 'My dear girl, you don't imagine that I'm trying to bribe you?'

'B-bribe me?' she uttered. Her saucer eyes, despite the smart hat, made her look like a surprised child, an effect considerably heightened by the bright colour which flooded her cheeks. She opened her mouth several times, only to close it again—speech, while her thoughts were so incoherent, would be useless. They clarified all at once into the tiresome fact that now it would be extremely difficult to show her true feelings—for if she did, he might construe them as the acceptance of the bribe he had so hatefully suggested she had suspected. He would never believe her. She choked upon a delicious morsel of truffle and swallowed it with as much pleasure as she would have downed a pill, then said finally, 'No, Hugo, I don't imagine any such thing—I tried to express my gratitude. You see, it's a marvellous present, even the most level-headed woman would be thrilled to have it.' She paused and went on briskly, 'Will you be busy in OP this afternoon?'

Hugo's mouth twitched a little at its corners, but he said in a perfectly ordinary voice, 'I expect so—there's a backlog of patients, naturally, but I'll do my best to get finished. By the way, I'm told the burns baby is doing well.'

They were on safe ground again; they talked amicably until he looked at his watch and said, 'I simply must go.'

They were on their way back from Rose Road after a busy evening, when Hugo told her that he was going to America. They were going over Putney Bridge and Sarah stared at the lights reflecting in the water below, as though she had never seen them before. She said at last, inanely:

'How nice. North or South?'

'North,' he answered casually. 'Philadelphia, Boston, Baltimore, Washington—not in that order of course, and a number of smaller places.'

For all the world, she thought, as though he were just

going into the next street. 'Will you be away long?' she asked. Her voice, she was pleased to hear, sounded politely interested, no more.

When he said laconically, 'Three weeks, give or take a day,' she felt her heart jerk and then resume its beating with a deplorable lack of rhythm. 'Isn't it all rather sudden?' she wanted to know.

He drew up in front of the house and turned to look at her in the dimness of the car. 'No,' he answered coolly, 'I've known about it for some months.' She waited for him to say something else; apparently he found that that was sufficient. She went ahead of him into the house, and wandered aimlessly in and out of the rooms, fiddling with the flowers until he came in from putting the car away.

'Why didn't you tell me?' she asked at once. She didn't look up from the chaos she was making of a vase of chrysanthemums.

'My dear girl, I saw no need; it isn't as though you are coming with me.'

She tried again. 'Why not?'

'What would be the point?' His voice was silky. 'We have just been on holiday, have we not? I shall be lecturing, shall I not?'

'You don't want me...?'

'Shall we not rather say that there would be no purpose in your coming?' The silky voice had a bitter thread in it.

She surveyed her wrecked vase. 'Oh! Is that why you bought me the coat?'

He bolted the front door with deliberate quiet and said over his shoulder, 'I shan't even bother to answer that, Sarah.'

She drew a breath. 'When do you go?'

'Tomorrow evening.' He had crossed the hall and had a

hand on the study door. 'I have to telephone St Edwin's—shall we say goodnight?'

He smiled at her quite kindly and in such a manner that Sarah felt she had somehow been at fault.

In her room, she sat down to think. Something had gone wrong somewhere. This morning at his rooms she had thought for a moment that he was going to tell her something—she wasn't sure what. Perhaps that he was a little in love with her—and she could have told him, and they could have started afresh. It was as though he wanted to get away from her, but if so, why did he bother to have her photograph on his desk, where he would have to look at it all day—and why did he buy her a valuable fur coat when her allowance was sufficient for her to purchase something quite nice for herself?

Perhaps it was some sort of fashion which dictated that doctors should have their wives' photographs on their desks…and as for the mink, could it be that Mrs van Elven, the wife of a highly successful consultant physician, was expected to wear nothing less? The thought was unworthy of Hugo, but she chose to ignore that. She sat on, stony-faced, while the same few ideas whirled through her aching head. At length, because she had grown cold, she went to bed, where she lay shivering with mingled chill and misery and hopeless rage.

Hugo greeted her the next morning with his usual placid manner. That he gave her a swift penetrating stare while her head was bowed over the coffee cups, she was unaware. She had taken great pains with her pale face, and was under the impression that she looked much as usual. She was surprised when he told her that he intended to go to Harley Street as usual. Somehow, because North America seemed so far away, she had imagined that the preparations would be lengthy, but Hugo was travelling light with one suitcase, which, he blandly informed her, was already packed.

She asked politely, 'Would you like us to have dinner early?'

'No, thank you, Sarah. I leave about seven—I'll take the car and leave it at the airport. I'll be home just after three, though—we could have tea together.'

He got up to go soon after, enjoining her to have a pleasant day, and she answered woodenly, 'Oh, yes. I'll take the dogs,' and then remembered to ask, 'You don't mind if I go to Rose Road while you're away?'

He paused in the door. 'Why ever not? You've got the Rover. I'm not your master, Sarah—you're free to do as you choose.'

The day seemed never-ending. At three o'clock she went to the kitchen and fetched the tea-tray, because Alice had the afternoon off. She had made a fruit cake, the kind Hugo liked, and Alice had made some muffins. Sarah arranged these delicacies upon a small table before the sitting room fire, with the muffins ready to toast. It was almost four when she heard his key in the door. She flew to the kitchen, and was putting the kettle on to boil when he strolled in. He said:

'Hullo, Sarah,' then asked casually, 'What shall you do with yourself while I'm away?'

She was prepared, for she had thought that he might ask it. She answered lightly, 'Tea won't be a minute. I shall go and see Mother and Father and perhaps stay for a day or two, and Kate wants me to go shopping—a real spree lasting two or three days—and the Coles asked me to go over weeks ago. Mary wanted me to spend a day with them. She's not very well, but of course you know that, and I want to shop for myself…'

He said, half laughing, 'Stop! My dear girl, I'd better extend my tour, so that you'll have enough time to do all you want.'

He took the tea-tray from her, and she went ahead of him into the sitting room, delighted that her exaggerated half-truths had sounded so plausible. She knelt in front of the fire, toasting the muffins, while he sat in his great armchair, glancing through his post with the relaxed air of one who has nothing better to do for the rest of the day. It was hard to imagine that in a couple of hours or so he would be starting on a three-thousand-mile journey… She became momentarily lost in a reverie in which she, with the ease of all dream happenings, accompanied him at the last minute, to be jerked back to reality by his voice enquiring if she liked her muffins burned to cinders.

She took the charred ruin off the end of the fork and started again, this time with more success, and presently they had tea. They had almost finished when Hugo said, 'I've arranged for the bank to cash any reasonable amount for you, Sarah—and Simms has everything in hand.'

She drank the last of her tea. 'Oh? What does he have to have in hand?'

'My affairs.' He spoke rather impatiently. 'This is an excellent cake—Alice has done us proud.'

Sarah said, her mind on what he had just said. 'I made it… Will you fly everywhere in America—could you not go by train?'

'Certainly not—I should be there for months if I did. The arrangement with Simms is merely routine. You can contact him if you need to—er—know anything. What did you put in this cake?'

She told him, her manner abstracted, while her imagination painted vivid little pictures of air disasters with Hugo injured, or worse still, dead—thousands of miles away. She looked unseeingly at him when he said, 'Don't Sarah. I've always considered you a woman of great good sense.'

His light derisive tone, more than his words, had the desired effect. She was making a fool of herself. She pulled herself together with an effort, uttering some not very intelligent remark about travel in America, then continued talking rather feverishly and with great brightness upon a variety of paltry subjects until Hugo got to his feet with the laconic remark that he had better change his clothes.

He came down again presently, just as the bracket clock on the mantelpiece reminded them in its silvery voice that it was seven o'clock, and went straight out to the car with his case. Sarah had gone out into the hall, but he had ignored her. It seemed that he neither wanted nor expected anything more than the most casual of farewells. He came back into the hall and shrugged himself into his car coat, looking huge and prodigiously handsome, and she wondered with a sudden spurt of jealousy how many women would meet him and think the same as she did. She went a little nearer, a smile pinned firmly to her pretty mouth, feeling cold and sick inside. He put a hand lightly, briefly on her shoulder and said, 'Well, *Tot ziens,* Sarah. I'll let you know how I'm getting on.'

He kissed her with an almost businesslike brevity, straightened up, and kissed her again, hard and fierce on her mouth, then went through the door before she could so much as say goodbye.

She was sitting over her solitary breakfast when the

telephone rang. She had been up for some time, and had taken the dogs for a walk because she hadn't slept too well, thinking about his kiss. She got up now and walked across the hall, calling to Alice not to bother to answer it, as she went. It was probably Kate.

She lifted the receiver and Hugo's voice, very close to her ear, said, 'Hullo, Sarah.' She was silent for so long that he said again, 'Sarah?' This time she managed to say 'Hullo, Hugo. I'm a—a bit surprised. I didn't expect you—did you have a good trip?'

'Yes—dull, though. I slept most of the time. What are you doing?'

'Having breakfast—I took the dogs out.' She stopped because her voice was wobbling so stupidly and he asked, 'Why are you crying, Sarah?'

She sniffed, and said at once like an unhappy child:

'Oh, Hugo, I do miss you, and you're so far away!'

Even as she said it, the sensible part of her brain told her that she was going to regret those words...but she was beyond caring. She heard him sigh—was it with relief or triumph? She didn't know until he said, 'I hoped you might. Do you know why I came, Sarah? Why I left you behind? Well, you will when I come home.'

Her heart beat faster. 'Can't you tell me now, Hugo?'

'No—I want to see your face. I have to go now, dear girl. 'Bye.'

He telephoned her every day, and the fourth or fifth time she ventured to say, 'Look, Hugo, if you're busy... I'm all right now. It's lovely to talk to you each day, but it's costing you a fearful lot of money.' The words weren't very satisfactory, but apparently he understood, for he said mildly, 'I'm lonely too, Sarah, and I can think of no better way of spending my money,' and then more briskly, 'How is Rose Road?'

After that, she got into the habit of saving up all the scraps of news to tell him each day—Alice's awful cold, the Christmas puddings they had made, the beautiful boots she had bought herself, and the utterly ravishing housecoat she intended to buy Miss Trevor for Christmas... It seemed he didn't want to talk about himself, although sometimes he made some small reference to his tour, and once he told her that he was a little tired and she had said quickly, 'Hugo, do take care!' and he had replied on a laugh, 'What of, Sarah? Too many parties or demos or beautiful girls?'

'All of them,' she said promptly, and then 'Are there a lot of beautiful girls?'

'I daresay—I haven't noticed. Did you think I would?'

She said carefully, 'Well, if I were you, I suppose I would because you're the sort of man women look at...'

'Dear Sarah, your delightful mind is as muddled as your grammar!'

His phone call became the high point of each day. She rushed back from her parents, terrified that she would be too late, although mostly he telephoned fairly early each morning, and it was on one such morning when he said, 'I'll be home tomorrow, Sarah. About eight in the evening.'

A day had never been so short, nor had there ever been so much to crowd into it. Sarah was happily busy—there was extra shopping to do, naturally, and a visit to the hairdresser and flowers to arrange, and of course, the careful planning of a meal which wouldn't spoil if Hugo arrived later than he had said. She went to bed that night tired and very happy.

She changed her mind at least three times during the following day as to what she should wear for his return. She wanted to look beautiful for Hugo—all the doubts and fears which she had experienced before he went away seemed to have disappeared; she felt almost sure that he was beginning to love her. Janet had become a wraith in a slowly forgotten past. She finally decided on a red wool crêpe dress, the colour of claret, with a whirly skirt of unpressed pleats and a soft scarf collar. It went very well with the red and bronze chrysanthemums she had massed in the downstairs rooms, and its colour gave a flattering warmth to the pallor of her excitement.

She was dressed far too soon. She toured the house once more to make sure that everything was perfect and then went into the drawing room, where the animals were drawn up in a tidy row before the fire. She sat down beside them and opened a novel—there was at least an hour to kill—and read the same page steadily for five minutes before throwing the book down and picking up her knitting, but after two rows of this, hopelessly botched, it went the way of the book…and barely fifteen minutes had passed. Her restless eye lighted upon the piano, and presently the room echoed to a hotch-potch of music, played rather inaccurately and far too loud.

When the animals rose suddenly from their sleep and looked towards the door, she stopped playing and told them to settle down again, because there was at least half an hour to wait. But they took no notice of her, but raced to the door, jostling each other to get there first. She got to her feet, her heart pounding, to stop and pound again even harder as the door opened and Hugo stood there. He caressed the animals with a kindly hand, and said quietly, 'Hullo, Sarah.'

Sarah started across the room, her face alight with happiness and not caring in the least that it might show. She had taken perhaps three steps when he spoke again. 'I've brought someone with me—you'll never guess who.'

She halted, suddenly and miserably certain that she was perfectly able to guess who her guest was. The happiness on her face was replaced by a look of polite welcome as he stood aside to allow a tall, dark woman to enter the room.

Sarah said in her charming voice, which, she proudly noted, held not one single tremor, 'But I think I do know. You're Janet, are you not?'

She looked at Hugo then, smiling a little, her brows raised in a faint enquiry. She derived some sort of satisfaction from his disconcerted look as he answered her, 'Yes, this is Janet—how did you know, Sarah?'

She gave a gay little laugh; listening to it, she wondered fleetingly why she had never taken up a stage career—obviously she was a born actress. Before he could say any more, she gave her hand to Janet and said smilingly, 'How very nice to meet you, Janet—you're exactly as I had pictured you, you know. I'm so glad Hugo brought you back with him.'

Janet smiled—a nice smile in a nice face—not pretty, but arresting and lively. Her eyes were brown and smiled too. Sarah was confused to find that she rather liked her.

'I didn't want to come like this, but Hugo persuaded me.' She looked at Hugo who was staring at Sarah. 'I met Janet on the plane,' he explained, 'and insisted on her coming back for a drink.'

Sarah said instantly, 'Of course—and dinner too. Alice and I have concocted a rather special meal, and you simply must stay.' She led the way to the fire and sat down beside Janet on the great chesterfield before it. 'You must see Alice, because she told me that she knew you when you were last in England. Have you returned to live here?'

She accepted sherry from Hugo with a smile that was quite empty, and held it in both hands, because they were shaking.

'I've a job here,' said Janet. 'Medical Registrar at St Kit's—it's a six-month appointment—that'll give me time to settle my future.'

Sarah took a long drink of sherry. Probably whisky or brandy would have done her more good, but the sherry would have to do. She was very cold inside; it prevented her from thinking, which was perhaps a good thing. Was her own future to be settled along with Janet's?

She put her glass down carefully and looked at Hugo, leaning against the side of the fireplace. 'And was the trip successful, and did you enjoy it, Hugo?' She tried to put some warmth into her voice, without much success—he hadn't even pretended to greet her or to ask how she was. He said now coolly, 'I hope it was successful. I can't say I enjoyed it. You've been all right, I hope?'

Sarah answered that yes, she had been fine, and would they excuse her while she just told Alice. She hurried to the kitchen, fighting a strong urge to go back to the drawing room and see what they were doing.

It was almost eleven o'clock when Janet got reluctantly to her feet saying that she really would have to go. Sarah, egged on by some perverse desire to hurt herself even more than she was already, begged her to stay the night, but it seemed she had already booked a room at a hotel and left her luggage there. Hugo had got to his feet too. 'I'll run you back,' he offered pleasantly, and when

Janet demurred, said, 'Nonsense, it will take no time at all, there's not much traffic about—besides, if it hadn't been for my insistence, you might have been tucked up in bed by now...'

Sarah accompanied them to the front door and wished a friendly goodnight to Janet, murmured meaninglessly to Hugo, and went back to the drawing room to wait for his return. She waited an hour, then went upstairs to bed, to lie awake until at last she heard his quiet footfall on the stairs. When he had shut his bedroom door, she turned on the bedside lamp and looked at the time. It was well past three o'clock.

She heard him go downstairs early, before seven o'clock, and go out with the dogs. Probably he intended to go through his post before breakfast. When she went down he was just coming from his study, a handful of letters in his hand. They exchanged civil good mornings, and talked during breakfast like polite strangers who find themselves at the same table. They had almost finished when Sarah mentioned Anne Binns' wedding in a week's time, followed the following week by Kate's. Anne's was to be rather a grand affair at a Knightsbridge church, and Hugo, frowning, said. 'Oh, lord, I'd forgotten. Top hats, I suppose. What did we send them?'

'Fish knives and forks in a magnificent case,' Sarah replied, and when he laughed briefly and asked why, she went on, 'Well, I should have loathed them myself.'

He looked at her in surprise tinged with amusement. 'My dear girl, you sound quite malicious! I have always thought of you as being the epitome of kindness.'

She shook her head. 'Then you will have to change your opinion of me. I can be as mean and nasty as they come.' She stared at him, and he stared back, his eyes searching and hard. He said suddenly:

'There was absolutely no need to have asked Janet for dinner last night, you know.' His voice was mild, at variance with his eyes.

She gave him an innocent look. 'But, Hugo, Janet's an old friend—more than a friend. To have sent her away after a drink would have been unthinkable. Besides, you enjoyed talking to her. You've a—a lot of time to catch up on. I thought we could have her to dinner again—or a weekend perhaps...'

He was angry, a quick peep sufficed to tell her that, but nothing of it showed when he spoke. 'You don't mind her coming here?'

She allowed a look of bewildered amazement to take possession of her face. 'You yourself,' she said gently, 'said we were level-headed and mature.' She took a slice of toast and crumbled it absently into fragments on her plate. 'It's marvellous that you should have met again, isn't it? Fate is remarkable!'

He said savagely as he got up, 'I'm glad you feel like that about it; I don't need to feel guilty when I see her,' and went out of the room without bothering to say goodbye, leaving her sitting there with a white face.

He didn't refer to their conversation when he returned home that evening, and there was nothing in his manner to indicate that it had ever taken place. On the surface they seemed to be back on their old footing, and during the next day or so this appeared to be the case. Janet was never mentioned, but neither were their daily telephone calls. Sarah found herself wondering if Janet had been with Hugo when he made them, although she was aware, deep in her mind, that he would never do such a thing.

It would be easier to bear if only she could think of him as a deep-dyed villain!

They went to Rose Road together, as they always had done. It had been far too busy for them to talk, and afterwards, in Dr Bright's flat, she had made a pretence of being busy in the kitchen, so that she had no need to join in the conversation. Only when they were on the point of leaving, John Bright gave her a penetrating stare and said:

'You're not your usual self, Sarah—does this work make you tired?' and she had said hastily, 'Goodness, no! I feel fine—perhaps I'm cooking up a cold.' She had smiled at him. 'And I hope I'm not, because you know how I like coming here.'

It was the Binns wedding the following day; it gave them something to talk about in the car on the way back to Richmond, but she couldn't help but know that Hugo's thoughts were far away.

The wedding was something of an ordeal, despite the pleasure of wearing the mink coat and a simply gorgeous hat, and being accompanied by Hugo. The bride looked almost pretty in her white satin and lace, and the bridegroom... Sarah studied him as he led his bride down the aisle. He was smiling, but the smile covered indifference and there were lines of ill-temper marring his good looks. She looked away from him and instinctively up to Hugo, to find his grey eyes fixed on her so searchingly that she coloured and looked away.

They were quickly separated at the reception. Sarah could see him towering above his companions, immersed in talk, and looking as though he was enjoying himself. She wandered from group to group, and when she could escape retired to a corner with Kate, who was quite obviously longing to talk. They settled themselves comfortably, sipping Mr Binns' excellent champagne, and Sarah said, 'You're bursting to tell me something, Kate, and do be quick, my dear, because we'll never be left to ourselves for more than a few minutes.'

Her friend eyed her doubtfully. 'I don't know whether to tell you or not, but I think I'd better, though I can't see that it matters now you're married to your nice Hugo. His old girl-friend—Janet, I think her name is—is back in London.'

Sarah said calmly, 'Yes, I know. She's been to dinner—and she's a perfect poppet. Not pretty, but attractive. She wears the most lovely clothes.'

Kate was not one to be put off by even so interesting a red herring as clothes. 'He's been seen several times at St Kit's, talking to her. She's Medical Registrar there.'

Sarah said airily, 'Oh, the grapevine!' and came to a stop as Kate went on, 'Sarah dear, this wasn't the grapevine—it was Jimmy. Sarah…oh, hell, why did the woman have to come back?'

'I've been wondering that myself,' commented Sarah, in such a forlorn voice that Kate said, 'You mind dreadfully, don't you? Can I help? Surely she can't make all that difference now you're married to Hugo. Perhaps it's just a flash in the pan.'

'After fifteen years?' Sarah asked bitterly.

Kate gave her a look in which doubt, suspicion and pity were almost equally blended. 'Sarah,' she began, when Hugo said from behind her, 'You two look as though you're conspiring to kill someone.'

Kate stood up. 'I don't know about Sarah,' she said sweetly, 'but that was exactly what I had in mind,' and went away without another word.

Hugo took her seat, removed the glass from Sarah's

hand and remarked mildly, 'A charming girl, but I fancy she rushes her fences sometimes. Do you suppose we've done all that's necessary here? The—er—happy pair are about to leave. I thought that we might slip away as soon as they've gone.'

It was still only a little after half past three; the November dusk was just beginning to cloud the river as they reached home. Indoors, Sarah said, 'Alice is out until six or thereabouts. I'll get some tea.'

Hugo looked at his watch. 'Don't bother for me, Sarah—I'll change at once. I've an appointment for five-thirty and I'll only just make it.' He started up the stairs, and she asked from the hall, looking up at his broad back, 'At Harley Street?' knowing what the answer would be before he answered shortly, 'No...if I'm not back by seven-thirty, don't wait dinner for me,' and disappeared into his room.

Sarah shrugged off the mink as though it were her old gardening coat, tossed her hat after it, and went into the kitchen. She hadn't eaten much at the reception; in fact, thinking about it, she couldn't remember eating anything except a morsel of wedding cake. She wasn't hungry anyway. She put on the kettle to boil, and walked up and down the kitchen with the teapot in her hand. A woman of courage and self-respect would doubtless go upstairs and ask a few straightforward questions, but even if she did, would she get straightforward answers?

The kettle boiled and she ignored it while she went to the back door to let Timmy in. He glared at her because she hadn't been quick enough and she picked him up, still in the open doorway, and asked, 'Timmy, what shall I do?'

'Do what?' Hugo had come into the kitchen. He turned

off the steaming kettle without comment and crossed the room and took the teapot from her and made the tea, then said, 'Well?' He shot her a keen glance, and went on casually, 'If you stay there, you'll catch your death of cold, as they say.'

She came inside then and shut the door. 'I was only asking Timmy if he wanted his tea now or later,' she said. She didn't look at him because she wasn't a very good liar and she wasn't sure how long he had been in the kitchen. She put Timmy down, and he stalked off to join the dogs in front of the sitting room fire. She picked up the tea-tray and followed him; it held only one cup and saucer, for she wasn't going to ask Hugo a second time. He followed her into the room, and asked, looking at the tray, 'Aren't you going to eat anything?' He was putting on his coat as he spoke.

'After all that lovely food at the Binns'?' she answered brightly.

'All you ate was a miserable slice of cake.' It seemed he had the eyes of a hawk behind those lazy lids. She said woodenly, 'I wasn't hungry.' Which remark he must have found unworthy of an answer, for he made none but walked to the door and when he got to it said:

'I think perhaps I had better say I won't be in for dinner, Sarah. I'll see you later.'

He lifted his hand in a vague goodbye, leaving her to pour her solitary cup of tea and vow that on no account would he see her later. So she went to bed early after telling Alice that the doctor had an important engagement and she herself couldn't face another morsel after the wedding reception. Alice listened and nodded, and presently when Sarah was in bed, she appeared with a nice hot drink. Sarah drank her Horlicks under her motherly eye, aware that nothing short of a blow on the head with some heavy instrument would ensure sound sleep for her that night, but she yawned to give Alice the satisfaction of seeing that her remedy was taking effect, and asked her to put out the light as she went away.

It was barely half past eight—the night was going to be long. She heard Hugo come in about ten, and closed her mind firmly to the vivid picture of him and Janet dining together somewhere quiet, where they weren't likely to be seen. She sat up in bed, hugging her knees, trying to decide what to do for the best. Should she go to him and say 'Look, Hugo, do you want a divorce?' She frowned, trying to remember if there wasn't a law about getting divorced before a certain length of time; but what length of time? She didn't know. Perhaps that was why Hugo had said nothing; perhaps he was waiting for her to say something. She remembered how he had kissed her when he had gone on his lecture tour, and how he had telephoned her; but that of course was before he had met Janet again.

It was very quiet in the house. Hugo was still downstairs, for she had heard the front door open and shut and the dogs scuffling in the hall, and a little later, she heard Timmy's low cacophonous grumble at her door. He usually slept with Alice, but it would be nice to have company. She let him in and got back into bed, holding his elderly furry body close. He fidgeted around for a bit and finally went to sleep, and later, much later, Sarah went to sleep too.

She overslept the next morning; by the time she got downstairs, Hugo had been out with the dogs and was already at breakfast. He wished her a pleasant good morning and she was shocked at the white weariness of his face. She said 'Hugo' before she could prevent herself, then stopped, because his expression would not allow her to ask him anything at all. There was no need, anyway, she knew how he must feel. To meet again the woman he had loved for so many years and not be free to marry her…it must be awful for Janet too. She drank some coffee and he said, 'You're not eating anything, Sarah. Alice tells me that you had no dinner. Do you feel all right?'

She said sharply, 'Yes, of course. I've a headache, that's all. A walk with the dogs will cure that.'

After he had gone, she went and sat at the little desk under the window and made out her shopping list. She would shop first, then come back for the dogs—it would fill an empty day. She put on her outdoor things and collected a dress for the cleaners and was reminded that there was a suit of Hugo's to take as well. She went to his room and found it, laid it upon the bed and began to go through the pockets—though she didn't expect to find anything; he wasn't given to hoarding bus tickets or bills. She remembered the inside breast pocket just as she was folding the jacket and swept a rather careless finger within it. There was a small box there—a red velvet jeweller's box. She looked at it for a long moment, then opened it. There was a ring inside; a gold ring set with precious stones—seven of them. Sarah frowned, for there seemed no pattern in their arrangement at all. She took it out and held it in her hand, looking at them. A diamond, an emerald, an amethyst and then a ruby, another emerald, a sapphire, and lastly, a topaz; a peculiar colour combination which struck a chord in her memory. She was putting the ring carefully back when she remembered. Such rings had been popular in bygone days—a man would give such a ring to the girl he loved; the gems spelled 'Dearest'.

There was a folded paper which had fallen out of the pocket at the same time as she had found the ring. She picked it up, and stood looking at it, and then very slowly opened it. It was a letter written in Hugo's handwriting— there was no address and no date. She folded it up again and then just as quickly, opened it again and began to read.

'My dearest darling,

It seems strange to write to you, for it is a long time since I have done so—and I shall be seeing you again very soon now, but in the meantime perhaps this ring will tell you a little of how I feel…'

Sarah read no further, but folded the letter and put it carefully back in the pocket, and the little box with it. She put back the odds and ends she had turned out of the other pockets too, and hung the suit back in the closet. She did it all mechanically, reflecting that she had got her just deserts for a mean and despicable action. When she had tidied everything away she went down to the kitchen where Alice was standing at the table, making a cake. She stopped her whisking when she saw Sarah and asked anxiously:

'Madam, are you all right? You're as white as a ghost.'

'It's only a headache, Alice—a brisk walk will cure it. I was going to take some things to the cleaners. I've put a dress out, but I haven't gone through the doctor's suit—the grey one. Would you do it for me and take them down to the cleaners? I meant to do some shopping, but I won't bother now. I'll take the dogs and have lunch out somewhere. Have the afternoon off, Alice—I'll get myself some tea when I come in.'

Sarah walked until she was exhausted and even the dogs began to flag. But she felt better for the exercise, and when she got home she was glad to see that she had some colour in her face again. Alice was still out; Sarah had tea and went upstairs to change her dress. She was downstairs again, in the kitchen with Alice, when Hugo returned. She had got into the habit of going into the hall to meet him, but now she stayed where she was, the kitchen slate held before her rather in the manner of a shield, but when he came into the kitchen, he said merely:

'Hullo. Something smells good,' and accepted the slice of cake which she cut for him, and went to sit on the kitchen table to eat it. He had eaten most of it when he asked, 'Has my grey suit gone to the cleaners?' giving her at the same time such a piercing look that she very nearly told him about the ring and the letter, but she could see his worried frown and the strained look around his mouth. She returned his stare with an innocent look of enquiry. She said, 'Yes—today.'

He still stared. 'Was there anything in it?'

She was saved from perjury by Alice, who answered for her.

'Yes, there was, Doctor. It's in the top drawer of your bureau—a little…'

'Yes, thank you, Alice,' he interrupted her swiftly, got off the table, went to the door and held it open. 'Come and have a drink,' he invited, his eyes still upon Sarah. She went, perforce, with him, and went and sat by the fire while he fetched their drinks before coming to sit down beside her. She was more or less prepared when he asked, 'I thought you usually went through my clothes before you sent them to the cleaners, Sarah.'

She said with a sangfroid which secretly pleased her, 'Yes, I do. But just this morning, I decided I'd go out with the dogs—my headache, you know,' she reminded him, 'and I asked Alice to do it for me. Do you mind? Was there something important?'

He said coolly, 'Yes…but only to me. I don't object to Alice doing such things; why should I? She always did, you know, before we married. Did you have a good day?'

She was at some pains to tell him just how good the day had been. When she had finished he made no comment but said:

'We haven't been out for quite some time, have we? Supposing we take Janet down to Rose Road one evening, and the four of us go out to supper afterwards?'

She agreed at once, for what else could she do? 'Shall it be tomorrow?' she wanted to know. 'Because it's Kate's wedding the day after that…and we're going to the Coles next week…or will Janet need more time?'

'I think not,' he answered carelessly. 'I mentioned it to her the other day and she thought it was a good idea.' He was staring at her again, waiting for her to make some comment. She said brightly:

'Well, that's settled, isn't it? Is Janet happy at St Kit's? I hope she's made some friends. Why don't we have her to dinner one evening? Saturday perhaps—if she's free?'

'By all means,' Hugo said smoothly, 'if you would like that.'

'Will you ask her when you see her?'

'Yes, of course. What makes you think I shall be seeing her?'

She flushed and avoided his eye; they were getting on dangerous ground again. 'Well, you know. The grapevine—and people…'

'Ah, yes, that grapevine,' he said evenly. 'And people—do you believe all you hear, Sarah?'

She shook her head. 'No,' and was taken by surprise when he asked then, 'Do you still love Steven, Sarah?'

She got up, making rather a business about putting her glass down on the little work-table beside her. She didn't know what to say—there were pitfalls whichever way she answered. She had better not say anything. 'I'll see if dinner's ready,' she said breathlessly, and sped from the room.

The following evening she met Hugo as she usually did, only this time they went to St Kit's to pick up Janet. Sarah, sitting in the back of the car, couldn't fail to see how Hugo and Janet suited each other, for Janet was big too—they looked wonderful together. She talked to Sarah over one shoulder on their way to Rose Road, but she talked a great deal to Hugo too with the ease of an old friend, and he answered her in like vein. Sarah was glad when they reached Dr Bright's and she could go to Sandra's little room, put on her overall and plunge into her work. She supposed Janet would stay with Hugo, and told herself that she didn't care in the least. But Janet spent the evening with John Bright, and chose to sit in the back of the car with him on the way to supper afterwards.

They went to a restaurant close to St Paul's and ate delicious steak and kidney pudding which Sarah was quite unable to appreciate. Hugo had brought up an interesting case of septicaemia he had been dealing with that evening, and though she was included in the conversation, they occasionally forgot that she was there and she was completely out of her depth. The look of interest on her face became a little fixed after a time, and when Dr Bright turned to her and said, 'Sarah, how quiet you are,' it was quite an effort to smile. She said, so softly, that only he heard her, 'Am I? It's all a bit above my head.'

He gave her a sharp look and to her consternation said loudly:

'Well, I don't know about anyone else, but I must get home.'

His words had the effect of breaking up the party, and although he didn't speak to her again on their way back, she was surprised and touched when he bent and kissed her when he got out of the car. His simple action made her feel sorry for herself, which was perhaps why, when they reached St Kit's, she was so gaily persuasive with Janet.

'You simply must come,' she urged. 'Hugo will fetch you.' She glanced at him and encountered a cold stare which she ignored. 'We never do anything on Saturdays.' And that was a lie—when they had first married, they had gone out to dine or to a theatre. 'Come to tea and stay for dinner.'

She talked with almost feverish gaiety all the way back to Richmond, pretending not to notice that Hugo's responses were both curt and abrupt.

It was Kate's wedding the next day, a small affair compared with Anne Binns' grand occasion, and yet a great deal more fun, for there were only family or close friends and everybody knew everyone else. Kate looked so beautiful that Sarah felt her own heart would break; she didn't dare to look at Hugo beside her for fear her own feelings would show. Luckily there were so many people to talk to at the reception that she had no time to think. The wedding had been at two o'clock, but it was well after five before they left the pleasant house in Finchley where Kate's parents lived. When they reached the Marylebone Road, Hugo turned left, and after she had waited a few moments for him to say why, she asked, 'The hospital?'

'No—I want to call at my rooms. I shan't be more than a minute or two.'

He went inside, leaving her in the car. She watched him cross the pavement and disappear inside, tall and elegant and distinguished and more of a stranger than he had ever been. She had Janet's reappearance into his life to thank for that.

He was back again within five minutes and as he slid into the seat beside her, she said waspishly, 'I suppose you telephoned Janet.'

She was horrified at herself the moment she had spoken, but he said mildly, 'Yes—I forgot to give her your message.'

She seethed silently. Presently, when she had her rage and her breath under control, she asked sweetly, 'Was she able to change her free time after all?'

He gave her a brief, unsmiling glance. 'Yes.'

Sarah took great pains with the dinner. Hugo had fetched Janet, apparently delighted to do so, and they had tea round the fire and Janet had been sweet—in any other circumstance, Sarah would have liked her very much. Now she went to the kitchen to make sure that everything was just so. They were to have *oeufs Maritchu* and *Poularde Niçoise* and an apple flan with clotted cream for afters. She went back to the sitting room, satisfied that the food, at least, would be a success, and found Janet and Hugo in earnest conversation which ceased abruptly as she entered.

Dinner was the success she had anticipated, so, for that matter, was the rest of the evening. Perhaps it was the excellent Pouilly-Fuissé which Hugo had opened, to mark, in his own words, a delightful occasion; or the fact that he laid himself out to be charming and amusing and

it was impossible not to respond. At ten o'clock Janet had
made as if to go, but Hugo had said at once:

'Not yet, Janet. There's an article in last week's *Lancet* I want you to see. There's something in it I can't
agree with.'

He got up and she with him, and Sarah watched them
go, side by side, across the hall to his study. He had
turned at the drawing room door and said quite charmingly, 'You don't mind, Sarah? We shan't be long—it's
hardly a drawing room topic.'

She nodded smilingly, longing to tell him that during the course of her nursing career she had listened to a
great many topics that were decidedly not fit for drawing
rooms, and had learned not to be squeamish about them
either. She remembered quite vividly several particularly
repellent subjects which he himself had discussed with
her not so many months ago.

It seemed like a hundred years of time before they returned, though it was barely ten minutes, and she said at
once, 'I'll get some more coffee,' so that it was another
half hour before Janet finally said goodbye, and then
only after Sarah had begged her to stay the night. She
stood on the step, shivering in the night air, waving in
answer to Janet's cheerful goodnight. Hugo had called
goodnight too. Presumably he would be back very late,
or, she thought with a faintly hysterical giggle, very early.

The weather had worsened in the morning and on Hugo's suggestion she didn't join him in their usual walk,
although she had never allowed the weather to keep her
indoors before. They were dining with friends that evening, which left the afternoon to spend in each other's
company. They spent it in the sitting room, reading the
Sunday papers by the fire and discussing the news with

a friendliness which wasn't quite effortless. Sarah welcomed it, and responded eagerly, with the dim idea that perhaps, if they could get back on to their old footing, it would be easier for her to talk to him about Janet. She longed to ask him what he had meant when he had telephoned her from America—he had said that he would tell her why he went. Had it been to meet Janet? She couldn't believe that somehow—meeting her had been one of those accidents Fate arranges from time to time. Rather desperately, she made one or two tentative overtures, to be checked by a blandness as effective as a high stone wall.

It was much colder the next day; Sarah hadn't intended to go out, but the day, viewed from the hour of half past nine, stretched endlessly, and Hugo had said he might be late home. She put on the mink coat and a little velvet hat; she would go shopping for Christmas presents. She was actually in no mood for such a pleasant occupation, but it would fill the day until teatime. She was in Fortnum and Mason's, having coffee, when Janet and Hugo came in. They didn't see her, for she was at a small table set against a wall, almost out of sight, and in any case, they were far too deeply engrossed in talk, and went to a table on the far side, at an angle to her. She sat watching them, unable to take her eyes away. Hugo was talking earnestly; his whole attitude expressed concern, and when he stretched out a hand and took Janet's, Sarah closed her eyes for a moment, knowing that she couldn't go on any longer.

She had already paid her bill, so she got up quietly, thankful that her table was so near the door. She went through it blindly and started down the stairs, to be almost swept off her feet by a man coming up at a great speed. He stopped his headlong rush long enough to set her upright, apologise with a strong American accent, raise his hat and smile rather charmingly before tearing on again, leaving behind him an impression of scarcely controlled excitement. She forgot him at once as she hurried down the stairs and outside, where she hailed a taxi. All the way to Richmond she sat in a corner of it, a look of deep concentration on her face. Presently she nodded to herself, by the time she alighted before her front door, she knew exactly what she was going to do.

Once inside, she went first to the kitchen, to tell Alice that she would be out until the early evening, and there was no need to worry if she was a little late home, and then to her room, refusing Alice's offer of a little something on a tray as she went. If she ate, she would choke; besides, she had a lot to do. She hung the mink carefully away and changed into a thick tweed skirt and a sweater, then packed a case with a modicum of clothes—more sweaters, slacks, a warm dressing gown and undies—before putting on the duffle coat she wore when she took the dogs out. This done, she went to the small locked drawer in her dressing table and took from it the diamond brooch and earrings in their boxes, added the pearls and then, after a moment's hesitation, her engagement ring, before taking them across to Hugo's room and locking them, with scarcely a second glance, in the top drawer of the tallboy there. Finally she sat down and counted her money. She had been to the bank that very morning and she still had a few pounds of her allowance, more than enough for her needs.

There only remained the letter she must write. She would have liked to have walked out of the house—and out of Hugo's life—without a word, but that would be hardly fair. It took her a little while, and a great many sheets of paper, before she was satisfied with her efforts. She wrote at last:

Dear Hugo,

I'm going away so that you can get a divorce and marry Janet. I tried to talk to you about it, but you wouldn't let me, and when I saw you both in Fortnum's today I knew we couldn't go on any longer. Make any arrangements you want; I'll agree to anything so long as you can be happy again. I'm taking the car—I hope you don't mind, but I've left the jewellery you gave me in the tallboy drawer in your room. I've plenty of money and I shall be quite all right because I can get a job very easily. I'll let Mr Simms know where I am, later.

She signed it 'Sarah' and read it through. It was a bit businesslike and bald, but that was a good thing, although the whole of her cried out to let him know how much she loved him. And a lot of good that would do, she told herself fiercely.

She could hear Alice in the kitchen; she picked up her case and went quietly downstairs, propped the letter on Hugo's desk in the study, and let herself out of the house, taking care not to look back.

There was plenty of petrol in the tank. Sarah flung her case on to the back seat and drove the Rover carefully out of the garage at the end of the private road. The AA map was open on the seat beside her; she had studied it with a hasty intelligent eye in her bedroom. Once she got to Smethwick she would be all right, because there she would join the road they had travelled on to Scotland. Once on it, she would remember it well enough. She reckoned she would have to spend two nights on the way, perhaps three. At any other time she would have been terrified at the idea of the motorways, but now she didn't care. She turned the car towards Watford, where she would join the Mi. It was barely two o'clock; she should be able to reach Manchester in the early evening and find somewhere to sleep in a nearby village. Not that the details of the journey bothered her; her one longing was to reach the cottage in Wester Ross and hide herself until the sharp edge of her grief had blunted itself a little.

Hugo, home later than he had intended, was met in the hall by an anxious Alice, who said without preamble:

'I'm worried about Mrs van Elven, Doctor. She came home about half past twelve, looking quite ill. She told me she would be going out and I wasn't to worry if she wasn't in to tea, but it's eight o'clock, sir, and no sign of her, and it's not like her not to ring up—she's always so considerate.'

Hugo had gone a little white, though he spoke calmly enough. 'Don't worry, Alice, I expect she's been held up. Did she take the car?'

'I don't know—she didn't say she was going to.'

'What was she wearing?'

'Her mink coat and that pretty little blue velvet hat.'

'Then she must be visiting. I'll telephone round and see if I can locate her—the car may have broken down, if she took it.'

He flung his coat on to a chair and went into his study and immediately saw the envelope on the desk. He stood looking at it for a long moment, his face expressionless, then opened it slowly and read Sarah's letter just as slowly and read it again before folding it neatly and putting it into a pocket, before going upstairs, two at a time, to her room. He saw the mink coat at once. He looked at it with a kind of quiet despair and went to search the closet—but Sarah had a great many clothes; it was difficult to see what she had taken with her, but he was reasonably sure that most of her things were still hanging there. Which meant that she had taken only sufficient for a few days. She was quite possibly at her home.

On his way downstairs again, he was already making a mental list of people she might be with. He telephoned them all in turn and was still at his desk when Alice came in to enquire for news. 'And your dinner's ready, Doctor,' she ended. But Hugo took no notice of this remark. He looked at his watch, and said, 'I'll try the hospitals…'

She came back presently with a tray. 'You can eat while you telephone, I'll take the dogs out, then you'll be here when Mrs van Elven comes.'

But Mrs van Elven didn't come.

Chapter 9

The first snowflakes were falling as Sarah took the unwieldy key from its hiding place and fitted it into the lock of the cottage's stout front door. It was very cold inside, but not in the least damp. She lighted a lamp and put a match to the Aga which the worthy Mrs MacFee had faithfully left ready, then wearily fetched her case from the car before putting it away in the garage. When she at length got indoors, she was shaking with cold and tiredness and the aftermath of driving hundreds of miles, spurred on only by the knowledge that Hugo would never love her now that Janet had come back into his life.

The journey had been a nightmare experience of icy roads, fog, wrong turnings and the dreadful monotony of the motorway, coupled with the dread of losing her nerve as the fast traffic tore past her for mile after mile. She had spent the night at Kendal and started off again in the dark, grey morning, which never really became any lighter. She had stopped for coffee and sandwiches, although she couldn't remember where or when; she only knew that she wasn't hungry. She made tea and unpacked, and presently went to bed without bothering about supper.

She slept the deep sleep of exhaustion and wakened in the late morning to find that it was still snowing. The countryside was blanketed, blotting out roads and hedges and walls. She dressed quickly in slacks and thick sweater, and went, rather anxiously, to inspect the store cupboard. But here again Mrs MacFee had kept her word. Sarah sighed with relief at the plenitude of its contents. She stoked up the Aga, made breakfast, and then, in gumboots and an old anorak, went to clear the short, steep run-in from the lane to the garage.

It took her longer than she had expected, and there was still the path to the top of the back garden where there was the potato clamp. She shovelled doggedly, uncaring of the snow falling steadily to obliterate her hard work—that didn't matter, she told herself with false cheerfulness, she could do it all again the following day, and the day after if necessary; it would give her something to do. When she finally finished, the early dusk was already darkening an already dark sky and it was almost three o'clock. She dug some potatoes, not very easily, from the clamp, put away her spade and went indoors. The little sitting room, once she had got the fire going and the lamps lighted, was warm and cheerful. She had a bath and changed into the warm dressing gown, to sit cosily by the fire, eating a meal, half lunch, half tea, and listening to the wind's whispered howling outside. It looked as though the weather was worsening…a sur-

mise confirmed by the weather forecast which predicted
heavy snow, gale force winds, and drifts to be avoided.

Sarah switched the radio off because she wasn't sure
if there were any spare batteries, then presently, in search
of something to do, she searched through the cupboards
and found some *gros-point* she had started when they
had been there in the spring. She sat with it in her lap,
remembering how happy they had been. She picked it
up and began to stitch carefully, but in a little while put
it down again, unable to see what she was doing for the
tears which filled her eyes.

The snow continued. Each day she cleared the paths,
glad of the work, then went back indoors to the warmth
to cook a simple meal and work or read by the light of the
one lamp she allowed herself. There was plenty of oil and
coal, but it was impossible to get down to the village, and
there was no way of knowing how long the bad weather
would last. Sarah had attempted to make her way down
the hill one morning and had plunged into a drift which
it had taken her so long to get out of, she hadn't dared to
try again. The telephone line was down, had been since
the day after her arrival, and she didn't think that anyone knew that she was in the cottage. Not that it mattered; she had enough of everything for a long time yet
and she was comfortable, and the longer she could keep
away, the more quickly Hugo would realise that she had
meant what she had written in her letter.

She had been there more than a week now, and the
snow, which had stopped for several hours, had started
again. She had seen the snow-plough on the road running
beside Loch Duich; it had looked very small in the sur-
rounding whiteness of the empty countryside, with the
Kintails looming in the icy distance. It had cleared the

road and disappeared again, but before any traffic which might have followed it could do so, the wind became a howling gale and obliterated its painstaking work. That same wind drove her indoors too, for it whipped up the snow into a blizzard which had made her painstaking shovelling a mockery.

She had her lunch early and spent the short afternoon turning out cupboards which were already as neat as Mrs MacFee's hands could make them, but it was something to do. She had thought that once she was alone in the peace and quiet of the cottage, she would be able to think calmly about the future; but that led to thoughts of Hugo, and she couldn't bear to think sensibly of him—not yet.

The wind died down towards morning and because she hadn't slept overmuch she got up early, before it was light, and had breakfast in the snug kitchen and did the chores, and because she didn't hurry over them it was after ten before she got outside. The snow had stopped, leaving great drifts against the garage door and blotting out the garden. She tackled the run-in first—not that she could have moved the car in or out, but at least she could get to it. The garden path was a more difficult job; she worked steadily at it until she reached the hedge which bounded its end and then stopped, leaning on her shovel, staring down the hill towards the hamlet below.

She didn't know what made her turn round, some slight sound perhaps. When she did, Hugo was standing quite close. He put up a slow hand and took off the dark glasses he wore when he drove long distances, and she could see how tired he was—there were lines she had never noticed before, etched deep between nose and mouth. She let out a sighing breath, unconscious that she had been holding it, put her spade down carefully, and went down the path towards him. She was bewildered and surprised and at a loss for words, and so, it seemed, was he. She said the first thing she thought of.

'How lucky I cleared the snow from the front of the garage. However did you get the car up here?'

His tired mouth cracked in a grin. 'I didn't. I left it at Glenmoriston and got a lift on a snow-plough as far as Shiel Bridge.'

She said in amazement, 'You walked? It must be six miles at least...the drifts are shockingly deep too. How long did it take you?'

He glanced at his watch. 'Four hours. The snow's pretty firm, you know, and there are plenty of landmarks.'

They stood and stared at each other until she said, 'You must be tired,' and went past him, down the path to the cottage. 'I'll get you a meal and then you can have a bath and sleep.'

She knew she sounded like a bossy schoolmarm, but at least it was better than just standing there...and it would be something for her to keep her mind on until she could collect her wits. She kicked off her boots at the back door and went to poke up the Aga while he pulled off his own gumboots and shrugged out of his sheepskin jacket. There was a covered milk can on the table. He saw her glance at it and said:

'I thought you might be getting a bit low with the tinned stuff.'

She was busy with the frying pan and the coffee pot and didn't look up. 'That was thoughtful of you—it must have been a nuisance to carry.'

He said politely, 'Not at all. I've some spare batteries for the radio too.' He had come to sit in the Windsor chair pulled up to the table. Sarah broke two eggs into the pan and then a third—he was a large man and would be hungry. She said at last, her thoughts once more under control:

'Why did you come, Hugo? I know there are papers to sign and—and things, but you could have gone ahead with whatever you needed to do. I told you I would agree. You didn't have to come all this way.' She drew a quick breath. 'How did you know I was here?' It was funny that she had only just thought of that. He didn't answer her question.

'I had to see you, Sarah.'

She dished up the bacon and eggs and put the plate down before him, and spoke her thoughts out loud without knowing it. 'No one knew I was coming here.' She picked up the coffee pot. 'It's something legal, I suppose,' she went on in a determinedly cheerful voice, 'and you're hung up until I sign something.'

'There's something I have to say to you, Sarah.'

She poured his coffee, studying his face. He was asleep on his feet.

'Yes, I know, Hugo.' She spoke soothingly and with authority, just as she would have spoken to a patient panicking in OPD. 'But you're going to eat now and then have a nap, and you can tell me after that and not before.' She cast around in her mind for a suitable topic. 'The telephone's out of order, I'm afraid—all this snow,' and before she could help herself, 'Did Janet know you were coming?' she interrupted herself and answered her own question, embarked on a spate of talk she couldn't stop.

'I hope you managed to telephone her from Inverness—at least she'll know you got there safely. If the snow stops they'll send out the plough and you'll be able to get a lift back to the car. I expect you can't wait to get back.' She stopped because of the look on his face; if he

hadn't been so desperately tired she could have sworn that
he was laughing silently. 'Was the journey very bad coming up?' she enquired. 'Where did you spend the night?'

'I came straight through.' his voice sounded harsh,
perhaps because he was so exhausted.

'Straight through?' she echoed, her voice a horrified
squeak. 'In this awful weather—it's hundreds of miles!'
She turned away and poured herself some coffee, swallowing back a great surge of tears. He must have thought
it worth while. She took a scalding gulp and said with
all the politeness of a good hostess, 'Do try some of this
bread—I made it. I've got quite good at baking.'

Hugo took no notice of this remark. He said again,
very quietly: 'I have to talk to you, Sarah.'

She put her cup down so sharply that some of the coffee
spilt, but her voice was gentle. 'Yes, I know. But not now.'
How could she explain to him that she was holding out for
a few more hours before she had to listen to him telling
her? 'You're too tired now and I must make up your bed.
The water's hot—you'll find all you need in the bathroom.'

She was already halfway up the little staircase as she
spoke, holding her thoughts fiercely in check. She had
almost finished making his bed when he came upstairs,
and without speaking to her went into the bathroom and
turned on the taps.

Downstairs, she cleared the table and washed up, then
went to the cupboard to collect the makings of a stew—
Hugo would want a meal when he woke; it would have to
be something that wouldn't spoil however long he slept. She
made some dumplings, then got out her boots and anorak
again and made her way to the shed halfway up the garden
where the apples were stored. Baked apples would go very
well after the stew and they could go on top of the Aga.

She managed to keep herself occupied with these homely tasks for quite some time, and then, forgetful of lunch, went into the sitting room and got out her *gros-point*. It was calming work, and she would need to be calm when he came downstairs. She stitched steadily, waiting for her mind to clear itself, so that she could plan what to say...but it did no such thing; indeed, her thoughts piled one upon another, each one more incoherent than the last. The only one that made sense and remained permanently clear was that she loved Hugo. The one fact, she told herself with hopeless, wry good sense, which was of no use to her.

The day wore on; when daylight began to fail she stopped her sewing and lighted a lamp, then went to look at her stew and then to find her handbag and make up her face with meticulous care and do her hair. She peered into the little mirror on the kitchen wall and decided that she didn't look too bad. She had got a bit thin and her face had little colour, but provided she remembered to smile... She tried out one or two smiles and was heartened to see how normal she looked. Hugo's pity was the last thing she wanted.

It was quite dark by now, and still no sound from upstairs. Sarah made tea and set a tray with a plate of scones and some jam Mrs MacFee had made and left in the cupboard, carried it into the sitting room and set it upon the little round table by her chair. She sat down then, to pour herself a cup of tea, only to leave it to get cold while she thought about Janet. It was absurd how much she liked her; she supposed she should really hate her for returning to England and ruining her life.

Which train of thought led, inevitably, to the future. She would have to decide what to do now. She would find a job, here in Scotland, and start again. She contemplated a bleak vista of years with something like loathing, and became so deeply immersed in her broodings that she failed to hear Hugo until he was at the foot of the staircase. He had put on the Aran sweater she had knitted rather laboriously while he fished, and some old corduroys, and he had found the red leather slippers they had bought together in Inverness. Her throat ached suddenly at the sight of them, but all the same, she remembered to smile.

'I've just made the tea,' she remarked simply. 'I hope you slept.' He looked as though he had—the lines had almost gone; he had shaved and he bore the well-scrubbed alert look of a well-rested man ready for anything. Well, so was she, she told herself.

He sat down opposite her and she poured his tea and handed it to him, and he in turn put the cup and saucer down again, staring at her in a silence so profound that she felt sure that he could hear her heart pounding. To forestall this possibility she made haste to ask him if he had slept well, quite forgetting that she had already done that, and when he replied that yes, he had, she added the interesting information that the beds in the cottage were very comfortable. This remark called forth no response, so Sarah took a sip of her cold tea, and picked up her embroidery frame and began unhurriedly to stitch, willing her hands to be steady, her lovely face bent to the glow of the little lamp; waiting patiently for him to tell her whatever it was that had necessitated his travelling almost six hundred miles in mid-winter. That he would tell her as kindly as possible she had no doubt. They had been—and still were—good friends. She thanked heaven silently that she had never allowed him to see that she loved him. All the same, when he spoke, she pricked her finger.

'It took me a week to find you, Sarah,' he said at last.

'You see, this was the last place I thought of. You said—do you remember?—that only the direst circumstance would force you to drive up here alone. I didn't remember that at once. I wasted precious days looking for you at your mother's and the hospital and Rose Road. I even went to see Mr Ives…and a dozen other people. You have so many friends. I tried Kate and Dick Coles and the bank, even old Simms…'

Sarah sucked her pricked finger. She said quietly, 'I'm sorry, you see, I didn't tell anyone because I didn't think you'd want to know.'

He said on a sigh, 'Sarah, my dearest Sarah! I've been half out of my mind.' He stopped. 'I love you,' he said suddenly and fiercely. 'I fell in love with you years ago… you were staffing on Men's Medical. It wasn't too difficult persuading Matron that you were just the type I wanted in OPD.'

She dropped her embroidery at that, and stared at him, open-mouthed.

'Oh, yes,' he went on, still fiercely. 'Only to discover that you and young Steven… I waited three years. And then I married you, knowing that I would still have to wait while you recovered from Steven; knowing that you weren't ready for my love. That's why I allowed you to go on believing in that hoary legend about Janet and me.'

Womanlike, she fastened on that. 'But you loved her!'

He smiled at her, with such tenderness and understanding that she caught her breath. He said quietly, 'Perhaps, for a year—two years.' And she nodded, remembering how she had felt about Steven. Her heart was thudding violently now; she picked up her embroidery again and began stitching as though her very life depended upon it, pushing the needle in and out of all the wrong holes with a complete disregard for the design. Hugo got up and took the maltreated canvas from her shaking hand, plucked her out of her chair and pulled her close so that her voice was muffled against his shoulder.

'Hugo!' she wailed. 'I've loved you for—months and months—long before I knew about it!'

Apparently this muddled remark made sense to Hugo, for he put a finger under her chin and stared down at her and kissed with slow gentleness and then, while she was catching her breath, kissed her again, not gently at all. When at length he loosed her a little she put her hands against his chest so that she could look up into his face.

'Janet—' she uttered. 'Why did you bring her home after you had been so—so nice when you telephoned? And why did you go away and leave me?'

'I thought that if I went away you might miss me—and you did, my darling, did you not? And as for Janet—my sweet Sarah, you gave me no chance to explain.'

'You didn't come back until after three o'clock,' she interposed pettishly.

He kissed her again before he answered. 'I parked the car and sat wondering how I could make you love me. You see, I had come home thinking…and you were quite waspish with me, dear love, and I began to think that you would never care for me.'

Sarah said in a rush of words that ended in a sob, 'Kate said you went to St Kit's to see Janet and you telephoned her, and you were in Fortnum's…' She was kissed into silence.

'Dear Sarah,' said Hugo. 'Listen. If you had shown me just once that I was more than just a good friend, I would have told you everything, but all you did was to fling Janet at my head. I would have told you that she's married and unhappy and had left her husband. That's why we were at Fortnum's—I persuaded her to meet him.'

'The man on the stairs who knocked me over,' observed Sarah, well pleased that the jigsaw of their conversation was making sense at last. Hugo lifted an enquiring eyebrow but forbore from questioning her; instead he said firmly, 'And now you will talk no more nonsense, dear heart, nor will you leave me again.'

He drew her close, but just for a minute she held back.

'Hugo, dear Hugo, there's something I must tell you.' She lifted a woebegone face. 'I—I found a ring in your pocket and I lied to you about it and I never will again; and there was a letter and I—'. She gulped. 'I read it— not all of it, just the first line or two, and I thought it was for Janet.'

She sniffed to hold back the tears, because if she cried it would look as though she was trying to get his sympathy.

Hugo crushed her so tightly to him that her ribs ached. 'You addlepated woman! Why didn't you read the whole letter while you were about it, then you would have known that it was for you. I wrote it in America and then decided that I would give you the ring myself. Of course, I didn't know that Janet was going to be there, or that you would ask her to stay to dinner.'

Sarah wriggled in his embrace. 'I told you I should be silly,' she murmured, and reached up and kissed him, to be kissed, most satisfactorily, breathless.

Outside the cottage the snow fell, unhurried and unheeded, and in the little kitchen, the stew, forgotten, bubbled fragrantly on.

* * * * *

If the Satler triplets were a definite, adding this client for July
would mean she could take off the first couple weeks of August,
which were always slow for Dream Weddings, and just be with
her twins.

Which would mean needing Nick Garroway as her nanny—
manny—until her regular nanny returned. Leanna could take some
time off herself and start mid-August. Win-win for everyone.

A temporary manny. A necessary temporary manny.

"Well, I've consulted with myself," Brooke said as she put
the phone on the table. "The job is yours. I'll only need help until
August 1. Then I'll take some time off, and Leanna, my regular
nanny, will be ready to come back to work for me."

He nodded. "Sounds good. Oh—and I know your ad called
for hours of nine to one during the week, but I'll make you a
deal. I'll be your around-the-clock nanny, as needed—for room
and board."

She swallowed. "You mean live here?"

"Temporarily. I'd rather not stay with my family. Besides, this way, you can work when you need to, not be boxed into someone else's hours."

Even a part-time nanny was very expensive—more than she could afford—but Brooke had always been grateful that necessity would make her limit her work so that she could spend real time with her babies. Now she'd have as-needed care for the twins without spending a penny.

Once again, she wondered where Nick Garroway had come from. He was like a miracle—and everything Brooke needed right now.

"I think I'm getting the better deal," she said. "But my grandmother always said not to look a gift horse in the mouth." Especially when that gift horse was clearly a workhorse.

"Good. You get what you need and I make good on that promise. Works for both of us."

She glanced at him. He might be gorgeous and sexy, and too capable with a diaper and a stack of dirty dishes, but he wasn't her fantasy in the flesh. He was here because he'd promised her babies' father he'd make sure she and the twins were all right. She had to stop thinking of him as a man—somehow, despite how attracted she was to him on a few different levels. He was her nanny, her *manny*.

But what was sexier than a man saying, "Take a break, I'll handle it. Take that call, I've got the kids. Go rest, I'll load the dishwasher and fold the laundry"?

Nothing was sexier. Which meant Brooke would have to be on guard 24/7.

Because her brain had caught up with her—the hot manny was moving into her house."

Don't miss
A Promise for the Twins *by Melissa Senate,*
available July 2019 wherever
Harlequin® Special Edition books and ebooks are sold.

www.Harlequin.com

HSEEXP0619

Need an adrenaline rush from nail-biting tales
(and irresistible males)?

Check out **Harlequin Intrigue**®
and **Harlequin**® **Romantic Suspense** books!

New books available every month!

CONNECT WITH US AT:

Facebook.com/groups/HarlequinConnection

 Facebook.com/HarlequinBooks

 Twitter.com/HarlequinBooks

 Instagram.com/HarlequinBooks

 Pinterest.com/HarlequinBooks

ReaderService.com

**ROMANCE WHEN
YOU NEED IT**

SGENRE2018

Looking for inspiration in tales
of hope, faith and heartfelt romance?

Check out **Love Inspired**® and
Love Inspired® **Suspense** books!

New books available every month!

Love Harlequin romance?

DISCOVER.

Be the first to find out about promotions, news and exclusive content!

f Facebook.com/HarlequinBooks

🐦 Twitter.com/HarlequinBooks

📷 Instagram.com/HarlequinBooks

P Pinterest.com/HarlequinBooks

ReaderService.com

EXPLORE.

Sign up for the Harlequin e-newsletter and download a free book from any series at **TryHarlequin.com.**

CONNECT.

Join our Harlequin community to share your thoughts and connect with other romance readers!
Facebook.com/groups/HarlequinConnection

HARLEQUIN®

**ROMANCE WHEN
YOU NEED IT**